MW01205022

THAT NIGHT AT THE PALACE

L.D. Watson

Reklaw

Contents

Rejoice always, pray continually, give thanks in all circumstances; for this is God's will for you in Christ Jesus.

I THESSALONIANS 5:16-18

Prologue

NECHES RIVER BRIDGE
8:35am Sunday November 16, 1941

Toad and Hunker were having no luck. Hunker blamed it on the stars, arguing that a full moon kept the critters away. Toad, being the older and wiser of the two Lowery brothers knew that it was most likely because it was November and there still hadn't been a cool spell. The two, thirty-six and thirty-five, respectively, had been hunting along the Neches every Sunday morning since they were old enough to hold a gun. For the third week in a row they had come up empty-handed. At this point they would be happy to bag just about anything. Ideally they hoped to get a deer or wild pig. Naturally, though, when it was warm like this, pigs and deer were hard to come by, but there's nothing wrong with a fat possum. Though admittedly greasy, a possum made a good stew with a little tomato and green pepper.

Unfortunately, they had sat for a good three hours in one of their best spots and hadn't spotted so much as a decent squirrel. This was bad news for the two Lowery brothers who were now going to have to find some work. There was always a job at one of the drilling sites, chopping timber or mowing. If that failed, they could haul hay, but neither looked forward to the backbreaking chore of lifting hay bales. Toad and Hunker lived on a few acres south of Elza where they grew some corn and a little tomato and they always ran a few head of cattle, all of which brought in a little money, but most of their income came from their Sunday morning hunts.

The two were a bit dejected as they crossed the old railroad trestle. For Toad the thought of hauling hay again was the worst possible option. Toad and his brother were both short, standing not an inch over five foot three with boots on, which made it a lot harder to lift those bales up to the side of a truck.

Unlike his brother, Toad was squarely built with no visible neck whatsoever. Toad had gotten his name because, according to family lore, the day he was born his grandfather took one look at the newborn baby and remarked, "That boy looks like a Toad."

Even Toad didn't know if the story was true, but for some reason the family began calling him that, and in 1910 when the census taker came around and started writing down the names of the kids, he asked about the little one with no neck, and his father answered, "You know, now that you mention it, we never got around to giving him a name. We've been calling him Toad since the day he was born."

So on that day, five years after he was born, Toad officially became Toad Alexander Lowery. The "Alexander" was the census-taker's name, and since no one could agree on a middle name, he just gave the kid his own.

No one in the family could recall how Hunker, who had a neck, got his name. Predictably, no one in or around Elza found that unusual considering these were the two youngest in a family of seventeen children, two of whom were killed in the war with Spain seven years before either Toad or Hunker were even born.

About mid-way across the bridge Hunker froze and suddenly whipped his old .30 Remington from where he had it casually cradled in his arm and put it to his shoulder in firing position. Toad stopped in his tracks. Hunker had heard something. It annoyed Toad that his little brother had such good ears. Hunker could hear a cricket a mile away. His eyes were good too. Hunker almost never missed a shot and would often pop a critter that his older brother never even saw.

Hunker held his gun in firing position as he scanned the river below. He cautiously, and without the slightest sound, crept forward. Toad then clearly heard the crackle of brush almost right below them.

"Gator!" Hunker yelled as he, with lightning speed, fired off two shots. Both men ran to the end of the bridge and looked down on the bank. Getting an alligator would be better than winning a grand prize at the fair for the two hunters. For starters, the meat in the tail could last them months if smoked right, but more importantly was the hide. There was a tanner in Jacksonville who would give as much as two hundred dollars for a good gator hide.

Everyone knew that there were gators in the rivers and ponds, but you almost never saw one. In fact, in all their years of hunting on the Neches, the Lowery brothers had not once seen a single alligator, though they had seen some tracks a few times. When they were boys a half-colored half-Indian fellow named Cherokee-One-Leg shot one over by Reklaw. Old Cherokee had been hunting in the bottomland around Mud Creek when a big old eight footer got a hold of his leg. Cherokee managed to shoot him and hobbled back to town but by the time he got there his leg was so infected that the doc had to cut it off at the knee. From then on they called the old man Cherokee-One-Leg. While he was laid up some of his kin went down in the bottoms and found the dead gator and collected his hide and cut out some of his teeth. Somebody took the teeth and made necklace with them. Old Cherokee was rightly proud of those teeth and wore that necklace almost all the time. When asked, he would say that he missed his leg, but he got one good alligator boot and a mighty fine necklace in trade.

From the time they were boys Toad and Hunker had hoped to someday get a gator. Granted, neither wanted to lose a leg, but they both wanted a tooth to wear around their necks like Cherokee-One-Leg.

This alligator was a big one, at least eight or nine foot.

"What is that in his mouth?" Toad asked, squinting from the morning sun.

Hunker didn't answer; he just handed his rifle to his brother and darted down the slope.

"Is that a person?" Toad asked as he began to make out the tangled mess of bloody limbs below.

Hunker cautiously made his way through the brush to the gator. He wasn't worried about the alligator being alive. He knew he got two good shots in the head but he was terrified of what he knew he was about to see.

"Yeah, it's a person. He's all wedged up between these trees."

Hunker made his way to the body. One leg was missing and the other was ripped to pieces as the alligator had been pulling on it for a while. The arms and body had been chewed at as well. One hand was mostly missing. The other hand held a stick. He had most likely tried to fight the alligator off.

Hunker reached down and touched the neck. He knew the fellow was dead but felt that he needed to check. Hunker had never touched a dead person before and didn't like it. It was especially hard because, after seeing him fully he realized, he'd known this kid since he was knee high.

"Is he dead?" Toad asked, though he knew the answer.

Hunker turned and started making his way up the bank. "Yeah, he's dead, but not long. He's still warm."

He climbed up to the tracks. Toad met him and handed Hunker his rifle, "Do you know who it is? I can't tell nothin' from up there."

Hunker looked sadly at his brother. Near tears, he answered, "It's Cliff Tidwell."

"Oh, no, not Clifford." Toad said softly as he looked down the slope.

Hunker had tears in his eyes, "His head's all bashed in like somebody hit him with somethin'."

Toad wiped a tear from his eye. "You mean somebody tried to kill Cliff?"

"Yeah."

"We gotta get the chief."

Chapter 1

ELZA CEMETERY
ELZA, TEXAS
1:30 p.m. June 14, 2014

The line of cars stretched for more than a mile. In fact, as the hearse was pulling into the back of the little cemetery, the last mourners had yet to leave the church parking lot. It was not a long service, but it was by far the most attended the little East Texas town had ever seen. Even more so than when Pastor Anderson died some twenty years before, when Elza was nearly twice its current size. The crowd was so large that a projector and screen and nearly a hundred chairs were set up outside to accommodate the expected overflow. Even then over two hundred people stood while nearly a hundred more sat in their cars and listened.

Jeana Yates and her grandmother Gemma Crawford Ferrell were two of those who chose to wait out the service in an air-conditioned car. Jeana insisted upon it. Gemma would have easily stood outside, but her ever-attentive granddaughter held firm. Gemma was nearing ninety, and though she showed little signs of slowing down, Jeana simply had to draw the line at letting the old woman stand in the heat, even though they had driven over three hours to be there. They could hear the service, which, quite honestly, was enough for Gemma.

Because they were already in their car, the two women were among the first to arrive at the little graveyard, and as a result they managed to get a reasonably close parking spot. Jeana was greatly relieved. She knew Gemma well enough to know that when the old woman had her mind set, nothing was going to stop her, and with the crowd at that funeral they could easily have parked hundreds of yards away. As it was, Jeana was terrified of what would happen if the woman stumbled and fell.

Dozens of people were headed to the little gate as Gemma and Jeana entered. Most of the people made their way toward the portable awning set up over the spot where the pallbearers were offloading the casket. Without warning, the older woman stopped and suddenly headed off to the left with Jeana following behind.

"Grandmother, the grave is this way," Jeana said pointing to her right as the elderly woman simply ignored her and hobbled in the opposite direction.

Gemma, cane in one hand and an oversized purse hanging from the other, made her way past dozens of gravestones as she carefully negotiated a path through the little cemetery. Finally she stopped in front of a marker to the left of a lone pine tree. Further to the left was a large family stone marked *Tidwell* surrounded by smaller markers with that surname. All alone in the shade of the pine sat a single pink granite stone. There was no epitaph, simply the name:

JESSE ROSE

CPL. US Army

FEB 3, 1922 – JUNE 6, 1944

The white-haired woman carefully knelt next to the stone and began pulling weeds from the base. Then, to her granddaughter's surprise, she reached deep into the purse and pulled out a small potted plant and centered it in front of the marker.

Quietly seated on her knees, Gemma Crawford Ferrell began to softly weep.

"Grandmother?"

Unable to control her emotions, the old woman fell from her knees and braced herself against the cold pink stone and began to cry. Jeana knelt next to her grandmother and attempted to comfort the woman, but Gemma waved her away. Gemma needed this time alone.

For well over an hour Jeana stood a few feet back while her grandmother crouched next to the stone wiping away tears. The massive graveside service finally broke up and throngs of mourners made their way back to their cars, all wanting out of the summer sun.

While the family of the deceased hugged relatives and friends, one woman fixed her eyes on the elderly lady leaning on a gravestone off in the distance. The woman excused herself from the group and walked up to Gemma as the elderly woman stood up to go.

"Are you my Aunt Gemma?" the woman asked.

Jeana stood stunned as she watched her grandmother smile at the woman and nod. Gemma then wiped away another tear and tenderly hugged the woman.

"Daddy had shoe boxes filled with your letters," the woman began as the two let loose their embrace. "He often told me that if I'm ever in Dallas that I should go see you and to call you 'Aunt Gemma.'"

Gemma smiled, "That's right."

The woman looked down at the pink stone, "That's him, isn't it?"

#

JACKSONVILLE, TEXAS
3:35 p.m. June 14, 2014

Gemma hadn't spoken a word all the way into Jacksonville. She simply stared out the window lost in her thoughts, or more accurately, lost in her memories. Jeana knew her grandmother well enough not to interrupt. Granted, she had a world of questions rolling through her mind, but she knew that this was not the time to ask.

"Pull in there," Gemma stated, pointing at a roadside diner built from an old railroad car.

"There's a McDonald's up ahead, grandmother. You know you like their burgers, and I'm sure they have a cleaner restroom." Jeana suggested, not liking the look of the place her grandmother pointed out.

"No. I want to go here," the older woman demanded in a tone that was more an order than a request.

Reluctantly, Jeana did as told and parked the Buick SUV in front of the dirty little diner.

Inside, led by Gemma, they seated themselves in a booth at the far end of the restaurant next to the window. When the waitress came, Jeana ordered coffee and hamburgers for the two of them without consulting her grandmother, who simply stared out the window.

After a lengthy silence the old woman said, "We had dinner here that night, the night of our last date. The night before he was arrested, the night of the murder. We sat at this very booth. Of course it was a lot different then. They changed the name. It was called 'The J-Ville Diner' in those days. It was a pretty nice place. At least we thought it was. Of course, there weren't as many restaurants in those days, and our standards weren't very high. This was as nice a place as any of us had ever been in at the time. We would drive all the way here to have a burger and then drive back to Elza to catch the movie at the Palace."

"You and that man in the grave? Corporal Rose?"

"Jesse, me, your aunt Jettie, and Cliff. I've been trying to think of how to tell you the story. Jettie always sat where you are. Cliff was next to her. She was so pretty then. She was as exasperating as ever," the woman commented, "but so pretty."

"Who was he, grandmother? And who was that woman?"

"Did you notice Jesse's stone? It was with the Tidwells. His family moved away right after the trial. They were ashamed. His folks were, well, not the sort to take the humiliation of a murder trial. I heard that they divorced. Jesse was probably the only thing that had been keeping them together. Once he left they probably realized that they didn't like each other very much.

I remember seeing his name in the paper listed as one of the local boys killed at Normandy. At the time I just assumed that he was buried over there, but later I heard that the Tidwells had him brought back here. It would make sense. I'm sure he listed them as his next-of-kin."

"What happened, grandmother? Who was he?"

"I don't know where to begin," Gemma said, with a little moisture forming in her eyes. "Cliff Tidwell's murder was so awful. Whenever I think of him I'm reminded of the pictures. He was half eaten by an alligator."

The woman stopped talking and began to weep.

"You don't have to tell me, Grandmother," Jeana said, sensing the difficulty the woman was having.

"No, I need to do this," Gemma explained. "I have to tell someone. I need someone to know what Jesse did. I just don't know where to begin. I guess it all started that night at the Palace."

#

PALACE THEATER
ELZA, TEXAS
8:07 p.m. Saturday November 15, 1941

"I told you we'd be late," Clifford Tidwell said as the two couples walked along Main Street to the Palace. "I swear, Jesse, you drive like my grandmother."

"Your grandma's never been behind a wheel, and you know it," Jesse countered.

"Well, if she drove, she'd drive faster than you. Look the lobby's empty."

Gemma and Jettie looked at one another and giggled as the four walked up to the ticket booth. They had listened to the two boys bicker all the way back from Jacksonville.

"How much did we miss, Able?" Cliff asked.

Able McCormack glanced at his timepiece, "Just the news reel so far, Clifford. There's still a Betty Boop before the movie starts."

"See, I told ya. We'll take two," Jesse interjected as he slid two quarters to Able.

"Us too," Cliff said as he passed a couple of coins.

"I shouldn't let you in, Clifford. I don't recall your mamma paying me for that time I caught you trying to slip in through that air vent." Able commented, more to the girls than Cliff. "This one somehow managed to climb all the way up to my rooftop and nearly fell straight through to the middle of the concession stand. He's lucky he didn't end up in the popcorn machine."

Both girls laughed politely. They had heard the story hundreds of times over the years, as had everyone else in Elza. Of course, it had been embellished to some extent.

The truth was that Cliff got stuck in an air vent and was in no risk of falling into the concession stand.

Cliff and Jesse's childhood antics provided plenty of amusing conversations at the domino hall and under the awning of McMillian's store. Naturally such yarns tended to grow to the point that they hardly resembled the facts.

As the boys took their tickets and headed for the door, Cliff remarked, "I swear, Able, do you have to tell that story every time I come here? If I hear it one more time I'm gonna start taking my business to the Plaza down in Sacul."

"It's a full house tonight, kids." Able commented, ignoring Cliff. "You may have to split up. Have Bobby make some people scooch over."

As the four entered the lobby, Bobby Weatherholt greeted them with a big smile and took their ticket. Bobby was well over thirty but wore the usher uniform with the pride of an army general. Tall and thin to the point of being unhealthy, he had worked at the Palace for most of his life, and as far as anyone could tell he had no intention of ever leaving.

He carefully separated the tickets and handed the stubs back. No one spoke. Bobby, though always smiling, almost never said a word to anyone.

He then opened the door and led the four into the auditorium. Inside he flipped on his flashlight and pointed it at the floor so as not to bother anyone watching the Betty Boop cartoon. He stopped about four rows down and, again without saying a word, tapped a man on the shoulder and motioned. In a moment seven people had moved to their left two seats, making room for Cliff and Jettie. Bobby then turned to the opposite row. By now everyone had already begun to move over. No one ever challenged Bobby's authority. This was the part of his job at the Palace that Bobby loved most. During these moments in the darkened theater he was in charge, and he took his responsibility seriously.

Gemma and Jesse slipped into their seats across the aisle from Cliff and Jettie. This was not the best of arrangements as far as Gemma was concerned. She and Jettie preferred to sit together with the boys on the outside of them. That almost never happened, however. The boys always liked to sit together so they could make jokes at the movie. They were usually quiet, but at least once in every movie Cliff would blurt out something which he and Jesse would find utterly hysterical, drawing angry looks from people all around the room and, of course, embarrassing the girls.

Sitting across the aisle wasn't as good as sitting next to her sister, but it kept the boys apart, and that, above all, was the most important task. It occurred to Gemma that she should enlist Bobby's help with this in the future.

#

ALLEY BEHIND THE PLAZA THEATER
ELZA, TEXAS
8:40 p.m. Saturday November 15, 1941

Irwin Stoker parked his 1929 Chevrolet pickup behind the Palace Theater. He had already crashed into a few garbage cans and an old Plymouth parked near the back door. The fifty-two year old farmer stumbled, almost landing on his face as he climbed out of the truck. He parked a little too close to the building and hardly had room to open the pickup door. When he managed to compose himself, he reached back into the cab and took a Remington Model-11 sixteen-gauge shotgun from the gun rack in the back window.

He stumbled a little more as he worked his way between the building and the truck to the back door of the theater. Homemade liquor will cause that. Then he reached down to pull on the steel door. It wasn't locked. There was no reason to expect it to be. Why would it be locked? Able McCormack had to take out the trash two or three times a night; locking the door would just make the task more difficult. Able was never concerned with people sneaking in without buying a ticket. He sold the tickets, and he knew everyone in town. All he had to do was look around the auditorium. If anyone had come in without buying a ticket, he'd spot the guy right away.

Occasionally, during the matinee, some boys would try get away with catching *The Dead End Kids* or an *Andy Hardy* by slipping in the back. Every time it happened Able would come down the aisle, grab the boys by the ear, and drag them out. There was a story around town that the Tidwell kid had tried to get in through the roof. Of course, Able caught him right away.

Able was a mean cuss. He didn't stop with dragging kids out of the place. He would leave Doris Broussard in charge while he took the boys all the way home. It didn't matter to him if they lived way over in Reklaw or as far east as Nacogdoches, Able would make sure the boys' parents were well aware of the criminal offense their sons had perpetrated. What's more, he made sure that they knew that no one from that household got to see a picture-show at the Palace until he received a nickel for the ticket the boys failed to purchase. Needless to say, boys rarely tried a second time to get into the Palace without paying full price.

Of course, it never happened on a Saturday night. And if it did, Elza's distinguished police chief, Thomas Jefferson Hightower, was there, as he was almost every Saturday night. There were no gangsters in Elza. The biggest crime Jefferson Hightower had dealt with in the past five years was when someone tried to break into McMillian's General Merchandise store. George Henry McMillian's cash box was an 1888 model from National Cash Register. The thing easily weighed two hundred pounds, maybe more. Whoever it was didn't get it as far as the back door before giving up. Old George Henry woke up and looked out the bedroom window next door and saw a car pulling away. He fired his shotgun a couple of times, but about all he accomplished was waking up every dog in town. By the time Chief Hightower showed up, the crooks were long gone, which, no doubt, was what the chief was hoping.

Irwin was quiet as he slipped in the door. It amused him at how easy it was. He wasn't concerned with getting caught, of course, he wasn't there to see a picture-show.

He was much more cautious now that he was inside. There was a long hallway down the side of the theater that most people didn't know existed. It was built to be a fire exit, but it served mostly as a storage area and a pathway for Able to take out the trash while the picture-show was going. At the end of the theater nearest the screen was a curtained doorway with an exit sign above. Irwin carefully peeked through the curtain at the audience. It wasn't hard to go unnoticed. Every eye was fixed on the Gary Cooper picture.

Scanning the room was easy, too. The bright screen lit every face. In just moments Irwin spotted the little punk sitting with that Crawford girl as if Jewel didn't exist.

That kid doesn't deserve to be alive, not after what he did.

Irwin checked the shells. They were there, naturally. There were always shells in his shotgun, but this was no time for mistakes.

His heart was pumping now. He could feel it pounding in his chest. He cocked the hammer back and slowly stepped out from behind the curtain and stopped. Not a single person noticed him.

Irwin held the shotgun to his side as he entered the auditorium. It was surprising that no one was paying any attention. Not a single person seemed to see him as he passed the first row of seats and then turned up the right-hand aisle. About halfway down, he raised the shotgun to his shoulder. Still, no one seemed to notice.

When he reached Cliff he stopped, pointed the shotgun at the boy and shouted, a bit too dramatically, "Clifford Tidwell, get ready to meet your maker!"

Jesse, like everyone else, hadn't paid any attention to the man walking up the aisle. People came and went all the time. It wasn't until he heard Cliff's name shouted out that he paid any notice. Afterwards he couldn't recall how he had managed to move or why. For some reason he leaped at the man. He almost missed him entirely because of the awkward way he had to get out of the seat and into the aisle. Luckily, his left hand hit the gun just as it fired, sending the shot into one of the chandeliers, causing broken glass to fall all over a group of people on the far side of the theater. By the time the blast was heard, two men had jumped on Irwin along with Jesse and wrestled the gun away.

The lights came on and the movie stopped. Everyone in the room began to realize that a gun had just fired.

As Jesse was getting to his feet, Able came running down the aisle with Police Chief Thomas Jefferson Hightower a few steps behind.

"He spoilt her!" Irwin shouted as the two men fought viciously to hold him down.

"What in God's name is going on here, Irwin?" Able shouted.

"He spoilt her, and I'm gonna kill 'im!"

Jefferson grabbed Irwin by the collar as Jesse picked up the shotgun, "Jesse, what happened here?" He asked as the boy handed him the gun.

"I'm not sure." Jesse replied with a shake in his voice, "I looked up just as he shouted that he was going to kill Cliff. I think I knocked him down."

"He spoilt her!" The man shouted again, this time with a slight crack in his voice.

"Who did what?" Jefferson demanded.

Irwin began to tremble. The man was on the edge of tears.

"He spoilt her. My, Jewel. My little Jewel. She's got a baby in her, and it's his." The man said as tears began streaming down his face.

"My God, Irwin. You almost committed murder," Jefferson said softly.

Clifford sat motionless. His face was white. "Mr. Stoker, I didn't do anything to Jewel."

"I'm gonna kill you, ya little punk!" The man shouted one more time as Jefferson dragged him out of the theater.

Jettie slowly stood to her feet, her eyes fixed on Cliff. Softly, with a hurt look she asked, "You and Jewel?"

"I swear, Jettie, I didn't."

Jesse was just as stunned as he stood staring at his friend. "You and to Jewel? After all we've been through? After what we promised her mamma?"

Cliff feebly stood, his legs still quivering from having almost been killed. "Jesse, you've got to believe me. I never touched her."

Jesse, suddenly and with all of his strength, punched his friend in the nose. As Cliff fell back onto the seats, Jesse jumped on top of him, pounding wildly on the boy's face. Immediately, Able and the two other men pulled Jesse away.

"If that old man doesn't kill you, I swear that I will," Jesse said loud enough for everyone in the theater to hear. He then reached out his hand to Jettie. "I'll take you home, Jettie."

"I swear, I didn't," Cliff uttered through his now bloody mouth.

Able put a firm hand on the boy. "We've heard enough from you, Cliff." He then turned to Jesse. "Take these girls home."

Jettie, awkwardly and with Jesse's help, managed to climb over her date and followed Jesse and Gemma up the aisle and out of the theater.

Able looked crowd, "The movie will start back in a minute folks." He then looked down at Cliff and said in a quiet but defined tone, "Get out of here and don't ever come back into my picture-show again, Clifford."

#

406 SUMAC LANE,
ELZA TEXAS
9:05 p.m. Saturday November 15, 1941

The instant Jesse pulled the 1930 Ford Sedan to a stop in front of the little white house, Jettie darted out of the car and in the front door. Tears were pouring down her face.

The problem with Cliff was that it was altogether possible that he was telling the truth about having never touched Jewel. Unfortunately for him, Jettie and everyone in the Palace knew that it was equally possible that he was the father of Jewel's baby. For a boy who had gotten in trouble for one thing or another every day of his life, he was a really good kid. He never once did anything to deliberately harm anyone. And it wasn't that he went around looking for mischief. Mischief just found him. He was just the kind of guy who had a tendency to jump without looking and without thinking for a moment about the consequences. Most of the time the consequences fell on Jesse.

Jesse shut off the motor and put both hands on the wheel. He was still trembling. Gemma, who had been sitting in the center seat, slid away from him. This was the opposite of their normal procedure when the two were parked alone together. She leaned back against the closed door and stared at him.

"I can't believe he did that to Jettie," Jesse remarked after a long silence.

"You want me to believe that you almost beat Cliff to death because of Jettie?" She asked in a steady tone that made it clear she wasn't buying any of it.

"It's not what you think."

"Why don't you start by telling me what I think?"

"There's nothing between me and Jewel."

"Yes there is," she replied, making it clear that there was no room for argument.

"I've never kissed her or anything like that."

Gemma just stared at him with almost no emotion showing.

"It's not like that."

"You can't lie to me, Jesse. I've known you all of your life. And why wouldn't you kiss her? She's tall, she's beautiful, she has all that blonde hair, and God knows you've had plenty of opportunity."

"Well, I haven't."

"I used to be jealous of her. You three would spend the entire summer playing together. I remember having to work in Mama's shop and I'd look out the front window and you three would be sitting on the curb laughing and sipping RCs. I was so in love with you back then, and you hardly noticed me at all. Why would you? You had the prettiest girl in town. She was as much a boy as either of you and twice the girl as me."

Jesse still had his hands on the wheel, looking forward. "Did you ever wonder why we sat on the curb across from your mom's shop drinking RCs?"

He turned to look at Gemma who simply shook her head.

"Your shop's two blocks from McMillian's, where we got the soda pops. We'd go there because I wanted to see you. We'd sit there an hour or more in the burning sun hoping you'd pass that window. The two of them were always laughing because they were making fun of me for not having the courage to walk in and talk to you."

Gemma continued to watch him. He was trembling more than ever, and there was a noticeable shake in his voice.

"Do you remember our first date? The carnival?"

"We rode the Ferris Wheel."

"It was Jewel who talked me into asking you. I was scared to death. I was convinced that there wasn't a chance you would go with me, but she insisted that you would."

"Okay, but that was when we were kids. What's going on now? And don't tell me that it's nothing. I've watched you and Cliff fight since first grade, but the two of you never fought like that. Cliff's nose is definitely broken, and when you said you'd kill him, I believed it - and so did everybody at the Palace."

"I lost my temper, Gem."

Gemma wasn't buying it, "And?"

As Jesse looked at her, his face began to change. His eyes began to moisten. He looked down at the seat between them, wishing that he could escape, but Gemma wasn't letting go.

"I can't tell you," he finally answered.

"Yes you can," Gemma countered, clearly not willing to yield any ground.

Finally he looked up at her. "We were there that night; the night her mama died."

Gemma's brow wrinkled as she tried to recall. "I always heard that her mother ran off with someone."

"Cliff made up that story. She was dying. We were just a couple of kids, and we didn't know what to do. She shot herself. I held her head. Cliff held her hand. She didn't want anyone to know the truth. She thought too many people would get hurt. She was going to have a baby, and it wasn't Mr. Stoker's. She had been raped. Don't ask me how I know that. I just know. When the chief started lookin' for her, Cliff said that he had seen her talking to one of the carnival men. I said that I'd seen the same thing. By then the carnival was long gone."

"You two stayed with her as she died?" Gemma asked, now trembling herself.

"Yeah. She was real beat up. I think she was going to lose the baby. She tried to kill the man that got her pregnant, but he smacked her around and left. She put the gun to her head, but I startled her just as she shot, so the bullet went through the neck and into her chest. We couldn't stop the bleeding. She begged us not to tell anyone about the baby or the men. She wanted to protect everybody. She asked us to hide her in the woods, then she made us promise to take care of Jewel.

"When Mr. Stoker said that about Cliff, I don't know, I just lost it. Me and Cliff, well, it's our job to take care of her. It's our job to keep things like that from happening to her."

Gemma was stunned. She slid over to Jesse, who had tears running down his face. The two held each other tightly.

"I always felt responsible for Jewel. Her daddy drank a lot. He was real rough with her mother. I don't think that he ever hurt Jewel, but he was real rough with Mrs. Stoker. She wanted Jewel to have it better." He paused for a moment, finding it hard to speak and then added, "I always thought we did a good job taking care of Jewel until tonight. I never imagined Cliff would do that."

#

301 RED OAK AVE.,
ELZA, TEXAS
12:01 a.m. Sunday November 16, 1941

Jesse was lying in his bed with his eyes wide open when he heard the familiar sound of pebbles hitting the window. Jesse's room was on the second floor. Though Jesse's house wasn't the largest on the block, it was still quite big by Elza standards, with two stories and brick outside walls. Jesse's father was an area manager for the Powhatan Oil Company, and though the depression had hurt almost everyone in Texas, the oil business continued strong. So when Mr. Davidson closed up the smaller of the town's two banks, Jesse's parents, Murdock and Garvis, got the house at the corner of Red Oak and 2nd Street for a considerable bargain. Of course, Jesse's dad would have been perfectly happy living in a tent, but when Garvis Hamilton Rose saw a chance to get a house on Red Oak, they were taking it "come hell or high water," as Jesse's grandfather would say.

Jesse climbed out of bed and pulled on his pants. He then opened the window and reached his hand out to pull Cliff in.

"Come on," Cliff said with a wave of his hand rather than climbing in.

"No. Get out of here, so I can go back to sleep."

"You weren't asleep, and you're not going back to bed, or you wouldn't have your pants on. Now, come on."

Jesse shrugged and grabbed a pair of shoes and a t-shirt, and then followed his friend out the window and onto the porch roof. At the corner of the house, the two jumped down to the ground and trotted up to Main Street where Cliff had left his 1929 Chevy Coupe. The car had almost no paint and sounded like the motor would fall out at any moment, but it was still a coupe. Short of a Packard convertible, there was just nothing better on the road.

Cliff drove out to State Highway 84 and then took a left onto a dirt county road for about a mile until they came to a railroad where he parked and the two got out.

"Come on." Cliff ordered.

"What are we doing out here?" Jesse protested as he stepped out of the coupe.

"Shut up and follow me,"

Jesse paused for a moment but finally complied. Cliff's disposition was normally quite jovial. For obvious reasons his mood was different, but Jesse had never seen his friend like this.

After a long walk along the tracks they came to an old iron railroad trestle that crossed the Neches River.

"Come on," Cliff ordered one more time as he began to climb to the top of the ironworks on the right hand side of the tracks. He then sat down on the wide beam high above the river.

Jesse hesitated, but it was too late to protest. Besides, it had been years since he and Cliff had sat on that bridge tossing stones into the river. Just before he began his climb, he reached down as he had done a thousand times before and picked up a few stones from beside the tracks.

Jesse climbed the trestle with ease just as he had so many times when they were kids. When he sat down, Cliff reached to his left to grab a long cotton rope that was tied to the trestle and hung down into the river below. He pulled up two beer bottles that had been cooling in the flowing water. He removed the bottles from the rope and handed one to Jesse. The two boys popped the bottle tops off on the side of the trestle.

"You want to explain what we're doing here?"

Cliff took a long pull on his beer. "The last time I saw Jewel was two months ago. We were sitting right here." He paused and looked at his friend. "I swear, Jesse, I'm not the reason she's pregnant."

Jesse paused for a long moment, looking at Cliff.

"Do you know who she's been seeing?"

"Some guy up in Jacksonville. I ain't ever seen him."

"I haven't talked to her in ages," Jesse confessed. "I know she's been working at that Chevy dealership. Do you know anything about the guy? Will he take care of her?"

"I hope so. He was all she could talk about. She said that she was in love."

"Why did her old man think it was you?"

Cliff shrugged, "He was on the porch when I drove her home. She didn't want me to take her to the house. You know old Irwin never liked us, but I figured, you know, we're practically grown."

"Yeah, he's never liked us hanging around with her. So he's not met this guy?"

"No. She's scared to death that he will find out. You know how he is with her. You can hardly blame him, after his wife leaving and all."

The two locked eyes.

"I told Gemma tonight," Jesse solemnly confessed.

"You what?"

"Just the part about Sarah dying. I didn't tell her the rest."

"If she talks...?"

"She won't," Jesse said, cutting his friend off with definitive assurance.

"You better be sure. If anyone finds her bones, our butts will end up in prison. I don't know what the charge would be, but throwing a dead woman into a mineshaft ain't legal, I can tell you that. And if anyone ever puts the pieces together, they'll find what else we did, and they'll put us in the electric chair for sure."

"No one's going to find out, and if someone does find the bones they'd never figure out it was her," Jesse said evenly as he took a sip of beer. "And if so, they couldn't connect us to it."

"That Texas Ranger came pretty close," Cliff replied. "He came real close, as a matter of fact. He knew that we did something. He just didn't know what."

"She won't say anything," Jesse repeated. Gemma was the one thing in the world that he was sure of. She wasn't about to tell anyone. He could have told her everything, and she wouldn't talk. Of course, there's no way he could tell her everything. It would hurt her too much to know what her father did, and he couldn't do that to the woman he planned to marry.

Jesse's life was all but planned out. In May he would graduate high school, and in the fall he would begin his career with the Texas A&M Corps of Cadets. Louie Sherman from over in Maydelle had arranged everything. Louie had just graduated from A&M and knew all the strings to pull. Jesse really wouldn't have had any problems anyway. He was going to graduate at the top of his class, and he'd already passed the Aggie Corps exams with ease. And it didn't hurt that the outgoing Corps Commander was an old family friend.

Gemma would bide her time at her mom's shop until Jesse got his army commission. With any luck they could get married at the chapel on campus. Jesse had heard that it was a real honor to get married there, but it was sometimes hard to get on the waiting list. He'd have to look into that as soon as he got enrolled. If not, Brother Bill at First Baptist Elza would happily marry them. It would just mean a lot more to both him and Gemma to do it at the University

Chapel with him in his new 2nd Lieutenant's uniform and the two of them leaving under the drawn swords of an honor guard.

The two hadn't openly discussed marriage just yet, but Jesse didn't doubt she would marry him. He knew she loved him. They had said it many times in the years that they had been together. He knew he loved her all the way back to third grade when he first could recall having seen her. Something about her stole his heart, and he'd not given a serious thought to another girl since. Everyone in town knew good and well that the two of them were made for each other. They were a regular topic of discussion at the First Baptist Church Women's Auxiliary, and Jesse's father, Murdock Rose, couldn't get a haircut without someone asking if he knew when Jesse would pop the question. That, of course, had little to do with people caring about the couple. Jesse and Gemma were both fully aware, though they never let on to one another, that the old boys at the domino hall had a couple of hundred dollars riding on whether or not he would pop the question before he left for College Station. A fellow stood to make a pretty penny if he could get a little inside information.

The fact was that Jesse himself didn't know. He'd given it a lot of thought, and he knew he had to make up his mind soon, but he just didn't know if it was a good idea or not. When he decided, he planned on sending Cliff down to the domino hall to place a bet, though it was unlikely that anyone would take it. It would be worth trying, nevertheless.

Either way, Gemma could never know everything that happened the night that Sarah Stoker died. Gemma loved him, Jesse was sure of that, but he was just as sure that there was no way she could marry the man who killed her father.

"Well, you make sure that she doesn't say anything. I don't want to die in Huntsville prison," Cliff remarked with a tone that made clear that he wasn't as confident in Gemma as Jesse.

"Perhaps you'd prefer to die in the Palace picture-show."

"Good-god, that scared the pee out of me. I never noticed the man until I saw the barrel of that shotgun right there in my face. I don't think I knew what was happening until I heard the shot. My ears are still ringing. And my nose hurts like hell!"

Jesse looked at Cliff, whose nose was clearly broken. The two began to laugh almost uncontrollably as over four hours of tension lifted off of them.

"You know she was always in love with you, don't you?"

"Gemma?"

"No, Jewel, you idiot."

"She was not."

"I swear, Jesse, you make the best grades in school, but you're as stupid as a pile of rocks."

Jesse just looked at him in disbelief.

"Every girl in town has been in love with you since the day you were born, and you haven't got a clue. God help the army once you're in charge. That's the reason I didn't tell you about Jewel's boyfriend. She wanted to be the one to tell you. Of course, after tonight it really doesn't matter. Anyway she's scared to talk to you about him. She's afraid you won't approve."

"What's it matter if I approve?" Jesse asked as Cliff began to climb down from the bridge.

"I don't know. She's a woman; they worry about things like that. Like I said, she always had a thing for you. I think she finally realized that with Gemma around she didn't have a chance."

Jesse followed his friend off the bridge and the two began walking back to the coupe.

Chapter 2

ELZA, TEXAS
June 4, 1936

"I'm telling you, you can't make it."

"Shut up, somebody will hear you," Cliff replied as he began climbing the rain drainpipe to the roof of the jail.

Jesse stood silent, nervously looking around the alley as his friend scurried up the side of the building.

"Come on, it's easy," Cliff urged in a loud whisper.

Jesse looked around again and finally started following Cliff up the back of the jailhouse. Surprisingly it was easier than he thought. He should have known it would be. He'd climbed the railroad trestle almost the same way hundreds of times.

Cliff scurried onto the top of the two-story building and looked over the side reaching out to help his friend. "Geez, you're a slowpoke."

Jesse took hold of Cliff's hand and made his way onto the roof. Looking back down, he thought to himself that it was much higher than it looked from the ground.

The boys went to the front of the building and peered over. Main Street was busy, but no one seemed to notice them. They went to the side of the building that connected to the Palace Theater, which was a much taller building. At the back, above the alley, the brick ledge on the jailhouse rose up two and a half feet. Cliff carefully stood on the ledge next to the Palace and looked up. "Here goes nothing."

The boy leaped as high as he could, which was just enough to grab hold of the edge of the theater roof. With some effort he was able to pull himself up and on top of the movie house.

"It's not so hard. You can make it."

Jesse hesitantly stepped up onto the ledge. He looked down and then up at the top of the theater, thinking that of all of the things Cliff had talked him into, this was easily the dumbest, but he couldn't chicken out. Not after Cliff had already done it. With all he had, he jumped up reaching for the theater roof. One hand caught hold, but the other missed. Hanging by one hand, his body began to swing out toward the alley. Cliff, who had already begun walking toward the front of the building, turned around just in time to leap back and grab Jesse's one clinging hand before the boy lost his grip. Cliff grasped tightly to his hand. "Pull!"

Jesse, swinging wildly, managed to whip his free hand to the top of the building. Together they pulled him on top, where they sat against the ledge with their hearts pounding. Suddenly Cliff started laughing uncontrollably. A moment later Jesse began to laugh, too. They looked at each other, and Cliff stood up. "Come on."

Though it wasn't visible from the ground, the roof of the Palace was arched. There was a three-foot ledge that circled the building, so the boys carefully walked alongside the ledge to the front. There they crouched down and peered over the ledge right behind the large neon "Palace" sign.

Directly across the street was an alley extending perpendicular to Main Street. Down the alley they could see a man in a suit and hat all alone smoking a cigarette. Jesse looked two doors to the left of the alley at a one of the shops. Above the storefront was a sign reading *Anna-Ruth's Dresses and Sewing.*

"Do you think she's in there?" Jesse asked.

"Who?" Cliff asked, his eyes still fixed on the man in the alley. Then he looked to his right and saw what Jesse was staring at. "Oh, she and her sister always come in to help their mom." He answered with an impatient tone.

"Do you know where she lives?"

"Down on Sumac," Cliff replied distractedly, having returned his attention to the alley.

"Let's go down there later."

"Why? You won't stop. You'll just walk by and look at her house like you do the store every day. Chicken."

"I'm not chicken."

"Yeah, you are."

"She doesn't know who I am. For all she knows I'm Frankenstein."

"She knows who you are. You know who she is. Besides, you're no where near as good lookin' as Frankenstein," Cliff replied as he spotted a woman walking along the sidewalk across the street. "There she is."

Jesse turned his attention to the woman. She was walking briskly, holding tightly to her purse. As she arrived at the alley, she looked around and turned in.

"I knew it. The second I saw him go into the alley I knew it!" Cliff exclaimed.

"That's Jewel's mom."

"Are you sure?"

"Yeah, I saw her and Jewel yesterday," Jesse replied.

The man in the alley dropped his cigarette and stomped it out. The boys watched as the woman cautiously approached the man. He reached for her, but she stepped back.

"Are they arguing?" Jesse asked.

"I think so. I wish we could hear 'em."

The man grabbed the woman and pulled her to him. As he tried to kiss her, she pushed him away. The man was now clearly angry and pulled her to him again. This time she slapped him as she pushed herself away. The man then hit her full fisted in the face. Both boys froze as the woman fell hard to the ground. They watched as the man said some things and then stormed out of the alley. When he reached the street he stopped and lit a cigarette.

"Do you know who he is?" Jesse asked.

"Yeah, he's Gemma and Jettie Crawford's dad."

Crawford started to turn and head up the street but hesitated and glanced up at the theater roof. Both boys dropped their heads below the ledge.

"Do you think he saw us?" Jesse asked.

"I don't know, but I'm not staying to find out," Cliff answered as he began to scurry to the back of the building.

Jesse began to follow but looked over the ledge one more time. The man was walking away. For the first time Jesse got a good look at his face. The man walked two doors up and into Anna-Ruth's Dress Shop but stopped one more time to look at the roof of the Palace. Jesse ducked down again and then rose up to look one more time. The man walked into the dress store just as Mrs. Stoker walked out of the alley. She had dusted herself off but was clearly upset.

Jesse scurried to the back of the building, keeping low. Cliff stopped just as he got to the ledge.

"Do you smell that?"

"Popcorn?"

Cliff fixed his eyes on a round air vent and headed for it.

"Come on. That guy saw us," Jesse insisted.

"Hang on," Cliff replied as he began to examine the vent pipe.

"Quit fooling around, Cliff. We're going to get caught."

Cliff took hold of the top of the vent and lifted it away. Surprisingly, there was nothing attaching it to the pipe but its own weight. He peered down into the pipe.

"I can see light."

"Cliff, you're gonna get us caught," Jesse urged.

"I'm going in," Cliff said without hesitation as he climbed into the vent.

Jesse ran over to the pipe, "What do you think you're doing?"

"I'm gonna get us some free popcorn."

"Knock it off."

"There's a vent down there. All I have to do is wait until the picture-show starts and I'll kick the vent out and drop in. I'll meet you at the back door." Cliff explained as he slid into the opening.

Jesse watched as Cliff worked his way about ten feet down the shaft until his friend came to a stop.

"Are you okay?" Jesse whispered.

"Yeah, but it's getting tight."

Jesse could no longer see his friend in the darkness and finally called out, "Cliff?"

"I'm stuck. Go get a rope." Cliff whispered somewhat loudly.

"Who's up there?" Echoed a loud angry voice from inside the theater lobby.

Jesse froze as he looked inside the shaft. Suddenly the tiny glimmer of light got much brighter as someone inside removed the vent at the bottom. He could clearly see Cliff's silhouette below.

"I'll be back," he whispered.

Jesse ran to the corner and dropped down to the roof of the police station and then quickly shimmied down the drainpipe, this time with no hesitancy or fear of the high building. When he hit bottom he darted around the corner and almost ran directly into Jewel Stoker, who was standing solidly with her arms crossed in the middle of the alley north of the police station.

"What are you two doing?" She asked in a tone that was not so much of a question as a demand for information.

Jesse froze, having no idea if Jewel was trustworthy, "Ah, nothing." He finally replied.

Jewel stood her ground, glaring at him.

Jesse needed to move. He didn't have time to waste on this girl. Still he couldn't help but want to stay a few minutes. He and Cliff spent many an hour fishing off the side of the bridge and debating who was prettiest, Jewel Stoker or Gemma or Jettie Crawford. Jesse had, until that particular moment, always argued in favor of Gemma, where Cliff held firmly in Jewel's camp. Gemma was girlier, and though that sort of thing was often annoying, Jesse just couldn't keep himself from looking at her whenever she was around. Jewel, on the other hand, was a bit of a tomboy. She was also a year older and often acted like it. However, at that moment as she stood in a t-shirt and a pair of jeans with her arms crossed like a parent, she sure looked pretty.

"I won't tell anyone, but I know you two are up to something," she said with a devilish smile that stopped Jesse's heart.

Jesse's eyes brightened. "Come on."

The two ran to the street, where Jesse stopped and peered around the corner. Nothing seemed out of the ordinary.

Jesse looked at Jewel. "Go to the Palace and look in the door."

"What's in there?"

"Just go look and tell me what you see."

She hesitated and then started walking up the street past the police station. When she got to the movie theater she turned and looked back at Jesse, who stood at the corner watching. She then went past the ticket booth to the doors and out of his sight. A moment later she stepped back into sight and bent over laughing. Finally she stood upright and waved for Jesse to come.

Jesse hesitated but walked cautiously to where she stood. Jewel started to speak but broke out laughing and pointed at the door. Jesse took a deep breath and walked to the door, carefully pulled it open, and looked in.

Across the lobby and directly in front of the concession stand stood Able McCormack on an a-frame stepladder. Able was wrestling with Cliff's legs, which were flinging wildly as they hung from an air vent. Alongside the ladder stood Doris Broussard the concession operator, a half-dozen onlookers, and Chief Hightower, who was also laughing.

"Hold still, and I'll pull you through," Able shouted angrily at Cliff.

"Let go of me." Jesse heard from the vent pipe.

"What were you doing on my roof?" Able demanded.

"I lost my kite. Now, let go of me."

"You lost your kite in my vent?"

Jesse watched as Cliff's shoulders and finally his head appeared. He then turned wide-eyed with fear and looked at Jewel who was still laughing. He turned and cautiously began walking away with Jewel alongside. Two blocks down they turned the corner and sat down on the grass under a sweet-gum tree in front of the Methodist church,

Jesse's heart was pounding, knowing that he was probably in as much trouble as Cliff. Then he looked at Jewel, who was still giggling. Suddenly the image of Cliff's legs swinging from the vent entered his mind, and he burst out laughing.

#

At exactly 7:00 a.m., Cliff Tidwell slung a homemade burlap shoulder bag of seed around his neck, picked a grubbing hoe from a pile of tools in a wheelbarrow, and began the start of what promised to be a very long week of hoeing and planting. The ground had been plowed a week earlier, but Cliff's father had not yet gotten to the chore of seeding the four-acre patch. Unfortunately, as a result of the previous day's ill-advised decision to try and steal a bag of popcorn, the job of planting that section fell to the twelve-year-old.

As Cliff began working, his eyes focused on the long straight row of red dirt ahead, about twenty feet away Jesse lifted one of the strands of barbed wire and slipped through the fence. He then held it up for Jewel to slip through. The two walked to the wheelbarrow and took a couple of hoes. As Jesse began hoeing the row next to him, Cliff looked up at his friend.

"What are you doing here?"

"We went up together, we might as well go down together. Besides, if you had gotten the popcorn I would have eaten it."

Cliff then noticed as Jewel on the third row began hoeing, "What's she doing here?"

"She saw us go up," Jesse answered. "How much trouble are you in?"

"I've got to plant this field. And Mr. McCormack said that I can't come back to the picture-show until after school starts. Does anyone know you were up there with me?"

"Everybody in town except my mom," Jesse replied with a smile.

Cliff began hoeing. "You know, if you had gotten caught and I got away I'd still be in bed."

"No you wouldn't," Jewel piped in. "I'd wake you up and make you come out here just like I did him."

#

WASHINGTON'S FEED STORE
ELZA, TEXAS
10:45 a.m., Sunday November 16, 1941

Thomas Jefferson Hightower breathed a long sigh as he shut off the motor of his 1941 Ford Police prowler. The car was the only good thing about that job. Being the chief of a one-person police department had very few perks. The brand new car was, for all practical purposes, the only perk. Six months earlier the town council had given him a choice - they could get him a car, or they could hire a second officer. He opted for the car because it didn't make sense to have a second officer to chase down a bank robber if they had to do it on foot. Not that chasing down a bank robber was an issue. Elza had very little real crime to worry about. Mostly he had some drunk doing something stupid, like Irwin Stoker walking into the Palace with a loaded shotgun. Still, it would be nice to have a second man to take a few of the midnight phone calls or block traffic for the occasional funeral.

For the most part, his ten years as the Elza Police Department hadn't been all that bad, until today. For the second time in his career in law enforcement, Jefferson was in way over his head. He hadn't had any real training. He'd been hired because his uncle Darrell was mayor and Uncle Darrell was only the mayor because Elza needed a city charter to get the state of Texas to give them money to put a traffic light where Highway 84 crossed Main Street. In the state of Texas, city charters required that there be an elected town council, an elected mayor, and a police chief.

It seemed like the best deal in the world at the time. It was a steady paycheck, and back in 1931 there weren't that many steady jobs. It wasn't hard work because there just wasn't that much crime, and he got to carry a gun right out in the open. On the downside, until recently, he'd had to drive around in a worn-out 1928 Model AA Flatbed delivery truck that he bought second-hand with the words "Bradford's Store" permanently faded onto the driver-side door.

It had been a long morning for Jefferson Hightower. First, at 5:36 a.m. on the one morning of the week that he got to sleep past five, his phone rang with Susie Tidwell on the line frantic because Clifford hadn't come home last night. Susie had heard about the events at the Palace through the Cherokee County Party Line News Service, which is what Jefferson called the local rumor mill. The telephone was the most remarkable invention in history, but at the very same time it was the worst thing that had ever come along. Almost every phone in town was on a "party line," which meant that a single phone line was shared by a half-dozen customers. This meant, naturally, that if your cousin in Memphis gave you a call, as many as six people were listening in, and within an hour, half of Elza would know that your cousin's wisdom tooth fell out the same day his wife ran off with a dentist. On the good side, the night that someone tried to steal George Henry McMillian's cash box, all it took was a single phone call and Jefferson was there in less than ten minutes. On the other hand, let some fool shoot off a scattergun at a coyote, and within thirty minutes Jefferson would be getting calls saying that no less than John Dillinger was robbing the bank. Never mind the fact that Dillinger had been dead since '34. And then something happens like Irwin Stoker marching in the Palace, and it didn't take an hour for most of Cherokee County to know that Jewel Stoker was pregnant with Cliff Tidwell's baby and Irwin darn-near killed him over it. It took a good ten minutes to convince Susie that Irwin didn't shoot Cliff because Irwin was sitting in jail sleeping off a fifth of back-forty hooch.

Then, just as Jefferson was about to sit down to his scrambled eggs and sausage, he got his second call of the morning. Apparently Cliff Tidwell's noisy Ford coupe was crashed into the loading dock at Nickel Washington's feed store out on Highway 84.

Ten minutes later Jefferson was looking at the second worst crime scene of his career. Nickel had said on the phone that there was blood and Jefferson had feared that Cliff might have knocked his head on the steering wheel. He rushed over because the poor kid most likely tried to make it home and was probably knocked-out, drunk, and bleeding someplace. Unfortunately, what had happened was a lot worse.

Jefferson hadn't seen so much blood since Peterson Crawford got run over by that train. The passenger seat was almost black. He didn't think it was really blood until he touched it. Sure enough, the seat was still wet and his fingers came up red as strawberry. The confusing part was that the stuff was only on the passenger seat and not on the driver side. Could there have been a passenger that got hurt? Only the car hadn't crashed into the loading dock all that hard; the car just had a tiny dent. Even more confusing was that Cliff didn't leave any footprints. The only tracks around the car were Jefferson's and Nickel's. The closest footprints that they could find were up by the highway, nearly a hundred feet away. Cliff must have gotten out of the car and let it roll down the hill into the dock.

Jefferson had responded to a lot of car crashes in his ten years as chief. He even had a couple with deaths, but he had never seen a crash that was anywhere near that bloody. And he certainly hadn't seen a bloody crash without a driver around.

Though he was a one-man police force, Jefferson wasn't completely alone. Back when Peterson Crawford got killed, it became clear that there were times when he needed some help, so the town council began to set a little money aside so Jefferson could pay temporary deputy police officers. Shorty Newman and Hobe Bethard had agreed to be on call for those times. It seemed like a good idea to get the car out of sight before the Cherokee County Party Line News Service had half of Elza coming out to see the bloody seat. So, before he headed over to the Rose's, he called Shorty and Hobe on Nickel's phone and had them move the car over behind the jail and cover it with a tarp.

Chapter 3

ELZA, TEXAS
June 26, 1936

The summer of '36 had settled into a regular routine for Jesse and Cliff. Like everywhere else in the country, Elza had been hit hard by what was being called the Great Depression. Jobs were hard to find for everyone and especially hard for a couple of twelve-year-old boys who were only looking for ways to make enough money for a few luxuries like soda pops and Moon Pies.

Cliff, though, was more enterprising than the normal twelve-year-old and managed to work out a deal with two of the merchants. As a result the boys started their day at eight in the morning at Washington's Feed Store sweeping and stacking sacks of feed. Then they went to McMillan's store where they swept floors and stocked shelves. Washington gave them five cents each but from McMillan they didn't get any cash but they got two RC's each a day and a Moon Pie each. George Henry McMillan, who had spent his entire life in the mercantile business, often remarked that he had never had to negotiate so long or so hard as he did with Cliff Tidwell, especially for a service that he really didn't want or need.

Nevertheless, the two boys spent their mornings working at McMillan's then would make their way down Main Street with ice-cold RC's in hand and usually a Moon

Pie or some peanuts. Generally by mid-morning they would meet up with Jewel, who spent the morning doing chores for her mother before joining the boys on the curb across from Anna-Ruth's.

"What are we goin' to do today?" Jewel asked as if they were loaded with options.

"We can go fishin'." Cliff replied as if it was an entirely fresh idea.

Jewel rolled her eyes. "How long's it been since the last time one of you caught a fish?"

Cliff and Jesse looked at each other and shrugged. "A couple of weeks."

"You know why?"

The two boys looked at one another and again shrugged.

"You two are morons. It's too hot. They don't bite when it's hot. Even I know that. If you went in the mornin' you might get somethin', but not now," Jewel replied somewhat smugly.

"We gotta work in the mornin's. Otherwise we couldn't buy the RC's." Jesse responded.

Jewel shook her head, "I know you have to work, and I appreciate you bringing me a RC every day. I'm just sayin' that it's dumb to go try to catch a fish every afternoon when there isn't a chance on God's green earth that you're gonna catch one."

"Yeah, I know. It's kind of like us sittin' here every day when we know good and well that Romeo's not going to go over there and talk to Gemma Crawford," Cliff joked, causing Jewel to laugh so hard soda came out her nose.

"Sorry, Jesse," she said once she regained control.

Jesse scowled at the two, "So what else is there to do besides fishin'?"

Cliff took a long sip of RC. "You guys want to go see a ghost town?"

Both Jewel and Jesse perked up.

"What ghost town?" Jesse asked, somewhat suspicious.

"There's a ghost town north of the highway."

Jesse and Jewel looked at one another and laughed.

"Honestly," Cliff argued, "My pa told me about it. Back in the old days there was a mining town called New Birmingham."

"What did they mine around here?" Jesse asked, sure Cliff was pulling one of his stunts.

"I think it was iron ore."

"So what happened to it?" Jewel asked, becoming convinced.

"Pa said that the ore played out."

Jewel's smile grew wide with excitement. "How long will it take us to get there?"

"I don't know, an hour or two. We follow the tracks to where they curve by the shantytown and then follow that old road 'til it plays out."

"My mom doesn't want me to go out by the shantytown." Jesse interjected, looking for a way out of following Cliff on another one of his adventures.

"We'll cut through the woods?"

#

Southern Hotel,
New Birmingham, Texas
June 26, 1936

Darnell "Shakes" Blankenship was two weeks and a day past his thirty-seventh birthday when he moved into his "summer home" in the Southern Hotel in New Birmingham, Texas. The Southern was a fine hotel in its day, but unfortunately it had fallen into some disrepair as of late. The roof, for example, had fallen in twenty or thirty years prior, and the three floors of guest rooms had long since collapsed into the lobby, leaving an enormous hole. Shakes liked to think of it as his own private solarium. His room was what he assumed had previously been a kitchen behind the lobby next to what once was probably one of the finer restaurants in the little boomtown. He had to climb over the rubble to get there, but the section he used had a roof, and the walls seemed solid. All things considered, it was far better than sleeping on the damp ground in a shantytown.

Shakes was a hobo.

In the spring of 1921, Shakes, then known as Darnell, graduated at the top of his class from Rusk High School not fifteen miles away. That September he enrolled in Stephen F. Austin Teacher's College in Nacogdoches where he studied mathematics. Most of the freshmen had their hands full just making grades, but for Darnell education was easy. When not in class he held down two jobs. Making money was important to Darnell. After two years he managed to save almost a thousand dollars and transferred to the University of Chicago where the tall, lean Texan earned a Bachelor's degree in accounting.

After graduation, Darnell Blankenship secured a job with the firm of Lockyer and Hornsby, two of the founding traders on the Chicago Stock Exchange. Darnell was on his way. The young man had a quick mind and calculated numbers like a human abacus. As a result he rose fast in the firm. In just two years Darnell had already been written up in the Financial Times as one of Chicago's bright young minds in the world of finance.

That same year he got word that both of his parents had been killed in an automobile accident on their way back to Rusk from a trip to visit relatives in Houston. Darnell wanted to go down there, of course, but he simply couldn't spare the time. The firm was swamped with work. He knew that it would take at least a week to go down to Texas on a train, handle the arrangements, and travel back. A week at the Exchange was like a lifetime; things happened so fast in the market. More importantly, the competition for jobs like his was unrelenting. If he left, there was a good chance that there would be no job to come back to.

So after a long, heated, and extremely painful telephone conversation with his sister, most of which he could hardly understand from all her sobbing, Darnell managed to talk his way out of the trip. But it was costly. He promised to turn over to her all of his inheritance, which amounted to a house, his father's hardware store, and what little money his parents had saved. Still, that wasn't enough for his sister, who never wanted to see him again. He had to promise that if he didn't have time to pay his respects to his parents that he would never come back to Rusk.

That part was easy. Darnell had no intention of ever going back to the little one-horse town.

That same year, he met her. Dianna Montgomery Bagwell. She was beautiful. What she saw in him - well, he knew exactly what she saw in him. Darnell was an "up and comer," and Dianna liked the best of everything. They dined in the finest restaurants and danced and gambled in the best speak-easies. If there was something expensive to do in Chicago, Dianna wanted to be in on it. They socialized with Chicago's finest and most notorious. On one occasion they dined just a table over from Al Capone himself at Coq d'Or in the Drake Hotel.

Their wedding was a simple affair. Only a few close friends and Dianna's family were invited. Though having a taste for the finer things, Dianna, it turned out, came from quite humble origins.

The couple took the train up the lake and honeymooned up on Mackinac Island. It was July fourth, and the Exchange was closed for part of the week, so Darnell only missed two days of real work. A man only gets married once, so he reasoned that he could miss a couple of days.

Those first few months were the best of his life. They were newlyweds, and Darnell had a very healthy income. Dianna found them an apartment right on Michigan Avenue. It was expensive, but she argued it would do nothing but go up in value, and of course, a man of his stature couldn't live just anywhere. She would have been right if nothing ever changed, but as Darnell "Shakes" Blankenship eventually came to know, in time, everything will change.

The first problem came when he got the bills for one of Dianna's shopping trips. She had spent a thousand dollars on clothes. One pair of shoes cost two hundred American dollars! That was the beginning of a series of fights that culminated when Darnell came home from a trip to see the New York Exchange with the two partners. It had been rumored that the firm might open a New York branch, something it had shied away from over the years. But the partners were seriously considering it now that they had someone dependable and smart to run it. Darnell was full of excitement when he returned home, knowing that Dianna would love New York, and hoping the move would help them iron out the problems in their marriage.

When he walked into the apartment the place was crowded with people, none of whom he had ever met. Dianna had been to the theater earlier in the evening and was hosting a party. That angered him enough, but upon searching the apartment, he couldn't even find her. Finally, she turned up in the bedroom, drunk, half-dressed, and with another man.

That night Darnell packed his belongings and moved into the Drake. The first thing the next morning he went to the bank to make sure Dianna didn't get a chance to clean him out. He was too late. The way she spent money, she had probably emptied it out before he went to New York. He didn't worry, though, because he only had a few thousand in there anyway. Darnell was a smart investor. He had money spread out all over the market. In fact, he had it so well spread out that her divorce attorneys would be hard-pressed to find out how much he had.

The divorce was as smooth as glass. Sure enough, her attorneys had no clue how much he was worth, and the settlement was based on less than half of what was really invested. She would keep the apartment, which he would pay for, and she would receive a monthly stipend for the next twenty years or until she remarried. Of course, Darnell made a grand performance, pretending that the stipend was far more than he could afford. But then, as soon as he walked out of the judge's chamber, he made arrangements for the stipend to be paid from the interest generated from just one stock. He actually laughed at the thought of how well he pulled that off.

All things considered, getting rid of Dianna would cost a lot less than staying married to her. The settlement and all financial arrangements required to finalize it were signed and settled on October 23, 1929, twenty-four hours before what became known as "Black Thursday," the day that millions of investors began to dump stocks.

The effects of the crash were devastating. Darnell had less than a hundred dollars in cash. His stocks had added up to something in excess of eighty thousand dollars. Now he had nothing but useless paper. At least that's how some people saw it. But Darnell knew the market as well as anyone. As he saw it, the market had bottomed out. This, he argued to his clients, was the time to buy, even if you had to borrow to do so. And that is exactly what he did. Then, five days later, came the big crash. October 29, 1929. That date would go down in history as the infamous Black Tuesday.

Not only did the stocks drop even further, he had bought on margin, which meant that he had borrowed to get them. He wasn't just broke - he was fifty thousand dollars in debt. Even if he could find someone to buy the stocks, he'd be lucky to come out with a thousand dollars for everything. Even that was a pipedream because anyone who had the money sure wasn't going to spend it on stocks.

The only thing he could do was sit on it. Of course, he moved out of the Drake right away. Then he arranged a meeting with Dianna and her attorneys. They would simply have to understand that there was no money. This, he was sure, was a temporary setback and in a few months the market would bounce back. In the meantime, she would have to sell the apartment and lower the stipend.

Dianna and her attorneys didn't understand. Dianna wasn't about to let go of her apartment, and there was no altering the stipend. Well, that wasn't completely true; it could be lowered, but it would be costly. It took nearly a month of negotiating during which Darnell was living in a south-side hotel where he shared a bath with five other people. He had long since fired his lawyers because there was no money to pay them. Actually, they had dropped him because they had seen his finances and knew full well what was about to happen. The stipend was cut, but to do so, he had to sign every stock he owned over to Dianna, and not just the stuff he had previously reported. They took everything, except the debt. Even when he turned everything over they weren't convinced, so it was finally agreed that until the value of all of the stocks returned to what they were on the day the divorce settlement was agreed upon, one week prior to Black Tuesday, he would pay her fifty-five percent of his salary from Lockyer and Hornsby. They had him, and they all knew it. He had no option. It was difficult enough signing the new settlement, but to add salt to the wound,

Dianna sat across the table with a smug expression while holding hands with her new boyfriend.

With payment on Dianna's apartment and the "stipend," Darnell would have almost nothing to live on, and he still owed the fifty grand. Yet he reasoned that he could hold off his creditors and manage living in the south-side hotel until the market began to climb back. He would eventually start collecting commissions again, and with some luck get his life back. At least that was his hope.

On New Year's eve the partners called them all into a meeting where they announced that they were closing the firm, effective January first. They argued that there was no money to keep it up. There was some truth to that. Darnell hadn't sold a single stock since October, but everyone was sure that it was just a matter of months or even weeks before things bounced back. Those two old crooks were simply covering their hindquarters. Unlike Darnell and most of their clients, Lockyer and Hornsby had invested heavily in real estate. It wasn't the best of investments at the time, but they hadn't lost everything from the Crash, and unlike almost everyone else in the country, they continued to collect revenue. Darnell, however, was out on the street.

It was then that he began to realize just how bad this crash really was. Lockyer and Hornsby weren't the only ones closing their doors. Most firms were closing. There wasn't a firm in town with a job opening. That being the case, Darnell began to try relentlessly to get hired as an accountant, but no one needed an accountant if they weren't making any money. By the spring of 1930 almost no one was making money. As mid-summer approached, Darnell Blankenship, the man who a few months earlier was on his way to owning Wall Street, was now five months behind on his payments to Dianna and living with a collection of out-of-work misfits in an alley behind a now closed toy factory.

Right after the crash, Darnell began drinking heavily. He hadn't been much of a drinker prior to that day, though he would have a little gin whenever he and Dianna went to a speakeasy. Now he had a bottle in his pocket almost all the time. It wasn't so much that he liked the taste of it. The cheap homemade stuff was strong and burned and had metallic aftertaste that lasted all day, but it calmed his nerves. He didn't know if it was from stress or something really physically wrong with him, but his hands had begun to shake most of the time, as if he was cold. The booze helped him relax, and when relaxed he didn't shake. So now he kept a bottle close by all the time. Whenever he got a job interview or some day-work, for that matter, he'd take a few drinks to settle him down.

It was his shaking hands that earned him the nickname "Shakes."

Finally one morning, as he was standing in line for day-work at a construction site, a private investigator and two thugs working for Dianna's lawyers found him. They dragged him into an alley and beat him so badly that he could hardly stand. Their message was a simple one: quit drinking and get a job.

Darnell already knew that he couldn't get a job because there weren't any. What he didn't know was that he couldn't quit drinking.

That night he hopped his first train, the first of many. Over the years he crisscrossed the mid-west a dozen times. Often he didn't even know what state he was in. All he had were the clothes on his back and a blanket to sleep on. He carried two tin bottles, one for water and one for hooch. He carried a third tin that he used for cooking and eating. Aside from those necessities, the only possession he had was the fedora made specifically for him at Johnny Tyus' shop on 79th Street and Racine Avenue back in Chicago. That hat was all he had left of his former life.

He lived in the shantytowns, and his meals came from the soup kitchens or the few pennies he could make from day-work here or there. One day he got off a train and realized that he was in East Texas. He had grown up in Rusk, just a few miles away, so he decided to walk into town and see his sister. He really didn't know what to expect. Their last conversation hadn't gone well at all. He didn't know where she lived, so he went to their father's old hardware store on the square across from the county courthouse. Just as he got to the door, she and two little boys came walking out.

When he said "hello" she stopped for a long minute and looked directly in his eyes. At first she had a look of surprise, but that quickly turned to disdain.

The older of the two kids asked her, "Who is that man, mommy?"

She turned her gaze to the child and answered, "That's a stranger. We don't talk to strangers."

She then led the kids away.

He left Rusk for the last time and headed for Elza where there was a shantytown. Everyone on the rails knew where to find a place to sleep or get a meal or a day's work. Elza didn't offer much work, and there wasn't a soup kitchen, but it offered a safe place to sleep without having to fear being run off. The shantytown, as it turned out, was on a bend in the track a little below New Birmingham. As a kid he and his friends had explored the old ghost town. So when he learned that the shantytown was just a little way from the old ruins, he decided to explore it again, this time with the idea of making himself a little home. In the back of the old hotel he found a room that no one would ever find without climbing over the debris, and that wasn't likely because of the chance of getting hit in the head by falling rubble. Before long, Shakes had himself a nice little apartment. It was the perfect little home. There were plenty of farms where he could get a little work or steal a few vegetables, and down the tracks was a river with fresh water and fish. When he needed money he could hop a train into Houston or Dallas, where he'd find a few day jobs to keep his little home supplied with canned food and hooch. It wasn't the apartment on Michigan Avenue, but it was a far cry better than shantytown.

#

After walking through wooded trails for more than half an hour, Jesse and Jewel had begun to feel that Cliff had led them on a snipe hunt. Basically it's an East Texas version of a wild goose chase, except your friend runs off and leaves you in the woods looking for a mysterious "snipe" while he goes home and has an RC.

"It ain't gonna work, Clifford."

"I promise; it's somewhere up ahead."

Jesse and Jewel stopped on the trail. Both knew better than to trust Cliff too far.

Cliff noticed them and pleaded, "I swear, I'm not lyin'. It's west of the river, north of the highway, and this side of the road. We've gotta be close."

Jesse and Jewel looked at one another and reluctantly began to follow.

"Cliff Tidwell, if there's not a town up here, I'm going to beat the snot out of you," Jewel threatened.

"Oh, like you could," Cliff retorted confidently.

Jewel stopped still, crossed her arms, and glared at him. "Do you want to try me?"

The two boys stopped and looked at Jewel. Jesse began to laugh at the thought of the two fighting.

"My money's on her, Cliff."

Jewel and Cliff stared at one another.

"It's too hot to fight a girl. Besides, there's a clearing up ahead," Cliff said as he shrugged her off and headed on up the trail.

"You're just afraid to have a girl give you a black eye," Jewel replied as Cliff headed away.

Jesse followed the other two, laughing as the trail led to a clear stretch through the woods that had once been a road. The road was almost waist high with grass, but there were the remnants of wagon ruts.

"This has got to be it," Cliff said, now relieved that the story he'd been told was probably true.

To their amazement, in the middle of the woods they walked into what was obviously a town. There was a main road lined with buildings and even some side streets with a few buildings and houses still standing. Most of the structures had been brick, but a few wooden buildings still stood as well. As they came to the main road, there was a sign.

NEW BIRMINGHAM, TEXAS

Pop. 1462

"THE IRON QUEEN OF THE SOUTHWEST"

Though the trees and brush had grown up, it was clear that there were once a lot of buildings and houses there. Most of the buildings had fallen down, but many had walls remaining. At the far end of the street was even a tall smokestack.

"That must have been the furnaces," Cliff pointed out.

Jewel walked along, wide-eyed with amazement. "This place is unbelievable. All this time we lived right down the road and had no idea it existed."

At the center of the town they came to a large four-story building. On the front was painted "The Southern Hotel." It was an enormous structure that was at least a city block long with a porch that extended the length of the front and a balcony on the second floor that did the same.

"That was a hotel?" Jesse asked in amazement.

"I've never seen a hotel that big before," Jewel interjected.

"I haven't either," Jesse added as he walked up the front steps toward the front door.

He stepped carefully, knowing from seeing all the rotted wood that the porch could easily break beneath him.

Jesse peered inside, but the roof had collapsed, and all four floors were now a pile of crumbled debris. Still, it was easy to tell that it had been a fine hotel at one time.

Deep in the building, past the former lobby, Shakes Blankenship peered from a dark shadow at Jesse as he looked into the building. In the year that he'd been living there, this was the first time anyone had wandered into his little paradise, and he wasn't at all happy about it. This tiny little crumbling boomtown was all Shakes had in the world. It was his refuge. It was a place where he could escape all the things that had gone wrong with his life.

But only a few feet away stood three kids who could, with only a few words, put an end to his private sanctuary.

Shakes watched with anger as Jesse looked around the hotel and finally walked back out to his friends. All this kid had to do was mention to a cop or a sheriff that there was a bum living in the old hotel in New Birmingham and it would all be over. One word and Shakes would be back on the rails.

When Jesse turned back to face the others, Cliff explained, "Pa said that this was once one of the fanciest hotels in Texas."

The three began to walk along the street in silence as they looked with amazement at what was once an enormous town, far larger than Elza and maybe even larger than Rusk or Jacksonville. Near the end of the street they came to an old mine. The building had burned down, but the smoke-stack from the smelter remained. There was also a mineshaft with a crumbling wooden framework around it. As they approached, Cliff picked up a pebble and tossed it into the shaft. The stone bounced and echoed, and finally they heard the splash of water. All three looked down into the deep shaft, making sure to maintain balance lest they fall in.

"How deep do you suppose it is?" Jewel asked.

"It's hard to tell. All I see is black," Jesse replied.

Shakes watched the kids peering into the mine from only twenty feet away. He had gone out the back door of the hotel and followed them along, keeping to the side street, out of sight. It occurred to him that all he had to do is run across the street and give the three a little push and that would be it. If someone came looking for them, all they would find was that three kids had fallen into a really deep hole.

All he had to do was run and give them a push.

The kids walked back through the town and came out the rutted road that led them in. When they came to the trail they had followed in, Jesse turned down it, but Cliff stopped. "Let's take this road. I think it'll be shorter."

"Do you have any idea where it goes?" Jewel asked.

"No, but it goes in the direction of the railroad tracks, so it has to put us out close to home," Cliff argued as he headed up the road with Jewel behind.

"Are you sure about this?" Jesse asked before following the other two.

"No, but we don't have anything better to do."

The three followed the lane to the railroad. It was obvious that before the tracks were built the road went straight through. When they climbed up on the tracks, the road on the other side that had once gone straight to New Birmingham now curved and followed along the tracks. Instead of leading to New Birmingham, the road now led to a little shantytown.

Jesse was wide-eyed with amazement. He knew about shantytowns. Lowell Thomas talked about them on the radio all the time, and he had seen one in a movie. He knew the place existed, of course - hobos wandered into Elza almost every day - but he had never seen the town and had no idea that so many people were there.

His mother called those people freeloaders and bums, but his father said that they were just normal folks who were down on their luck. Most had lost their jobs and then their homes because of the Depression and were trying to make their way to California.

The town covered about an acre of land where the railroad tracks curved to the south next to a county road that led out to the highway near McMillan's. There were around a hundred men and women and children, most living in tents and lean-tos. Some were living out of cars and wagons. All had the same downcast look upon their faces.

Until that moment Jesse had never thought of his family as wealthy. He knew that they were one of the better-off families in Elza. Just living on Red Oak Avenue said it all. There were only a few two-story brick homes in town, and they were all on Red Oak. In fact, there were only two houses bigger than his. One belonged to the bank president and the other was Fitches Funeral Home.

He also knew that they had it a lot better off than Cliff's and Jewel's families. Both of their fathers were farmers who had to take part-time work at the mill to make ends meet. Farming, his father had often told him, had made pretty good money before the depression. Crop prices dropped dramatically after the crash of '29, and many of the farmers had to find jobs. Others lost their farms to the banks. Elza was lucky to have the pulp mill even though his mother complained constantly about the smell of burned wood and tar. According to Jesse's father, the only reason the town survived was because there was one good business that continued to hire workers. Murdock Rose often liked to remark, to Garvis's utter humiliation, that Jesse's grandfather, the late Horace McCracken Hamilton, would still be in business had he the wisdom to convert his lumber mills to pulp rather than investing in whores and cheap whiskey.

Jesse realized, as he Cliff and Jewel followed the tracks past the little village that the Rose family might not be rich, as his mother regularly informed him, but he had a home and a bed and a meal every night, which was considerably more than these people.

Just ahead, where the railroad tracks turned to the south, Chief Thomas Jefferson Hightower slowly drove along the corrugated road toward the three in his old 1928 Model AA Flatbed truck. The chief had bought the truck second-hand from old Mr. Bradford over in Maydelle whose son used it to deliver groceries and feed for their family store. The Ford's cab was powder blue and was so faded and oxidized by the sun that if you rubbed your hand on the door it would come up a dirty white. On the side door you could still see where the word "Bradford" was once painted.

Jefferson had been fighting with the town council for years to get a police prowler. He argued, quite rightly, that a police chief shouldn't have to go running down the street every time someone called for help. He also made the sound argument that it was embarrassing to the entire town that on those rare occasions that he made an arrest he had to buy bus tickets for him and his prisoner to go before the judge at the county seat in Rusk. The town council naturally understood, but argued that the town, quite frankly, could barely afford to pay his salary, let alone buy him a car to drive around in.

It was finally agreed that if he bought his own vehicle, the town council would keep him supplied with gas and oil. It soon became a running joke down at the domino hall that if the town council knew beforehand how much oil that Ford leaked they would have bought him the prowler he wanted.

"Hey, Jefferson!" Cliff shouted with a wave as the old Ford rambled toward them.

The chief pulled the truck to a stop and the three kids walked up to the window.

"What are you kids doing out here?"

"We went up to the old ghost town," Jesse answered.

"New Birmingham?" the Chief asked smiling.

"You know about it?" Jewel asked excitedly.

"Sure. We used to hike up there all the time when I was your age."

"What are you doin' here, Jefferson?" Cliff asked.

"I like to come out and check on these folks now and then, that's all."

Jesse looked around at the little town, "I bet you make a lot of arrests out here."

"Nope, not a one. Once in a while one of these fellows gets drunk and I take him in and let him sleep it off, but they never cause any trouble. I really just take them in so I can give them a good meal and a decent place to sleep. Most of these folks don't get much to eat."

Jesse looked around somewhat ashamed at his remark.

"You kids want a ride back to town?"

"Sure, Chief," Jesse replied for the three of them.

"Hop on the back," Jefferson told them unnecessarily as Cliff and the other two were already climbing onto the flatbed truck.

#

The Chief pulled over at McMillan's and stopped. The kids hopped off the flatbed, and Cliff walked over to the cab.

"Thanks for the lift, Jefferson."

"Anytime," the chief replied as he pulled away and headed up toward Main Street.

"Hey, Jefferson!" Cliff suddenly shouted as he ran up to the truck.

The chief stopped and looked back at Cliff who, followed by the other two, came to the window.

"Jefferson, if you could give those people down there some food, would you?"

"Well, sure," he answered, "do you have a stockpile of food that you want to take down there?"

"No, I was just wondering," Cliff said, and then he turned to walk off.

Jefferson watched Cliff walk away. If it were any other kid, he'd be a little puzzled at the question, but Jefferson knew better than to try to figure out what was on Cliff's mind. That kid, he had long since decided, would either end up rich or in jail. Cliff was one of those people who had no fear of taking a risk and less fear of the consequences. He smiled and waved at the kids and then pulled away.

"Okay, what are you cookin' up?" Jewel asked Cliff as she and Jesse caught up with him.

"Nothin'."

Jesse and Jewel look at each other, neither buying it.

"Nothin', my butt," Jewel replied.

"Let me think on it a while, and I'll let y'all in on it when I have a plan."

#

COUNTY ROAD 36,
ONE MILE SOUTH OF ELZA, TEXAS
12:31 a.m. June 27, 1936

Cliff and Jesse walked quietly along the long gravel road. It was after midnight, and neither boy wanted to get caught. Under his arm Cliff carried a rolled up tarp. Finally they came to a road crossing, where Cliff stopped.

"Now will you tell me what we're doing out here?" Jesse asked in a loud whisper.

From across the road and hidden by the shadow of a large live oak tree, Jewel answered, "Stealing watermelons."

Jesse and Cliff both turned their heads in her direction in shock.

"What are you doing here?" Cliff asked in even a louder whisper.

"Same as you. Stealing watermelons," she answered with both innocence and sarcasm as she walked over to the two boys.

"How'd you know?" Cliff asked.

Jewel rolled her eyes at Cliff.

"The only person you fooled is him," she said somewhat loudly, glancing at Jesse, "I'm surprised Chief Hightower isn't out here."

"How'd you know we'd be here and not someplace else?

"You won't feel bad about stealing from Mr. McAlister. Everyone knows that he plows half his crop under.

In the distance a dog started barking.

"Be quiet," Cliff demanded and then added, "Well, as long as you're here, you may as well help. Here's what we'll do. Jesse and me will go into the field and bring you watermelons. You pile them up in the ditch next to the road. We'll cover 'em with the tarp and some dirt and come get them tomorrow."

Jewel saluted mockingly. "Yes, sir, Colonel."

Jesse laughed as a perturbed Cliff led the two of them through a barbed wire fence into a watermelon patch.

The field belonged to an old man by the name of Jeremiah McAlister, whose farmhouse was about a quarter of a mile further up the road. Mr. McAlister had been a pig farmer for most of his life. In fact, his house was practically wallpapered with ribbons from his many grand champions at county fairs and one ribbon, of which he was particularly proud, from the Texas State Fair in Dallas. For years, most of his crops served only as food for the pigs, but a few years back he decided that he was too old for pigs and sold off his stock. He still farmed a few crops like turnips and corn and watermelons, the best of which he loaded each week into the back of his '34 Ford pickup and hauled them up to Jacksonville to sell at War Memorial Park. The rest of his crops, the watermelons that were too small, for example, he simply let rot and then plowed under. This made for a good fertilizer, but, in Cliff's opinion, was a terrible waste of good watermelons.

Within minutes Jesse and Cliff were carrying large handfuls of smaller watermelons to the fence, where Jewel would take them and stack them neatly in the ditch. Within an hour the three had at least two hundred watermelons stacked orderly in the ditch. When they finished, they covered the watermelons with the tarp and then added some dirt and brush, so that if a car passed, which was pretty unlikely, no one would notice.

As they stood admiring their labor Jesse asked, "Okay, wise guy, we got the watermelon, how do we get 'em to the shantytown?"

Cliff rolled his eyes, and Jewel began to laugh.

"What?"

"I swear, Jesse," Cliff began, "you make the best grades in school, but if you had to match wits with a jack-ass you'd need crib-notes."

#

It was a little after noon when Chief Thomas Jefferson Hightower's faded powder blue Model-AA Flatbed rolled up the dirt road. Cliff sat in front with the Chief while Jesse and Jewel rode in back.

"Pull over to the right where the roads intersect," Cliff instructed.

Jefferson didn't know what the kids were up to, but knowing Clifford it probably wasn't good. Obviously there couldn't be too much mischief involved, or else they wouldn't have invited the Police Chief. The chief had to admit that he was both a little flattered and entertained that the three kids chose to include him in one of their little escapades. Still, as he pulled the truck to the side of the road, Jefferson couldn't help but fear that giving Cliff Tidwell and his two accomplices a ride could cost him his job.

As Cliff climbed out of the truck, Jesse and Jewel were standing on the flatbed scanning the area for witnesses.

"Anything?"

"No, we're clear," Jesse replied as he climbed down.

Jewel stayed in the back of the flatbed while the two boys pulled the tarp off the watermelons. The three had worked out their plan as they walked home. In order not to raise suspicion in case anyone found the watermelons, the boys followed their normal routine of working at McMillan's.

At around noon the three would have a soda across from Anna-Ruth's (that was mostly for Jesse). Then they would head over to the domino hall where, if he held to his normal schedule, they would find the chief, and Cliff would talk him into giving them a ride in his truck. Once they were out of town, the rest would be easy.

"And as soon as Mr. McAlister notices that his crop is missing a couple of hundred watermelons, everybody in town will come after the three of us," Jesse said, putting an ending on Cliff's plan.

"Don't you get it?" Cliff argued, "Jefferson is our alibi. No one is going to accuse us of stealing watermelons when everybody at the domino hall knows we were with the police chief."

Of course, Jesse and Jewel knew full well that, chief or no chief, if Mr. McAlister notices those watermelons missing, those two boys would get the blame.

When Jefferson stepped out of his truck and saw the enormous pile of watermelons, he almost blew his top, "What have you three done?" he said, almost yelling.

"Jeez, Jefferson, do you want the whole town to hear us?" Cliff scolded.

"You three are going to get me fired. Jeremiah McAlister will be in my office screaming to have you kids arrested."

"All we're going to do is haul them down to the shantytown. Besides, he can't blame us. Everybody in town saw us leaving with you," Cliff reasoned.

"That's the part that'll get me fired."

"Oh, come on, Jefferson," Cliff went on as he and Jesse began picking up watermelons and handing them up to Jewel, "You said yourself that you'd help those people if you could."

"I didn't say that I'd commit larceny, which is exactly what this is."

Jesse and Jewel began to laugh a little, knowing that the chief had lost this battle to Cliff before it even began.

It became obvious to Chief Hightower as he watched that the kids had no intention of stopping. Realizing that he was involved whether he wanted to be or not he said, "Well, if we're going to do this let's make it quick. Cliff you get in the ditch and hand them up one at a time to Jesse. Jesse, you hand them to me and I'll hand them up to Jewel."

In moments the four had the truck loaded. The kids covered the watermelons with the tarp and tied it down. Then, all four hopped into the cab and the chief drove the truck right down Main Street and out to the highway and then up the old dirt road to the shantytown.

#

The people of shantytown stayed back at first as the three kids pulled the tarp off the watermelons. Usually when they encountered a police uniform it was to beat them and drag them off to jail or beat them and run them out of town. Either way, it involved a beating.

The boys seemed unaware of the situation, though the cop clearly understood. It was Jewel who caught on and broke the ice. She spotted a pregnant woman with two kids and picked out one of the biggest melons and took it over to the woman, broke it open, and began handing chunks to the two kids. The little ones scarfed the melon down like it was the best meal they had ever eaten. As the children finished it up, the girl went back to the truck and grabbed another melon and took it to the lady.

"Have it for supper," she said as she handed her the melon.

By this point a few of the other homeless men and women began walking over to the truck, and the two boys handed out melons. The police officer simply stood next to his truck and lit a cigar.

Soon three lines formed, one in front of Cliff, one in front of Jesse, and a third in front of Jewel. Shakes Blankenship was in Jesse's line.

When he stepped up to the boy, Jesse handed him a melon and turned to grab another. As Shakes started to walk away, Jesse said, "Hold on, take another one. We have plenty," and handed the former stockbroker a second melon.

Shakes looked at the boy who only the day before he had contemplated killing and said, "Thank you," and turned and walked away.

Jesse watched the man walk off into the woods as he continued to hand out melons to the hungry people.

#

MCALISTER'S FARM
7:00 a.m. June 28, 1936

Jesse, Cliff, and Jewel were all three standing in one of Jeremiah McAlister's fields, each with a burlap sack of seed hanging off their shoulders and a hoe in hand working their way down a two acre stretch. When Mr. McAlister saw that his field had been raided, he didn't bother to go to the police station. Instead he went directly to Cliff's father. Ned Tidwell didn't bother listening to any of Cliff's claims of innocence; he simply searched out his son's two accomplices and took them all to Mr. McAlister and worked out a deal.

McAlister, in reality, wasn't all that angry but would have preferred the kids asked rather than just stealing from him. If he had known they were taking the melons to the poor people down at the shantytown he would have given them all they wanted. It was Cliff's dad who insisted that the kids work off the price of the watermelons. Had McAlister shown up at Jesse's house, Murdock would have simply handed the old pig farmer twenty dollars and sent him on his way. But Ned didn't have twenty dollars, and more importantly, he wanted the kids to know just how hard old Jeremiah McAlister worked to plant those melons. So for the next week or so the kids would, as Ned Tidwell put it, "become re-acquainted with the fine art of planting watermelon seeds."

Cliff was angry. He had a well-planned and, quite frankly, foolproof alibi that would prove there was no possible way the three were involved in the disappearance of old man McAlister's crops. Unfortunately his own father refused to even hear his defense.

Jewel was, in all honestly, pleased that her involvement in the caper was assumed, making her feel like a real part of the gang and not just a sidekick. She would have preferred that if she had to get caught it could have been for a less strenuous infraction, though.

Jesse had no doubts that the three would get caught from the very beginning. Being friends with Cliff Tidwell, he had long-since learned, was often adventurous, but those adventures almost always had a price tag.

"Jewel," Jesse began, "have you noticed that every time we get into trouble it's because of something Cliff got us into?"

Chapter 4

301 RED OAK AVE., ELZA, TEXAS
10:45 a.m., Sunday November 16, 1941

There are few people in this world with the patience of Murdock Rose. Twenty-five years in the oil fields will do that to a man. Contrary to popular belief, you won't get oil by simply stabbing a pipe in the East Texas soil. Sometimes it takes weeks and even months of drilling to get anything up, and that's if you're lucky. More often than not you find yourself picking up and moving on to the next lease. Once, he recalled, they dropped fifty wells before hitting pay dirt, but it was worth it. That strike was one of the biggest since the old days when Kilgore had pump-jacks on the school playground. Of course, Murdock didn't get a piece of it. He was a lowly roughneck in those days. He was lead-man on that rig, which was quite an honor since he was barely out of his teens, but he was a roughneck nonetheless, which meant that all he got were his simple wages. Unlike the company owners, landowners, leaseholders, and bankers who became millionaires off that one hole, he did the labor and only got a day's pay.

It was a long hard road, but Murdock went from being a roughneck to manager of a region that covered a territory larger than the state of Rhode Island. As such, he could now get a piece of every hole drilled. Mind you, it was a very small piece of the pie, but in four or five years he'd retire quite comfortably. More importantly, Garvis was happy that he no longer came home smelling of sweat and crude. For over twenty years Murdock sank pipe, a job that had taken its toll on his back and had put a lot of good men in an early grave. Those days were over. Murdock rarely drew a bead of sweat these days. His white shirt was always crisply pressed, and his tie was never loose. And, thanks to Monroe's Tailor Shop and Dry Cleaners, his suits were always clean and freshly creased, even in the brutal August heat. It didn't hurt, of course, that he could now afford to drive a 1940 Cadillac complete with the miracle of weather-conditioning.

The Caddy was about the only luxury Murdock allowed himself. He had the unimaginable luck to stumble on it while in Houston for a manager's meeting. It was a rare find. Murdock stopped in the Cadillac dealership because his old Ford spent more time being fixed than rolling. At least that's how it seemed to Murdock. He really didn't want a Cadillac. A Chevrolet or Buick would have suited him just fine, but Garvis insisted he needed an automobile that suited his station. Murdock didn't care in the least about his "station," but when he spotted the red Cadillac LaSalle through the showroom window, for some reason that now escaped his memory, he pulled the old Ford over and walked in.

The LaSalle, of course, was absolutely ridiculous and without question the worst possible automobile to use driving to and from oil fields. It was bright red with a shine you could comb your hair in and had a chromium hood ornament that looked like a shiny buck-naked angel in flight. After only five minutes in the dealership, Murdock came to his senses and started to walk out when the salesman mentioned those two magic words - "weather-conditioning." According to the salesman, the automobile had been ordered straight from the factory for a rich oilman, but his wife hated the color and thus he refused to take delivery. Apparently, Cadillac red was not a deep enough tone to suit her sensibilities. That same salesman went on to say that this was the only Cadillac in all of Texas with weather-conditioning, a fact which Murdock Rose knew to be wholly untrue. Three of the board members of Powhatan Oil drove Cadillacs, and all three had weather-conditioning, a fact that Murdock did not hesitate to make known. Furthermore, it made no small commotion in the showroom when he proclaimed he was not about to purchase an automobile from a bold-faced liar.

He was back in his Ford with the motor running when the sales-manager, along with the dealership owner, convinced him to come back in and hear the apology from the salesman and re-consider buying the LaSalle. Murdock, by that point, had long since made up his mind that he wasn't going to drive around East Texas in a hot automobile as long as one with weather-conditioning was sitting there available to him. His calling the salesman a liar simply served to point out to the salesman, his sales manager, and the dealership owner that he was well acquainted with three of the wealthiest men in Houston and was most certainly the only person who would walk in the dealership that day or even that week or maybe even that entire month who had the means to buy what was very possibly the most expensive automobile in all of Southeast Texas. Murdock ended up in a sit-down meeting with the owner of the dealership who, out of "his apologetic spirit," took five hundred dollars off the asking price. That "apologetic spirit" naturally was nothing more than a bribe that hopefully would bring Murdock back to buy next year's model, a bribe that had no chance of paying off. The Ford had served him well for over ten years, and if the Cadillac did anything less he would never consider buying another one.

So late that Friday evening, Murdock Rose cruised into Elza in weather-conditioned comfort. The automobile didn't garner too much attention because by that time of night the streets were almost empty, which pleased Rose considerably. The only thing that caused him to have any hesitance of buying the LaSalle was that the blasted thing was such a bright red that from now on he would be the center of attention every time he so much as drove to church, a benefit that pleased Garvis well beyond his understanding.

Despite being worn out from the long drive up from Houston, he had to take Garvis for a ride as soon as he got into the driveway. He fully expected Jesse to come along, but he'd made the mistake of telling the boy that the Ford was sitting at the Cadillac dealership in Houston and it was his if he wanted to go down there and bring it back. Thirty minutes later Jesse and Clifford Tidwell were halfway to Conroe in that noisy coupe Cliff drove. They camped out somewhere along the way, and by lunchtime Saturday they had that old Ford on blocks in the driveway with the motor scattered in a hundred pieces all over the yard. By Monday morning those boys had that car running like it was brand new, a talent that Murdock was utterly unaware the two possessed. Had he known, to his wife's chagrin, Murdock Rose would most certainly still be driving around town in an eleven-year-old Ford.

As much as Murdock liked the weather-conditioned Cadillac LaSalle, Garvis liked it at least ten times more. Murdock saw the weather-conditioning as simply an added perk, albeit a very nice one. Garvis rather, loved the fact that it was a Cadillac. And, more importantly, a LaSalle, the top of the Cadillac line. Even more importantly, it was bright red with lots of chromium, unlike the plain black

Ford sedan. She loved the fact that every eye turned when they drove through town. As she had said more than once, "The Roses are the envy of every 'dirt farmer' in East Texas." Whenever she said such things, Murdock would point out that those "dirt farmers" bought the petroleum that paid for the overpriced collection of bolts.

Murdock resented her condescension. His father and grandfather before him had at some point in their lives worked the fields. More importantly, had it not been for the oil boom, he himself would more than likely be picking cotton or herding cattle.

Garvis, however, was never put off by Murdock's remarks. She didn't like living in a small town, let alone one that didn't have so much as a decent restaurant. When she married Murdock she never envisioned that they would spend their entire lives in tiny Elza. Her father, Horace McCracken Hamilton, God rest his soul, had been owner of the Hamilton Lumber Company and Timber Mill in Henderson, and as such did business with just about everyone in the oil fields.

One such oilman was Mr. Nehemiah Rice Nightingale, who had been President and General Manager of the Frelinghuysen-Nightingale Petroleum Company before he sold the company to the Powhatan Group in Houston, when it became Powhatan Oil. Mr. Nightingale was a wealthy man long before he sold Frelinghuysen-Nightingale Petroleum but after the sale he was, for a time at least, very possibly the richest man in all of Texas, which was saying a great deal.

Mr. Nightingale also happened to like betting on the horse races at Fairgrounds racetrack down in New Orleans. In the early 1920's, Garvis's father desperately needed to lock up a lumber contract with Mr. Nightingale, so he arranged a little trip to the track. Horace McCracken Hamilton made a huge event of the little junket, as he called the trip, by arranging for no less than three private rail cars complete with sleeping berths, a cook, and a free-flowing bar. That was no small feat, considering it was the beginning of Prohibition and would have landed all of them in jail if caught. Thus, no less than a thousand dollars was invested to ensure that the railroad conductor kept any passengers from knowing what was going on in the back of the train.

The alcohol was the easy part. Garvis's father supplied lumber to the Whittlesey Brothers and - though it was only rumored, but Garvis knew it to be a fact - he also supplied grain and cane sugar for the Brothers. The Whittleseys operated stills all over East Texas, and some people claimed that they were at least partly responsible for the grain alcohol that kept New Orleans' infamously decadent Vieux Carrie lubricated during those times.

Garvis's role on the excursion was to help serve Mr. Nightingale's needs - most specifically to make sure that his liquor glass stayed full. But her real purpose, at least according to her mother, Mrs. Horace McCracken Hamilton, was to make sure that her father didn't get so drunk that he began saying insulting or offensive remarks to one of the most important oil men in all of Texas.

Mr. Nightingale accepted the invitation, and though it was specifically stated that the invitation extended only to him and his immediate family, the oilman chose to bring along a dozen of his drinking buddies. One of those buddies was a young, tall roughneck named Murdock Rose whose family, Nightingale bragged, had been in Texas all the way back to the Alamo. An honor only a true Texan could appreciate. Garvis's father, though, was not at all impressed with the man's pedigree; the Hamiltons had been Texans back in the days of the Republic when Horace's great-grandfather had migrated from Louisiana. As far as Hamilton was concerned, Mr. Rose, like all of the men

Nightingale had brought along, was not invited, and thus they were enjoying a very expensive vacation at Hamilton's expense.

Unlike her father, Garvis was awe-struck by the tall young man. First, because he was rugged and very good looking, but also because she had heard Nightingale remark more than once that Mr. Rose was a natural oil man and would someday be running Frelinghuysen-Nightingale Petroleum.

So naturally as they made the long trip to New Orleans, young Garvis made every effort to get to know this young man who was destined to become Texas' next tycoon.

Murdock, however, showed little interest in the girl, regardless of how much effort she took to make herself look irresistible to him.

Garvis naturally had no clue that Murdock was way out of his element. Up to this point in his life he had never so much as been on a train, let alone in a private car. As a matter of fact, he had never traveled more than fifty miles from Nacogdoches, where he grew up. Nightingale insisted that he come along and "help spend this lumberjack's money." That meant he had to go out and spend a week's wage on a suit of clothes since his wardrobe amounted to a half-dozen work shirts, two pair of work pants, and one well-worn pair of bibbed-overalls.

Garvis also did not know that although Murdock's great-grandfather had in fact been at the Alamo, he had been the only one of our brave heroes to run away from the battle; thus, instead of going out in glory, he brought nothing but shame on his family. This family disgrace was something of which Murdock mysteriously seemed unaffected. Of course once they were married Garvis was reminded of it every time she had to write her last name. Unaware of Murdock's family's humiliation and the fact that he was not a tycoon in the making, Garvis fell head-over-heels in love long before they got anywhere near New Orleans.

During their day at the track where, as her father later said, "Nightingale and his boys tried to gamble away the lumber mill," she made every effort to look her best and was rarely more than a few feet away from Mr. Rose.

It wasn't until that night that he showed any real interest in her at all. Mr. Nightingale insisted that they have dinner at The O'Dwyer Brother's Original Southport Club despite the fact that Hamilton had arranged for a steak dinner to be prepared back on the train. Nevertheless, at Mr. Nightingale's insistence they all hopped into some Packard limousines and headed to this "restaurant." Had her father known that The Original Southport Club was in reality a notorious speak-easy and casino, there was no way he would have allowed his "precious princess" to come along.

The "restaurant" was a large, beautiful old home on Monticello Avenue and sat at a bend in the river surrounded by other such homes. Behind the house was a lovely garden with fountains and waterfalls and a spectacular view of the Mississippi. As they walked in the door, Nightingale explained that although the business was totally illegal, there was little risk of a raid because of the relationship the owners had with certain members of the local law enforcement and government. He said that it was not unusual to see Senators and even movie stars at the tables. Sure enough, they were there less than five minutes before someone pointed out Fatty Arbuckle playing roulette.

Horace Hamilton was in a bit of a quandary; he had to take care of Nightingale's whims, regardless of how costly, but he could not tolerate his daughter sitting around in a speak-easy with the Jezebels that he saw hanging on the arms of the fools gambling away their hard-earned money. Thus he asked Murdock if he would be so kind as to sit outside in the gardens with Garvis while he tried to keep Nightingale from spending what was left of her dowry. Hamilton had recognized his daughter's infatuation with Murdock almost as soon as they had left Henderson. Had the young man been like any of the other oil stains that Nightingale had brought along, he would have made sure that Garvis was kept a safe distance away. But Mr. Rose was considerably different from those other gentlemen. For one thing he had the hands of a man who worked for a living. The others in the group appeared to be accountants and lawyers, but not this man. This was a young man who earned his living through hard work. More importantly, he was a man who showed considerable promise. Nightingale was not the kind of man to toss around compliments lightly; if he said Rose would go far in the oil business, he would probably do so. More importantly, he probably wouldn't have invited the young man along if he didn't expect him to be very important one day.

For Garvis it couldn't have worked out any better. Not only did she get out of that smoky gambling hall, she got to sit on a beautiful terrace on a lovely spring evening alone with what might possibly be the most eligible young man in the oil industry. Unfortunately, the most eligible young man in the oil industry didn't say a single word for the first half-hour they were out there. As a matter of fact, he did almost everything he could possibly do to keep from even looking at her. Every time she spoke he would look at her for a long moment and then give a one-word answer and quickly turn his head away.

Garvis had all but given up when after at least ten-minutes of silence he asked, "Would you like to go to the movies with me sometime?"

Hooked.

Little did she realize that he had wanted to ask from the moment he first laid eyes on her. He'd never seen a girl so beautiful in his life. Girls who look like her did not come out to the oilrigs. More importantly, they didn't date roughnecks, and he was a lowly roughneck. Still, she was more stunning than any woman he had ever met.

It took no time at all to reel him in. He was love-struck. He just didn't know it. Garvis had spent a year at SMU and knew all too well how to bring in a catch, and Murdock Rose was as easy a catch as ever there was. Three months later, in June of 1920, Horace McCracken Hamilton walked her down the aisle at the South Main Baptist Church of Henderson, Texas.

Otherwise, the junket to New Orleans had not proven all too successful. Hamilton watched four thousand dollars go to the roulette tables at the O'Dwyer brother's club and not one thin dime of Frelinghuysen-Nightingale Petroleum money came back his way. As he often liked to point out, "All I got out of that train ride was a dead-beat son-in-law."

Of course, Murdock Rose was no dead-beat. Granted, contrary to what Horace McCracken Hamilton felt he had been led to believe, Rose was a long way from wealthy. Nevertheless he had a good job and managed to save a little from each paycheck, despite sending money back to his elderly parents. Which, as it turned out was considerably more than Horace Hamilton ever did.

Less than a month after they were married the Henderson Star reported that Hamilton had, in fact, been supplying cane sugar and grain from his timber leases to an enormous boot-legging operation and, after a subsequent raid on Hamilton Lumber Company and Timber Mill, no less than six hundred gallons of the Whittlesey's top grain whiskey was found hidden behind stacks of two-by-fours. Notoriety such as a bootlegging arrest would send most businessmen over the edge, but not Horace McCracken Hamilton. In fact, in some social circles in Texas, an arrest for bootlegging was a badge of honor. Unfortunately, though, the enormity of the liquor raid led to a United States Treasury investigation of Hamilton Lumber Company and Timber Mill finances. The Treasury investigators learned, and later proved in a subsequent raid, that the highly respected Mr. Hamilton was not only involved in bootlegging but also had significant financial dealings with a number of houses of ill-repute throughout East Texas and Louisiana. Still, such a reputation did not bring down Horace Hamilton. His father and grandfather before him had earned a good, if not completely respectable, living in that same industry. No, what brought him down was the fact that, unlike his son-in-law, he himself was a dead-beat. He had outstanding loans with banks all over the state. In fact, though he had once joked to Murdock about Nightingale gambling away what was left of Garvis's dowry, Hamilton had already done just that. The fifteen thousand dollars he spent on the junket to the Fairgrounds (plus about four thousand for Nightingale's evening at the tables) had been the last of a near two hundred thousand dollar line of credit, all of which had been lost to failed business deals. The Frelinghuysen-Nightingale Petroleum contract, which, as it turned out, never materialized, was a last ditch effort to save the lumber company. Worse still, according to the United States Treasury investigators, Horace McCracken Hamilton had been cheating on his Federal taxes almost from the day that the tax bill was passed in 1913.

For a man like Horace McCracken Hamilton it was acceptable to be thought of as a bootlegger and even tolerable, though be it somewhat embarrassing, to be called a…"procurer of pleasure." But a man of Hamilton's status just couldn't be thought of as a dead-beat, much less go to prison for the un-American act of not paying his taxes. Therefore it did not surprise Murdock in the least when, after missing one of his many court dates, Horace McCracken Hamilton was found hanging by the neck in his lumber mill.

Garvis, naturally, could not accept that her father took his own life. She insisted all along that her father had been set-up. She often remarked that, "Daddy was murdered by those dreadful Whittlesey boys, who framed him and hid all of that liquor in his mill."

Murdock had long since learned to accept Garvis's denial of her father's guilt. She had railed on about her "daddy's" innocence for so long that it was no longer worth the debate. She was adamant that the Whittleseys had killed her father despite the fact that both of the Whittlesey boys were sitting in jail at the time of Hamilton's death. She also refused to accept that he was a bootlegger and a... "procurer of pleasure" despite the fact that he had confessed everything to two Texas Rangers when he was arrested, drunk and naked, at Miss Delilah's Tomato Farm southeast of Maydelle.

It came as no surprise to Murdock when the papers began running stories about his father-in-law and the subsequent investigations and indictments. Mr. Nightingale had warned him about Hamilton's dealings before he married Garvis. Nightingale may have liked to drink and gamble, but he had no respect for a man who took advantage of young women the way Hamilton did. Even if he was loosely connected to those houses, he was still in Nightingale's opinion, "the worst kind of crook," which is why he refused to even discuss a lumber contract with the man.

When it came to Hamilton at least, Murdock knew what he was getting into when he married. Unfortunately, he was not in the least bit prepared for Garvis. The woman was beautiful; there was no question about that. Even in her late thirties, she was a looker, but she was also a handful. She had married Murdock knowing that he wasn't rich but her father was and the two would be able to live comfortably with Murdock's income and a little help from "Daddy." But right after the wedding ceremony, Hamilton took Murdock aside and explained that some business deals had not worked as well as expected and it would be a month or two before he could get them the house he had promised. Murdock, of course, could not possibly care less about any house from the man he now thought of as a glorified lumberjack, but Garvis absolutely hated that the two had to live in a dirty little old rented shack of a house on the back of a smelly chicken farm. Still, she was in love and often said that it would be fun to tell their grandchildren that they started their life together in the absolute worst possible conditions. Besides, it was only temporary. She and her father had already picked out a lot in Henderson where they would build their dream home. "This one," she would say with a laugh, "will have indoor-plumbing and a swamp-cooler." As if not having either was not only intolerable but also somewhat humiliating. Murdock, conversely, had never lived with indoor plumbing and wasn't sure what a swamp-cooler was.

The day Garvis learned that her father didn't have enough money to pay his legal bills, let alone buy her a house, she was distraught to the point of being ill. On top of that, her mother, who in her opinion had, "never appreciated daddy," filed for divorce and moved to Dallas the very day the, "horribly ridiculous accusations about illicit houses," hit the papers.

There were a lot of long, difficult years, five of which were in that little farmhouse without plumbing. Though there were moments when Murdock thought he could not tolerate another minute with her, there were other times when he knew he couldn't live without her. For all her faults, Garvis was a good mother. She had raised their son Jesse almost by herself while he had been working the rigs. For that he loved her more than he could ever express. So if it took a little patience to live with Garvis, well, he had patience.

Thus, that Sunday morning after what he later thought of as the, "Incident at the Palace," Murdock Rose was patiently waiting for Garvis to get ready for church. It wasn't that she was late getting ready. Murdock had long since learned that she could get herself ready with less than a half-hour notice. What kept her was that she knew precisely how long it took to drive the half-mile to the First Baptist Church. She also knew at just what time the most people would be in the parking lot, about five minutes prior to the service starting. Therefore she knew just what time they needed to leave the house to be seen by the most people when they arrived at church in the big red LaSalle. So that Sunday, like all Sundays, Murdock patiently waited for his wife to come out of the bathroom, one of three in the house, at precisely the right moment for the two of them to arrive at the First Baptist Church Elza to be seen pulling into the parking lot with the windows up as they drove in weather-conditioned comfort. After over a year, Murdock would have thought that she would have gotten over making such a show, but she hadn't.

#

Jefferson stepped out of the prowler slowly and walked up to the porch of the Rose's home. There were very few people in Elza that Jefferson didn't like. For the most part, just about everybody obeyed the traffic laws and showed Jefferson a reasonable amount of respect whenever he asked them to move a car out of a No Parking zone or to drive slowly past the school and such. In all honesty, Murdock always did even though he sometimes acted as if Jefferson was just being a pain in the posterior. Garvis, on the other hand, looked down her nose at Jefferson and just about everyone else in Elza. Quite frankly, Jefferson did his best to not come in contact with her. The woman was just plain rude. Frankly, he had no idea how she managed to raise such a good kid as Jesse.

As he stepped to the door, he secretly hoped that Murdock would be the one to answer. Murdock, though somewhat infuriating, was a man Jefferson could reason with.

Just as he raised his hand to knock, the door suddenly opened as Murdock held it for his wife to come out. The two were obviously dressed in their Sunday finest, which in the case of Garvis meant a dress that cost about what Jefferson made in a month.

"Chief Hightower," Murdock said, "what brings you here?"

"Murdock, I apologize for interrupting you two on your way to church, but I need to speak to Jesse for a minute."

"Is he in some trouble?" Garvis asked, the tone of her voice causing Jefferson to feel as if he was being told to get off her porch.

"No ma'am, I just need a word."

"Can this wait, Chief?" Murdock asked. "We're running late."

"I know, and I truly am sorry, but I need to speak to him right away."

"You're making me scared, and you are not speaking to my son until I know exactly what this is about," Garvis ordered loud enough for the neighbors to hear.

"Garvis, enough," Murdock said in a firm tone, sensing something from Jefferson. "Chief, let's go inside, I'll get Jesse."

Murdock held the door open as a fuming Garvis walked back in, followed by Chief Hightower.

"Exactly why do you need to see my son, Chief?" Garvis demanded.

"Enough!" Murdock ordered in a way Jefferson hadn't expected.

Garvis suddenly shut up and stared wide-eyed at her husband. Jefferson sensed that she had rarely heard him speak like that before.

A sleepy but awakening Jesse came down the stairs wearing a pair of jeans and pulling a t-shirt over his head.

"What's going on? I heard dad all the way upstairs."

"The chief needs a word with you, Jesse," Murdock replied.

Garvis was still staring at her husband but now with an expression of anger.

"Good morning, Jesse," Jefferson said with a bit of a smile. He had always liked Jesse.

"Good mornin', Chief. What's up?"

"Do you know where Cliff Tidwell might be?"

"He's probably home asleep, unless he went to church. But after what happened last night I doubt that. Why?"

"He didn't come home last night. Did you see him after the shooting at the Palace?" Jefferson asked, feeling sure that he knew the answer. Those two boys had been sneaking out at night since they were nine or ten years old. About the only two people in town that didn't know it were Jesse's parents.

"What shooting?" Murdock asked in a tone that demanded an immediate answer.

"I'll explain in a minute, Murdock," Jefferson said in a commanding voice that let everyone know that this was serious, and he was in charge.

Jesse was a little uncomfortable with his parents there, but Jefferson was not joking around. He just used his serious "Police Chief" voice and Jesse had no choice. "He came by here at about midnight. We slipped out like we did when we were kids and drove over to the railroad bridge."

"In your car or his?"

"Now, Chief, I'm starting to think that I need to know what this is about," Murdock demanded, beginning to feel that something serious was happening.

Jefferson never took his eyes off Jesse. "In a minute, Murdock."

"His car, Chief."

"And then what?"

"Chief?" Murdock began.

"I said that I'll explain in a minute, Murdock," Chief Jefferson said with a lot more authority than he realized he could muster.

Murdock suddenly stood silent; no one had spoken to him like that since he was a child.

"He dropped me off over on Main, and I walked back here. We always did it that way so," Jesse paused and looked at his parents, "so mom and dad wouldn't hear his car."

Jefferson was well aware that the two boys did that. Mrs. Cunningham had called him a dozen times after midnight over the years because of Cliff's noisy Ford. Before the coupe the two used to drive around in Nickel Washington's old Model-T pickup, which was even nosier than the coupe.

Jefferson turned to Murdock. The man's face showed that he was angry, but for the first time since Jefferson had become chief, Murdock Rose looked as if he respected the badge.

"Cliff didn't come home last night, and this morning we found his coupe crashed into Washington's Feed Store," Jefferson said, feeling a little empowered.

"Where's Cliff? Is he okay?" Jesse asked, clearly worried about his friend.

"We don't know. He wasn't there."

Outside, Shorty Newman pulled up to a stop in his black Dodge pickup behind the police prowler. Jefferson glanced out the screen door with some curiosity but turned his attention back to Jesse.

"What time did you get home?

"It was a little after one-thirty," Murdock replied.

Jesse froze as he looked at his father.

Garvis looked at her husband, "You knew he was out?"

Murdock looked at Jesse, "I always hear you coming and going, son."

As Shorty stepped up to the porch, Jesse felt a little cold chill, realizing that every time he had climbed out the window his father knew full well what he was doing.

"Chief, I need to talk to you," Shorty said from outside.

"I'll be out in a moment, Shorty."

"I think you need to come right now, Jefferson," Shorty replied with a shake in his voice.

Jefferson looked out at Shorty who was covered in mud from the knees down. "Good lord, Shorty, what did you get into?"

"You've got to come, Jefferson. Quick."

Jefferson looked at Jesse and his parents, "It looks like they've found something. Jesse. I'll call you when we find Cliff."

"I'm coming," Jesse said as he headed to the door.

"No." Jefferson ordered just as he stepped out, stopping Jesse in his tracks. "I'll call you."

"Wait. What's this about a shooting?" Murdock demanded as his patience ran out with Chief Thomas Jefferson Hightower.

Jefferson paused in the doorway, "Irwin Stoker came into the Palace last night with a shotgun and tried to shoot Cliff. He thinks Cliff got his daughter pregnant. Jesse here stopped him. He saved Cliff's life."

Murdock and Garvis were stunned as they watched Jefferson turn and walk out the door.

When they got about halfway to the prowler, Shorty started to speak, but the police officer halted him. When they were finally by the cars and out of earshot he nodded for Shorty to explain.

"The Lowery boys pulled up just as we were about to tow off Cliff's coupe. They had been out huntin' and, well, you just need to come down to the river."

"What is it, Shorty?" Jefferson asked, a little annoyed.

"It's Cliff, Jefferson. I ain't never seen nothin' like it."

Jefferson looked at the porch. Jesse and his parents were watching. He nodded in their direction, smiled, then turned to Shorty, "Lead the way."

"One other thing, Jeff. The coupe. There was a bloody tire-iron under the seat."

#

Jefferson parked right behind Shorty's Dodge pickup. They'd just driven about a quarter mile alongside the railroad line to the trestle on a rutted road made by hunters and fishermen. Jefferson hated doing that to his brand new prowler. He felt sure that the springs wouldn't take much of it, and he doubted that the town council had allotted much cash for repairs.

Toad Lowery came walking toward him and Shorty as they approached the trestle. Jefferson found Toad to be a bit amusing. He'd known Toad all of his life and had always thought that "Toad" was just a nickname because he actually looked like a toad. He was short and broad-chested with no visible neck at all. On top of his shoulders, Toad had a melon shaped head that looked as if it was two sizes too big for his body. Naturally, given his appearance, kids would nickname him "Toad". Then one weekend a few years back he had to run Toad and his brother Hunker into his jail for getting drunk and driving their father's flatbed Buick all through Mrs. Hollis Harrison's prize winning azaleas. Two years earlier Mrs. Hollis Harrison had won second prize at the State Fair of Texas Floral Competition. Mrs. Hollis Harrison was convinced that she had not won first place because, as it was learned after the fair, one of the judges, an editor from the Dallas Morning News, was also a cousin of that Galveston woman who did win. Mrs. Hollis Harrison was bound and determined to go back to the State Fair and win first place, and might have had it in the bag had the Lowery brothers not driven through her garden. Apparently it takes two or three years for a "competition quality" azalea to blossom. Understandably, Mrs. Hollis Harrison was not happy with the Lowerys and wanted them to go to prison. She settled for them spending two weeks on the county road gang.

When Jefferson booked the boys, he asked Toad for his real name. Obviously drunk, the boy kept telling him that his name was Toad. Finally, the next afternoon when their parents came and tried to bail them out, Jefferson finally realized that the boy was given the name "Toad" at birth and had somehow grown up to look like one.

"Chief," an excited Toad began, "We been huntin' on the other side of the river and came walkin' across the bridge when Hunker seen a gator on the bank eatin' somethin'. Well, he killed the gator with his first shot and then he climbed down the bank to get a look and seen that it was eatin' some fella."

Hunker walked up with a hunting rifle across his shoulders, holding it casually with both hands loosely hanging on it. "His head's awful bloody, Jefferson, but I'm pretty sure it's Cliff Tidwell."

"Have you two told anyone else about this?"

"No, Chief," Toad replied, "Just Shorty and Hobe. I seen Hobe tryin' to tow that coupe; he said he'd get you, and we came back here."

Jefferson walked out on the bridge and looked over at the body.

"Right by those trees," Toad said as he pointed.

Jefferson took one good look and then turned away, feeling the scrambled eggs he had eaten for breakfast coming to his throat. The alligator was a big one, at least eight or nine feet. It lay dead with a leg in its mouth. The human was lying on his side, the leg almost ripped off.

"You boys stay here. I don't want any more tracks down there." Jefferson told the three as he made his way down the bank. When he got close enough, he swallowed hard and took a good look at the body. The head had been bashed in to the point that there was as a dent the size of a cantaloupe in the skull. Jefferson turned his head and began climbing back up the steep bank to the bridge. Out of sheer willpower, he kept himself from throwing up in front of those watching from above.

When he reached the top the boys met him.

"You ever seen anything like it, Chief?" Toad asked with a big smile, garnering a disgusted look from Shorty who was clearly close to losing his breakfast.

"No," Jefferson said solemnly. "Toad, you and Hunker are now deputy police officers. You'll get a day's pay, just like Shorty. I'm going back to town to make a few calls.

Shorty, you're in charge. None of you are to go down to that body. And if anybody comes along, don't let them near the bridge or down the hill. If anyone tries, arrest 'em. This is a crime scene."

"What about my gator?" Hunker asked.

"You can have it after the investigator gets here."

"You gonna call Sheriff Cadwalder? You know Jonas Cadwalder don't like us," Toad said reminding Jefferson that the Sheriff did, in fact, dislike the two boys. When the two brothers were working on the county road-gang, they made an attempt to escape by driving away on a road grader. Unfortunately, the big machine had a maximum speed of about six miles per hour. When the Sheriff's deputies caught up to them, they drove the grader into a creek. It took Sheriff Jonah Cadwalder nearly a month to find a tow truck large enough to pull it out of the ditch.

"No, Toad, I ain't callin' Cadwalder."

Chapter 5

301 RED OAK AVENUE. ELZA, TEXAS
5:15 p.m. Sunday November 16, 1941

Jesse and Gemma sat quietly on the front steps of the house. Jesse had his arm around Gemma. It had been a long day for both. News of a death moves quickly in small towns, regardless of how hard the police chief tries to keep it quiet. Gemma first heard about it when she was walking out of church with her mom and sister, Jettie. It was obvious that something unusual was happening. There was a group of men gathered around Hobe Bethard who was sitting in the parking lot in his wrecker. Usually, after the service, there was a group of men gathered under the sycamore tree to smoke cigarettes and tell each other what a good sermon the preacher had given. It was considered impolite, if not an outright sin, to smoke too close to the church. It always seemed amusing to Gemma that the sycamore was somehow the appropriate distance from the building to allow one to smoke without bringing down the wrath of God Almighty. She also found it amusing that those men pretended to know if the preacher had given a good sermon, since most of them had been asleep.

This time was different. The same men were gathered, but there was a considerable commotion. Pretty soon some of the men began walking off to talk to their wives, and an even bigger commotion seemed to stir. Though Jettie and her mother seemed oblivious, it was clear to Gemma that everyone kept looking their way as if whatever was happening had something to do with them.

After visiting with some of the ladies, Gemma and her mom and sister shook hands with Brother Bill and told him what a good sermon he had preached. That, of course, was a bold-faced lie, because Gemma hadn't heard a word Brother Bill had preached. Her mind, and Jettie's too, was on Cliff and what had happened at the Palace. What Cliff had done was unbelievable. The humiliation Jettie was feeling was more than Gemma could stand. She wanted to break down and cry. Everyone was looking at them as they walked into church, which she expected, but after the service, well, it was getting worse with everyone huddled in little groups gossiping and looking at them.

As Gemma and her mom and sister walked to their car, Gemma felt as if all eyes were on them. In fact, as it turned out, they were. Before they got to the car Mrs. Greer started toward them. Mrs. Bertha Greer had been the children's Sunday School teacher since, well, no one could remember how long she had been teaching, but Gemma suspected that it was altogether possible that she also taught Mary Magdalene.

Mrs. Greer was as sweet a lady as there was in all of Elza, and no one would question that. Whenever someone died, she would be the first to bring a pot roast and a pound cake, and there was no doubt that she worked harder than anyone at First Baptist Church Elza when it was time to get ready for the annual spring revival. But there was equally as little doubt that there was anyone in all of Elza as accomplished at spreading gossip as Bertha Greer.

As the woman approached, Gemma prepared herself for a confrontation. Whatever Mrs. Greer wanted couldn't be good, and Gemma was bound and determined to protect her little sister even if meant telling her former Sunday School teacher to go mind her own damn business.

Mrs. Greer walked over to Jettie and took the girl's hand. Suddenly everyone outside the church was quiet.

"Mrs. Greer, what's going on?" Gemma asked, knowing that at least forty people were straining to hear, and also knowing that one of the town's most notorious gossips was about to say how sorry she was that Jettie's boyfriend had gotten another girl pregnant.

Mrs. Greer, ignoring Gemma looked tenderly at Jettie, "Sweetheart, you may as well hear this from me. Cliff's dead. He was in a terrible car accident last night."

In moments half the women of First Baptist Church Elza were gathered around Jettie. Gemma held her sister as she went from shock to tears. Soon, Brother Bill was there. He took Jettie by the hand and quieted everybody down. He then led everyone in prayer, first for Jettie to get though this tragedy, secondly for Cliff's family, and then finally for the community who has lost a beloved son. He then admonished the congregation to go home and try not to gossip or speculate. Rather, he asked that they all pray and wait for the police chief to do his job.

Of course, gossip and speculation were the two things that the people of Elza were best at. Before they got in the car to leave, Gemma had heard that Cliff had wrecked his car into the feed store. She also heard that he had somehow fallen off the railroad bridge and gotten eaten by an alligator. Both stories were a little unbelievable. First, the feed store was at least a hundred feet off the highway, and it seemed highly unlikely that he would accidently run into a building that far off the road. And, though she had heard all of her life that there were a few alligators in the Neches, she had never met anyone who could say that they had actually seen one. More importantly, what would he be doing in the river that late at night? All she knew was that apparently Cliff was dead, and she needed to get to Jesse as soon as she could get Jettie home and away from all these people.

On the way home, Jettie insisted that they stop at the police station to find out what had happened. Gemma didn't like the idea of going there for fear of what they might find out, which quite honestly she couldn't imagine. She would have preferred to drop her mom and Jettie off and then go find out for herself and report it to them later. That wasn't going to happen. Jettie was determined to go to the police station, and that was that.

Naturally, the police chief wasn't there, and against Gemma's pleading, Jettie and her mother insisted that they go to see Cliff's mother. Even if she didn't know what had happened, she certainly needed to be consoled. Of course, when they got to the house there were eight or ten cars parked all around it, one being the police chief's new prowl car.

Their mother led the way as they approached the porch where Chief Hightower stood with a glass of tea, fuming because one of his deputies was running around town telling anyone he could find that the Tidwell boy was laying dead next to the river. When he saw Jettie he stepped off the porch and met the ladies.

"I'm so sorry, girls. I had planned to stop by your house after I came here."

"What happened, Chief?" Gemma's mother, Anna-Ruth demanded, somewhat impatiently. She had no love for the chief. She had long held the suspicion that he was the reason that they never knew exactly how her husband ended up dead on a railroad track.

"Ma'am, we really don't know yet. Some boys found him by the river. His head was cracked open. He may have just fallen off the bridge. I just don't know yet. I called down to Austin and they're sending out a Texas Ranger to investigate. He'll be here this afternoon."

"Thank you, Chief," Anna-Ruth said sharply, showing her impatience with the man. She walked up the steps and into the house, followed by Jettie. Gemma stayed.

"Have you seen Jesse, Chief? He and his parents weren't at church."

"I stopped by to see him earlier, but that was before we found Cliff."

"Why before?" Gemma asked, sensing something.

"We found Clifford's car down by the feed store, but no one was around. I was hopin' he was with Jesse."

"Oh," Gemma replied, understanding that there was more that she wasn't being told. "Thank you, Chief."

As she began up the steps and into the house, Jefferson took her arm to help her. He always liked Gemma. She was smart as a whip, and he knew full well that she was aware he'd not told her the entire story. He also knew that she was smart enough to know not to ask. There were times like this that Jefferson Hightower hated his job. By being vague he was doing the same as lying, and he didn't like lying to this girl. But the fact was that he didn't know what had happened, and he couldn't tell her that Cliff was half eaten by an alligator. There were few people in Elza whom Jefferson had as much respect for as Gemma Crawford. When her father was killed, Gemma, even though she was a little girl, took on the weight of handling the funeral arrangements because her mom was too distraught. She even ran her mother's store for a time. It occurred to the Chief that Gemma didn't buy the story that her dad had gotten drunk and was hit by a train either. She accepted it like they all did, but she didn't believe it.

When Gemma walked in, the house was already crowded with friends and relatives. Most of the women were huddled around Mrs. Tidwell, who had her arms around Jettie. Most of the men were on the porch where Chief Hightower continued trying to calm speculation.

After about an hour Gemma began persuading her mother and Jettie to get out of the house as more and more people began showing up, most with dishes of collard greens, black-eyed peas, turnips, and almost every casserole imaginable. Just as Anna-Ruth was finally ready to go, Jesse walked through the door. Gemma immediately met him and hugged him tenderly. Then, without saying a word, he walked toward Cliff's mother who was sitting on a couch with her sister and a cousin. Before Jesse got close she stood to her feet and rushed to the boy, throwing her arms around him. For the first time through this, tears swelled in Gemma's eyes.

Jesse just stood there hugging Mrs. Tidwell without saying a word. Finally, he lost all control and tears began streaming down his face. Gemma, now crying, was holding tightly to Jettie as they watched Jesse sobbing. He and Mrs. Tidwell sat down on the couch. With her arms around him, Susie Tidwell tried to console him as all of his emotions poured out. Everyone in the room was silent as they watched her holding him, stroking his head. It occurred to Gemma that she was probably the only one in the room who knew the real source of this breakdown. Cliff was more than a friend. Cliff was a brother.

Jesse was an only child, and he had a distant relationship to his parents, to say the least. He had told Gemma on a number of occasions that Susie Tidwell was much more a mom to him than his own mother had ever been. He felt the same way about Ned, Cliff's father. It was Ned Tidwell who taught him to fish and hunt. Murdock was never around for such things. In fact, he had once confided that he couldn't remember his father ever so much as tossing a ball with him. Worse still was that he couldn't recall his mother ever giving him a hug. Most people in town held a little envy for the Roses. They thought of Jesse as the kid who had everything. Only Gemma knew that he would much rather have grown up on the east end of town with the Tidwells than in that big brick house on Elm.

After a few minutes Ned Tidwell walked in from the back porch where he had been with his two brothers. Ned was a stern, proud man who didn't want to be seen sobbing in front of half the town, but when he approached the couch, tears began pouring down the man's face. Jesse stood, and Ned wrapped him up in a big bear hug, both sobbing openly. Finally they sat on the couch where the large man held his wife and his adopted son.

A half-hour later Gemma was in the kitchen with her mother and several of the other ladies, washing dishes and taking care of the other needs as at least half of Elza came through to spend a few minutes with the Tidwells. It would seem natural that the food would disappear with as many people as were showing up, but instead, the number of casseroles only increased.

Gemma had just finished drying what must have been the hundredth tea glass when she noticed that the living room become eerily silent. When she looked through the door, she saw Jewel Stoker had just walked in. By now everyone in town had heard about what happened at the Palace the night before, which meant that everyone in town knew that Jewel was pregnant and that Cliff was most likely the father. Most of the people there were, no doubt, thinking that the Stoker girl had a lot of nerve to show up at such a time. Gemma though, couldn't help but admire the courage it took.

Jewel was accustomed to stares and whispers. She was tall with a head full of long blonde hair and was, in

Gemma's opinion, the most beautiful girl to ever grow up in Elza. But the stares and whispers had nothing to do with how she looked. It seemed to Gemma that almost any time the subject of Jewel Stoker came up, it immediately transitioned to gossip about her mother. Most of the time there would be comments like, "That girl will turn out just like her mother," or "She'll probably run off and leave her kid and husband, just like her mother."

There had been rumors around town about Mrs. Stoker for as long as Gemma could recall. Some claimed that she ran off with one of the carnival workers. Others said that she just ran off. And still others suggested that Irwin Stoker ran her off. That part had seemed the most likely to Gemma since he didn't seem to miss her at all. Some claimed that the reason Irwin didn't try to find her was that she was once a prostitute. Gemma remembered that her own father claimed he'd heard that Irwin met her when she worked a whorehouse over by Maydelle. Until Jesse had revealed the truth to her, Gemma had believed some of the rumors could have been true.

Amazingly, Jewel never let on that she was aware of such talk. She just went on about her business as if the whispers and condescending glares didn't exist. Only Gemma knew better. The two had a quiet, unspoken kinship that only they could understand. It was partly because one had lost a mother and the other had lost a father only a few weeks apart. It was also partly because they were both in love with Jesse Rose. It was mostly, though, because of something that happened the night of the carnival, the night Jewel's mother disappeared. Gemma had found Jewel kneeling down behind one of the tents crying. That night Gemma learned that Jesse loved Gemma. She also learned that Jewel didn't miss a thing. She knew about every rumor and whisper.

Gemma watched as Jesse stood and went to Jewel and wrapped his arms around her. The two stood for a few minutes until Susie Tidwell came and took Jewel in her arms. If Mrs. Tidwell had any ill thoughts about Jewel or Sarah Stoker, she never let them show. Gemma and Jesse had enjoyed many a Saturday dinner at the Tidwell's table over the years, as did Jewel. Where most of the ladies in Elza gossiped behind Jewel's back, Susie Tidwell treated the girl like a daughter. Susie didn't seem to care why Sarah left, all she cared about was a poor girl was without a mother that was being raised by an old farmer who drank and didn't know the first thing about raising a daughter.

After Mrs. Tidwell finished hugging Jewel, Ned came to her and did the same. Jewel then walked directly to Jettie, whispered in her ear and led her into the kitchen, an action that was not lost on the condescending eyes of most of the people in the house.

When they got in the kitchen, Jewel took both sisters aside, and Gemma's mother led the other ladies out, though there was more than one ear trying to hear the conversation.

Jewel took both Jettie's hands and looked her in the eye, "I've heard all about last night. Please believe me. There was nothing between Cliff and me. Daddy has it all wrong."

"But why?" Jettie asked hesitantly.

"I've been getting sick in the mornings. Daddy figured it out," She paused and swallowed, trying to hold back the tears, "I have a boyfriend up in Jacksonville. I let things get out of control one night. Daddy doesn't know about my boyfriend. I'm afraid he won't approve. He's a little older. About a month ago Cliff and I went out to the railroad bridge where we used to go fishin'. We just talked, like we always do. I hadn't seen him in months. I told him all about my boyfriend. When he drove me home, my Daddy saw him. Yesterday when he saw me sick again he thought Cliff was the father. Daddy and I had a big fight yesterday, and I left and went up to Jacksonville. He spent the day drinkin'.'"

To the amazement of everyone in the living room, Jettie and Jewel hugged tenderly then and again when they all left.

#

It was late afternoon when Gemma got her mother and Jettie home. She stayed only a few minutes before going to Jesse's. He pulled into the driveway just as she was getting out of her mother's car. The two met halfway to the porch and sat down without saying a word. Gemma felt like there were no words to say, yet there were a million words waiting to be said. Finally, out of the silence Jesse blurted, "It wasn't an accident. Somebody killed Cliff."

Gemma turned her head to look at him. This was something that hadn't entered her mind.

"But who...?"

Jesse shrugged as if to say that he had no idea, but inside Gemma knew that there was something he wasn't telling. Jesse was troubled. It was like he had a deep dark secret eating its way out. She also knew that sooner or later he would open up completely. She just needed to be patient. But this frightened her. If he knew something, he needed to open up about it soon.

They sat for a few minutes, then Gemma leaned her head against Jesse and whispered, "I love you," as he pulled her close to him. For the second time that day, tears began rolling down both of their cheeks.

#

MAIN STREET
ELZA, TEXAS
June 25 1936

Jesse led as he, Cliff, and Jewel strolled down Main Street, all three carrying R.C. bottles.

"Here we go again," Jewel said as Jesse stopped and sat on the curb and the other two follow suit.

"You know she's not in there," Cliff said.

"Who?" Jesse asked with his eyes fixed on the front window of Anna-Ruth's.

Jewel and Cliff giggled and looked at each other.

"You could always just walk in there and talk to her," Jewel suggested.

"Who?" Jesse asked again, with more attempted innocence.

"Gemma, you idiot," Jewel answered, this time with disgust.

"Oh, her. She doesn't know who I am."

"Oh, she knows," Jewel replied with assurance.

"Did you guys hear what happened in Jacksonville?" Cliff asked, changing the subject. He had been down this road enough times and knew full well that Jesse was way too much of a coward to ever walk across the street and talk to Gemma Crawford.

"Some girl got killed is what I heard," Jesse replied, relieved to get the conversation on anything but him.

"I heard it was a colored fellow that did it," said Cliff. "Someone named Davis."

Jewel spotted a commotion in front of the domino hall. A number of men were gathered and began to get into cars.

"Mr. Davis from over in Pleasant Grove? He works on the rigs for my pa."

"I think it's his son."

"Guys, something's going on," Jewel said as she pointed toward the end of the street.

"What do you suppose is up?" Jesse asked as a line of cars and pickups began heading their direction.

"I'll find out," Cliff replied as he stood to his feet and waved down a pickup. "Hey, Toad, what's up?"

Toad Lowery pulled to a stop as Cliff, followed by Jesse and Jewel walked up, "We're gonna go watch a lynchin'."

"Was it Mr. Davis?" Jesse asked.

"His son, Bucky." Hunker Lowery answered from across the cab. "I can't believe it, either, I know'd Bucky and he's a nice kid."

"Well, I don't care if he's a nice kid or not, if he did what they say he did, they oughta hang 'im from the highest tree," Toad clamored.

"I didn't say that they shouldn't hang 'im. I just said that he's a nice kid," Hunker replied.

"Can we come?" Cliff asked.

"Fine with me," Toad answered, as Cliff was already climbing in the back of his pickup, "but if you get in trouble with your ma and pa, don't come crying to us."

"Come on," Cliff said, more aimed at Jesse than Jewel.

Jewel hopped right in but Jesse hesitated.

"You can't come," Cliff said to Jewel.

"Why not?"

"A girl can't go to a lynchin'."

"If you two can go, I can go."

Then both kids looked at Jesse who was still hesitant.

Toad looked at him, "If you're comin', get in."

Jesse shrugged and climbed into the back of the truck just as Toad pulled away.

Cliff looked at Jesse and Jewel and rolled his eyes. "My first hangin' and I'm going with a girl and a chicken."

As the truck pulled away, Gemma Crawford watched them leave from inside the dress shop.

#

Jacksonville was about twelve miles north of Elza, and by 1936 was considerably larger. Twenty-five years earlier the two towns had been about the same size, but the Santa

Fe railroad put a depot right in the middle of Jacksonville, which brought all sorts of businesses. Jacksonville's newspaper *The Jacksonville Statesman* eventually put all the papers in Cherokee county out of business, and by 1930, Jacksonville got Chevrolet and Ford dealerships and a Sears and Roebuck's.

The line of cars and trucks from Elza circled through town past the jailhouse where fifty or sixty men had gathered. Jesse watched the crowd of angry men as they passed and felt a sense of fear run through him. Until that moment it had been a bit of an adventure, but suddenly there was a frightful reality to what was taking place.

A block south of Commerce Street was a big square park with parking spaces all the way around it. Jesse often thought it reminded him of a county seat without a courthouse. In the center of the park stood a monument to the soldiers of the Great War. Every Saturday farmers from all over circled the park with their pickups to sell produce. On weekdays like this only a couple of farmers took the time to come into town.

Toad parked next to the only farmer on the square. "Hey, Clovis," Toad said to the farmer as he got out of his pickup. "We gonna have a lynchin'?"

The old man just shook his head with disgust. "It sure looks that way."

Jesse, Cliff, and Jewel climbed out of the back of the old Ford as Hunker walked around to where Clovis and Toad stood.

"What's the matter Clovis?" Hunker asked. "Don't you think he deserves to get hung?"

"Nope. He ain't killed nobody. He might ought to go to prison for a while, if he did it."

"I thought that girl was dead," Toad said with surprise.

"Naw. She's laid up over at Doc Mahoney's. She's been hurt pretty bad, but she's gonna make it. "

Cliff, Jesse, and Jewel listened to the conversation as they watched the commotion across the park.

"Well, a fellow that does something like that to a girl still ought to get hung," Hunker argued.

"Maybe, if he done it. But I don't think he done it," the old man said with conviction.

"Who did it if he didn't?" Hunker asked, somewhat angrily.

"A lot of folks have seen her carrying on with a white fellow from down your way."

Toad suddenly got angry. "Ain't nobody from Elza did that!"

"I didn't say he did it. I'm just sayin' that nobody knows if that boy did it or not. I've known Bucky all his life, and he's as good a young man as I've ever met. By god he don't deserve to get hung just because he ain't white."

Toad started to open his mouth when Hunker put his hand on his brother's shoulder and pointed toward the police station, "Somethin's happenin'."

"Come on," Toad said as he and his brother began to hurriedly head over to the crowd.

Toad looked back at the kids who were following behind, "You kids stay close to us. If you get separated, head for the truck."

"We will, Toad," Cliff answered as they headed to the crowd, which has now swelled to well over fifty or sixty.

Crossing through the park, Jesse noticed something moving over their heads. Looking up he saw a rope tied into a hangman's noose slung from a telephone pole and swinging in the breeze.

As they approached, Jewel grabbed Jesse's arm. "Do you think they're really going to kill him?"

"I don't know," Jesse replied.

The three stayed back from the crowd. Looking around, they saw several cars and trucks pulled into the town as more and more men from the surrounding communities arrived. The kids found a spot on the curb across the street from the jailhouse and sat down to watch. In minutes the crowd, which moments before had been no more than sixty men, was turning into a mob of over two hundred.

"What if that old man's right?" Jewel asked the other two. "What if he didn't do it?"

"By the looks of this crowd," Cliff answered, "they're going to hang him no matter what. The chief here ain't like Jefferson. My pa says this guy is really bad. He says that when this chief finds hobos down on the tracks he don't just run them off. He likes to beat 'em up first."

Suddenly Jesse recognized a man in the crowd and elbowed Cliff.

"I see him," Cliff replied as he watched the man work his way through the crowd, yelling along with all the others.

Cliff stood, "I'm gonna get a closer look."

"Stay here," Jesse said to Jewel as he too stood and then followed Cliff into the crowd.

"I'm not going anywhere," Jewel replied emphatically.

The two boys worked their way through the angry mob, trying to keep the man in sight. Finally they got to where they could see him up close. He was the man from the alley, Peterson Crawford, Gemma's father.

The boys tried to keep an eye on the man, but the mob around them kept pushing and shoving. The boys soon got separated. In moments, Jesse found himself standing almost next to the man.

Suddenly, the mob became silent. Behind them in the street a black Oldsmobile pulled to a stop. A man got out of the car and went to the back door and opened it. As he did, the mob split into two, making an open path to the front of the jailhouse. Jesse was standing to the left of Peterson Crawford with another man between them. Across the open path he saw Cliff, who also was keeping an eye on Mr. Crawford.

Then Jesse noticed that the crowd's attention turned to the jailhouse steps. Looking up, he saw the police chief stepping out of the door. Behind him two officers came out with a young black man between them. Each officer was holding the young man's arms, which were handcuffed behind his back. The Chief led as the four headed down the steps. The young man in handcuffs was clearly terrified and tried to resist, but the two officers made sure he came along.

At the same time, at the other end of the opening in the crowd, the man who had opened the car door helped a young blonde haired woman timidly step out. Her face was bandaged, and she couldn't stand without help. The man insisted, and she hesitantly walked as best she could with him.

At the same time, the officers with the black man came toward the girl and stopped directly in front of Jesse. The man and girl also stopped. Jesse looked at Mr. Crawford, who was staring intently at the girl. Suddenly she noticed him and the man between Crawford and Jesse. She tried to turn and go back to the car, but the man holding her arm wouldn't let her. Jesse watched as she glanced up a second time at Crawford and then the other man, both of whom had their eyes trained on her face. Jesse glanced at Cliff, who had noticed the same things that he did. The girl was terrified as everyone could clearly see. Most thought it to be because she was standing directly across from the black man who attacked her, but only Cliff and Jesse could see that she was afraid of Crawford.

The chief stepped to his right so that the girl was standing face to face with the young black man.

"Gladys, is this the man who raped you?" the Chief asked, but it seemed to Jesse to be more of a statement than a question.

There was complete silence as every man in the crowd strained to hear her answer. Jesse looked back at Crawford, whose angry scowl was bearing down on the girl.

She looked at the chief and started to shake her head, but then glanced back at Crawford. His left hand slightly opened his suit coat revealing a Smith and Wesson .38 Special that he had tucked into his belt. She glanced back at the chief with tears streaming down her face and just nodded.

Suddenly the crowd began shouting and pushing.

The young black man pulled back and shouted, "It wasn't me! I didn't do it!"

The larger of the two officers punched him with all his might. With blood streaming down his face, the young man kept proclaiming his innocence while the screaming mob closed in around him.

The man holding the girl managed to get her back to the Oldsmobile as Jesse and Cliff began frightfully trying to work their way out of the crowd. People were pushing and shoving all around them. At one point Jesse looked back to see that the police officers had let go of the young black man and were watching the mob drag him away, beating him as they went.

Fighting his way through the mob, Jesse suddenly felt a hand on his shoulder. He stopped and looked up to see Peterson Crawford holding on to him. Jesse looked at the man and darted away. With the crowd all around them, he managed to easily get free and soon was across the street where Jewel and Cliff were waiting.

"Let's get back to the truck," Jewel demanded, clearly frightened.

Jesse and Cliff led the way, neither wanting to reveal that they were as terrified as Jewel.

When they got to the pickup they climbed into the back and watched. The mob was dragging the young man, beaten to the point that he was unable to walk. The noose had been lowered, and they held him as the crowd put the rope over his head. Jewel turned her head to hide the tears. Cliff and Jesse watched in stunned silence as the young man was being pulled up by his neck, his limbs flinging wildly. Finally, after what seemed like an eternity of shouting, his legs stopped moving as the last breath of life slipped from his lungs.

Toad and Hunker approached the truck with their heads down.

"That chief oughten't done that. They should have given him a trial," Hunker said in disgust.

The two climbed into the cab of the truck.

"I knew that kid," Toad said. "He's a good kid. That girl didn't say he done it. She just nodded her head a little."

Jewel and the two boys looked at the mob that was boiling over with chaos and anger. Suddenly there was a single gunshot from behind them. All three looked back as a man on horseback slowly rode into the park. The crowd immediately fell silent. The man wore a broad cowboy hat and held a six-shooter in his right hand just like Gene Aurty or John Wayne.

"Cut him down," he demanded to one of the men in the crowd.

No one in the mob made a move to stop the horseman as he tossed a pocketknife to the man.

Hunker and Toad stepped out of the cab and onto the running boards of the pickup to get a good look at the horseman.

"That's Brewster McKinney," Hunker announced.

"Who?" Jesse asked.

"Corporal McKinney?" Cliff asked.

"That's him all right," Toad agreed.

"Who's Corporal McKinney?" Jesse asked.

"Texas Ranger," Cliff replied. "One of the toughest men alive from what I hear."

"He must 'ave just got here," Toad injected. "A ranger wouldn't have let them lynch him."

They watched as the now silent crowd lowered the man from the telephone pole. Jesse and Cliff both had tears in their eyes.

To their right an old black Ford pickup stopped in the middle of the street. A black woman got out of the truck and began running toward the mob. When she got to the young man who was then lying on the ground, she began wailing and threw herself on his body. The only sound that Jesse could hear was the woman's wailing.

Jesse spotted a tall black man walking along the path the woman had taken a few moments before, "That's Mr. Davis," he said softly, breaking the eerie silence.

Davis walked past the ranger to whom he looked at with disdain and over to his wife who lay across her son sobbing. He had to pull hard to get her free from her son. The woman was now wailing without stopping as Davis held her. Finally, he led the woman back to his pickup. About half way to the truck the two stopped walking. The wailing turned to silence and the two looked around at the mob. Davis looked over at the pickup and at the three kids. Then the man and wife, holding tightly to one another, stood as straight and tall as they could and walked back to their pickup with their heads held high.

Chapter 6

MAIN STREET,
ELZA TEXAS
4:40 p.m.,. Sunday November 16, 1941

Corporal Brewster McKinney was tired when he climbed out of his 1937 Ford Model 74 coupe. The fifty-year-old Texas Ranger had spent the night before on a stakeout with another Ranger at an old Roadhouse on the Trinity River. It was after five that morning when he finally got to sleep, and then a little before noon he got the call to go down to Elza.

Elza was the only black mark in the otherwise perfect career of Brewster McKinney. The Rangers prided themselves in always solving their cases. Unfortunately, the fact was that the world-famous law enforcement agency left a lot of cases unsolved or "open" as the Rangers preferred to say. Most Rangers had a number of "open" cases on their record, but Corporal McKinney only had one. Some years earlier a local playboy had gotten drunk and driven out on some railroad tracks just in time to get hit by the Santa Fe headed up to Dallas. The problem for Brewster McKinney was that the man didn't have a history of getting drunk. He did, Brewster learned, have a history of carrying on with women other than his wife, and there were husbands all over East Texas who had reason to kill him. There was also a dent in the back of the man's head that matched perfectly with a bloody tree limb they had found about a few hundred feet up the track. So though he couldn't prove anything and he had absolutely no leads, Corporal McKinney knew in his soul that he had let a killer go free.

McKinney put on the 5x Stetson he had bought two years prior at the Paris Hatters in San Antonio, carefully closed the door to the Ford, and walked into the Elza Police Station. Brewster loved both the car and the hat. The Ford was the first vehicle the Ranger had ever bought new off the showroom floor, and he suspected that it would be the last. Thus, the car was tuned-up once a year, and the oil was changed at exactly three thousand miles, no more, no less. The hat was as fine a Texas style hat a man could buy, and the price reflected it. He suspected, as with the car, that he'd never be able to afford to buy another one, so he took care of it.

Elza wasn't a county seat so there wasn't a town square with a large courthouse in the center. Before 1910 the town barely had enough population to justify a post office. In fact, back in those days the town was called Azle, after the family that founded it. Then when they tried to open a post office they found out that there already was an Azle, Texas. After some head-scratching they spelled the founder's name backward and came up with Elza.

In the early days of the oil boom, the town swelled to over two thousand people. The result was a busy main street with two banks - one sitting on the corner that was as much a centerpiece as any county courthouse. Clearly the population was down some, but Brewster could tell that this was still a busy little town. Even on a Sunday with the stores closed, there were quite a few people about.

When he walked in the door Brewster immediately remembered the police station and police chief. The police headquarters was little more than a storefront wedged between the movie theater and an alley. The second floor had been outfitted with four jail cells, though, as Brewster recalled, they sat empty most of the time.

Inside the door was a large, open room with a simple desk and two chairs. Behind the desk was a long hallway leading to the back door and a staircase leading up to the jail. The little building had once been a tobacco shop, and even after nearly ten years the wood floors and walls still had the scent of fresh tobacco. Brewster found the odor disgusting. The Ranger, unlike virtually all of his fraternity, was a life-long non-smoker. He personally found the habit intolerable. Brewster was a large man who took pride in his physical ability to handle any crook he encountered, as he had done on many occasions. He held to the unpopular belief that sucking smoke in to one's lungs had to inhibit one's ability to chase down a bandit. That theory, which he espoused regularly, was not at all popular with the majority of his fellow lawmen at his Division Headquarters back in Dallas.

Brewster stood silent for a moment. There was a little sound coming from the back of the building. "Chief Hightower?"

Faintly, from another room he heard, "Just a minute."

There was the sound of a toilet flushing, then a ruffled Chief Thomas Jefferson Hightower came up the hall as he tucked his shirt in his belt, which was almost completely hidden by his belly. A law officer who didn't maintain a reasonable weight wasn't tolerated among the Rangers. It was a very rare occasion when a Texas Ranger ever had to chase down a bandit, but he was expected to be capable of it. More importantly, to Brewster's thinking, a peace officer needed to command respect. In the 1890's Captain Bill McDonald had been called into Dallas to squelch an uprising of a group of very unhappy and probably drunk boxing fans who were threatening to riot over a canceled boxing match. When he got off the train, a reporter asked if he was the only Ranger sent. McDonald, it is said, answered, "One riot, one Ranger." The story had made the afternoon paper and, as the Captain himself put it, "There never was any riot."

Brewster didn't believe a word of it. He suspected that some reporter made the story up. He had met Captain McDonald early in his career, and he doubted that the man, though an excellent Ranger, was eloquent enough to conjure up such a clever retort. Still, the story caught on, and the point was quite valid. If you looked and acted as if you could handle a riot, you would never need to handle a riot.

Police Chief Thomas Jefferson Hightower looked as if he had difficulty fastening his belt, let alone handling a riot.

"Corporal McKinney?" Jefferson asked as he walked up to Brewster, holding out his hand.

The Ranger hesitated, confident that the unkempt chief hadn't bothered to wash. Finally he shook the man's hand, "Chief," Brewster replied.

"You probably don't remember me. I was chief when you handled an investigation here several years back."

Brewster smiled, something he didn't do often. "I remember, Chief." The man he recalled had been thirty pounds thinner, though.

Jefferson motioned to the chair in front of the desk. "Have a seat, Corporal. You must be tired. I just made some coffee, you want some?"

"Thank you, Chief. I'll take it black," Brewster said as he took his seat.

Jefferson poured two cups from a pot sitting on a hotplate behind his desk. The coffee pot was a sore spot to Jefferson's pride. He had charged it to the town account at George Henry McMillian's store as an office expense.

It only seemed reasonable that the town would cover the cost of coffee. He gave a cup to everyone who came in the door, he reasoned. Then, Samuel Hastings, the mayor, town manager, and overall pain in Jefferson's backside, got the bill and darn near soiled his trousers. The result was Jefferson paying for the coffee pot.

"What have you got for me, Chief?" Brewster asked as Jefferson handed him a cup of coffee. McKinney was thankful that the Chief had held it by the handle.

"There's a kid down by the river. He's got his head bashed in. We found his car first. It was crashed into the feed store with the passenger seat all covered in blood. Then a little later this mornin' some boys were out huntin' and came across the body, half eaten by an alligator."

"Any suspects?"

Jefferson breathed a heavy sigh. He really didn't want to do this. "Last night the kid, his name's Cliff, and his best friend, Jesse Rose, got into a fight at the picture show. Jesse yelled, right there in front of fifty people, that he was gonna kill Cliff."

Brewster's eyes widened. It sounded pretty open and shut, but these things were never open and shut.

"I broke up the fight and sent 'em home separately, but they got together later and had a beer down by the river."

"Same place as you found the body?"

Jefferson nodded, "Yeah. Look Corporal, I've known Jesse all of his life. I think he was angry, and those words just came out of his mouth. Those boys have been best friends since they learned to walk. It just don't make sense."

"Do you know what they were fightin' about?"

Jefferson sighed again and rolled his eyes, "It was a girl. The two boys used to be pretty sweet on her, I think. But the last few years they have been courtin' these two sisters. Hell, half the town is bettin' on when Jesse is gonna ask the older one to marry him. So then last night this other girl, Jewel Stoker, well, her old man came into the Palace with a shotgun and darn' near killed Cliff. As a matter of fact, Jesse's the one that stopped it. Well, we get the lights on and I grab Irwin, Jewel's old man, and take his gun, and he says that Cliff got his daughter pregnant. No sooner than the words came out of his mouth, Jesse jumped on Cliff and started beatin' the daylights out of 'im."

Brewster leaned back in his chair and took a long drink of coffee. He suddenly realized how tired he really was. "Where's this girl's daddy?"

Jefferson looked up at the ceiling. "He's sober now, sitting in a cell. I'm gonna drive him to Rusk tomorrow. I suspect Judge Buckner will put him on the road gang for a week or two."

"And both these boys have girls?" Brewster asked, knowing the answer but asking more as part of processing the information.

"Yeah," Jefferson replied. "That's what I don't get. Jesse's as in love as anyone I've ever seen. There's nobody in town that would disagree with me either. He's goin' off to join the Aggie Corps next fall. Just about everybody thinks he's gonna ask her to marry him before he leaves."

"What about this other kid, Cliff?" Brewster asked, "Do you think he got this girl pregnant?"

Jefferson grimaced, "Corporal, if there was trouble to get into in this town, Cliff would find it. He's not a troublemaker. I mean he's never done anything really bad. He just does things without thinking them through. And that girl, well, she is a bit of a looker. She finished school last spring and's been catchin' the bus into Jacksonville. Works at the Chevy dealership up there."

"The boys are in school?"

"Yeah, worked out at the timber mill all summer. They've been doing that for the past two or three years. Like I said, Jesse's headed down to College Station. Cliff, I hear, got accepted into Stephen F. Austin Teacher's College. I suspect he was plannin' to keep working at the mill and drive into Nacogdoches. His folks don't have the money that Jesse's family has."

"They're pretty well off?

"His daddy's a big dog with Powhatan Oil. I think he manages all of their rigs around here."

Brewster sat silent holding the warm coffee cup on his lap for a long moment, "So where's this body?

"Still sittin' where we found it. I deputized a couple of boys, and they're watchin' over it. I figured that you'd want to look at it before we handed it over to the undertaker."

"I appreciate that, Chief. We better get out there. It'll be dark soon"

"The car's out back if you want to look at it first."

"Yeah, take me to it," now remembering that although Chief Hightower looked a bit sloppy, he was a pretty decent police officer.

Jefferson led the Ranger through the hallway to the back door. The coupe sat next to some garbage cans, covered in canvas.

"I didn't want anyone to see it until you got a look," Chief Hightower said as he began pulling the tarp off the car.

Brewster walked around the car, looking closely for any sign of a clue. He then began looking at the bloody seat.

"I haven't had time to look, but the boys who towed it in said that there's a bloody tire-iron under the seat."

Brewster opened the door and reached under the seat. He pulled out an angled tire wrench. The socketed end was covered with blood.

"In the morning I'm going to need to go over the car for fingerprints. I doubt that I'll find anything, but you never know. Is there a place where we can keep the car locked up?"

"One of the boys I deputized has a mechanic shop. He'll let me keep it over there."

"Do you have a camera or someone who can take some crime scene pictures for us?"

"I've got a boy up there waiting. I told him not to leave the bridge until you've looked at the scene first."

"How about a doctor? I'd like to get a time of death."

"I forgot to tell you. I had him down as soon as we found the body. He says that the poor kid died a half-hour or so before my boys found him."

Again Brewster was reminded that despite being overweight and a little unkempt, Chief Jefferson Hightower was a decent lawman.

"Good. Now take me to see this body. Call your undertaker, and have him meet us out there."

#

Corporal McKinney had seen quite a few bloody crime scenes in his time as a Texas Ranger. Most were the result of a robbery or a fight in an alley behind a gin-joint. Once there was a housewife who used a carving knife to turn her cheating husband into a pincushion. In that last instance, both Brewster and the judge on the case felt like the wife was completely justified. Her husband was a louse. Had she stabbed him once or twice she might be walking scott-free right this minute, but there was just no possible way a judge could let a woman off after she stabbed her husband two hundred and thirty-five times with a twelve-inch knife right after she bopped him over the head a dozen times with a rolling pin.

Still, as bad as that poor hacked-up cheating husband looked, he didn't compare to this. One side of this poor kid's head was completely caved in, no doubt from the tire iron. From the looks of things, he had lived for quite a while after the beating. He had vomited at least twice. Once up the hill a little and then again right where he lay, after the gator dragged him down the slope. Brewster had only seen one killing that was anywhere close to this bad, and that was just a quarter of a mile up the those same tracks. That time the guy's skull was broken and he had been slung out of a car that had been hit by a train.

Brewster prided himself in not getting ill at a crime scene. It was unprofessional and showed weakness, two things a Texas Ranger couldn't afford. But this one got to him. He made sure to not let the deputies up on the bridge see his face as he looked over the body. Chief Hightower was standing a little up the slope, but he doubted the Chief noticed. The Chief had already contaminated the crime scene once and looked as if he was about to again.

Finally, after walking around the body a couple of times, he went down the slope to the water's edge and looked up. The alligator was just a few feet up the embankment. Above the gator to the right lay the victim. On the top of the slope was a small tree with some broken limbs. The muddy slope was smooth but there were alligator tracks all around. The body was hung on some small broken bushes and partially wedged between a bush and a small tree. The gator had been trying to pull the boy between the two. By the look of things, the tree would have to be cut just to get the body free.

One of the victim's legs was ripped away and one hand had been chewed on. The victim's remaining hand was holding a two-foot stick that he most likely had used to fight off the gator.

"What do you think, Corporal?" Jefferson asked.

"He definitely died after the gator dragged him down here."

"Seriously?" Jefferson asked in shock. "How can you tell?"

"There's vomit next to his face. Someone bashed his head with that tire-iron. They probably put him in the car and drove to the bridge and shoved him down the slope. I suspect they thought he'd float downstream some. He got hung up on that broken tree," he said, pointing. "He probably hung there a while until the alligator smelled the blood and came up the slope and grabbed hold of his legs. From the looks of the mud the gator worked at him a while and finally broke him loose and dragged him down here where he got hung up again. The alligator most likely fought with him for quite a while. There's a lot of smoothed-out mud. I suspect the gator went into a roll and ripped off the leg. At some point the kid finally died. The gator was still trying to get him loose from these bushes when your boy there shot it."

"Dear God."

"Look at his right hand. He's holding on to that tree limb. Your undertaker will have to pry it free." Brewster answered as he looked around. Then he spotted something at the tree on the slope above. "Chief what is that at the base of that tree?"

Jefferson worked his way back up the slope toward the bridge. On the ground there were a few rocks stacked up. Jefferson looked at them and then back at Brewster. "Someone stacked up some rocks."

Brewster climbed to the slope to where Jefferson stood. He was a little put out with himself. He had been looking at the body where it lay and hadn't thought about the fact that it had been moved by the gator. It was a rookie mistake. A seasoned investigator such as he shouldn't have made such an error.

He looked at the rocks and the trees and the marks on the ground. When the boy was pushed off the bridge he landed wedged in the small trees. He was probably weak from the blood loss, not to mention the pain. Most likely he didn't have the strength to stand up, let alone get out of the trees. He must have made a pillow with the rocks while he lay there, probably so that he could keep an eye on the gator.

Brewster walked back down to the body. The kid had grabbed the limb when the gator dragged him into the bush. The Ranger looked at the leg that was still attached. The heel of the boot was dug into the ground. He was still fighting to the very last.

The Ranger turned his head away from the chief and the deputies and looked out at the water. Part of him wanted to vomit. Another part of him wanted to cry. That gator may have worked on him for hours before he died. No human should have to go through anything like that.

Brewster turned and began walking up the slope to the Chief, somewhat disgusted with himself that he was still nauseated. The long-time peace officer considered himself above such things. It occurred to him it was because this was just a kid, and a good one at that, that it bothered him so. He couldn't help but wonder if he would have felt that way had it been a bank robber or a cop killer lying on that slope. Blood is blood, but when it's a bad guy you don't mind seeing it spilt. Conversely, when it's a decent kid like this, it breaks your heart.

When he reached Jefferson, he walked past the chief toward the trestle, "Have your boys go ahead. I've seen enough."

"Sure," the Chief replied as he followed the Ranger up to the tracks.

Alongside the tracks, behind the prowler, sat a black hearse with two men leaning on the hood beside Bobby Weatherholt, who was there holding a camera. Jefferson motioned to Bobby and the three began walking to the river. "Let Bobby get his pictures before you boys touch anything." He then turned to his four deputies who had been standing on the trestle watching the corporal, "Toad, you and Hunker give 'em a hand," he ordered.

As the chief was talking to his deputies, Brewster began walking to the far end of the bridge, away from everyone else. After a few minutes Jefferson walked up. "What do you think, Corporal?"

Brewster, stopped walking and leaned on the bridge and watched as the four men began trying to lift the body. "Do you go to the movies, Chief? Charlie Chan, the Thin Man, Mr. Moto?"

"Sure, every week."

"Well, it's never like that. Killers don't plan it out. They don't try to frame-up someone. Killers get angry and they shoot, or in this case, clobber someone over the head. Tell me about these two boys."

"They're good kids. Oh, sure, Cliff got in a little trouble now and then, but, like I said, he never did anything bad."

"You said earlier that they were together a lot?"

"They were best friends. You almost never saw them apart. They were in school together, they worked together, and even last night they were out on a date with their two girls together. Corporal, there's just no way Jesse did this. He's a good kid."

"Someone who was really mad stopped that boy in town last night and hit him with that tire iron. It was rage. He didn't just hit him once or twice. He hit him a dozen or more times to make a dent like that.

"Then the killer drove the kid in that coupe down here and tossed that body down off the bridge, knowing that he'd bleed out and the critters would eat up the body. It's just dumb luck that those two found him."

"Why would anybody want to do that?"

"If his buddy didn't do it, then it was someone who had a real good reason to hate that boy."

"Do you think it was someone he knew?"

"Whoever did this definitely knew him. Murderers kill for a reason. This kid doesn't look like he had any money, so it wasn't robbery. The fact is, most murderers are family members or co-workers, people who know the victim well enough to have a reason to hate him."

"I can't believe his family did this and, damn-it, I just ain't buyin' that it was Jesse."

"Okay, let's say it's not this Jesse kid. Let's say there's someone else out there, someone who has a reason to kill this boy," Brewster began, thinking out loud, "These two kids are best buddies. They probably know just about all the same people. And they were together most of the time, which means that if someone had reason to kill one of the boys, then he probably has reason to kill the other. You say this kid and the other one were out late last night, and this one dropped the other kid off and headed home?"

"Right."

"So..." Brewster paused in thought, "he sees some guy fixing a tire on the side of the road late at night and stopped to help."

"That makes sense, Cliff would have turned left off Main onto the highway a few blocks to get to his house. He would have gone right past Washington's Feed Store, too."

"So let's say the guy's on the side of the highway out in front of the feed store with a flat, and this kid stops to help, and the guy whacks him over the head with a tire iron then puts the boy in his own car and dumps him here."

"Then it was just some random guy who suddenly decided to kill?"

"No, this wasn't random. The kid's head is too bashed in. There was passion behind it. The human skull is pretty thick. If you hit it once or twice with a tire iron you'll get one or two fairly small dents. He would probably die, but this killer hit him over and over. You don't do that randomly. You do that out of rage."

"But Cliff wouldn't have stopped for someone if he knew he might get killed."

"So we've got a killer who hated this kid enough to beat him to death, and the kid didn't know anything about it."

"If he wanted to kill Cliff, then…"

"Chief, you have a killer right here in Elza. Chances are that this Jesse is on his list. Bring him in for questioning. He's better off in jail than he is on his own. We need to question him anyway. He's probably talked to the killer and doesn't even know it."

In the distance a '37 Ford Woody rumbled along the rutted road that was becoming congested with cars.

"Just what I need. Onlookers."

The law officers began walking toward the end of the bridge where Toad and Hunker stood watching the men below pulling Cliff's mangled body from the brush.

When the chief reached Toad, who was still standing guard, he pointed to the man getting out of the Woody. "I don't know who that is, but if he tries to get a look down at Cliff, slap some cuffs on him."

"I don't have any cuffs."

Jefferson pulled some handcuffs off his belt as the man, with great determination, made his way through the high grass toward the tracks.

"Let's go, Corporal," Jefferson said to Brewster. "Toad can take care of this."

The two began walking along the tracks to the prowler as the man from the Woody came toward them. Before he got to Jefferson and Brewster, Toad, hunting rifle still in hand, intercepted him.

"Sir, you're gonna have to turn around and go home. We have police business here," Toad ordered in a tone that impressed himself far more than the other man.

The man reached into his suit pocket and pulled out a notepad. "I'm David Roberson with the *Jacksonville Statesman*. I need a few words with your chief."

"I said no," Toad replied emphatically, growing more impressed with his importance.

"I hadn't thought about this," Jefferson said softly to Brewster. "I'll deal with it, Toad."

Brewster followed Jefferson to the reporter.

"Are you sure, Chief? I've got this." Toad said, disappointed that he didn't get to use the handcuffs.

"Go back to the bridge and see if they need any help," Jefferson ordered his deputy.

The reporter watched the deputy leave and turned to Jefferson and asked, "Really, his name is Toad?"

"What can I do for you, Mr. Roberson?"

"I hear you got a bad one," the reporter said, a bit too cheerfully for anyone's taste.

"We don't have any information for you. Come back in a day or so."

"Is he down there? I'd love to get some pictures." Roberson said, ignoring the Chief and walking past Jefferson and Brewster to the bridge as he pulled a Spartus camera out of the side pocket of his coat.

"No pictures," Jefferson ordered, grabbing the camera as Roberson passed him by.

"Chief, you can't stop me. The press has a right to be here," Roberson defended just as he got a look down the bank at Cliff's twisted and mangled body. "Good God almighty."

"No pictures," Jefferson repeated as he walked up to the reporter and handed back the camera.

Roberson stared down at Cliff. Then he raised and unfolded the camera. "I can't print it, but I gotta take one to show the guys back at the paper."

"No pictures. That kid was a friend of mine."

Roberson sighed as he relented, and then asked compassionately, "What happened here, Chief?"

"We don't know yet," Brewster answered with authority.

"Who are you?"

"Brewster McKinney, Texas Rangers."

"THE Brewster McKinney?" Roberson said as he excitedly tried to write notes while holding the camera.

"We have a murder. The kid's name is Cliff." Brewster paused and looked at the Chief.

"Cliff Tidwell."

"Cliff Tidwell. He was hit in the back of the head. We think with a tire iron," Brewster looked at Jefferson and then continued. "He died immediately. Put that in your paper as a quote from me. You got that. You do not mention the gator. His mom and dad don't need to read that in the paper. Besides, like I said, all that happened after he was dead. If I read one word about an alligator in that paper of yours, I'm going to come find you and I'm gonna tie you to one of those trees down there and leave you overnight and see what happens. You got that?"

The reporter stared at the tall, gruff old Ranger and nodded his head.

Jefferson couldn't help but smile. It never would have entered his mind to threaten to kill a reporter, but he wasn't Brewster McKinney. Over the years since their first meeting, the chief had read many newspaper accounts of the Ranger's exploits. The man was famous, and he had a reputation for being tough and ruthless. A law officer making an arrest was common news, but a law officer single-handedly apprehending four armed robbers was the sort of thing that legends are made of. McKinney is a walking, talking legend. It was, for instance, well known that the he carried a Colt .45 automatic pistol in a shoulder holster under his coat like a gangster. Some claim that his draw was so fast that there wasn't a man alive who could match him. Jefferson, conversely, had never taken his weapon from its holster and prayed that he never would. The only time he came close was the night that George Henry McMillan's was robbed, and thankfully the burglars were long gone before Jefferson got the call. Of course, that's why McKinney could make threats to a reporter. He knew full well that the reporter had read the same articles that Jefferson had read, and though it was unbelievable that the Ranger would follow through with his threat, no man alive would take that risk, not when they knew McKinney's reputation.

"Do you have any suspects, Mr. McKinney?" Roberson asked timidly.

"Yes, and we're going to make an arrest. Make sure you put that in your paper."

#

ELZA, TEXAS
June 26, 1936

Jesse and Cliff were sitting on the steps of George Henry McMillan's store sipping RCs. On hot days like this the boys worked their way around town. First they tended to their chores at home - that mainly applied to Cliff. Then they would meet up downtown at eight in the morning and head over to McMillan's to sweep and stock shelves. Then they would go to Washington's Feed Store to see if they could do a little work there. If they were lucky, they could get a dime for cleaning the place up. Sometime around ten Jewel would join them and they would all spend the rest of the day either hanging out downtown or heading to the bridge to fish. If Mr. Washington didn't have any work, they would usually head back to McMillan's and sit on the steps listening to the old men argue.

This morning they were sitting on the steps of McMillan's.

To their left, Shorty Newman and one of the older men were sitting on a couple of old wooden chairs playing checkers. In Elza there were the men who had work, like Jesse's and Cliff's fathers, and there were the young men who couldn't find work (or didn't want to find work), who spent most of their days at the domino hall. Lastly, there were the old men who had long since done their work. These old men spent their days sitting around George Henry's discussing the world's problems while playing checkers. As a rule, the boys preferred to hang around with the older men. The old men had great stories, although rarely true, and they never asked the boys to go do anything without offering to pay a nickel or dime.

George Henry's, being the best place to buy groceries in town, naturally got a lot of traffic. Everybody, young and old, came through the store sooner or later, and the boys found the conversation amusing.

Some days a couple of the younger men like Shorty Newman and Elza Police Chief Thomas Jefferson Hightower would be there. Shorty had a reputation for being the best checker player in town, and he'd been in the process of proving his prowess all morning long.

The events in Jacksonville the day before had both boys confused and even depressed, but neither understood exactly why. First, neither boy was prepared for the sight of a man being hanged. When they hopped in the back of Toad Lowery's truck, all they were thinking about was the excitement of the moment. They had heard of hangings and lynchings, and somehow it seemed entertaining, but the thought that a man would actually die didn't become a reality until they saw it happen. More importantly, both boys had felt that they were going up to Jacksonville to watch justice take place. A bad man was going to get what he deserved. But, Jesse, for one, felt sure that an innocent man was murdered by an angry mob, and the two of them, along with Jewel, were a part of the mob. And if, in fact, an innocent man was killed, they were as guilty of murder as anyone.

None of them had spoken all the way home. When they had gotten to Elza they were all three ready to go home even though it was still early in the day. So when Toad stopped in the middle of Main Street, the kids had simply said goodbye and headed their separate ways.

All morning long Jesse had wanted to bring up the subject to Cliff but didn't know what to say. Sitting there on George Henry's steps, he was still churning it all in his mind when an old Ford Model-AA pickup pulled to a stop at the gas pump.

The two boys knew the truck, as they did every truck around town. One glance and they knew exactly who was coming down the road. This truck was of particular interest to them. There wasn't a man in all of East Texas that fascinated the boys more than old Cherokee-One-Leg. There were all sorts of stories about the man - that he had lost his leg to an alligator, that he had been a Buffalo Soldier and fought alongside Teddy Roosevelt at San Juan Hill, and, some said, that he even helped track down Geronimo.

One day the boys were at George Henry's with Cliff's dad when some of the men began talking about how they should bring the Klan back and run all the blacks back to Africa. Before that Jesse had never seen Cliff's dad angry. Both boys had gotten whippings from the man, more than once, generally for some trouble Cliff thought up, but even then he was only a little angry. That day at George Henry's, Ned Tidwell was flat-out mad.

He had argued that many of the black folks in the area had a lot more right to live in this country than any of those men in the store. There were blacks, he had said, that fought at the Alamo. Then he said that there were six hundred black men who had stood alongside Andy Jackson and Jean Lafitte when the British tried to take New Orleans. As a matter of fact, he added that Cherokee-One-Leg's grandfather was one of them. Then he said that Cherokee's grandpa went on to become one of the first mountain men, and his father had scouted alongside Kit Carson. Cherokee, he said, fought alongside Teddy Roosevelt.

With this new information, combined with the fact that Cherokee-One-Leg had survived an alligator attack and wore the gator's teeth around his neck as proof, the two twelve-year-olds were in absolute awe of the old black man. All things considered, the boys, quite rightly, held a lot more respect for the old, crippled man named Cherokee than they did most of the white men in and around Elza.

The two watched in wonderment as the lean old man gingerly climbed out of the cab of his Ford with his one good leg and the peg attached to the other. He had an old homemade crutch that he pulled out of the truck and used it to stiffly hobble over to one of the pumps to begin filling up his pickup. In Jacksonville and Henderson some fill-up stations had the new electric pumps, but McMillan's had the old visible pumps with the glass tank at the top that bubbled as gas flowed down into the vehicle.

The old one-legged man used the pump handle to pump a couple of gallons of gasoline into the globe and then watched it drain into his tank. When he finished, he took his crutch and hobbled toward the front door. As he began up the steps where Jesse and Cliff were sitting, Shorty, who had been in the delegation from Elza the day before, asked, "So Cherokee, what'd you think about that hangin' yesterday?"

The old black man stopped still. He slowly lowered his good leg off the step and turned to face Shorty. Standing tall, he stared icily at the man and said, "That boy didn't do nothing'. They hung him like a damn criminal and all he done wrong was be born black."

Jesse and Cliff froze as both felt a cold chill from the tension.

"Well that girl said he did. I know. I heard her," Shorty cockily replied.

Jesse watched as the old man's eyes, which had been yellowed with age, burn almost red with anger. "Bucky didn't do nothin'. He was at my house. He was reading to me. My eyes is bad and I can't read no more. He was readin' the Bible. When he went home some of you boys grabbed 'im and put 'im in jail. And then yesterday ya lynched 'im. No one bothered to ask. Nobody cared to ask if he did it or not."

Jesse looked over at the police chief, who was sitting on a bench sipping a Dr Pepper, not appearing interested in involving himself in a scuff with Cherokee-One-Leg.

Shorty looked at the man, realizing that he may have started something that he shouldn't have. "She said he did. You said he didn't. Who are we to believe?"

The old man's anger now burned. Jefferson tensed, knowing that he may have to do something.

Jesse and Cliff sat wide-eyed as Cherokee flung his crutch to the ground, straightened up, and walked without the slightest hint of difficulty to Shorty, who was now visibly frightened.

Standing directly over Shorty, the old Indian fighter said, "Bucky was with me. Are you calling me a liar?"

Shorty shrunk before Cherokee, who was easily forty years his senior, and with his head down, softly said, "No."

Jefferson then stood to his feet, "We don't want any trouble Cherokee. Shorty went too far. The fact is I should have shut him up before he opened his stupid mouth. Bucky was a good boy. I known him all his life. I don't need you to tell me he didn't do it. Anybody who knew him knows he didn't do it. I'm sorry, Cherokee. I'm truly sorry."

The old man looked Chief Hightower in the eye and nodded his head. The anger had altered slightly to sadness, and Jesse could see that there was a hint of a tear in the old warrior's eyes.

As Cherokee-One-Leg walked back to the steps, Cliff got up, picked up the old man's crutch, and handed it to him. The Indian fighter took the crutch, nodded his head to Cliff, and climbed the steps past Jesse and into McMillan's store.

Jefferson sat back down on the bench, and Shorty got back to his game, but no one said a word. Jesse looked at Cliff, who motioned with his head for them to leave. Jesse got up and silently sat his empty RC bottle in the bottle crate by the steps, and the two boys started walking toward Main Street.

Once out of earshot of the store Cliff said, "Gemma Crawford's daddy raped that girl."

Jesse didn't know what to say. He knew it was true but he had no words. He just nodded.

"We're the only ones who know."

"I know," Jesse replied. "And he's gonna do somethin' bad to Jewel's mama, too."

"We've gotta tell somebody. Maybe we should talk to Jefferson."

"He ain't gonna listen to a couple of kids, especially one that got stuck in the Palace air shaft."

"Should we tell Jewel?"

"What are we gonna tell her? That her mama is carrying on with Gemma's daddy? We don't even know if it's true. She'll just get mad at us."

The two boys walked along the side of the road, silently in thought for a few minutes, when Cherokee-One-Leg pulled up beside them in his Ford pickup.

"You boys hop in the back," the old man ordered without further explanation.

Jesse and Cliff looked at each other and then did as they were told. It wasn't that either felt obligated to obey, but they both sensed something in the man, and they respected him.

#

Cherokee turned the truck off the highway and headed down the old road toward the tracks. He turned left and followed the worn ruts along the tracks to the old trestle across the Neches. When he got to the bridge, he stopped and climbed out with what Jesse thought was amazing agility for a man in his eighties with only one leg.

The boys climbed out of the bed of the truck and without a word followed the old Indian fighter as he walked out onto the trestle.

"You boys come out here and fish, don't you?" The old man asked, but it was really a statement.

Cliff and Jesse looked at each other, curious about what the old man wanted with them. Cliff finally answered the man, "Yes, sir, but we don't catch much."

The old man rested his arms on the crossbeam of the trestle and looked out at the river below. "This is a good spot. I fished here when I was a kid. That was before they laid these tracks."

Jesse and Cliff climbed up and sat on the crossbeam that Cherokee was leaning on, just as they did almost every day.

"Did you grow up here?" Jesse asked, wondering if all the stories he had heard about the man were true.

"I was born here. My grandpa was the first black freeman to own land in these parts."

"Is it true that your grandpa fought with Andy Jackson in New Orleans?" Cliff asked in awe.

"Grandpa Cort Bradford came over here from Spain, though I think he was probably born in Morocco. He was sailin' with Jean Lafitte when the British attacked. After that he went west and explored the Rockies. He was there twenty years before white folks like Jim Bridger and Kit Carson showed up," the old man answered with pride.

"Did you really help get Geronimo?" Jesse asked, full of excitement.

The old man was saddened by the question. "Yes, sir, I did. I was assigned as a scout for the Fourth Cavalry. We chased him all over Mexico and New Mexico."

Jesse recognized that it was painful for the man to answer. "I'm sorry, sir. I didn't mean to…"

"It don't bother me none. Everybody asks about that. But they wouldn't ask if they know'd that my little brother was ridin' with that old Apache. I had a good life in the army, but that expedition ain't one of my favorite memories," the old man said with pain in his voice.

Jesse and Cliff were silent as they thought about how the old man they so admired for his courage was a man suffering from a lot of pain.

Cherokee-One-Leg knew what the boys were feeling. He had been asked about Geronimo a hundred times but only mentioned Augustus twice and got the same reaction both times.

Cherokee wasn't from the Cherokee nation as most people thought. Texans had given him the nickname when he was a child. He and his brother were born half Arapaho. Their father and grandfather were great admirers of the Roman Empire, so they were named Julius Caesar and Augustus Caesar, no last name. Their great-grandfather had no last name when he got off the ship in New Orleans. He was simply Cort the deckhand. Upon seeing the face of slavery in the south, Cort chose to go west, first to Texas and finally on to Santa Fe and even California.

Because of his experience in the west and having learned a number of native languages, Cort had become a valuable scout and had spent time with Bridger, Kit Carson and even John Fremont. In the area now known as Colorado he met and married Nizhoni, the daughter of an Arapaho warrior. Cort's family grew, and in the 1840's he took his sons and their families back to Texas. He needed a last name in order to purchase property, so he took the name of his closest friend, Ephraim Bradford. Thus, Cherokee's legal name was Julius Caesar Bradford.

Life was hard for a free black family in Texas in those days. Texas was a Republic, but it was a slave-holding Republic. It was worse on children who were as much Arapaho as they were black. Comanche raids had still been common, so the half black sons of a squaw were not welcome in the schools and often were not even allowed to play with other boys. In 1850, Cherokee's father, Titus, went to meet his mother's family in Colorado. There he eventually married an Arapaho named Cocheta. Five years later he returned to Texas with his wife, where their two sons, Julius Caesar and Augustus Caesar Bradford were born. When the War Between the States broke out, Cherokee's father took the family back west, where he had spent the rest of his life scouting for the Union Army.

Cherokee turned and looked solemnly at the boys and asked, "What happened yesterday?"

Jesse felt coldness in the pit of his stomach, recalling just how angry the old man had been at Shorty and knowing that they were as guilty of Bucky Davis's death as anyone.

Cherokee saw the hesitance in the boy's faces. "I know y'all was there. Mert Davis seen ya,"

The man then looked directly at Jesse. "You are Murdock Rose's boy, aren't you?"

Jesse froze for a moment and then answered, "Yes, sir, we were there."

"Last night a bunch of folks gathered at the Davis's house over in Pleasant Grove. The young men all want to riot. That Ranger came out and settled things down, but they're gonna get bad if we don't do somethin'.

"Mert said that there was a hundred men there, maybe two hundred. This mornin' I went up to Jacksonville, and everybody I talked to said they weren't there. You'd think Bucky went and hung himself."

"A white man did it," Jesse said softly with his head down.

The old man looked at him again with a wrinkled brow.

"There's this man here in Elza," Cliff began. "Mr. Crawford. We saw him a few weeks ago talkin' with this woman, Mrs. Stoker."

"Irwin Stoker's wife?" Cherokee asked.

"Yes, sir," Cliff continued. "We've seen him get her to go into the alley a couple of times. She always comes out real upset. So one day we seen them go into the alley, so we climbed up on top of the Palace so we could see what they was doin'."

"That's why y'all went up there? I heard you two were tryin' to steal popcorn."

Jesse grinned. "That was after," he interjected. "When we were about to climb down, Cliff decided he was hungry."

"So anyway," Cliff began again with a glare at his friend, "We saw him hit her a couple of times."

"What's that got to do with Bucky?"

"Yesterday," Jesse started solemnly, "we got in the back of Toad's pickup and rode up to watch. When we got there the crowd wasn't that big, but cars and trucks started comin' in from all over. It was like you said, maybe two hundred. We were stayin' back 'cause the crowd was getting scary, but then we saw Mr. Crawford and decided to go up into the crowd to get a good look."

"That's when the police chief came out with Bucky," Cliff added.

"They walked him right down in the middle of the mob," Jesse continued, "and then this car drives up and some man walks the girl out. They were right in front of me. Bucky on one side, the girl on the other."

Now the boys are getting excited and Cliff added, "So Mr. Crawford gets to where the girl can see him. At first she didn't seem to notice him. Then the chief asked if Bucky did it, and she shook her head. But she looked up at Mr. Crawford, and she got really scared."

"Yeah," Jesse said, "Even more than she was before, but she still shook her head. Then Mr. Crawford opened his coat a little and she saw his gun."

"He had a gun?" Cliff asked in surprise.

"Yeah, I think me and her were the only ones who saw it. Nobody was payin' any attention to him except us. So then when the chief asked her again if Bucky did it, she nodded, but I think she just did that because she was scared of Mr. Crawford."

"When she nodded, the chief just got out of the way, and the mob dragged Bucky into the park and hung 'im," Cliff finished.

Saddened, Jesse looked at the old man, fighting tears. "I'm sorry we didn't stop it. I don't know what we could have done, but Bucky didn't need to die."

Cliff wiped a tear from his eye, "I was up thinkin' about it all night, Cherokee. I don't know what I expected to see when we got in Toad's truck, but I sure didn't expect to be part of a murder."

"You boys didn't do nothin'," Cherokee said with sensitivity. "There's a lot of bad people in this world, boys. Some are real bad, like that Mr. Crawford. Others, like those who lynched Bucky, are bad because they let hate build up inside of 'em 'til days like yesterday when they let it all out. Others out there are bad because they watched and didn't do nothing', like that fool back there at McMillan's. To him, Bucky's just another dead black. But, you boys, y'all were just a couple of witnesses."

"Mr, Cherokee?" Jesse asked. "Do you think there'll be riots?"

"I don't know. Those boys want blood, and they got the right. A white man done it, and a black man got hung."

"What if we tell them what we know about Mr. Crawford?"

"Lord almighty, don't do that. Have you told anyone?"

Jesse and Cliff shook their heads.

"Don't. The law don't care about black folks, and if he's that bad he'll come after you. I'm gonna come into Elza tomorrow with a load of tomatoes to sell. You boys point him out to me."

Chapter 7

301 RED OAK AVE.

ELZA, TEXAS

6:40 p.m. Sunday, November 16, 1941

Garvis Rose prepared two plates with roast beef, mashed potatoes, collard greens, and carrots. There was a lot left since Jesse hadn't eaten lunch. Sunday was pot roast day. Garvis wasn't much of a cook. Her mother hadn't cooked at all; they had had Nelda to do all the cooking. She would have preferred to have someone to do the cooking for her, but Murdock wasn't about to pay someone to cook. Of course they could afford it, but he was a bit old fashioned in that way. It took several years for him to concede and hire their housekeeper, Miss May, from over in Pleasant Grove. Cleaning up after the man was where Garvis absolutely drew the line. From day one in their marriage she refused to clean his filth. As it turned out, that decision was one of the wisest of her life because Murdock Rose didn't like cleaning up after himself either. Therefore, as soon as they could afford it, Miss May was hired.

Cooking, though, was something from which she couldn't find a way to escape. She fumbled through the first few years. Of course, they were young newlyweds and Murdock didn't mind a burned hen or a dry turkey, but it wasn't long before he began to complain. She, naturally, tried to convince him that she was hopeless and they needed to hire a cook, but such reasoning simply fell on deaf ears. Then one day he came home with a brochure for a cooking class at the Henderson community center. She, naturally, pretended that he had hurt her feelings but, like all men, Murdock could be exceptionally dense. Thus, every Tuesday and Thursday she took the bus into Henderson where she and the East Texas hillbilly housewives learned how to baste a chicken and whip eggs. Eventually she began to somewhat enjoy cooking, but it was still humiliating that even though they could afford proper kitchen help, she still had to spend a couple of hours a day standing over a hot stove.

She sat the two plates on the dining room table, along with flatware and two glasses of iced tea and then walked to the front door. Jesse and Gemma were sitting on the steps holding each other. It had been a dreadful day for Jesse, and the two had been sitting there for over an hour without saying a word.

It was just terrible about poor Cliff. Over and over Garvis had asked herself how it could possibly have happened. Sadly, that dumb cluck of a police chief sure wasn't going to get to the bottom of it. Poor Jesse was just lifeless with sorrow. Garvis hadn't heard him say two words all afternoon. This was the one and only time that Garvis was thankful for Gemma Crawford.

It wasn't that Garvis had anything against Gemma, of course. She was a delightful girl, but her father was a drunk who got hit by a train and her mother was a seamstress, of all things. Jesse deserved better. Nevertheless, if he had to spend his time with one of the girls in this two-bit town, Gemma was, as Garvis' daddy would say, "the pick of the litter." Garvis was just thankful that he hadn't taken up with that Stoker girl. That would have been a real problem.

At any rate, Jesse would be in College Station in a few months, and Mrs. Murdock Rose felt sure that he would be over this little infatuation with Gemma by Christmas. Still, it was exceptionally annoying that every time she walked down Main Street some bumpkin would ask if Jesse had "popped the question yet." As if it was a foregone conclusion.

Well, it wasn't.

That very subject had been the cause of the only real difficulty in her relationship with her son. Jesse was a wonderful boy. Garvis, and Murdock too, couldn't be more proud. He would graduate at the top of his class. Granted there would be only six graduates, but Jesse was unquestionably the smartest. He was always respectful and had never given his mother a single problem. He was so sweet, too. And Garvis felt they could talk about anything.

Well, almost anything. The biggest worry in Garvis's life was that Jesse would get himself engaged to that girl before going off to college. That was the one thing that Mrs. Murdock Rose was just not going to stand for.

It shocked her when she sat her son down to have a conversation about his intentions with Gemma, he steadfastly refused to listen to her. Garvis said she had no intention of trying to separate the two. She simply felt that it would be wise for him to finish at Texas A&M, get his Army commission, and after a couple of years, once he had been promoted to First Lieutenant, or god willing, Captain, he could then think about marriage, once he was making a reasonable living. Of course, by that time he would have long since forgotten about a high school sweetheart.

Jesse's response was appalling. Not only had he refused to discuss it with her, he told his mother in no uncertain terms, that his plans regarding Gemma were not her business. Then he stormed off to his room and wouldn't come out. Understandably, Garvis had been appalled; no mother wants to hear such talk from her baby.

When Murdock came home, she immediatly sent him up to have a stern talk with Jesse. But when he came downstairs Murdock simply said that, "The boy knows what he's doing," and she was not to worry.

Murdock spent that night in the guest room.

As far as Garvis was concerned, this was not over. She may not be able to keep him from getting engaged, but she would see to it that he didn't get married without getting his commission first.

The worst part of that little incident was how Jesse had talked to her. It was simply shocking. She thought they had been so close for all those years. Which, now that she thought about it, is why it was so surprising to learn that he had been slipping out the window at night and running around town with Cliff. Jesse just didn't keep secrets from his mother, did he?

It was the influence of that Tidwell boy. The two had been best friends since they were in diapers. Garvis had heard stories about Cliff's mischief, but fortunately, Jesse never partook in the antics. Obviously, Cliff Tidwell had convinced Jesse to sneak out a few times. Garvis was going to have to have a little discussion with Jesse about that. But the really concerning part was that Jesse had never told her about it. Jesse was not one to keep secrets from her.

As she stepped out on the porch, that waste of tax revenue of a police chief and another man were getting out of the prowler. Garvis had always thought Chief Hightower was worthless, but she now despised him for the disrespectful way he had spoken to her husband that morning. Murdock Rose was one of the leaders of the community, and this civil servant treated him like he was a pea farmer.

"I've got dinner on the table for you two, Jesse."

"I'm not hungry, mom. Besides, the Chief is here. Maybe he has some news."

Garvis stood patiently with her long-practiced and most pleasant smile as their town's only law enforcement officer and his companion approached the porch.

"Hi, Jesse, Ms. Garvis, Miss Gemma," Jefferson said as Jesse and Gemma stood.

Garvis glared with disdain, but as quickly as she could, she replaced her glare with her pleasant-though-somewhat-condescending smile.

"Did you find out what happened?" Jesse asked.

Brewster recognized the boy.

"Well, Jesse," the Chief began, "we've got a pretty good idea, but we have some unanswered questions. Would you mind coming down to the station with us?"

"No, of course not."

"Hold on just a minute!" Garvis exclaimed at a volume that was just shy of a shout.

"Ms. Garvis," the chief began.

"Any questions you have you can ask right here on this porch," Garvis ordered, having not forgiven the tone with which this public servant had spoken to her husband that morning.

"Mom."

"Murdock, come out here. They're arresting Jesse."

"Ma'am, I didn't say anything about arresting him."

"Then you can do your talking right here."

Murdock came to the door where his wife had been standing. Garvis was now on the porch with both hands on Jesse's shoulders.

"What is this about, Chief Hightower?" Rose asked in a commanding tone intended to let everyone know that he was in charge at his home.

"Murdock, we-,"

"That's Mr. Rose to you Chief," Rose interrupted.

Jefferson paused, glanced at Brewster and rolled his eyes. This had been a long day, and Murdock and Garvis Rose were not making it any shorter.

"Murdock. We have a murder, and your son may be able to answer a number of questions. Now, he's comin' with us and that's that."

Gemma grabbed tightly to Jesse's arm with fear in her eyes.

"Chief Hightower," a belligerent Murdock began, "get off my property and don't come back without a warrant."

"We don't need a warrant," said Brewster, who had until now remained silent.

"And who the hell are you?"

"You're Corporal McKinney, aren't you?" Jesse asked, but he knew the answer to the question. For the first time since this confrontation began, Jesse was frightened.

"We've met before haven't we son?

"You came to town when I was a kid."

Brewster began putting it all together. "You were one of the two boys we questioned."

"Yes, sir."

Brewster looked at Murdock and Garvis. "Brewster McKinney, Texas Rangers."

"Well, I don't care if you're the governor himself; my son isn't leaving my porch."

"Mr. Rose, your son is hereby under arrest for suspicion of murder."

Jesse tensed and Gemma clenched her hands on his arm.

"He's not going anywhere," Garvis ordered. "Murdock get your gun."

Brewster opened his jacket revealing the Colt .45 automatic pistol in his shoulder holster, "Ma'am, this ends one of two ways. Your son comes with us peaceably, and we hold him overnight and ask him some questions, or I arrest your husband for obstruction of justice."

"Damit," an unhinged Jefferson Hightower began, "everybody calm down. Corporal, with all respect, please fasten your coat. Jesse get in the prowler. Now, Murdock we're taking him in for questioning. He's not under arrest," he said with a glance toward Brewster. "You can see him in the morning."

Murdock and Garvis froze, both fuming.

"Come on, Jesse," Jefferson ordered with way more authority than he knew he had.

Jesse timidly stepped off the porch, glancing back at Gemma.

"Gemma, you're welcome to come down to the station," Jefferson said compassionately to the girl.

"My lawyer will be there first thing in the morning," Murdock proclaimed.

"I'm sure he will," the Chief replied as he led Jesse to the prowler, with Gemma following.

#

MAIN STREET
ELZA, TEXAS
June 27, 1936

Jesse and Cliff were walking up Main Street after finishing up at McMillan's store. Up ahead, Jewel was walking toward them as she did every day at about that time. Just past the Palace, Cherokee had his Model-T parked nose-in to the curb and was sitting on the tailgate selling tomatoes.

"You gotta get Jewel out of here."

"Why me?" Jesse protested.

"She likes you more than me."

"Bull."

"Well, somebody's gotta do it. What if her mama comes out and meets Mr. Crawford?"

"They ain't done that in a while."

"I know. Somethin's up."

"Well, I ain't doin' it. I'm gonna visit with Cherokee."

As the two were debating, a Plymouth sedan pulled into one of the parking spots just in front of them. Peterson Crawford was driving, and Gemma and Jettie were sitting in the front seat beside him. Crawford got out of the car and stared at Jesse as he and Cliff came to the front of his car.

As Jesse and Cliff stopped in their tracks at the sight of Crawford, Jewel approached them.

Jesse turned his attention from Crawford, trying to avoid eye contact with the man. In an attempt to appear casual, he said, "Hi, Jewel."

"Hi, Jewel," Cliff echoed.

Gemma and her sister started climbing out of the car as Crawford continued looking at Jesse. Jewel knew something was up but assumed it was just Jesse freezing up in front of Gemma.

"Hi, Gemma," Jewel said, looking past Jesse and Cliff.

Gemma looked at the three kids as Jewel stepped between the two boys toward her.

"Hi."

"We're going McMillan's to get some RCs if you want to come along. Jesse'll buy you a soda," Jewel said with a grin toward Jesse. "Won't, you Jess?"

Jesse froze, staring at her.

"Gemma," Peterson Crawford called to his daughter as he turned to head across the street toward his wife's dress shop.

"I'll be there in a minute, Daddy."

Crawford took Jettie's hand and led his younger daughter across the street but glared back at Jesse.

"I've gotta help my mother with her shop."

"Maybe some other time," Jewel replied after a long glance at Jesse.

"Sure," Gemma answered and then, after looking at Jesse, turned to walk away.

Once her back was turned, Cliff shoved Jesse in the shoulder causing the boy to stumble off the curb.

"Uh, Gemma," Jesse blurted out.

Gemma turned back around to look at him.

"Uh," Jesse paused. "Uh, hi. I'm Jesse Rose."

"I know."

"I, uh. Hi," he repeated.

Gemma looked at him for a several seconds before replying, "Hi."

"Bye."

Gemma looked at him for a moment then said, "Bye," and turned to walk away.

When Gemma was inside Anna-Ruth's, Cliff said, "Well, you finally did it. You finally said two words to her. Of course, Harpo Marx could have said something more eloquent."

Jewel started laughing, "Come on, let's go to McMillan's."

"Y'all go on, I'm gonna hang here a while."

Cliff glared at him.

"We'll bring you an RC," Jewel replied. "Cliff will buy."

"If he wants an RC he can get it himself."

"Come on, can't you see? He's in love," Jewel replied as she grabbed Cliff and began leading him away.

Jesse couldn't keep himself from smiling as he walked up Main to where Cherokee-One-Leg sat on the tailgate of his Model-T selling tomatoes.

As Jesse arrived at the truck, Cherokee had just finished putting some tomatoes in a brown paper bag and handing it to a woman. The lady politely handed him some coins and walked away.

Jesse climbed up on the tailgate next to Cherokee.

The old soldier looked down the street at Cliff and Jewel who were heading away, "Where's your pardner goin'?"

"He and Jewel are goin' down to McMillan's. She hangs out with us some. We wanted to get her out of here. Her mom was the woman Mr. Crawford was meetin' in the alley."

The old man nodded. "I know her. Irwin Stoker's girl."

"Well, did you see the guy that got out of that Plymouth over there?"

"Naw, I saw you tryin' to talk to that other girl."

Jesse shrugged.

"Kid, I've fought Apaches, Comanches, Mexican bandits, and Spanish soldiers, but there ain't nothin' like a woman to put a shiver up a man's spine."

Ignoring this, Jesse continued. "He walked across the street with his girls and into Anna-Ruth's. I think they live over on Sumac."

Cherokee looked across the street. Crawford was at the shop window looking out.

"He's lookin' at ya."

Jesse looked over his shoulder at the shop. Crawford was standing at the window looking at the two of them.

"He knows you suspect he did somethin'. You boys stay away from that man."

Crawford walked out of the shop, crossed the street, and got into his car. As he walked, he kept his eye on Jesse and the old Indian fighter. When he pulled away, he drove past them, staring.

"We will, Cherokee."

#

ELZA, TEXAS POLICE STATION
Sunday November 16, 1941

Jesse was sitting on an iron cot. He was scared, but he felt somewhat reassured by some of the things Jefferson had said as they drove over. Despite Corporal McKinney's protests, Jefferson had told Jesse that he wasn't under arrest and that Jefferson knew full well that Jesse hadn't killed Cliff. Jesse's parents had made it difficult, and they needed to question him in private.

Across from Jesse sat Brewster McKinney and the Chief on a couple of chairs they had to bring up from the office. Jefferson was embarrassed that there were no chairs up there, but he had never had a need for one. He'd never questioned a prisoner before. Drunks usually slept it off and went free the next morning. Everybody else stayed the night and then got to ride down to Rusk where the judge either fined them or put them on a road gang.

In fact, first thing in the morning, Jefferson had to take a prisoner down to see the judge. When they brought Jesse up, Jefferson had suddenly realized that Irwin Stoker was still in one of the two cells. Thank goodness he had a slop bucket, or the poor man would have soiled himself. The Chief sent him to sit downstairs to wait while they talked to Jesse. Jefferson didn't worry much about Irwin leaving or running off. Stoker knew he was headed to the county farm. If he ran off, he'd just end up on the farm a lot longer.

Fortunately, Gemma had followed in her car. Jefferson asked her to run up to the diner in Jacksonville for hamburgers. He told her that she couldn't stay while they questioned Jesse, but she was welcome to stay as long as she wanted to once they were done. If she ran to Jacksonville, it would give her something to do, and it would be a big favor to him.

When she left, McKinney began to laugh. "You got some gall, Chief."

Jefferson looked at him, confused.

"You just dragged her boyfriend down to the jail in connection with a murder, and you ask her to go get you a hamburger."

Jefferson cringed. He really hadn't thought about it that way. Actually all he was thinking about was if the town council was going to pay him back for five hamburgers, fries, and shakes.

"Jesse," the Chief began, "like I said before, I know you didn't kill Cliff, but we need to know what happened last night."

"Sure, Chief," Jesse replied, still frightened.

"Why did y'all go out to the bridge?"

"Just to talk, you know. We've been going out there since we were kids."

"When was the last time you were out there?" Brewster asked.

"I don't know, a few months, maybe a year."

"Why last night?"

"Cliff wanted to talk."

"About why you attacked him?"

Jesse froze.

"Look, I just flew off the handle, that's all."

"The Chief said that it took three men to drag you off him. That doesn't sound like someone flying off the handle to me. It sounds like someone who really wanted to hurt a man."

"Why, Jesse?" The Chief piped in. "Why'd you start hittin' Cliff?"

"Look, Chief, that didn't have nothin' to do with Cliff gettin' killed."

"How do you know?" asked Brewster.

"I just know it was about some stuff that happened a long time ago."

"Something that happened the last time I was here?"

Jesse looked wide-eyed at Brewster. His heart was pounding, "No."

"You're lyin', Jesse."

Jefferson looked at Brewster as the Ranger studied the boy's face.

"That girl's his daughter, isn't she? The guy on the tracks, that girl who went for burgers is his daughter."

"Yeah, but that's got nothin' to do with Cliff."

Brewster sat back in his chair, still studying the boy's face.

"Are you in love with that other girl? The one Cliff got pregnant?"

"What? No. Jeez, no. She's just our friend, that's all."

"But Jesse, that's what you got everybody in town thinkin' after last night," Jefferson explained. "Let's face it, it makes sense that you'd attack 'im if you were in love with her."

"Jefferson, you know I'm not in love with Jewel. Hell, the whole town's bettin' on whether me and Gemma get engaged before I go to A&M."

"Then how come you got mad when you found out he got Jewel pregnant?"

"He didn't get her pregnant," Jesse said softly.

"You sure thought so last night."

Jesse looked at the door to the stairs.

"Can Mr. Stoker hear us?"

"I doubt it," Jefferson said, glancing back at the door.

"Would you mind closing that door? He doesn't need to hear this."

Jefferson looked at Brewster, who motioned with his head, and Jefferson went to the door leading to the stairway, shut it, and returned to his chair.

"The reason Cliff and I were on the bridge last night," Jesse began, "was that he wanted me to know she's been seein' some fellow up in Jacksonville. I haven't talked to her in a while on account of I've been spending so much time with Gemma. Her pa doesn't know about the fellow either. A few weeks ago she and Cliff went out to the bridge to talk. She told 'im about the guy she's been goin' with. It started to get dark, and Cliff took her home and old Irwin saw her gettin' out of Cliff's car. He ain't seen her with any other guys, so when he found out about the baby he went gunnin' for Cliff."

Brewster sighed. "That explains why you were on the bridge, but it doesn't explain why you attacked him."

Jesse sat silent with his head down. He knew that he couldn't tell them the truth, but he wasn't getting out of this without telling them something. Jesse swallowed. This was no longer about fear. This was a memory he had long tried to suppress. "Because we promised her mother."

"Her mother?" Jefferson asked with a wrinkled brow.

"Yeah."

Brewster looked at Jefferson for more information.

"The girl's ma, Mrs. Stoker, ran off with some carnival people a few years back."

"We saw her before she left. She was all upset. She said that she had to go and she knew me and Cliff ran around a lot with Jewel. You remember Chief, it was that summer you helped us steal Mr. McAlister's watermelons."

"I remember, Jesse," Jefferson said sympathetically, seeing that the kid was near tears.

"She made us promise to look after Jewel. Mr. Stoker used to hit Mrs. Stoker some. I don't know if he ever hit

Jewel, but we promised to take care of her, you know, just in case. Over the years she had become kind of like a sister. You take care of your sister. When I thought Cliff…" Jesse paused, tears swelling in his eyes, "well, I lost it."

Brewster and Jefferson looked at each other, and finally Brewster offered, "Let's take a break for a while. That girl should be back soon with the burgers."

Jefferson was relieved. He had a lot of things going on in his head, and he didn't know how to sort any of it.

The two lawmen stood. "Relax, Jesse. I'll send Gemma up with some supper in a bit."

Jefferson and Brewster came through the hall to the front of the station from the staircase in the back. Irwin Stoker was sitting at Jefferson's desk.

Jefferson had, again, forgotten all about him. "I'm sorry, Irwin. I shouldn't have left you here all this time. Why don't you go on home? I'll come get you in the morning, and we'll go to Rusk and see Judge Buckner."

"Is he gonna put me on the road crew?"

"I suspect so. Damn, Irwin, if you hadn't shot off that gun I might have got him to let you off with a few days in the county jail, but you know Nehemiah Buckner ain't gonna' let that go without at least a couple of weeks on the crew. And you're gonna have to pay Able McCormack for that chandelier you shot out."

"Now, Chief, that wasn't my fault. I wouldn't of shot that chandelier if that kid upstairs hadn't of hit my shotgun."

"Good God, Irwin. If Jesse hadn't done that you'd be headed to the chair down in Huntsville right this minute."

"Okay, tell Able I'll pay for it when I get off the road crew," the man said as he headed toward the door. "Hey, Chief, did that kid up there kill Clifford Tidwell?

"We don't know yet, Irwin."

"Well if you find out that he did, tell him thanks for me," the older man said as he walked out the door.

Jefferson just scowled as he sat down behind his desk. He wasn't used to days like this.

"What do you think, Corporal?" Jefferson asked as Brewster sat in the opposite chair.

"He's lyin'."

Jefferson's eyes opened wide, "You think he made that up about Mrs. Stoker?"

"No. They made a promise to look after that girl," Brewster answered as he processed, "but there's more to it. He didn't tell us everything. Somethin' doesn't make sense."

Brewster started thinking, "That gal ran off with a carnival, you said?"

"Yeah, we think she was runnin' around with one of those carnival workers."

"If a woman came up to you and said that she was going to run off with another man and leave her husband and daughter, would you feel a lot of sympathy and make a promise to look after her kid?"

Jefferson thought about it a moment, "Well, when you put it that way, I don't know that I would."

"I don't know how it is here, but where I came from nobody has anything nice to say about a woman who runs off on her family. Those are the women people gossip about."

"It's the same way here. She was the subject of a lot of talk at the domino hall."

"So she's leaving her husband and daughter, and just before she goes she asked these two boys to look after her daughter, and these kids, some five years later, feel obligated. There's somethin' more to this story. I could see it if she was dyin' or somethin'." Brewster paused in thought. "Did anyone ever hear from that woman again?"

"I don't think so. I think Stoker gave up lookin' for her after a week or so."

"How do you know she ran off with a carnie?"

Jefferson paused, partially in thought, but also because he realized Brewster was onto something. "Cliff Tidwell told me he saw her sneakin' off with one of the carnival boys."

The two men sat looking at each other.

"How long ago did this happen?"

"It was that summer you were here, the same summer that Peterson Crawford got hit by that train."

"That woman's dead. Those boys were with her as she died and promised to look after her daughter. When this boy found out that the other one got the girl pregnant he went off on his buddy. Chief, we have three murders, and that kid upstairs is in the middle of all of it."

"Three?"

"That woman didn't run off with a carnival, and that Crawford fellow didn't get killed by a train."

#

ELZA, TEXAS
July 1, 1936

Jesse, Cliff, and Jewel walked past the end of Main Street and turned onto Texas State Highway 84, Cliff leading.

"Now will you tell us where we're goin'?" Jewel asked with a tone of frustration.

"Boy, I suggest we take a little walk, and the two of you get all bent out of shape."

"You didn't suggest anything," Jesse told him. "You said, 'Come with me, I've got an idea,' which usually means that we're gonna end up hoeing a watermelon patch."

"You two get into a little trouble, and you'd think it was the end of the world."

"I've got blisters on top of blisters, thanks to you," Jewel argued. "Now where are we goin'?"

Cliff just smiled and remained silent as he crossed the highway and walked into the wide gravel parking area in front of Washington's Feed Store. Jesse and Jewel hesitated and looked at one another, but like always, they followed as he walked around the back of the building and stopped with his arms crossed.

The area behind the feed store, for longer than the three kids had been alive, had been a catchall for farm implements, tools, vehicles, and various junk items that had accumulated over the years. Like merchants in small towns throughout the country during the Great Depression years, Nickel Washington sold a great deal of his inventory on credit. Unfortunately, many of his customers, like thousands upon thousands around the country, were unable to pay. Most customers tried to find ways to make it right, many working out installment plans, which Nickel always accepted although he didn't particularly like it. Still, it was better to get something than nothing. A few offered something as collateral, or in many cases, as payment. Usually this meant getting a worn out tractor or a dull plow blade, or in one particularly annoying case, a mule that was so old that he died not two weeks after Nickel took ownership.

Anything that was in good enough condition to use, Nickel would sell just as soon as he could find a buyer or hold until the customer had the cash to pay off his bill. Naturally, though, much of the "collateral" was nothing more than junk that sat rusting in the weeds.

Directly in front of Cliff was a badly rusted 1919 Model-T Ford stake bed truck. The stake bed looked a lot like every other Model-T except it had a heavier, all-wooden bed. This one once had an all-wooden cab, too, but it had long-since succumbed to weather and was broken away to the point that all remaining were a bench seat with doors and a bed.

Jesse and Jewel looked at the truck that Cliff so proudly stood before and again looked at each other, somewhat baffled.

Finally Jesse asked, "I give up, what are we doing here?"

"Don't you guys get tired of walking all the time?"

"What are we gonna do, drive around in that?" Jesse asked.

"Why not?"

Jesse and Jewel began to laugh.

"I bet we can get it to run. I looked at it this mornin'. It needs a few parts, but I bet we can make it go."

"Even if we could, Mr. Washington isn't gonna give us his truck," Jesse exclaimed.

"He won't give it to us, but he said he'll let us use it to make deliveries, and he'll pay us five cents a run. And George Henry McMillan will pay two cents a run and give us all the gas and oil we need."

"Well, smart guy, that all sounds good, but where are we gonna get the parts to make it go Jewel asked.

"First of all, *we* won't. You keep forgetting that you're a girl."

"So?"

"A girl can't fix a truck. Y'all aren't smart enough, and you're not strong enough to make deliveries," Cliff answered sensibly.

Jewel angrily put her hands on her waist and glared. "I know as much about fixing a truck as you do."

Exasperated, Cliff turned to Jesse. "You tell her."

"Don't bring me into this. I'm still wondering where you're gonna find parts."

"I don't know. There's old Model-T's all over the place. We'll find somebody to give us a few parts."

Jewel smiled and started to walk away. "I've got a Model-T."

Jesse and Cliff watched as she turned.

"Where?"

"Under the shed behind our barn. The axel's broke, so it's just been sittin' there for years. I could talk my dad into lettin' us get some parts off of it. But, you know, I'm just a girl and I don't know nothin' about trucks. And I'm not smart enough to help and I'm too weak to make deliveries."

Cliff watched as she walked toward the highway, realizing that he had no option, "Okay, you're in."

Jewel turned around with a smirk on her face, "Equal partners."

"Equal?"

Without waiting for anything further Jewel turned back around and started for the highway.

"Okay," Cliff finally conceded.

"And two RCs a day."

"What?"

Jewel stopped and looked at him, "Two RCs or nothin'."

"No way. If you're getting an equal share, you buy your own RCs," Cliff protested, walking toward her.

"Okay," Jewel answered and turned and continued to walk away.

Cliff looked back at Jesse.

"You shouldn't have told her that she couldn't help."

"One RC."

Jewel stopped and thought for a moment and finally turned around.

Then Cliff added, "But you don't get to drive."

Once again Jewel began walking away.

"Okay, you can drive, but only one RC."

Jewel looked at him and smiled. "Deal."

Cliff walked to her and they shook hands. Then Jewel added, "I'm smart enough to get you to buy me a free RC every day."

Chapter 8

ELZA, TEXAS
November 17, 1941

Corporal Brewster McKinney hadn't gotten much sleep, but then neither had the poor kid upstairs. After he and Chief Hightower questioned the kid, McKinney walked across the street and took a room in the only hotel in town. The bed was old and the mattress sagged in the middle, but that wasn't what kept McKinney from getting any sleep. Cases like this one kept his mind churning. Every time he dozed off, another thought came into his head, and he'd be up for another half-hour, thinking.

The first thing he planned to do the next morning was head over to the garage to get prints off the coupe, but he had little hope. Good prints are hard to get, and finding a match could be like looking for a needle in a haystack.

The bottom line was that he had nothing. The kid in the jail almost certainly didn't do it. The only reason to keep him was to protect him from becoming a second victim. If the killer was smart, he'd be long gone by now. But killers were rarely smart.

So if the woman hadn't gone off with a carnival, and she instead had died, where was her body? And this Crawford fellow - what was his connection? And what did those two murders have to do with this one? Could it be the same killer coming back to finish the job?

Brewster rolled around in bed until five that morning when he finally got up. Downstairs, the lady who ran the hotel was already making breakfast. Her few other guests were oilfield workers who ate early, and Brewster was not unlike them in that respect. For the Ranger, a workday began at five in the morning and ended whenever it ended.

Brewster ate four pancakes, three scrambled eggs, and a half-dozen sausage patties before heading across the street to the Police Station. As he walked in the door, he could hear Chief Hightower snoring. The chief lived in a few rooms in the back. The Ranger first went to the hotplate to make a pot of coffee. He'd had two cups with breakfast, but that was just to get his blood flowing. He would drink at least six before the morning was over. After going to the bathroom, filling the pot, and setting it on the hotplate, he headed up to check on the prisoner.

At the top of the stairs he could see the boy sitting on the cot with his feet on the ground and his head in his hands. The poor boy probably hadn't slept either.

"You need anything? I'll have some coffee made in a few minutes."

"Thank you, Mr. McKinney. I'd like some."

"Sure."

As McKinney turned to head back down, Jesse asked, "Mr. McKinney, what happens to me now?"

Brewster hesitated; he knew that it was not wise to get into conversations with prisoners. He'd seen a lot of criminals make fools of jailers by cozying up to them. They didn't manage escapes like in the picture-shows, but he'd seen them really mess up a prosecution. Those, though, were real criminals - psychopaths who were always looking for an edge. This kid wasn't a psychopath.

"Your lawyer will be here in a little while, and I suspect you'll go home."

"Corporal, do you think I did it?"

"No, kid. I'm with the chief on that."

"Then why'd y'all keep me all night?"

Brewster saw his opening. "Because you lied to me last night. You didn't make a promise to a woman who ran off with a carnival. You made a promise to a woman right before she died. And you know who killed her. You also know who killed that Crawford fellow. Whoever killed them probably killed your friend and is still out there right now, and you're next on his list. We kept you here because here you're safe. But when you walk out that door, you're his. Maybe not today or tomorrow, but sooner or later you're his."

Brewster headed on downstairs. Best let the kid stew on that for a while.

A few minutes after six, just after Brewster settled behind the chief's desk, Chief Hightower came into the office. He was looking ruffled. Most likely he'd only been awake a few minutes, but he was in a freshly pressed uniform.

"Good morning, Corporal. Have you checked on Jesse?"

"Yeah, he's a little stressed."

"I don't think he slept much. Gemma left around midnight. After that I heard him pacing a lot."

"He'll be pacing a lot more now. I told him that I didn't believe him about the woman running off. I also told him that I think he knows who killed the woman and who killed Crawford."

"How'd he react?"

"He didn't say anything, but he's scared."

Jefferson poured himself a cup of coffee and settled into one of the chairs. Normally he wouldn't put up with someone walking into his office and taking over, but for Brewster McKinney he made an exception. Frankly, if not for McKinney, Jefferson wouldn't have a clue about the case.

"I would be scared too."

"Is there any connection between the woman that ran off and Crawford?"

Jefferson thought on it for a while and finally replied, "Honestly, I can't recall them ever being around each other. I'm not sure if they ever met."

"What did he do?"

"Nothin'. He always strutted around in a suit and hat like the big city people you see in the movies, but I never knew him to have a job. There were a lot of people out of work in those days. His wife owned a dress shop across the street. She still does. I suspect that was their only income."

"Was he from here?"

"As I recall, a lot of folks from Jacksonville came to his funeral. I expect that's where he came from."

"What about the woman? Where was she from?"

"Irwin's family's been here for a while. That farm belonged to his father, but I don't know much about her. She used to own a produce store across the street. That's about all I remember."

Jefferson finished his coffee and stood. "Speaking of Irwin, I need to go get him and take him over to Rusk. Do you mind keeping an eye on Jesse?

"No. Go ahead, Chief. I'm going to sit here and think on this a while."

#

RUSK, TEXAS
November 17, 1941

Nathaniel Elbridge Cockwright, County Attorney for Cherokee County Texas, was a man of stature and standing. At forty-five he aspired for much but had accomplished little. This was not, of course, for lack of persistence. Nathaniel's singular goal when he graduated from the University of

Texas School of Law, at the top of his class, was to be the youngest man ever elected Governor of the greatest state in the union. He missed that boat back in '27 when Dan Moody got elected at age thirty-three. Still, his aspirations to be governor had not subsided.

The problem Nathaniel had was that he had made a crucial mistake early in his career. He moved to Cherokee County. Not that Cherokee County was a bad place. There quite frankly are few places in Texas to have as beautiful of a view as the view from Love's Lookout just north of Jacksonville. And he couldn't ask for a better place to raise his children. The problem with Cherokee County was that the place was a political dead end. Nathaniel had moved there at the suggestion of one of his law professors who happened to know that the County Attorney would not run for re-election. Nathaniel was told that if he moved there and opened a practice he would be a shoe-in for the kind of job that most attorneys wait years for. Once in, he'd bide his time a few years while earning a reputation as a tough prosecutor and then run for the state Attorney General. The next step, of course, would be the Governor's Mansion.

The problem was that for a prosecutor to get a reputation as a tough litigator, he has to have a crime to prosecute. The thing that made Cherokee County such a good place to raise children was that there was almost no crime. The closest he came to getting any headlines in the eighteen years he'd spent as County Attorney was when a train hit some fellow down in Elza and a Texas Ranger thought he had a murder on his hands. Unfortunately none of the doctors who examined the body would testify that the guy had been murdered or if he got the dent in back of his head from bouncing around after the train hit him.

During all those years, Nate, as his wife and only his wife called him, had seen three real murders cross his desk. One was a jealous wife who confessed, so it never got to trial. The second was a fellow getting run over by a tractor plow, but that imbecilic judge, Nehemiah Buckner, tossed the case out, claiming that it was an accident, which Nathaniel considered to be a ridiculous judgment even though he had no solid evidence to suggest otherwise. The third case, and the one that had promised to be by far the best opportunity to make some headlines, was a lynching that had taken place in Jacksonville back in '36. Unfortunately the police chief stood by and watched while half of the city's council members took an active part. There was no problem finding the key players, but if Nathaniel had sought to prosecute, the chance of getting a penny of campaign money out of the county's largest city would be next to impossible.

Therefore, Nathaniel was forced to run for minor state offices in order to build a reputation as a contender in state politics. He had run for a State Senate seat, a State House seat, State Comptroller, and State Railroad Commissioner, all of which were disasters. The local seats were uphill battles from the beginning because the incumbents in both the State Senate and State House had been sitting in those seats since the '20s and were so well known and liked in their districts that campaign donations were almost impossible to find. Worse still, every time Nathaniel put up a campaign sign, some good old boy would shoot holes in it.

Those failures paled in comparison to the humiliation of his live radio debate with his opponent for Texas Railroad Commissioner. That attempt went badly even before the radio debate when Nathaniel lost the primary election and made the degrading decision to switch parties and run for the office as a Republican, which immediately alienated just about everybody in his home county, the one county where voters knew his name.

So on the day of the big debate, Nathaniel and his wife packed up the kids and drove all the way to the Will Rogers Coliseum in Fort Worth where radio station WBAP was to broadcast the event live to every major city in the state. Nathaniel's opponent, a former judge and oil company lawyer, the Honorable Aaron Daniel Haymans, a resident of Fort Worth, had at least two hundred supporters in the audience. Nathaniel had only his wife Rebecca and three daughters, Hannah Denise, Melissa Mae, and Georgia Carolyne. Naturally, when Haymans got up to speak, he was welcomed with cheers and resounding applause. When Nathaniel was introduced he was welcomed by, on state-wide radio mind you, his wife clapping and the faint echo of his oldest daughter yelling, "Daddy."

That alone was humiliation enough, but then the moderator, a newspaper political reporter from Dallas named Matthew Hendley, kept mispronouncing Cockwright's last name. Instead of calling the East Texas litigator by his proper name, Nathaniel Cockwright, that incompetent journalist kept calling him Nathaniel Cockfight, which naturally garnered near-endless laughter and even some applause from the coliseum full of Haymans' followers. Nathaniel should have expected it when he saw that the moderator was wearing a Texas A&M class ring. You can't trust an Aggie to do anything right.

The fact of the matter was that Cockwright's political career had almost no chance of succeeding so long as he remained in Cherokee County. He had come to East Texas to make a reputation as a tough criminal prosecutor, but he lived in a county with absolutely no notable crime. Oh, there was the occasional break-in, and a few times a year he'd handle an armed robbery case, but most of the crime in the county consisted of drunk and disorderly charges or some sort of traffic violation or an occasional domestic case.

All of those cases were well beneath the dignity of the office of County County Attorney, and thus Nathaniel passed them on to one of his two deputies. The truth of the matter was that it had been a good six months since he had so much as walked into Judge Buckner's courtroom.

So naturally, when he sat down at his desk at exactly 7:59 a.m. on Monday morning with his cup of piping hot coffee and fresh-off-the-press copy of *The Jacksonville Statesman*, Nathaniel almost spilled an entire cup of coffee on his lap when he read the headline: BRUTAL MURDER IN ELZA.

Nathaniel quickly read over the article and then pressed the mechanical lever on his newly installed office intercom. He had wanted an office intercom from the moment he was sworn-in as County Attorney, but the budget simply hadn't had any room for the device. It was 1941, and the twentieth century was just getting to Rusk, Texas.

"Anita," he ordered to the speaker on his desk.

"Yes, Mr. Cockwright?" His secretary answered after far longer than Nathaniel preferred.

Across the hall gossiping with the County Clerk's secretary again, no doubt.

"Assemble the staff in my office immediately."

"Roosevelt isn't in yet, Mr. Cockwright."

Roosevelt was Roosevelt Primrose, the youngest of Nathaniel's two deputy D.A.'s. Primrose was a decent young lawyer with a lot of promise despite having the handicap of acquiring his law degree from Southern Methodist University. What the young man lacked in legal knowledge he made up for in appearance and attitude. Although short, he wore impeccable-looking suits despite their being off-the-rack from such places as Sears and Roebuck's or Montgomery Ward's. How in the world the kid managed to look that dapper in a mail-order suit was beyond Nathaniel's understanding, but when the boy walked into a courtroom, he looked like a lawyer who knew he was going to win his case. Unfortunately it didn't seem to bother him in the least that his secretary regularly called him by his given name in spite of the fact that he was a board certified, licensed attorney in the state of Texas.

"Has Mr. Primrose called in?"

"No, sir. I suspect that he just overslept."

"Well, assemble the staff as soon as he gets here. Oh, and get David Roberson at *The Jacksonville Statesman* on the phone."

"Yes, sir."

Cockwright picked up the paper again, angry at the fact that his junior assistant C.A. was already nearly five minutes late for work. Nathaniel was not at all happy with his two deputies. One was young, inexperienced but so organized and well prepared that he sometimes won his cases because he wrote such a good brief. The other was old, grouchy, and often looked like he had slept in his suits. The only good thing about Deputy C.A. Mason Coleman was that he was a walking encyclopedia of legal knowledge without which Cockwright would sometimes be completely lost. But that's the reason to have a staff. A single person can't be expected to know how to do everything. Together, as annoying as his staff might be at times, they made a decent team. Coleman handled the legalities, Primrose wrote up the briefs, and Nathaniel managed.

Nathaniel's intercom buzzed, and the attorney pressed the lever.

"I have Mr. Roberson on the line, sir."

She calls the reporter "Mr."

He pressed the lever on his new speakerphone, not bothering with the handset.

"Mr. Roberson. This is County Attorney Nathaniel Cockwright."

"Yes. Hello, sir."

"I was just looking at your article on the killing of this young high school student down in Elza. Your headline says that it was a "brutal" murder. Exactly what was so brutal about it?"

"I take it you haven't spoken to anyone down there yet?"

Nathaniel clenched his teeth. Of course he hadn't talked to anyone. No one there had bothered to call him.

"No, your article is the first I've heard about it."

"Well, I have to tell you, it was the saddest thing I've ever seen. From all accounts this was a nice kid that everybody in town liked. Someone bashed his head in with a tire iron, or at least they think it was a tire iron. They hit him so hard that a big section of his skull was caved in. Then they dumped him off the side of a bridge, still alive, I think. and an alligator chewed on him a few. The Ranger told me that he died before he was tossed off the bridge but one of the deputies claimed that the kid fought off the gater for several hours before he died. Just an awful scene all the way around. "

Nathaniel cringed at the thought of how painful that must have been but then realized this was the case he'd been waiting for his entire career.

"Why wasn't any of this in your article?"

"You mean the gator?"

"Well, that and the head bashing."

"I talked it over with my editor, and we decided that the bloody stuff wasn't necessary. I mean, his family is going to read that article. Their kid was murdered; they don't need to know that he died quite so horribly, do they? Besides, Ranger McKinney was there, and he made it real clear that the kid died from the head wound and didn't want anything about the gator getting out."

Nathaniel's rage was building.

"This is an important story," Nathan began angrily. "We have a vicious killer on the streets, and the people of Cherokee County need to know about it. I don't care what some damn Ranger says. It's your job to report that story."

"I'm pretty sure they arrested the guy after I went to press. He apparently had threatened to kill the kid a few hours earlier. I'm about to go down there for a follow-up story."

Nathaniel looked at his watch.

"I'll be there at about ten with sheriff's deputies to take that murderer back here to Rusk. You be there and get the story. Also, it wouldn't hurt to have a photographer along. And tomorrow morning I want you to print the whole story about how that kid died. In fact, you should do a side story all about this kid. You said yourself he was well-liked. Son, this is the biggest story of your life. It's certainly the biggest story that ever happened in this county, and you're sittin' on it."

"First of all, Nate,"

"The name is Mr. Cockwright."

"Mr. Cockwright, I'm not sure if my editor will want me to run that, and we don't even have a photographer, and, quite frankly, I don't want to lock horns with Brewster McKinney."

Nathaniel closed his eyes. This idiot, back-woods journalist was beginning to give him a headache.

"What is the big deal about this McKinney? A Ranger is nothin' more than a glorified street cop."

Nathanial heard laughing over the phone.

"Mr. Cockwright, Brewster McKinney is not a street cop. He's just about the last of the old-school shoot-first-and-ask-questions-later Rangers. He's worked a million cases and has been in more shootouts than Wyatt Earp. He learned under the likes of Frank Hamer and Eli Bradford.

He practically threatened to feed me to a gator if I ran that story, and I'm pretty sure he meant it."

The C.A.'s blood was boiling.

Nathaniel looked at his watch. "Listen, I'll be in Elza at ten o'clock. You be there and have a camera. And tomorrow I want to read the full story - every gruesome detail. I want the people in this county to know what kind of bloody killer we captured. You let me worry about this cowboy. If your editor objects, you tell him to call me. One other thing - if I don't see that full story along with a background story on what a good kid this was, you had better hightail it out of this county because if you get so much as a speeding ticket, I'll see to it that you do two months on the road crew."

Nathaniel clicked off the phone and grinned.

That fool's probably wetting his pants.

A moment later Anita knocked at his door and opened it without waiting to be invited.

"The staff is ready, sir."

He simply shook his head at the incompetent disrespect.

"Bring them in."

Within minutes, seated in a semicircle around his desk, were his two deputies Primrose and Coleman and his legal assistant Vivian Yates. Vivian was the one bright spot on his staff. She was trained at Gaston Avenue School of Business in Dallas and as a result was one excellent researcher. Her only professional flaw was that she had the tendency to call everyone "hun," and that included her boss and on at least one occasion, Judge Buckner. Cockwright had been trying to break her of the habit for at least five years with no luck what so ever.

"Now that we're all here," Nathaniel began, with a glare at Primrose, who completely missed the insinuation, "I'm sure all of you have heard about the murder."

Primrose and Coleman glanced at each other and then looked back at Nathaniel. Vivian sat staring at the C.A. with her notepad and pencil in hand; she clearly had no more knowledge about any murder than the two deputies, but the facts of the case were of no interest to her. Her only purpose was research. The attorneys did the rest.

"Clearly, I'm the only person around here that reads the newspapers. There was a young man murdered down in Elza Saturday night. I haven't spoken to the police chief yet, but I intend to go down there later."

"Elza?" Primrose interrupted.

"Yes, Elza," Nathaniel, replied with another glare at his junior deputy. "As I was saying, I don't know much about the case just yet, but I believe..."

"Nathaniel, I-," Primrose interrupted again but was immediately cut off.

"I'll take questions, in a few minutes, Primrose. I'm going down there to talk to the chief. I understand that he's made an arrest."

"Nathaniel, the Elza chief is here. I just saw his new prowler out front."

"What?"

"I just saw the new prowler with "Elza Police" printed on the side door. It has to be him. I'm pretty sure that's still a one-man department down there. He's probably dropping off his murderer with the sheriff. If we hurry we can probably catch 'im before he leaves."

Nathaniel leapt to his feet and rushed out the door. As he passed through the outer office he ordered Anita, "Call downstairs to the Sheriff's office. Tell him that I'm coming down. If the Elza Chief is there, tell them not to let him leave."

Vivian just sat there while Primrose and Coleman looked at each other, "Should we go?" Primrose finally asked.

"I'm not runnin' down those stairs after some cop. You can if you want."

Primrose thought for a moment and then got up and trotted after the C.A.

The sheriff's office was in the basement of the large Cherokee County Courthouse building, and Cockwright's office was on the third floor. This meant the C.A. had to run down three flights of stairs, across the atrium and down one more flight of stairs before reaching the sheriff. Cockwright prided himself on his appearance. A man of his position absolutely had to look as professional as possible, so his suits came straight from Neiman Marcus in Dallas and his spit-polished shoes came from Milton S. Florsheim in Chicago. Granted, the suits and shoes were expensive, but being the C.A. required a professional demeanor, especially a C.A. who would soon be governor.

Sheriff Jonas Cadwalder had been a large man when he played football for the Sam Houston State University Bearkats, but in the thirty years since his playing days Jonas Cadwalder had gained weight significantly, to the tune of two hundred plus pounds. With a six-foot five-inch frame that tipped the scales at well over four hundred pounds, the sheriff was a very large and intimidating gentleman. At the farm where at any given moment a half-dozen or so prisoners were doing as much as a year or two on the county road work detail, Cadwalder was more often than not referred to as Sheriff Fat-walder, though understandably not in his presence or in earshot of one of the bulls.

Cadwalder was sloppy on his best day and the complete opposite of Nathaniel Cockwright. For starters, to Nathaniel's disdain, the Sheriff of Cherokee County Texas had never, on any occasion that the C.A. could recall, worn a tie. Secondly, as far back as Nathaniel could remember, he couldn't think of a single time he'd seen the man without a food stain of some sort on his shirt. But then what could one expect from a hillbilly version of Sidney Greenstreet?

It was bad enough that the county Sheriff had a less-than-professional personal appearance, but more annoying was the fact that the man showed absolutely no respect to the office of County Attorney.

Cadwalder didn't see his appearance as a problem. The fact was, he dealt with the vermin of Cherokee county on a daily basis and saw no reason to put on a clean shirt every morning only to spill coffee on it right before he drove a hot, sweaty squad car out to the farm to check on the inmates. If it displeased that "thinks he's too good for Cherokee County" County Attorney, then all the better.

So a few minutes earlier when his girl, Beverly,took a call from that clown of a C.A.'s girl ordering him to keep the Elza police chief in his office, Cadwalder didn't budge. Sheriff Cadwalder didn't take orders from anyone save Judge Buckner, and he had a tendency to ignore those, too. More importantly, Cadwalder didn't like that prissy little C.A., and he liked the C.A.'s two prissier little assistants even less. So since the Elza police chief had already walked out of his office not ten seconds prior to his receiving the call from that pinstriped circus clown upstairs, Cadwalder wasn't about to get himself out of his chair and go running after the man. If the C.A. wanted to talk to Jefferson Hightower, he could go running after the Chief himself.

Two minutes later when Cherokee County County Attorney Nathaniel Elbridge Cockwrght barged into his office demanding to see Chief Hightower, Cadwalder showed no interest in getting out of his chair except to refill his coffee cup. C.A. Cockwright, naturally, was not particularly impressed with the sheriff's department's nonchalant attitude toward obeying orders from the County Attorney's office. That dissatisfaction would have probably escalated into a world class shouting match had it not been for Cockwright's urgent desire to speak to Chief Hightower, and thus the C.A. rushed out the door as soon as he learned that the Chief was at that moment up on the second floor in Judge Buckner's courtroom with a prisoner who, according the C.A., should have been handed over to his office and then the sheriff's office.

It was a shame that Sheriff Cadwalder didn't know exactly why Cockwright, whom he couldn't help but think of as Cockfight, needed to see the Chief until it was too late. Irritating that prissy little C.A. was one of the few pleasures of his job, and he had missed a golden opportunity.

County Attorney Cockwright was furious and out of breath when he, followed by Primrose, burst into Judge Buckner's courtroom after climbing back up two flights of stairs. He knew that it was ill mannered and unprofessional of him to do so, but it couldn't be helped. He'd wasted enough time already. Had that fat slug of a sheriff told him that Chief Hightower was up there instead of stammering around arguing with him, he might not have had to barge in while the Judge was arraigning the prisoner. There were times, Cockwright suspected, that the grossly obese sheriff did these things on purpose just to irritate him.

Of course, had the dumb bumpkin of a police chief done his job right in the first place, Cockwright would not have to barge into the judge's court. Minor cases that were uncontested naturally didn't require the C.A. office's involvement. These cases, usually traffic violations or drunken and disorderly behavior, were presented before the judge. Judge Buckner would then issue some punishment and they would be handed over to the Sheriff to either pay a fine or go to the county farm. But this idiot Police Chief from Elza had a major murder on his hands. Even if this murderer made a complete confession, it was still the C.A.'s job to handle the arraignment. This melon-headed cop was treating a murderer as if he was dealing with another drunken hobo.

A case like this had enormous implications to public safety and had to be handled with the public in mind. Frankly, the press should be there so that the public could rest assured that this killer was off the streets. Furthermore, the citizens needed to see their duly elected officials performing their jobs.

The problem with being a C.A. in a place like Cherokee County was dealing with these small town police departments. People like this chief had no legal education and therefore had no understanding of proper jurisprudence. A few of these hillbillies had little more than a grade school education and were hired simply because their brother-in-law happened to get elected mayor.

Proper or not, Nathaniel made a grand show of marching into the courtroom even though, besides the judge and the chief, the only people in the court were the bailiff, the clerk, and the murderer. The chief, fool that he was, was standing in front of Judge Buckner's desk with his hand on the murderer's arm. He didn't even have handcuffs on the man.

"Your Honor," Nathaniel began, "I must interrupt this proceeding. I insist that my department take over the processing of this case immediately."

Jefferson looked over his shoulder in dismay at the County Attorney as he was rapidly approaching the bench.

"And why would that be?" Judge Buckner asked nonchalantly.

"Your Honor, surely you will agree that a case like this one cannot be handled the same way you would some drunken brawler."

Judge Buckner looked down at the notes handed to him by the clerk moments before and then, with a smirk, asked Nathaniel, "And why not?"

"This man, allegedly, committed a major crime, your Honor. We owe it to the public to handle this case with the utmost care. I'm sure that the last thing we want is for a case of this magnitude to get overruled on some technicality."

"Well we certainly don't want that," the Judge retorted. Judge Bucker had been on the bench in Cherokee County for almost fifty years. In those years he'd seen a lot of C.A.'s come and go but none as irritating as Nathaniel Cockwright. Cockwright treated the office of County Attorney as an inconvenience he was forced to endure until he got elected to the job that he seemed to think he deserved. This performance was a perfect example of what Buckner thought of as Cockwright's incompetence. Had he bothered to step into the clerk's office before storming into the courtroom, he would know that this was a drunk and disorderly case and not a murder. Buckner had read the same article in *The Jacksonville Statesman* as Cockwright, but unlike Cockwright, the judge finished the article. Had Cockwright done so he would know that the Texas Rangers had sent one of their best men down to investigate the murder in Elza. And if Cockwright was half the County Attorney that he thought he was, he would know that the Rangers never march into court without consulting the C.A.'s office. The reason the Rangers were so well respected was that they only presented cases that were sure to get a conviction.

"So you will agree that I need to take over this arraignment immediately."

"This is not an arraignment, Mr. Cockwright. Mr. Stoker here has foregone his right to a jury trial, and I am about to present his sentence."

Nathaniel's jaw dropped. He had never imagined such a thing. Buckner was an old crotchety judge, but the C.A. never thought the man incompetent. A first year law student could get this sentence overthrown on appeal.

"Judge, you can't tell me that you're seriously going to handle a murder case this haphazardly."

Judge Buckner looked up at Cockwright, fighting the temptation to laugh, and then looked at Chief Hightower. "This is a murder case, Chief? I don't see anything about a murder in my case notes."

Jefferson's eyes widened. Up to that moment he was just wondering why the County Attorney was interested in Irwin Stoker getting drunk and firing a shotgun off in the Palace, but suddenly he didn't know what to think.

"No, sir. He threatened a kid, but he was stopped before anyone was shot."

Nathaniel had a sick feeling in the pit of his stomach. "This isn't the man who murdered that boy in Elza Saturday night?" He asked the chief.

"No."

The judge held his notes up, pretending to be looking at them as he fought the urge to smile.

"You said he threatened someone. How do you know he didn't commit that murder down there?"

"Because he was sitting in my jail sleeping off a drunk, sir," the chief answered, still not realizing that the judge was playing with the C.A.

Nathan suddenly realized that the judge had let him make an ass of himself. He glanced at Primrose, wishing there was a way he could blame this mess on him, but there was just no escaping it.

"Your, Honor, I seem to have made a mistake. Please continue."

The judge, feeling like he deserved an award for his acting performance looked at Stoker. "Mr. Stoker, I sentence you to six weeks on the farm. If you're back in my court again because you fired a gun while drunk, you'll be there for a year. Is that understood?"

Jefferson nudged Stoker to answer.

"Ah, yes, sir."

"Bailiff."

The bailiff put handcuffs on Stoker and led him away.

The judge slammed his gavel. "Court adjourned."

Cockwright stood there humiliated as Judge Buckner rose, glared at him, and walked out of the room.

County Attorney Nathaniel Cockwright was fuming when the judge left, but he still had business to do. His office had a career-changing murder to prosecute, and this dimwitted police chief had his ticket to the Governor's mansion sitting in his jail.

"Chief," he said while trying to control the anger that he now was directing at Jefferson, "tell me about this murder investigation. I understand you've made an arrest. Why haven't you contacted my office?"

Jefferson was dumbfounded, wondering just how the C.A. knew that they had picked up Jesse and asked, "How do you know we made an arrest?"

"That's not the point! Why haven't you contacted my office?"

Primrose stepped back. He felt for the police chief. He'd been on the receiving end of more than one of Nathaniel Cockwright's tirades and could see a world-class example on the way. Primrose was less than two years out of law school and knew almost nothing about being a C.A., but he felt sure that he knew more than Cockwright. This was no way to talk to a police chief, especially one with a major crime on his hands. If justice was the sole objective then the two departments should be working together to make sure that they presented a case that put the culprit behind bars.

"Look, Mr. Cockwright..."

"County Attorney Cockwright."

Jefferson rolled his eyes. He'd never had any encounters with Cockwright, but he'd heard a few stories from the sheriff and other police chiefs. "We picked up someone, but we're not finished with the investigation."

"I'm the one who will decide when you've finished your investigation. As I understand it, you're holding a young man who threatened the victim in front of witnesses only hours before the murder?"

"Well, yeah, but there's more to it."

"Like what?"

"Well, these kids were friends, and I've known them all their lives, and I don't think this kid did it."

"You don't think he did it?" Cockwright began sarcastically. "Well, then, let's go find someone you haven't known, Chief. Why did he threaten the victim?"

"It was about a girl, but I don't think it was a serious threat."

"Okay, you have motive. Where was this kid when the murder took place?"

"Well, we think he was home asleep, but he'd been with Cliff, the victim, a little before the murder."

"Good god, Chief. What are you waiting for? You have your man."

"I brought in a Texas Ranger to help with the investigation, and we think that there's more to this."

"Why is everyone impressed with the damn Texas Rangers? You two are making this case harder than it needs to be. You have your man. Clearly, you and this Ranger can't handle this, so my office is taking over."

"Primrose," Cockwright ordered.

Primrose rolled his eyes behind Cockwright's back, a move not missed by Jefferson.

"Yes, sir."

"Go tell the Sheriff that we require two of his deputies immediately to go to Elza and pick up this prisoner."

Primrose froze; the last thing he wanted to do was speak to the sheriff. "Me, sir?"

"Yes, you. Is there anyone else named Primrose around here?"

Primrose debated with himself for a moment. Did he want to take a lashing from Cockwright or one from the sheriff? Finally he decided on the sheriff. He didn't have to work for him every day. "Yes, sir," he said and headed off to the sheriff's office.

"We'll be leaving within the hour. I want you with us." Cockwright ordered the chief.

#

ELZA, TEXAS
November 17, 1941

Reporter David Roberson had been taking calls all morning from other papers about the murder. He'd done the same thing a dozen times over the years. In the big cities, helping a competitor is unheard of, but these papers weren't really competitors. Some of these cities were forty to sixty miles away. This murder in Elza was front-page news on his paper because Elza was just a few miles down the road, but over in Nacogdoches or Palestine or Henderson, this was page-three stuff. The same was true when something of interest happened over in their cities. He could make a few phone calls and basically repeat the other guy's story, giving him a contributor credit.

After his little conversation with the County Attorney, Roberson found himself in a bit of a pickle. On one side, he had a Texas Ranger who threatened him. On the other he had a C.A. who did exactly the same thing.

Then, while talking to a reporter from down in Crockett, a thought came to Roberson's head.

There's safety in numbers.

So, Roberson happened to casually mention that the murder was considerably more vicious than he'd previously thought. Apparently, Roberson explained, the killer had fed the poor kid alive to an alligator. Also, there had been an arrest, and the C.A. himself was headed down to Elza to pick up this brutal killer. It was probably the part about the alligator that had gotten the ball rolling.

He made six calls in fifteen minutes. Anyone who could be in Elza by ten got the word.

Sure enough, Roberson wasn't able to park anywhere near the Elza Police station. There were reporters around that he hadn't even called. There was even a guy from Natchitoches, Louisiana. He must have broken a land speed record getting to Elza. Roberson arrived as late as he possibly could. The last thing he wanted to do was run into Brewster McKinney. The way he saw it, he could just stay in the background and let the other reporters do the work.

The little town was alive. All the good old boys were out to see what was going on. They weren't used to so many strangers all at once. Roberson could see many of his various competitors interviewing the locals. Everyone wanted to get the facts on this killing. What kind of person would feed a dying man to animals?

Roberson suddenly had a sinking feeling. That would be the headline on some of these papers tomorrow. From what he could tell, the kid in jail was not a bad kid and may not have done it, but when the evening papers came out, thanks partly to Roberson, this young man's picture would be on every front page as the monster who fed his friend to an alligator. Roberson knew that he was partly to blame. But, it was this C.A. who pushed him into it. The fact was that the C.A. would hang this kid regardless. It didn't matter if there was a real killer out there walking free. This story was big enough to hit wires and would probably be all over the state by the evening editions, which, of course was exactly what Cockwright wanted.

The reporter had grown to hate politicians like Cockwright. Those types insisted on nothing short of total integrity from the press but would lie right to your face and demand that it be printed without challenge. It was an end-justifies-the-means world to those people. Politicians like Cockwright seemed to think that their personal agenda was all that mattered. Cockwright probably hadn't even given a thought to guilt or innocence.

Roberson was stewing on that thought as a small caravan of cars turned off the highway onto Main Street. The lead car was a county sheriff's Ford, followed by two other county Fords, with the Elza Police prowler in the rear. The three county cars all stopped in a line stretching from the Police Station to midway past the movie theater. All the reporters suddenly came running. Roberson saw that a few of his fellow journalists had photographers with them, a luxury the *Statesman* couldn't afford. Roberson was shocked to see just how many reporters had made the trip to Elza. It occurred to him that he wasn't the only one who had made phone calls.

That arrogant priss had his staff working the phones making sure their boss got his headlines.

Then the back door of the second car opened and out stepped, smiling for the cameras, Nathaniel Cockwright.

Roberson watched with disdain as Cockwright made his grandiose performance for his colleagues and then walked to the front door of the Police Station. This was all backwards. These journalists, himself specifically, were doing the bidding of an ambitious, incompetent, and borderline corrupt politician for the sheer purpose of helping him further his political aspirations. A journalist's job was to be the voice of the oppressed, the vanguard of the people. They should be holding politician's feet to the fire, exposing corruption, and demanding justice for the masses. Cockwright may have won this round, but he wouldn't win the match. This journalist would not be used, at least not by the likes of Nathaniel Cockwright. McKinney was right. That kid's family needn't read the details in the papers. The kid in jail may yet be innocent, but Cockwright was perfectly willing to send him to the chair to springboard himself into the Governor's mansion.

#

Brewster McKinney was on his sixth cup of coffee. After Chief Hightower had left Brewster went upstairs two more times to question the boy. Obviously he had struck a nerve. The kid, who had shown a few signs of fear the night before, was now seriously frightened. He tried to conceal his feelings, but he showed the signs - avoiding eye contact, fidgeting, sweating. It was only a matter of time before he broke, if Brewster had a couple of days to wear him down. But he didn't have a couple of days. The kid's daddy would be in with some big-city lawyer, and Brewster wouldn't have another minute with the boy.

It was around nine-thirty when the first reporter showed. Brewster"s been dealing with reporters his entire career. Many of his fellow Rangers hated journalists. Conversely, a few loved the limelight. Brewster neither liked nor hated them. He simply saw them as a necessary evil. They had a job to do just like he did. The only problem as far as he was concerned was that they tended to be annoying, and they often wanted to over-play his personal role in the investigation. The simple way to deal with journalists, he had long since learned, was to give them a story. The trick was keeping from becoming part of the story. By nature of being a Texas Ranger, he tended to get mentioned in the papers. Reporters loved to get quotes from Rangers, especially when it was a small town case like this. So, Brewster had a simple method of dealing with newspaper mosquitoes. He'd give them a story - the story he wanted them to print. The story would be true, and they would get a quote from a Texas Ranger, but they wouldn't get the whole story. Brewster always kept a few cards in his hand.

So when the reporter burst into the Elza Police Headquarters, Corporal Brewster McKinney of the Texas Rangers was prepared to hand out the same basic facts he had given the reporter who showed up at the bridge the night before.

Then the reporter told him, "I understand you have the murderer in custody."

Brewster was explaining that the investigation was still in progress when another reporter came into the office and asked, "Is this where the press conference is being held?"

Before the second reporter got his question out, another reporter, followed by his photographer, entered the little office. They were all tossing out questions, but from the clatter Brewster managed to get that the county C.A. was on his way and was going to hold a press conference to announce that the "Alligator Killer" had been apprehended.

Brewster told the reporters that he didn't know anything about any press conference and that they should leave. Getting them to go was easy. He stood and casually revealed the Colt Commander concealed in a shoulder holster under his jacket and told the reporters that they needed to go. It didn't hurt that he was larger than all of the journalists, and showing the Colt certainly helped, but he knew that it was the Ranger's badge on his belt that sent the mosquitoes scurrying. There was an intimidation factor with being a Texas Ranger. He was a member of a no-nonsense fraternity. The very last thing Brewster McKinney would ever do is draw his weapon on a journalist, but those fellows didn't know that.

They weren't out the door thirty seconds when the telephone rang. Brewster took the call thinking he was helping out the chief, but to his surprise the caller was his immediate superior, Company B Commander, Captain "Little Bigfoot" McCullough. Contrary to what one would expect, Captain McCullough didn't have large feet. As a young ranger the Captain was partnered with a much older Corporal who took to calling him "Little Bigfoot" because he claimed that McCullough reminded him of legendary Texas Ranger, William "Bigfoot" Wallace. Captain McCullough hated being called "Little Bigfoot" but the nickname stuck, as these things tend to do and, as he once said, "There's worse things in life than being named after a Texas legend."

Initially Captain McCullough wanted to know how the case was going, to which McKinney answered, "A dead end, for now."

Captain McCullough then informed McKinney that he was being temporarily pulled off the case. Apparently the local County Attorney had called the Ranger headquarters in Austin complaining that McKinney was interfering with the prosecution in a major murder case and demanded the Ranger be immediately removed. Texas Rangers Director Calvin Anthony then called Company B Commander McCullough and "suggested" that Corporal McKinney take a few days off but, and this part was an order, "Keep an eye on the case."

McKinney took that to mean that both Captain McCullough and Director Anthony felt that the reputation of the Rangers for getting their man was much more important than soothing the ego of an overly zealous County Attorney.

Brewster McKinney had long since come to the conclusion that if the only battles a law enforcement officer had to fight were with criminals, then the job would be a piece of cake. Unfortunately, politicians were the biggest enemy of the crime fighter. A perfect example was back in '33 when Governor "Ma" Ferguson shut down the entire Ranger organization. Almost immediately afterward Bonnie Parker and Clyde Barrow went on their shooting spree all over the state, and there was nobody the Governor could send to chase them down. Eventually a laid-off Ranger, Frank Hamer, had to put a stop to it.

This time the problem was a small town C.A. trying to make a name for himself. Brewster had run across such before, but they tended to let him do his job. They just wanted the glory. Brewster cared nothing about the glory, but he did want to make sure that he put the right man behind bars. The only thing he knew for sure about this case was that the kid upstairs wasn't the killer.

When he had finished talking to Captain McCullough, he walked to the front door of the Police Station and locked it. He looked out the front window and saw that there were several men standing around. None of them looked like they were locals. Among them, just getting out of his car, was the reporter from the bridge the night before.

This C.A. called more people than just Director Anthony.

Brewster then walked down the hall to the back of the station and up the stairs to Jesse's cell.

Jesse was sitting on his cot with his shoes off.

"Come on kid, get your shoes on," McKinney said.

"I'm going?"

"Yeah, but hurry."

Jesse put on his shoes and followed Brewster down the stairs to the back door.

"What's going on, Corporal?"

"I'm not sure but we need to get you out of here. Don't go home. Go to that girl's house. No, wait. Last night the chief told me that you and that other boy once got in some trouble for climbing up on the roof."

Jesse nodded.

"Do you think you can do it again?"

"I suppose."

"Climb up there and wait until me or the chief come for you."

"What's this about?"

"Your lawyer's not here yet and some idiot C.A. wants to make a big show of arresting you. We're not gonna let that happen."

Jesse hesitated, not knowing what to do. Then they heard the front door rattling. Someone was trying to get in.

"Go," Brewster ordered.

Jesse went out the back door and over to the rain gutter he had climbed some five years before. McKinney watched to make sure that the kid made it and then closed the back door and headed to the front of the Police Station.

#

As the caravan pulled into Elza, Nathaniel Cockwright watched with a smile on his face while a group of a dozen or more journalists gathered in front of the Police Station. The C.A. was on his way to having the biggest day of his career. Granted, that little incident in the courtroom was a bit embarrassing, but the only ones who witnessed it were Judge Buckner, Primrose, and that dimwitted police chief - and really it was the chief's fault. That fool should have come to his office the moment he arrived at the courthouse. The County Attorney should not be left in the dark when there was a crime of this magnitude in his county. The number one item on that fool's agenda should have been to meet with the C.A. about what to do with "The Alligator Killer."

But even this clown of a police chief couldn't stop what was coming. Neither would that Texas Ranger, Nathaniel thought with a smile. That was a stroke of genius. Coleman out-did himself with that one. Nathaniel would like to take the credit for it, but it was all Coleman. As the deputy C.A. pointed out, the Rangers were only there at the request of a police department. When the C.A.'s office took the case, the sheriff's department could take over the investigation.

"Let's face it," Coleman explained, "the Sheriff is too lazy and too close to retirement to buck us on this. We'll build the case any way we want."

"More importantly," he continued, "a simple call to the Ranger's headquarters in Austin, complaining that the Ranger is interfering with the C.A.'s case, will result in the Ranger being sent back to where ever he came from with his tail tucked between his legs."

The boys had done their job. By the look of things, every paper in East Texas was represented. Thanks to that alligator, this story might just get picked up by the wire services, and if Nathaniel played it right it would make the headlines again on the day of the arraignment. If all went well, he could probably get headlines again when he met with the deceased family to promise a quick end to this painful ordeal. He'd be out front again, of course, throughout the trial, and he'd surely get to make a speech or two after the conviction and again after the sentencing. Finally, and this part would take some string pulling, but with some luck, he could get a picture of himself holding hands with the victim's mother right before they threw the switch on the "Alligator Killer."

The nickname had been his own idea. Thank God for that alligator. Hitting the boy and leaving him to die would be little more than a run-of-the-mill murder case. But to leave the helpless dying kid to get eaten alive by a vicious reptile was reprehensible. That was the sort of thing that could get picked up in papers all over the country. And that was just the start. The jury would eat this up. Nathaniel had half his opening remarks already written in his head. There was absolutely no possible way they'd give this kid anything short of the chair.

Nathaniel was all smiles as he stepped out of the car to be greeted by a throng of reporters.

"Gentlemen, let's go inside and I'll answer all of your questions," the C.A. said as he led what amounted to a small parade to the front door of the Police Station.

Reaching down, he grabbed the doorknob and simultaneously turned and pushed. Unfortunately for Nathaniel Cockwright, the knob didn't turn and the door didn't open and he slammed his face into the glass.

There was a round of smiles and muffled laughter from the reporters as Nathaniel jiggled the doorknob in a futile attempt to open the locked door.

Smiling back at the reporters Nathaniel said, "Just a minute, gentlemen. The office seems to be locked."

Primrose, a few steps behind him among the reporters, pushed his way through the crowd to the door. "Let me try, sir."

He took hold of it and, like Cockwright, tried with no success to open the locked door.

"Where's the Police Chief?" Cockwright asked with an obviously counterfeited smile.

Jefferson, unlike the rest of the caravan, had chosen to park the prowler in a parking spot rather than leave it in the middle of Main Street. Of course, with all of the reporters in town, along with the normal Monday morning business, there were no spots, and he had ended up parking almost all the way down by the domino hall. When he got to the Police Station, Cockwright had been standing there several minutes, fuming but smiling for the reporters.

"There's our good Police Chief. Chief, the door to your office seems to be locked," Cockwright said, still smiling broadly.

Jefferson had had about all he could take from the C.A. He wished that he could have talked with Corporal McKinney before turning Jesse over. Jefferson had no experience with this sort of thing and, frankly, had no idea if any of this was legal. Normally when he had an arrest, he took it before Judge Buckner and the judge took it from there. This was the first time he had ever even spoken to the County Attorney. He'd come across Primrose and Coleman a few times, but only because they happened to be in the courtroom, not because he had any business with them.

"I lock it when I'm out of the office," Jefferson commented as he worked his way through the crowd of reporters to the door.

Cockwright continued his simulated smile but managed to give an aggravated glare at the chief.

"Well, it wouldn't do to have the police station robbed, now would it?" Cockwright said with a broad smile.

There was again a little laughter, but much less than when the County Attorney slammed his head into the door.

Jefferson unlocked the door and let the C.A., his two deputies, and a mob of reporters into the office. Just as they came in, Brewster McKinney came down the hall.

"I thought I heard someone at the door," McKinney said as the approached the chief.

"Corporal," Jefferson began, "this is the C.A., Nathan Cock-"

Jefferson paused, trying to remember the C.A.'s last name. All he could think was Cockfight, but he knew that wasn't right.

"Nathaniel Cockwright," Nathaniel said with a glare to the chief and a broad, fake smile, "I assume you're the famous Texas Ranger I've been hearing about."

Brewster shook hands with the C.A., "Well, I don't know about being famous, but yes sir, I am a Texas Ranger. Brewster McKinney."

Suddenly everyone with a camera began taking pictures of McKinney, and Nathaniel seized that opportunity, smiling broadly for the photographs.

"Well, Mr. Ranger," Cockwright began, "we're here to take the 'Alligator Killer' off your hands."

"I'm sorry, what killer?"

"The 'Alligator Killer.' The young man you arrested last night."

Brewster looked at Jefferson, "Someone killed an alligator?"

There were a few muffled laughs from the reporters.

"They're here to take Jesse," the Chief answered.

"Oh, the kid. I let him go this morning."

Nathaniel's eyes flared, "You what?"

"I sent him home."

"You sent a murderer home?"

"Well, we didn't have a case, and there's no real reason to think he did it."

Stunned, Cockwright looked around at the reporters who were all jotting down notes.

"Ah, perhaps you two should brief me on the status of the investigation, and then I can fill in our friends in the press," Nathaniel said in effort to save face. "Gentlemen, would all of you mind stepping outside a moment? When I get an update I'll fill all of you in."

Naturally the journalists were reluctant to leave and asked a barrage of questions, none of which Cockwright was capable of answering. The most notable and obvious question was, "Does this mean that the 'Alligator Killer' is still on the loose?"

To Primrose's amusement, Nathaniel had to do a lot of sidestepping on that one. He was quite proud of the label he'd put on the killer and insisted that Primrose and Coleman reference the moniker to every newspaper they called. Now it had quite ironically, come back to bite him. Still, ever the politician, Cockwright managed to get everyone out the door, including his two deputies to help manage the ever-growing disaster.

Once all of the reporters were safely out, Cockwright turned to Jefferson and Brewster and demanded, "What are the two of you doing to me?"

Jefferson looked at Brewster and the Ranger simply shrugged and said, "The kid's daddy has a lawyer on the way here, and with what we've got on the boy, the case would be tossed out in no time anyway."

"That is for me to decide, not you," the now fuming C.A. shouted.

Brewster glanced over Nathaniel's shoulder through the wide glass front window at the reporters. Sensing he was being watched, the C.A. regained his composure and glanced back at the reporters with his broadest smile.

"Look, you two nincompoops, this is my case. I want every detail." He looked at Jefferson. "Get me your report."

Jefferson went over to his filing cabinet. He had spent two hours the night before typing the thing up. This was, by far, the longest, most detailed, and most difficult report he'd ever written.

"And you," Cockwright said to Brewster, "you're no longer on this case. The sheriff's department is taking over. Your captain should be calling. I spoke to the director this morning."

Jefferson handed the report to Cockwright, which amounted to one single spaced typewritten page, "That's it. Not much to it."

Cockwright took the paper and began reading.

"My captain," Brewster began, "called just before you got here. I was waiting for the chief to return before heading back to Dallas."

Cockwright glared at Brewster and then looked back down at the page. He knew McKinney was being sly.

After a moment Cockwright said, "Let me get this straight. He threatened the victim at the movie and then attacked him over something to do with a girl. Then the two were together at the bridge at the time the murder took place?"

Brewster crossed his arms and leaned back against the counter behind the chief's desk.

"Well, yes," Jefferson replied, "but there's more to it."

"What?"

Jefferson thought and then answered, "Well, there was this killing a few years back."

"The murder was the night before last!"

"I know, but..." Jefferson looked over at Brewster for help.

Brewster smiled, "I think what the Chief is trying to say is that the kid didn't do it."

"How can you say that?" Cockwright demanded again in a voice loud enough to be heard outside.

Brewster smiled at the reporters who were straining to hear and then replied in a calmer, more even voice, "We know because we are professional law enforcement officers, and we know when we've got our man. That kid is not our man."

Cockwright almost blew his top. "Professionals? You two couldn't solve this case if the killer walked in here and confessed. In this county I can get a conviction in five minutes with what I have right here in my hand.

"Now see here," he said to Brewster, "you're off the case and I want you out of this town today."

Then he turned to Jefferson. "Right now, you're going to take me to this kid's house where we're going to arrest him for the murder of," he looked back at the report, "Cliff Tidwell."

Jefferson looked at Brewster, having gained a little nerve from working with the Ranger and then looked at Cockwright. "I don't work for you. If you want to arrest him, go do it yourself."

The C.A.'s eyes lit up again, but then he glanced over his shoulder and smiled at the reporters. He then looked back at Jefferson and Brewster and said calmly, "You two mark my words. By the time I'm finished with this case I'll have both of your badges. Now, where does this kid live?"

"Go a block up Main, turn right to Red Oak. It's 301, on the corner. You can't miss it."

The County Attorney glared at the two and turned to head out the door.

"My report, Mr. Cockfight?" Jefferson asked.

Cockwright stopped at the door, took a deep breath, and looked back at Jefferson.

"My report. I need it for my files. I'll make you a copy and get it to you later today."

The C.A.'s eyes were red with anger as he handed the paper to Jefferson, and then he put his smile back on and headed out the door.

Jefferson felt some pride as the turned to look at Brewster.

"Well, Chief," Brewster offered, "I believe that between the two of us we have a pretty good enemy in that C.A."

They watched out the window as Cockwright, along with his deputies and the sheriff's deputies, got into their cars and pulled away, followed by the throng of reporters.

"Poor Jesse," the chief commented.

"Yeah, we should probably go get him."

Jefferson looked at Brewster, "You didn't send him home?"

"He's on the roof waiting for us to get him down."

A few moments later Jefferson and Brewster were standing at the base of the storm drain as Jesse shimmied down from the roof of the police station.

"Now, what do we do?" Jefferson asked Brewster.

"Well, I've got to go back to my headquarters in Dallas, but the case is still yours as far as the Rangers are concerned. If you want me back, you just need to call my HQ, but it'll probably be a good idea for me to stay out of town a few days while that Cockwright fellow cools down."

Jesse came to the ground between the two men.

"What about Jesse? I can't take him home."

"I've been thinking about that."

"What do you mean, I can't go home?" Jesse asked.

"The C.A. wants to make a name for himself by puttin' you in jail for killing Cliff. They're at your house right now, so we got to get you out of here as soon as we can."

Jesse's face showed the fear he felt.

"Can they do that?"

"They're going to try, but we know you didn't do it," Brewster explained. "You know more than you're tellin', but you're not a murderer. But they're going to give you the chair if you don't open up."

Jesse looked him in the eye. He fought the urge to cry but just shook his head.

"Okay. We've got to take you somewhere to keep you out of their hands. Is there a friend who you can stay with? Someone out of town?"

Jesse just shook his head.

"Chief?"

"Nothin' comes to mind."

"Wait. I know where I can go," Jesse replied.

Just as Jesse started to say where, Jefferson stopped him. "Don't tell me. I don't want to have to lie to the C.A."

"Okay, I'll take you," Brewster offered. "Chief, I suspect you need to get ready. That C.A.'s gonna be back here screaming at you in a minute."

Jefferson smile. "I'm beginning to enjoy rufflin' his feathers'."

#

Police Chief Thomas Jefferson Hightower had just enough time to make some fresh coffee and sit down behind his desk before his eminence, County Attorney Nathaniel Cockwright, came barging into his office demanding to know exactly where Jesse was hiding. The C.A., of course, didn't believe him when he said that he had no idea.

"I don't know what you think you're doin', Chief Hightower, but this isn't over. I'm going to get that kid."

"Anything I can do to help," replied Hightower with a smile as the C.A. stormed out the door and got into one of the cars and drove away.

#

About ten minutes later Brewster, with Jesse beside him, drove his coupe through a small community of about a hundred homes. The streets were all reddish dirt, and most of the homes needed some repair. There were lots of kids about playing, and most of the homes had large porches with one or two adults sitting on rocking chairs, shucking peas and carving potatoes. Every face Brewster saw was black.

At Jesse's direction Brewster turned down a long narrow road that went on for about a quarter of a mile and ended at a single house. On the porch sat an old black man, alone in a rocking chair. The man had a stern face and the cold look of someone who had experienced a hard life. Brewster had seen such men many times. Most were criminals, but a few were Rangers. It struck him that there was often a fine line between bandit and lawman.

As the car approached, the old man stood. Brewster noted that he had only one leg.

"Are you sure about this?"

"I'm sure," Jesse replied.

"You're not going to be able to hide out long. That C.A.'s not going to give up. He'll be here looking for you."

"I suspect they'll get me at the funeral," Jesse replied drily.

"Funeral?"

"I'm going to Cliff's funeral."

"I'm sorry, I hadn't thought about that. I'd hoped we could keep you out of their hands until I got back."

Jesse shrugged. "I can't miss the funeral. He was my best friend."

"No, of course not," Brewster replied. "Your dad's lawyer will be in town soon. I'll call Chief Hightower and have him get in touch with this lawyer and fill him in on everything. I'll have Hightower come get you Wednesday morning and take you home. You can see your parents and meet with the lawyer. He'll probably have you turn yourself in after the funeral."

"Okay."

Brewster looked at the stern-faced old man on the porch. "Are you sure you'll be alright here?"

Jesse smiled, "Cherokee's my friend. I'll be okay."

"Cherokee?"

"Folks call him Cherokee-One-Leg because he's half Indian. His real name's Julius Caeser Bradford. His mom was Arapaho. People around here don't know the difference, so they've been callin' him Cherokee since he was a kid."

"Now I remember him."

Jesse stepped out of the car and reached back to shake Brewster's hand.

"Thank you, Corporal."

"We're going to get you out of this, kid, but you're going to have to tell us what you know."

Jesse looked him in the eye. "I wish I could help, but I can't."

Chapter 9

Jesse and Cliff rumbled along through the old black community in the noisy old Model-T truck. It had taken almost a week to get the thing running. They had ransacked almost every Model-T in East Texas for parts. Jewel's father's old truck had a good fuel pump, distributer, carburetor, and gas tank, but both trucks had rusted-out radiators. As it turned out, there were a lot of old Model-T's around; many were still running, but the ones that didn't run almost always had a rusted-out radiator. Finally they learned that Mrs. Bertha Greer, Jesse's and Cliff's Sunday School teacher, had an old Model-T car sitting in an over-grown shed in the woods behind her house.

All three of them went to check it out before talking to Mrs. Greer, partly because they expected it to be rusted just like the others, but mostly because the boys knew full well that before she would let them so much as look at it, she'd make them go home and memorize a half dozen scripture verses. So far, Jesse and Cliff, mostly Cliff, had managed to get through Mrs. Greer's class with memorizing almost no verses, with the exception of the mandatory John 3:16, Romans 3:23, and Romans 10:13 - there was no escaping having to memorize those three. Jesse and Cliff, again mostly Cliff, always managed to find something to help

Brother Bill with that required their immediate attention at the time during class that was allotted to scripture memory. They regularly volunteered to set up or put away the folding chairs in the "fellowship hall" or pour water into the baptism tank.

The boys had pretty good success in avoiding Mrs. Greer's memorizing assignments, but that was mostly because Brother Bill made sure the boys had something to keep them occupied. About a year earlier they had volunteered to help fill the baptism tank, which had to be filled by hand since there was no running water in the church. The tank itself was a modern marvel and had been purchased from Sears and Roebuck and installed right behind the choir loft. Unfortunately, since almost everybody in Elza had already been baptized, the new tank didn't get a lot of use, especially in the summer months when the water level tended to go down due to evaporation. The tank also tended to leak into the choir robe room. So when they did have someone to baptize, the tank had to be re-filled. This particular task was not one that the boys preferred to volunteer for, but carrying buckets of water was still better than getting any more of Mrs. Greer's memorization assignments. That summer Sunday morning the boys told Brother Bill that they would be happy to fill the tank. It was a considerable amount of work, requiring the boys to fill three gallon buckets at Mrs. Williamson's well next door and carry them into the back of the building and then pour them into the tank.

That particular Sunday had been right after the annual spring revival, and there were five freshly saved lives to be baptized. The group, all members of the same family, had recently moved to Elza from over in Louisiana. They had previously been Presbyterians, but Elza didn't have a Presbyterian church, so they all needed to be re-baptized to become full-fledged, honest-to-God Baptists.

Jesse and Cliff had just finished their first trip with a bucket when Cliff had noticed Brother Bill's fishing waders hanging in the dressing room behind the sanctuary next to the baptism tank. Brother Bill would put on the rubber waders so that, rather than completely disrobing to baptize the newly saved Christians, all he had to do was pull the waders over his pants and put on a white robe over his dress-shirt. That way, while the choir sang Amazing Grace, which they did after every baptism, all Brother Bill would have to do is take off his robe and waders, put on his suit coat, and walk out just after the chorus and deliver his sermon.

By the third time the boys passed the waders hanging on the wall, Cliff could no longer resist the opportunity and took out his pocketknife to cut a small hole in the seat of the rubber waders. Later, when Brother Bill had stepped into the pool to baptize the five newly saved believers his rubber pants began to fill with water. The professional that he was, he never let on before anyone, but as the choir sang it had taken almost all five new Christians/Baptists to help him climb out of the tank. Worse still, he had to borrow some trousers from the newly baptized - Baptist style - believers to deliver his sermon. So that Sunday he had stood in front of the whole congregation wearing his black suit coat and a pair of tan pants that were eight inches too short.

Naturally, the pastor knew exactly who was responsible, regardless of how innocent the boys tried to appear. The following week the two drained the tank, which again had to be done by hand. They then scrubbed the tank, helped repair the leak, and then re-filled the tank, which took almost a full day. After that Brother Bill made sure that the boys had tasks to perform each Sunday morning. Little did he know that he was doing them a favor by getting them out of Mrs. Greer's class right before she issued memorization assignments.

So when Jesse, Cliff, and Jewel saw that Mrs. Greer's Model-T sedan had not only a good radiator but also four wheels with no broken spokes and a seat that was in almost new condition, they had no choice but to go knocking on her door. It took considerably less begging than Jesse or Cliff would have thought. Mrs. Greer was delighted to let the three kids have parts off the old car. The car had belonged to her late husband, God rest his soul, and since he had sold the motor out of it for parts before he died the thing was doing nothing but rusting away.

They were just about home free without the subject of scripture memory even coming when Jewel asked, "Is there anything you would like us to do for you, Mrs. Greer?"

If Cliff had owned a gun he would have shot her right then and there. Another moment and they would have gotten away without so much as quoting the words, "Jesus wept," had Jewel managed to keep her big mouth shut.

As a result of Jewel's generosity, the two boys were given the memorization list for the entire summer. Jewel was exempt from the task because her family went to the Methodist church, so Mrs. Greer didn't feel responsible for her spiritual development. Mrs. Greer had never met Jewel but confessed to be extremely impressed at what a thoughtful young lady she was when she promised, to Cliff's chagrin, to make sure that the boys worked on their memorization every day.

Nevertheless, regardless of how much it ended up costing them, the little stake bed Ford turned out to run pretty well. To drive it the boys had to wire a couple of two-by-four blocks to the pedals because Jewel was the only one tall enough to reach the floorboard. And of course the top had long since rotted away, so when it rained, which wasn't often, they got wet. But aside from the occasional backfire and a lot of noise, the truck rolled along just fine.

In fact, the only problem they had at all was getting tires, but Cliff solved that issue by offering to make three free deliveries per tire for George Henry McMillan. Cliff wanted one delivery per tire, but the fact was that they were in no position to negotiate. They weren't going anywhere without tires, and George Henry was the only person in Elza with tires for sale.

The day they finally got it running they proudly drove right down Main Street on a busy Saturday afternoon to show off their achievement. Of course, by then everyone in Elza knew what the kids were up to, mostly because they had gone through every shed and barn in town looking for parts. Still, they made quite a show with Cliff at the wheel as they triumphantly demonstrated their mechanical skills. There had been quite a debate as to who had the right to be the first to drive the truck. Jewel made a good case for herself given that without her father's truck they would probably still be looking for parts. Jesse's argument was probably the weakest, but it was he who found out that Mrs. Greer had a Model-T in the woods behind her house. Cliff shot that one down because he, rightly, figured that they would have found it sooner or later. In the end Jewel had to give way to Cliff, even though he wasn't tall enough to reach the pedals, another argument in Jewel's favor, but fixing the truck had been Cliff's idea. All things considered, building up that old truck was nothing short of genius as far as all three were concerned.

The possibility of the kids getting it to run had been a subject of a great deal of deliberation at the domino hall and out in front of McMillan's store. Not an insignificant amount of money had been wagered, which encouraged Cliff's determination all the more. Once he learned that the boys at the domino hall were placing bets, there was no amount of scripture memorizing that could have stopped him from driving that rusted collection of bolts.

Thus their proud parade down Main Street garnered the attention of just about everyone in town. People all along the street came out of the stores to see that the kids actually got the old, long-forgotten truck to roll. Even Gemma and Jettie Crawford stepped out of Ruth Anne's shop to clap and wave as the Model-T rolled by. Their father, Peterson Crawford, who had just parked his Plymouth sedan, stood stern-faced and watched as the kids passed.

Just as they reached the end of the street, Police Chief Thomas Jefferson Hightower stepped off the curb into the middle of the thoroughfare with a cigar in his mouth, displaying the most official look he could muster. Cliff pulled to a stop and the chief walked around the truck, looking it over carefully and finally stopping next to Cliff.

Chief Hightower had been approached a number of times on the street by concerned citizens warning him that three mischievous kids who were way too young to drive were building an automobile. Most of the warnings, naturally, came from the same people who complained about Toad Lowery's noisy truck or that Hobe Bethard's dogs barked too much. The chief, of course, already knew about the kids - in fact he had bet a dollar fifty that Cliff would get it done. He also knew, of course, that they were too young. He'd even checked with Judge Buckner who, upon considerable thought said, strangely, that there was no law prohibiting kids from driving.

And Jefferson also knew that their parents were the only ones in the small town who didn't know what they were doing. So the chief, without the kids knowing, which in Elza was no small feat, had a discussion with some of their parents. He made no effort to talk to Murdock and Garvis

Rose, who never knew or seemed to care what Jesse did with his time. For Jefferson's money, life was better that way.

Cliff's father, Ned Tidwell, was not at all surprised at what the kids were doing, but he expressed a lot of concern for their safety, as did Irwin Stoker. In the end they both came to the same conclusion - the kids were putting their time to good use and staying out of trouble. More importantly, their idea of doing deliveries for Washington's and McMillan's was a darn good one, and they would probably make a little money at it. Among the three, however, Jefferson was the only one who thought the kids would actually get that old Model-T to run. In the end it was decided that the kids could go through with their plans and no one would interfere. If they got the truck running, which was doubtful, Jefferson would give them a good talking to about safety and responsibility of driving an automobile.

All in all, the only real concern was that Irwin Stoker didn't like his little girl spending her afternoons with those two boys. Jefferson just smiled and assured him that he and Sarah had done a good job raising that girl and that the boys had much more to fear from her than she did of them.

So when Jefferson walked up to a proudly smiling Cliff Tidwell, he gave the best performance of a professional lawman he could possibly manage. Cliff, as usual, had long since suspected that the Chief might possibly try to deny them the right to drive and had prepared an admirable case in defense of his position. Jefferson, though, was not at all interested in Cliff's oratory and gave a good ten-minute lecture to them about all the auto accidents he had seen in his time as chief. It was a grand performance, though at that point in his career, other than a few fender-benders, he had only seen one serious accident, and it didn't involve a serious injury. Because of the size of Elza, most of the town, the three kids included, had come out to see that wreck. Still, Jefferson made his point that the driver of that car could have easily ended up dead.

Eventually, the kids had to agree to some safety requirements or else, Jefferson, as chief, would take the truck away. First, they had to drive no faster than twenty-five miles per hour. That part, he suspected, was easy because he didn't think that the old truck would actually go that fast. Secondly, they couldn't go more than ten miles from downtown Elza, and not into Jacksonville or Rusk because the police in those towns might not be so accommodating, and he wasn't about to go to either of those towns to get the kids out of jail. Thirdly, they were not to drive after dark. That part was all the more important because it looked like the headlamps on the old truck were broken.

All three readily agreed, mostly because they had no choice, though none of them had any idea if they could obey Jefferson's rules. They could keep from driving at night and they knew that they'd get in trouble for going up to Jacksonville or Rusk, but the ten-mile rule and the speed limit were different stories. The car's speedometer and odometer didn't work, so they had no idea how fast they were going or how far they had driven.

The two boys turned up the long, red dirt, tree-lined lane leading to Cherokee-One-Leg's house. Their daily routine had changed once they became mobile. Both boys started getting up extra early to do their chores at home. They then met up at Washington's where they, as quickly as they could, swept the floors and stacked feed. Then they would load up for a delivery, if Nickel had any. At first there weren't any at either store, but as soon as the local farmers heard they could get feed delivered, they began calling in orders.

When finished at the feed store the boys would rush over to McMillan's and sweep and stock, and if they were lucky they would get one or two deliveries before picking up Jewel at noon. Cliff made a reasonable case that they should keep the profit from any deliveries that they made before she joined them. Jesse, by that point, stayed out of Cliff's arguments with Jewel, realizing that Cliff never won and was more likely to go home with a black eye than with any extra profit. Jewel made her position clear that Cliff would not have had a truck without her dad's parts and they had a deal, making them equal partners. The two were in quite a standoff until Jewel was ready to put up the dukes, to which Cliff would mutter that he wasn't going to beat up a girl and would storm off in defeat.

So Cliff and Jesse would make a couple of deliveries in the morning without Jewel but sharing all profits as if she were along. They had been hoping for a chance to go out to Cherokee's without Jewel from the start, but this was the first opportunity they'd had.

Cherokee was sitting on his porch wearing his cavalry hat, enjoying the cool of the morning as the two boys came bouncing along the lane in the old truck. He, like everyone in the area, had heard that they had the truck and stood to watch as they approached.

When they pulled to a stop, Cliff shut off the motor, but the old engine continued to rumble, sputter, and backfire for at least twenty seconds after they got out of the car and walked to the porch.

"Hi, Cherokee," Cliff said cheerfully once the noisy old truck shut down.

"Some new sparkplugs might help that racket," Cherokee offered as the two boys got to the porch.

"We're plannin' to get some if we ever pay off the tires," Jesse replied.

"Come sit down boys. I got some tea made."

The old man hobbled into the house and a moment later returned with a couple of Ball-Mason jars. He picked up a crock jug he had sitting in the shade on the porch and filled the two jars.

Jesse took a sip of tea from one of the glasses. "Wow, that's cold."

"An old Indian trick. I make the tea at night with cane sugar then lower the jug into the well before I go to bed. It cools overnight down there in that water, and by mornin' it's nice and cold."

The old man settled in his rocker, "You boys sit-down,"

The two kids took seats, Jesse in the porch swing and Cliff in the opposite rocker.

The old man smiled at Cliff. "That was my wife's chair. We spent twenty years rockin' on this porch."

"Where is she?"

"She went to be with the Lord almost five years ago."

"I'm sorry, Cherokee," Cliff replied.

"Don't be, she was a good woman. She was a good army wife. She never once complained when I went off to chase Indians or fight the Spanish. She was, by far, the best part of my life."

"Do you have any kids, Cherokee?" Jesse asked, wanting to change the subject.

The old man reached for a cane that he kept next to the door and stood. "My first son died at birth. My daughter died in the winter of '85. But my other son, Romulus...." the old man stopped speaking and hobbled into the house. A moment later he came out with two velvet-covered cases. He handed them to Jesse.

"Romulus started out with the tenth cavalry like me but transferred to the ninety-third in 1917. They created two colored divisions, the ninety-second and ninety-third."

Jesse opened one of the boxes. Inside was a medal with a green and red striped ribbon. The medal was a cross with crossed swords.

"That's the Croix de Guerre. It's the highest medal the French give to foreigners."

Jesse handed the box to Cliff and then opened the second one.

"That's the DSC, Distinguished Service Cross," the old man said with obvious pride as he seated himself. "It's the second highest honor given in the American army."

The boys looked at the two medals and handed them back to Cherokee.

"Romulus was a captain in the three-hundred and seventy-second Regiment." The man paused and took a sip of tea. He was killed in the assault on Champagne."

The old man clutched the two boxes with his head down. Jesse couldn't help but feel for the man who was so proud but had lost so much.

"Y'all seen any more of the Crawford man?"

"No," Jesse replied. "We see him drive off almost every day. I think he goes up to Jacksonville."

"I wish there was somethin' we could do," Cliff uttered.

"You're doin' it. Just keep your eyes open and let me know if you see anything. I'll do what needs to be done. I've chased down savages like Apaches and Comanches. Men like that one, they make mistakes. We just gotta be patient."

#

Twenty minutes later Cliff and Jesse rumbled down Main Street in the old truck. This time Jesse was at the wheel. He pulled to a stop in front of the Palace just as Jewel and her mother Sarah came out of one of the stores. Jesse shut off the motor, but as usual it sputtered and backfired before shutting down.

Jewel walked over to the boys.

"Don't be late for dinner," Sarah said as her daughter walked away.

"I won't, Mom."

"Hi, Mrs. Stoker," the two boys said almost in unison.

"Hello, boys," she said. "Y'all be careful, now."

"We will."

Jewel walked to the driver's side where Jesse was still seated.

"Scoot."

"What do you mean, 'scoot'? You just got here."

"It's my turn. Now scoot over. You two have been drivin' all morning. Now, it's my turn."

Cliff sat opposite Jesse, smiling broadly because it was Jesse and not him facing off with Jewel.

"I'll just drive over to McMillan's. You can drive then."

Jewel put both hands on her hips and glared at Jesse.

"Are all girls as aggravatin' as you?" Jesse asked as he slid over.

Jewel smiled and climbed up behind the wheel. "Pretty much all of us."

Jewel started the motor and pulled out of the parking spot and drove up Main Street to McMillan's store. As they drove by, Jesse noticed Peterson Crawford sitting on a wooden box in front of the domino hall staring down the street. Jesse looked behind him and saw Mrs. Stoker walking down the block. Jesse nudged Cliff, and they both looked at Crawford. As they passed, the truck backfired and Crawford took his gaze off Mrs. Stoker. He looked at the truck and noticed the two boys staring at him. He watched them as they drove away.

#

Sarah Stoker turned the corner on Elm Street to make the long walk home. She was just crossing Red Oak when a brown Plymouth sedan pulled up beside her.

"Hop in, Sarah. I'll give you a ride home," Peterson Crawford yelled out the passenger side window.

Startled, Sarah nervously looked around and then bent down to the open window. "Go away. I don't want to talk to you."

"Oh, Sarah, relax. No one around here cares. And old Irwin's off workin' the fields somewhere. Hop in."

"I'm not going anywhere with you. I'm a married woman."

"Oh, Sarah, there's no reason to act like that. You and me are old friends, and besides, we both know what kind of woman you are."

She looked around again, now showing real anger.

"Go away."

"You got anything for me?" he asked with a broad smile.

"I told you before, we don't have any money."

He looked leeringly at her. "Well, Sarah, you're gonna have to come up with somethin', and I'm sure you've got somethin' I'd like, unless you want everyone in Elza to know who and what you really are."

She froze and stared at him as he opened his suit coat and revealed a Smith and Wesson .38 Police Special tucked into his trousers.

"Come on. Go for a ride with us," she heard from behind.

Sarah swirled her head around to see Richard Crawford standing behind her. Startled, she tried to rush away, but he grabbed her arm.

"Come on, Sarah. Let's go have a little fun," Richard said with an evil grin that sounded more like an order than a request.

"You know, Rich, we could always wait a couple of years. That little blonde we saw in that old Ford will be lookin' good before long," Peterson added.

Sarah looked into the car at him. Her heart sank at the disgusting remark.

"Stay away from my daughter."

"Get in the car, Sarah," Peterson added, this time without a smile.

Dejected, Sarah watched as Richard opened the car door. She wanted to turn and run, but he still had hold of her arm. Finally she got into the Plymouth and slid over as Richard got in after her.

#

MAYDELLE, TEXAS
June 15, 1915

Juanita Burney had the look of a woman who had far exceeded her thirty-six years. Sometimes one ages from things other than years, as is often the case of women like Juanita. Life tended to be hard for an unmarried mother who operated a business. Still, she was an attractive woman with long black hair and a shapely figure, and of course she took great pains to wear the right amount of rouge.

Juanita lived in a little shack that had once been a henhouse behind the farm house. She preferred it that way. She could have easily made for herself a place inside the main house, but she didn't want to raise Sarah in such an environment. Sarah, she hoped, would not have to age beyond her years. Sarah, she promised herself, would never set foot inside such a place as The Maydelle Tomato Farm.

In 1898, at age nineteen Juanita, then Juanita Carrillo, began working the counter at the Alamo Laundry and Cleaning service less than a block from the actual Alamo and almost directly across the street from the Menger Hotel in downtown San Antonio. Juanita had beautiful dark eyes and long black hair. She was a rarity in San Antonio. Her mother was white, and her father was a descendent of Mexican aristocracy. Though her grandfather had been in Texas since before 1800 and fought for Texas in the revolution of 1836, to the whites that she grew up with, Juanita was always a "Mexican."

Her grandfather had done well after the revolution, and though it took some years he had managed to get much of his family's fortune out of Mexico. He eventually purchased real estate in San Antonio. Over the years the city continued to grow, as did the Carrillo wealth.

Following her grandfather's footsteps, her father invested heavily in real estate. He also opened and managed the Crockett Street Bank and Trust, the largest and most prestigious bank in town. All things considered, the Carrillo family owned, managed, or collected payment on about twelve percent of San Antonio, a sizable fortune at that time. They lived in one of the first and largest homes in the King William District.

Eduardo Carrillo was a hard man who expected much from his children, so, like her brothers before her, Juanita had to take a job as soon as she graduated from Ursuline Academy. Her father chose the Alamo Laundry and Cleaning Service for her because he saw investment potential in this new service and wanted his daughter to learn all about the laundry business. Eduardo did not want his daughter to become like the women of the social class that he saw almost daily having lunch in the restaurant of the Menger or lounging at the Polo Club. His daughter was going to understand the value of a dollar and would be as capable of managing a business as any man. So rather than watching polo ponies or playing tennis with her friends, Juanita learned the business of Laundry and Cleaning.

It had been all the news when the famous Teddy Roosevelt came to San Antonio to train his newly established volunteer cavalry, known as the Rough Riders. The river city buzzed with excitement. Juanita, like everyone else, hoped to catch a glimpse of the former Navy Secretary either at The Menger or possibly at the fairgrounds where they trained.

So Juanita was surprised that morning in April 1898 when Colonel Roosevelt walked into the Alamo Laundry and Cleaning Service to have his uniforms cleaned and pressed. In all honesty, had he not been in uniform and wearing his trademark glasses, she may not have recognized him at all. That was partly due to the fact that he was not nearly as tall as she would have expected, and he was considerably unassuming in his manner.

But the most important reason that she did not notice the Colonel, however, was the other man in uniform. This man, standing right behind the Colonel, was taller, with dark skin and a broad smile that she couldn't help looking at.

Juanita Carrillo was in love. She knew it the moment she first glimpsed Captain Jamison Ernest Burney. She tried to keep from showing that she was stricken by the man, but she was certain that she had failed. In fact, she was so smitten that it was only after the Colonel handed her his laundry and she took down his name that she realized that she had one of the most famous men in America standing right in front of her.

As difficult as it was, Juanita managed to take the young Captain's laundry also and write down his name without making a complete fool of herself. Up to the point when he was walking out the door, she had no clue that the handsome young Captain had paid any notice of her at all because she was so preoccupied with her own feelings.

She quite easily could have gone her entire life thinking that the Captain hadn't even seen her had the Colonel not said, "I believe, my boy, that you are smitten. Don't you think that you should invite the young lady to join us at the hotel for dinner?"

Captain Burney paused, looked at her, marched to the counter, and did just that. She was a bit amused that he seemed nervous. Naturally, of course, she agreed, but only if he would come to her home, meet her parents, and assure them that she would be home before ten. The captain agreed, and at precisely five o'clock that evening he knocked on the door of the house on Prince William Street.

Captain Burney, as it turned out, was not a boy that was easily intimidated. Most boys she met feared courting a girl from that part of town and feared courting her even more when they learned that her father was Eduardo Carrillo. Still, Carrillo was not in the least impressed with the young captain. But since the young man would only be in town a few weeks, and they would be dining at the Menger, where the Carrillo family was well known, Eduardo relented and allowed Burney to escort Juanita to dinner.

They dined in a private room in the hotel restaurant that had been reserved for Roosevelt and the other officers. Juanita was the only woman present, which made her the center of attention. Colonel Roosevelt saw to it that she was seated in between himself and Captain Burney. The night was one of the most memorable of her life. Colonel Roosevelt kept everyone entertained with stories of his adventures in North Dakota. Unfortunately, though fascinated by the exploits of the famous adventurer, Juanita was far more interested in learning about Captain Burney, whom the Colonel tended to refer to as Jay.

After dinner, which seemed to last for hours, the Colonel ordered all of the officers to their quarters. All the officers, except Captain Burney, who he suggested might enjoy taking Miss Carrillo for a walk down by the river. The captain escorted Juanita to a little coffee shop overlooking the San Antonio River just south of downtown where the two talked right up to until there was just enough time to get home before Eduardo called for the police. Over coffee she learned that he had graduated Harvard the same day that she graduated from Ursuline Academy. She also learned that he had received his commission because he was a family friend of the Colonel's. It was highly unusual to be commissioned directly as a captain, but the Colonel had ways of pulling strings to get what he wanted. He continued to explain that he served as Roosevelt's aide-de-camp. Juanita had no idea what any of that meant, but it made no difference. Juanita was in love, and she simply enjoyed the sound of his voice.

Every night for the next two weeks Jay and Juanita had dinner at the Menger and would then take a walk to the river. Some evenings they ate with the officers, and others they dined alone. On those occasions when they joined the officers, she found herself becoming a de facto mother of the group. Most of the officers, unlike Jay and the Colonel, were not so well-educated and refined. Accordingly, she took on the job of correcting behavior and manners. Of course, she did so with great charm and somewhat in jest, thus all of the senior officers, and especially Colonel Roosevelt, were wholly entertained, endearing her even more to the group.

Nevertheless, no matter what the young man did, Eduardo Carrillo was not becoming endeared to Captain Jamison Burney. In fact, as the second week of their courtship was coming to a close, Eduardo decided that it was time to put an end to this romance before his little girl became too infatuated. For Eduardo it was a simple matter of reasoning with the girl. He would sit down and explain that this romance needed to end. Captain Burney was a nice young man, but he had no future, and at best she would end up as nothing more than a camp follower. No daughter of Eduardo Carrillo would become the wife of a soldier, and his grandchildren would not grow up in military housing. The decision was made, and she would have to live with it.

There was considerable commotion in the Carrillo house the night Juanita came home from her evening with the officers of the First Volunteer Cavalry and her father issued his directive. All four of Juanita's brothers hid in their rooms, and her mother, though somewhat sympathetic to Juanita's cause, stayed out of sight. Juanita, with a hard-headed determination comparable only to that of her father, did her best to stand her ground and, sobbing, only agreed after Eduardo promised to allow her to spend one more evening with her soldier.

That next night would have been the worst of her life had it not been for the fact that she had spent all of the previous one crying. Fortunately, Jay did not take her to dinner with the other officers. Instead they ate alone at a café on the river. All the while she was trying to think of a way to explain what her father had said the night before. But while she was trying to think of a way to tell him, he had even worse news for her. The Rough Riders had received their orders, and early the next morning they would catch a train for Tampa, Florida and then, most likely, to Cuba.

Then he did what she had not imagined. Captain Burney got down on one knee beside her chair, took small a black box from his pocket and asked Juanita Carrillo to marry him. He admitted that he should ask her father first and she should come to New York to meet his family, but there just was no time. In fact, the officers had already moved out of The Menger and into tents with the men, and he would join them soon.

She knew that it was impossible and her father would never approve, but smiling broadly with tears streaming Juanita said, "Yes."

When they got home, Captain Burney officially asked Eduardo Carrillo for Juanita's hand. Carrillo, of course, was furious with both of them and refused, ordering the Captain out of his house and his daughter to her room. Tearfully, Juanita watched Burney go.

Early the next morning, long before anyone awoke, Juanita Carrillo slipped out the back door of the house on King William Street and walked downtown to the railroad station. The troop train, actually two trains, had already departed, but she caught the nine o'clock for New Orleans. As it turned out she was not the only "camp follower" going to Tampa. There were at least a dozen other women like herself on the train.

Once in Tampa she had no trouble finding Jay. Everyone in the little town knew where the Rough Riders were bivouacked, and that night Jay and Juanita were married. She wouldn't have minded waiting until he returned. She actually tried to insist that they go to meet his parents before marrying because she knew full well that they could not return to San Antonio. After the war they would need help getting started, and eloping was no way to win his family's approval. He argued though that they needn't worry about "getting started," he had plenty of money, and it was more important to him that she had his name. That way, heaven forbid, if something happened in Cuba, she would be cared for.

Juanita had no idea what he meant by that. She knew that Captains didn't make much money, but she accepted it because, well, she was in love.

They had one night together in Tampa before the Rough Riders boarded a ship for Cuba. The fact was that a quarter of the Rough Riders didn't make the trip, and none of their horses went along because there was no room.

Juanita stood tearfully waving as hundreds of blue shirted cavalry solders, one being Captain Jamison Ernest Burney, waved back as a tug pushed the ship out to sea. That was the last time she saw her beloved Rough Rider.

She and five other war wives rented a small house in Tampa and worked as waitresses in a nearby café while they waited for their heroes to return. Like everyone else in the country, they anxiously and proudly read the newspaper reports of how the war was going and about the Rough Rider victories at Kettle and San Juan Hills. Finally, in mid-August, they got word that the unit had returned to Camp Wikoff on Montauk Point, Long Island New York. Juanita and the other wives booked seats on the first train north.

After a week she finally got to Camp Wikoff where she and the other wives were escorted to a waiting area at a makeshift tent/office to reveive for word from their soldier. One by one each of her companions either saw her beloved or was informed that he was in the hospital - or in one case had been killed. Finally, after nightfall, Juanita began to get upset that no one seemed to know the whereabouts or condition of Captain Burney. After screaming to see Colonel Roosevelt, who was apparently in New York, she was finally escorted to the tent of a Major Pevoto who, fortunately, had been one of the officers with whom she had shared so many dinners back in San Antonio. The major explained to her that the Captain had been taken ill with yellow fever in Cuba, and upon their arrival at Camp

Wikoff he was met by his family who had a letter from the Secretary of War requesting that he be released to the care of his private physician.

Before being allowed to take Burney, his parents had had to sign a release with an address where he could be contacted. Major Pevoto reluctantly gave Juanita the address, which, coincidentally, was only a few miles away at a place called Southampton. Though the hour was already late, she refused to wait and rushed to be by her husband's side.

It was near midnight when she arrived at the house, though the word house could hardly describe the place. Her home, rather her parents' home, in San Antonio was easily, and by no accident, one of the largest in the city; this house was at least four times its size. The house was set back from the road by at least two hundred yards and had a long lane up to the door from the gatehouse by the main road. The road was fronted by a stone wall that would have kept the house from being visible had it been any smaller. A night guard at the gate refused to even consider letting Juanita in until, after almost an hour of pleading, she convinced him to look at the marriage license. Upon seeing the document he made a call on a telephone to the main house. Then after she waited almost another hour, an automobile arrived at the gate and a large man dressed in a dark suit escorted her to the home.

The front door opened to a large three-story atrium where she was introduced to a kind but stern looking older gentleman who claimed to be Jay's father. Juanita, exhausted and in tears, pleaded for the opportunity to see Jay. The man explained that his son was quite ill and not in shape for visitors. In fact, he said, Jay was possibly near death, and a physician was with him. Juanita was now near frantic, demanding to see him. The gentleman asked her to calm down and took her by the arm into a library off to the side of the main atrium. He then asked to see the marriage license. Juanita was hesitant but agreed to show it to him in hope that he would realize that she was, in fact, Jay's wife and had every right to be with him at this time.

Upon reading the document the man looked at her and asked, "How much do you want?"

Juanita was stunned and simply stared at the man.

"Will a thousand dollars take care of this?" He asked as he reached into a desk drawer and removed some cash.

Juanita began to cry, when suddenly the doors leading out to the atrium opened and a woman burst in. The woman ran to the man, sobbing, and said, "Hamel, Jay's gone."

Juanita was stunned as she realized that her husband was dead, and she never even got to tell him that he was going to be a father.

While holding his wife the man looked at Juanita with fire in his eyes and ordered, "Get out of my house, now!"

Juanita just stood there with tears streaming when he said again, "Someone get this Mexican whore out of my house!"

Suddenly the man who drove her to the house grabbed her from behind and carried her out to the automobile and drove her back out of the gate and into the little town where he shoved her out and ordered her never to return.

Two weeks later, broke and desperate, Juanita arrived at the door of her parents' house. The commotion that took place the night before she ran away had been quite calm compared to her welcome home. After thirty minutes being yelled at, Juanita was finally told that she no longer had a home. She never got to explain that her soldier was dead or that she carried his baby. She was told that she had made her decision when she ran away and that she was not ever to return.

Sarah Burney was born in Houston, where Juanita found a sympathetic cousin who gave her a place to live. That refuge only lasted a few weeks. For the next year Juanita and baby Sarah bounced from relative to relative, and finally she found a room at a boarding house and a job as a waitress in the small town of Crockett. By the time Sarah was three, Juanita was no longer the bright happy young girl she had been when she met her Captain in the Alamo Laundry and Cleaning Service. She had become hardened and bitter.

She shared a room in the boarding house with another waitress named Elaina who worked some evenings at a brothel on First Street. Elaina tried for months to get Juanita to join her there, but Juanita had no interest in such thing. Then one evening they were told that the café was closing. This was the worst possible news. Juanita had run out of relatives and had no place left to go. Finally, realizing that there were no options, she went to the house on First Street. At the beginning the work disgusted her, but when the money began to add up, her perspective changed. She and Elaina started alternating nights, one working and the other staying with Sarah. Soon Juanita, only working three nights a week, was making far more than she had made working six days a week at the café.

Not long after she began her new profession, a lumber mill owner by the name of Horace McCracken Hamilton came to town. Mr. Hamilton lived way up in Henderson but came all the way down to Crockett because, as he put it, "it was wiser to find one's 'pleasure' away from home." Mr. Hamilton became one of Juanita's favorite customers, partly because he was pleasant and kind but mostly because he gave her a healthy tip. Men who left tips were always treated better because tips were not shared with the house.

One evening while sitting in the parlor downstairs at the house on First Street Juanita and Mr. Hamilton began to talk about investments. Juanita, of course, had no education in the stock market, but she had overheard a lot from her father all those years. Hamilton was quite impressed with her knowledge, realizing that Delilah, the name she used while inside house on First Street, was not just pretty, but she was also smart.

One evening after "business" was finished, Mr. Hamilton made a job proposal to Delilah. Naturally, of course, she thought he was just full of wind, but as he persisted she realized that he was quite serious. He explained that he had come in possession of an old tomato farm in the southern corner of Cherokee county. The house, he said, was quite large, looking a lot like an old South plantation home with a huge porch and Roman columns across the front. He could have a crew fix it up and in no time they would be in business. She would run it, of course, and he would serve as a silent partner.

She agreed to think about the deal, and one week later they made a "formal" agreement. It was a handshake deal because one could hardly expect a lawyer to draw up a contract for an illegal business.

Juanita and Sarah, along with Elaina, packed what things they had and moved to the tomato farm. Immediately upon arriving at the farm Juanita saw the small house out back and decided it was the perfect place to raise Sarah. It had once been a hen house, but with some work and a new floor it made a nice little home. With the money she made, Juanita was able to hire Marie as a housekeeper to look after Sarah while Juanita worked.

As she grew, Sarah was strictly forbidden from entering the main house. In fact, she was never even told what kind of work her mother did, but naturally by the time she reached her teen years she learned about these things, as kids that age will tend to do. Though her mother tried to keep her separate, Sarah knew all the girls who lived in the house and talked with them frequently - but always in the yard behind the house because even as she reached her late teens she never actually went inside.

Sarah attended school in Maydelle, walking the three miles each way every day. On Sundays she and Marie attended the little church there. Unfortunately there were no Catholic churches in town, so the two had to become Baptists. Juanita never attended church with them. None of the local men ever came into the Farm, but she knew from visits to the Bradford's General Merchandise Store that everyone knew who and what she was. Because she was known, she went to great pains to keep from being seen with Sarah.

Of course, people knew that a little girl lived in the house behind The Farm but there were several people who worked on the farm who were not part of the "business that took place there." Juanita had gone to great lengths to make the business an actual working farm. Out on the highway, three miles from the farm, she had a "tomato stand" where they sold not only tomatoes but all sorts of produce, including black-eyed-peas, butter beans, corn, and even turnips, all grown on "The Maydelle Tomato Farm." Of course, those seeking the other services the farm provided knew it as "Miss Delilah's Tomato Farm," or "Miss Delilah's Tomato Farm and House of Pleasure," or, more often than not, it was just "Miss Delilah's."

As it turned out, Juanita really had inherited a good head for business. The Farm was the largest and most successful farm within miles. Eventually she had houses built for the people she hired to work the fields and tend the cattle. Granted, none of it would have been possible without the money generated by the "business," but as Mr. Hamilton joked, "If the house ever burned down, Delilah would still turn a profit off corn and turnips."

One Saturday afternoon just a few weeks after Sarah's sixteenth birthday, she was walking home from spending the day at her friend Clara's house in Maydelle. Clara's parents had come to know and love Sarah, though they were initially slow to accept the girl. They knew where Sarah lived and were, understandably, hesitant to let their daughter become friends with someone from such a background. They, of course, knew Marie from church and admired her dedication and hard work each year at the annual spring revival. Marie explained that although she lived on The Farm, Sarah had never been in the house, and she doubted the young girl knew any more about what took place inside than did Clara.

So that Saturday as she turned off the main road onto the lane leading to the house, as she had done a hundred times before, she had no cares in the world. She was running later than normal, and as the rays of sunlight gave way to dusk, she picked up her pace as much as she could, knowing what trouble she would be in if she didn't get home before dark. Not many visitors came along during the day, but on the occasion that an automobile passed as she walked up the road, she paid no attention to them, and they, understandably, were too focused on their destination to notice her.

Then, as it was just about dark, a sedan with two young men in it pulled up beside her. The young man driving asked, "Hi! Would you like a ride up to the house?"

Sarah was a little frightened by the boys and shook her head, continuing on her way.

But the men were not so easily deterred. "My name's Peterson and this is my little brother, Richard. He's never been to the farm."

Sarah tried to ignore them, but they persisted.

"Do you live here at the farm?"

"Please leave me alone."

"Look she talks," Richard joked.

"Come on, get in. We're goin' the same place as you. There's no reason you should walk all that way."

Sarah stopped and looked at them. She was not out much when men were coming to the Farm, so she didn't see many of them, but the ones she did see were always much older than these two. These men were not much older than she. Sarah looked up at the sky; it was almost dark. She then looked down the lane, knowing that she was still a long way from home.

"You're going to the house?"

"Yeah," Peterson answered with a smile.

She hesitated for a few moments and then nodded. Peterson, the driver, got out of the car, and she climbed into the seat between the two men.

As soon as Peterson was back in the car Richard asked Sarah, "So what's your name?"

"Sarah."

"Isn't that haunted cemetery around here?"

"Sure. It's right down the road," Peterson responded.

"I've never seen a ghost. Have you, Sarah?"

"I need to get home."

Richard put his arm around her. "Oh, come on, we won't be long."

Peterson put the car in reverse and headed back to the main road.

"Please," she pleaded, "I need to get back."

"You look frightened," Peterson stated as he headed the car up the road and away from the lane, "there's no reason for a girl like you to be afraid of a couple of boys like us."

"I really need to get home."

Richard produced a bottle from bottle from the floorboard, "Here, have a drink. It'll make you feel better."

Laughing, he pushed the bottle to her lips. She tried to resist as alcohol splashed all over her dress. She swallowed some. It burned and caused her to cough.

Peterson pulled the car up to a cemetery gate.

"My little brother's never been to the tomato farm. Why don't you give him a little taste of what he can expect?"

Richard started kissing and groping her.

Now in tears she pleaded, "Please stop."

She began trying to push him away as Peterson took a long pull from the bottle. Richard finally opened the door and stepped out of the car. He pulled on Sarah, ripping her dress completely open.

"Come out here with me. There's no room in the car."

Standing outside the car he tried to pull her out, but she continued to resist. Laughing, Peterson gave her a shove, and she started sliding off the seat. Continuing to fight, she kicked at Richard and he fell into a slight ditch on the roadside. Sarah tumbled out of the car on top of him. Seeing her chance, she took off running down the road in the direction of the house. Richard got to his feet and began to run after her while Peterson sat laughing.

Sarah slipped through a barbed wire fence on the roadside, leaving a piece of her torn dress hung on the wire. Richard tried to pursue but got hung up in the fence. Having played in these fields all of her life, she had no trouble finding her way through the corn rows and woods and easily found her way back home.

Richard eventually got through the fence but lost her once she got into the corn and finally gave up. In the distance, Peterson could be heard laughing.

It was another thirty minutes before Sarah got home. Her dress had been torn to shreds, and she had scratches and cuts all over her arms and legs from running through bushes, woods, and cornfields. With tears streaming down her face, she recounted what had happened to Marie, who, upon hearing the story, ran into the house to get Juanita.

Embarrassed and still frightened, Sarah re-told her ordeal to her mother. Though hardened and bitter from life, Juanita had surprising compassion when it came to Sarah. Regardless of what hardships life had thrown her, Juanita was a good mother who worked tirelessly to give her baby a future.

Early the next morning Juanita and Marie took the farm truck into Jacksonville. Juanita decided that Sarah should not be living behind the house. She needed to be away from that environment. It had happened once and it could easily happen again.

After a little looking, they found a nice little whitewashed building just off Commerce Street. Juanita had often thought about opening a produce store, and this was a good opportunity. Sarah and Marie could live in the apartment on the second floor, and they would sell vegetables in the store downstairs through the summer and dry goods during the winter. The place really didn't need to make money; the other business provided plenty of income, but still, it wouldn't hurt if it turned a profit.

So Sarah and Marie began their little produce store. A year later Sarah finished her education, and at her mother's insistence, she enrolled in the Alexander Collegiate Institute there in Jacksonville. She was not a good student and hated school. There were very few women in the institute, and every man there reminded her of the two brothers who drove her to the cemetery that terrible night. Finally, after a couple of long nights of arguing, Juanita finally relinquished and Sarah left school to work full time at the produce store.

Sarah worked hard, and the little store flourished. Soon she began taking produce from several local farmers. And since farmers were coming in almost every day, she began selling other things that they needed such as farm tools and feed, and of course overalls and tractor parts.

A couple of years after she began working full time at "The Farm Produce Store" Sarah noticed a young man hiding behind the grubbing hoe display looking at her, but she couldn't get a good look at him. She really didn't give him any more thought until the next day when she walked out to the post office to buy stamps.

She didn't see the car following her as much as she sensed it. Finally after she looked back a couple of times the car drove on past her and parked on the street a little ahead. Still not concerned, but curious, she continued on along the sidewalk. She tried not to look at the car, but she could tell that the driver was definitely watching her.

Then as she passed Richard Crawford, the younger of the two brothers, stepped out of the car and asked, "Hey sweetie! Remember me?"

Sarah froze; even before she turned around she knew the voice and was terrified. Turning, she looked at the face that she had tried to block from her memory then spun and began walking quickly up the sidewalk.

Richard, smiling broadly, chased after her.

"Come on, I just want to take you for a ride."

"Please go away," she pleaded without stopping.

"Don't be that way. I just want to have some fun."

"I've got to go."

"I'll get my brother; he's married now, but he still likes to have fun."

She began walking faster to get away from him. Finally he grabbed her arm.

"Come on," he began, still smiling. "We'll pay whatever you want."

Terrified and in tears she tried to pull her arm free.

"Please let me go," she said much louder than she intended.

People along the street looked at them, and Richard quickly let go. His smile quickly went away.

"I don't know why you think you're too good for me, but I don't have to take insults from a whore."

Tears streaming down her cheeks, she turned away from him and began running up the street. With fire in his eyes Richard watched her run away. He then noticed people along the street looking at him. He quickly turned and went back to his car.

For the next two weeks Sarah lived in terror, almost never leaving the store or apartment above. Finally, after a week and knowing that Marie had long since concluded that something had happened, Sarah sat down with both her mother and Marie and told them about Richard. It was decided, though Sarah objected, that they would sell the store and open a new business much farther away.

The following day Juanita paid a visit to the First American Bank of Jacksonville Texas where she discussed the value and potential sale of "The Farm Produce Store." The bank assistant manager, Mr. Grover Beckwith, not only helped the pretty lady assess the value of the store, but out of kindness, he found a local businessman to take the store off her hands.

Juanita, of course, was no fool. She knew before walking into the bank what price she expected to get for the store, and she also knew that, looking her most attractive, she would get a senior representative who would do his best to "lend a hand" and help her find a buyer who would give her a "fair price."

The businessman that Mr. Beckwith introduced Juanita to took a good look at the store and several good looks at Juanita and made an offer that was considerably more than the price the banker thought the store was worth. Juanita, to Mr. Beckwith's surprise, smiled broadly and declined the offer, to which the gentleman naturally countered. The negotiation continued over a delightful lunch at the only steakhouse in Jacksonville, where Juanita eventually agreed to a price that was ten percent more than she had hoped and thirty percent more than the stupid banker thought the store was worth.

Juanita split the proceeds three ways. Twenty-five percent went to Sarah and twenty-five percent went to Marie since the two of them had managed the business and, frankly, were the reason it had done so well. The other half went to an account Juanita kept for Mr. Horace McCracken Hamilton. Again, Juanita was no fool. One does not skim on business partners, especially those who claim to be in the lumber business but were actually bootleggers.

Sarah and Marie were given a month to find a place to go, but for the time being they could continue living in the apartment while they helped the transfer of ownership. Juanita, of course, had to go back to her real work. Businesses like The Farm didn't manage themselves.

A little before midnight on the same day the sale was finalized, "Miss Delilah's Tomato Farm" was raided by Texas Rangers, Texas state highway patrol officers, and United States Treasury investigators. Everyone in the house was taken to jail. As it turned out, Mr. Horace McCracken Hamilton, who happened to be in the house at the time, was the subject of an ongoing investigation into his finances.

Mr. Hamilton, of course, had legal representation and was released on bail almost immediately.

The ladies who worked at the farm were not quite so fortunate. Because Mr. Hamilton had been making some headlines as a result of his bootlegging connection, the judge was not so quick to let them go. Normally they might spend a night or two in jail, but under the circumstances each of the ladies of "The Maydelle Tomato Farm" were sentenced to six months at the Goree Unit of the Texas prison system outside Huntsville.

Almost all of the men arrested at the raid were released within hours, the judge not wanting to destroy any of their reputations for a simple lapse of good judgment. Only two men received any jail time, and those two, Peterson and Richard Crawford, would have been released had they not tried to escape from the raid by attempting to fight off the officers. Assaulting an officer of the law would have gotten both of them at least six month to a year in the state penitentiary, but after hitting a state patrolman Richard grabbed a Texas Ranger from behind while his brother smashed a wooden chair across his face, breaking his nose. As a result the two were given five years each in the Eastham Unit near Weldon.

For Juanita, the consequences of the raid at the farm were far worse. Though Mr. Hamilton received half of the profits as the Treasury Department Investigators concluded, the title to the property was in her name, and therefore the business belonged to her. That did not stop the Treasury Department from confiscating all of her property and bank deposits in their investigation of Hamilton. Thus she had no money for representation. So, two weeks to the day after the raid at "The Maydelle Tomato Farm," Juanita Carrillo Burney pleaded guilty to charges of prostitution and money laundering and was given a ten-year sentence at the Goree Unit of the Texas Prison System.

Sarah, upon hearing about the raid, tried repeatedly to visit her mother in jail, but Juanita refused the visits in an effort to shield her daughter from any connection to the farm. But then, three months after arriving at the little prison farm, Juanita received her first and only visitor during her incarceration. Eduardo Carrillo made the trip to the Goree unit to see his daughter. During the visit Juanita sat stone-faced across a table while her father told her how disappointed he was in her and that he hoped she realized how much shame she had brought upon the family. He continued to tell her that there would be no help from her family when she was released.

She never mentioned to Mr. Carrillo that he had a beautiful granddaughter.

Twenty-four hours later Sarah Burney received a telegram informing her that her mother was dead. She made repeated attempts to get someone at the prison to tell her what had happened to her mother, but she was simply told that her mother had taken her own life.

With the money Sarah and Marie got from the sale of the store, the two women settled in the small but prosperous town of Elza, south of Jacksonville and east of Rusk. On Main Street across from the movie theater they opened another produce store. Sarah went to all of the neighboring farmers and cut deals to sell their crops. This business was much smaller than the one in Jacksonville, but they made enough money to survive and live comfortably in the apartment above. The two women attended church on Sundays, and on Saturdays they walked across the street to see the movies. Life, for a time, was good.

One afternoon a new farmer walked into the store asking to do business. He was quite a few years older than

Sarah and seemed extremely shy. This behavior baffled the girl who had little experience with men, especially potential suitors, and even less with shy ones. He explained that he had recently been discharged from the army and had moved into his parent's old place on the edge of town. She naturally signed the man up and began selling his corn, potatoes, and collard greens.

For the next two years he came into the store at least once a week. He always had on clean overalls with his hair slicked back, and he always kept his head down and had trouble looking Sarah in the eye. Marie saw from the start that the man was in love, but Sarah couldn't believe that it was possible given that he had hardly spoken more than a dozen words since she'd met him. Still he continued to come, and finally one day he swallowed up all of his nerve and asked Sarah to go to the movies with him. The following Saturday night Sarah Burney and Irwin Stoker went on their first date. Four weeks later, when he walked her across the street after their fourth date, he asked her to marry him.

Sarah didn't know what to say and asked if she could have a few days to think about it. She immediately ran upstairs to tell Marie, who had already surmised that it would happen. Sarah was terrified, but Marie argued that he was a good man who worked hard and would take care of her into her old age. So the next Saturday night Sarah agreed to become Mrs. Irwin Stoker, and two months later at the courthouse in Rusk the two, with Marie as a witness, became husband and wife.

Before they married, Irwin insisted that Sarah would not work, so she and Marie began the process of closing. Marie made arrangements to go live with her sister in Houston. They each shed many tears and promised to stay in touch. They exchanged letters every few weeks until about a year later when Sarah received word that Marie had passed away.

A few days before the wedding, a woman had come to town to buy the store building. Her name was Anna-Ruth Crawford. She told Sarah that her husband was away in the army, and she wanted to open a dress shop so that when he got out they would have a little business to get them started. Sarah sold her the building and promised to come by and visit right after she and Irwin got settled in.

About a week after the wedding day, Sarah dropped by with some freshly picked cucumbers to welcome Anna-Ruth to Elza. Anna-Ruth had not yet opened her store but had moved into the apartment, and she invited her new friend up for a cup of coffee. As they sat at the tiny kitchen table sipping coffee Sarah noticed a picture hanging on the wall. Her heart stopped. She felt a cold chill run through her and almost dropped her cup. Somehow she kept her composure enough to not reveal her feelings as she looked at the picture of Peterson Crawford. Anna-Ruth saw Sarah looking at the picture and took it off the wall and showed it to her. She said that it was her husband who was away in the army.

Sarah had never made the connection with the last name of Crawford. She had probably seen it in the paper, but it never occurred to her that he was Anna-Ruth's husband. She did know that he wasn't in the army. After the raid at the farm, she and Marie had kept an eye on the newspapers. One article mentioned the two brothers who were sentenced to five years for assaulting a Texas Ranger. Above the article were two small pictures of the men. At the time she was relieved because she knew that she and Marie would move and she'd probably never see Richard and Peterson Crawford ever again.

Sarah tossed and turned all that night. Sooner or later the two men she feared most would be right there in little Elza. She was fraught with despair. Should she tell Irwin?

He would surely protect her, but then she would have to tell him about The Farm. Would he understand that she never worked there? Would he believe her?

After two sleepless nights she sat her new husband down and told him where she grew up. Irwin was infuriated. She never got to the part where she told him about Mr. Crawford and his brother. From that moment on he hated her and everything about her. He began to drink, and from time to time, in fits of anger, would strike her. Their life was that of two people who shared a house and a bed but never love. She did all that was expected of a farm wife, and he put food on the table. He worked the fields and rarely spoke to his wife.

A little over a year later Jewel Stoker was born. Irwin, who had so little love for his wife, had nothing but love for his baby girl. Sarah, who until then had so little reason to live suddenly had every reason to live.

That same day, unbeknownst to Sarah, Peterson Crawford and his brother Richard were paroled from prison.

Chapter 10

301 RED OAK AVE. ELZA TEXAS
12:00 p.m. November 19, 1941

Jesse and Gemma slowly climbed the steps to the porch and approached the front door of the house. Jesse was wearing the same jeans and t-shirt he'd had on the day Brewster and Jefferson arrested him. Gemma was wearing her best Sunday dress. There were some cars out front, and Jesse prepared himself for what he knew was going to be a difficult encounter.

The two days with Cherokee-One-Leg had mostly been spent trying to figure out what had happened and who had killed Cliff. Both he and Cherokee missed their friend and had shed some tears, but they also knew that there was work to be done; they knew that business they had hoped was long-since behind them had come back and cost Cliff his life. Cherokee blamed himself. Deep down he knew that the things from the past weren't finished. The boys had been too young at the time to understand, but he knew better. Inside he knew that they should have told everything to the Texas Ranger years ago, but that would have hurt the two people Jesse cared for most`, so he wouldn't allow it then, and he wouldn't allow it now.

It was Cherokee who had come up with a plan. Jesse was determined to be at Cliff's funeral and, of course, so would the C.A. and some sheriff's deputies.

After Jesse left his office with Corporal McKinney, and after the C.A. had left, Jefferson went to Gemma and told her that Jesse was hiding. She didn't have to think about it to know where he was. Cherokee-One-Leg was Jesse's one and only hero. Whenever Jesse had a problem, no matter how big or small, he always went to Cherokee.

It had taken several years for Gemma to understand the relationship Jesse had with the old black man. In a small East Texas town in the 1930's, you rarely saw a young white boy even speaking to old black men, let alone run and hug them as if they were long lost uncles. But as Gemma began to see the relationship Jesse had with his parents, she slowly understood. In the same way that Cliff's dad had taken the place of a father to Jesse, Cherokee took the place of a grandfather. She had heard, through the Elza gossip mill, how Jesse's real grandfather had killed himself before Jesse was born because he'd had some connection to a prostitution business. Naturally, as a boy, Jesse was drawn to the old man who was part Indian and had fought in wars, not to mention that he wore an alligator's tooth around his neck. As they grew to adulthood, Jesse and Cliff had come to love the man as if he was family.

Gemma, of course, was a little afraid of an old man who rarely smiled and always seemed a bit gruff. He was kind to her, of course, but distant. She especially could not understand why Jesse put so much faith in him. But Jesse was steadfastly insistent upon spending as much time as he could with the old soldier rather than with his father's lawyers. On that point Jesse was unyielding. He constantly reassured Gemma, "Don't worry, Cherokee will know what to do.

Jesse was nervous when he reached for the doorknob. He expected there to be lawyers, of course. It was possible that there would be sheriff's deputies. Sooner or later he was going to have to face them, but what made him the most nervous was that behind the door was his mother.

Gemma had come by Monday after seeing Jesse to tell them, as per his specific instructions, that she had heard from him and that he was okay and would come home soon. He had specifically told her not to say that she had seen him. If she did, his mother and his father's lawyers would not leave her alone. None of this information sat well with Garvis, but there was nothing she could do, which irritated her all the more.

Gemma knew that she wasn't one of Garvis Rose's favorite people. Garvis was always exceptionally kind and polite when Gemma was around, but venom has a way of working its way out, and Gemma had felt the bite of Garvis Rose more than once. When she was younger Gemma tried especially hard to be accepted by Garvis, and it bothered her that Mrs. Rose seemed to look down upon her. But in time she had learned that Jesse had little regard for his mother's opinions. Conversely, he had the highest regard for Cliff's parents' opinions, and Mrs. Tidwell treated Gemma like she was a daughter.

Sure as he expected, when he opened the door, Garvis wrapped her arms around him, sobbing and insisting that he should not have hidden out from them. Jesse simply accepted the rebuke. He'd been dealing with Garvis all of his life and knew that there was no point in fighting over something as minor as this. There would be other fights before the day was over.

Also as expected, the house was full of lawyers, all anxious and happy to meet Jesse and all assuring him that he had little to worry about. The C.A.'s case was far too weak, and they were confident that they could keep him from spending a single night behind bars.

Jesse went upstairs to take a bath and dress for the funeral while Garvis and Gemma made sandwiches for Murdock and the lawyers. When Jesse returned, he grabbed a quick bite and then announced that he and Gemma were leaving for the funeral. Garvis, naturally, protested. She insisted they would attend the service as a family, and afterward he would surrender to the sheriff or C.A., with his lawyers present, of course. The lawyers would negotiate with the C.A. to allow Jesse to return home and await the arraignment and, heaven forbid, trial.

Jesse had other plans.

#

TIDWELL FAMILY FARM
ELZA, TEXAS
3:54 p.m. November 19, 1941

Cherokee County Attorney Nathaniel Cockwright was furious. Nothing had gone as planned. First, the family of the deceased refused to allow him into their home before the funeral. Cockwright had met with this poor family immediately after that stupid Texas ranger and idiot police chief had let the murderer run away right out of their jail. Actually, that wasn't an accurate description of what had happened. Those two fools released him and sent him away as if it was the most natural thing in the world.

Then, during his first meeting with the family, as Nathaniel assured them that the kid who had killed their son would get the electric chair, the father, in an excellent display of how the uneducated think, insisted that the fugitive was not the killer and that Nathaniel was after the wrong man. The father seemed to think that somewhere out there was some unknown assailant. Obviously he had been talking to that incompetent police chief, even though he claimed he hadn't. Nathaniel, naturally, understood the delusion the man was under. In all small towns, Elza being no exception, everyone knew one another. It was understandable that they would have trouble accepting that one of their own was capable of committing such a crime. From all the interviews that his two deputies had conducted, not a single person in Elza believed that this Jesse kid was responsible, even though almost half of them had heard him threaten to do it just a couple of hours before the murder. In his years as Cherokee County C.A., Nathaniel had run across this kind of backwoods mentality before, but never to this great of an extent. The people of Elza were so confident in their belief that they began to refuse to even talk to the deputies.

Then came the funeral. Nathaniel had planned every minute of the event. First he was going to arrive with the family in a limousine rented at the C.A. office's expense. That part went out the window when the family had refused to see him or let him into their house.

Nevertheless, the day could still be salvaged.

He had spent more than an hour the previous day with the pastor and the funeral director. The funeral director agreed to help the C.A. make sure that the funeral went smoothly and without any problems. By smoothly, the C.A. meant that if the murderer happened to show up, which was unlikely, the pastor would have someone point him out to one of the two C.A.'s office deputies who would be discretely standing in the back of the church. The brutal killer would then, again very discretely since it was a funeral, be taken into custody by one of the sheriff's department deputies.

That morning the two deputy C.A.'s made the appropriate calls, and thus the press had arrived, this time in far greater numbers than before. There were easily fifty or more reporters and photographers out front when Nathaniel arrived. As he predicted, the wire services had picked up the story of the "Alligator Killer." By Tuesday evening Vivian and Anita were fielding calls from as far away as Atlanta and Denver. Everyone wanted to see this evil kid go down.

The funeral director's other job, which he had failed at miserably, was to make sure to arrange the seating so that County Attorney Cockwright would sit next to Cliff's mother. Nothing would look better on the cover of the papers than for the next Texas Attorney General, or possibly even Governor, to be at the funeral consoling the grieving mother. Unfortunately, the idiot running the funeral couldn't even get that simple task correct.

Since he couldn't get into the parents' house, Nathaniel's backup plan was to stand out in front of the church to greet the family when they arrived. He would open the car door for the mother, give her a consoling hug, all before the cameras, and then escort her and the senseless father into the church where he would continue to hold the mother's hand throughout the service. As arranged with the funeral director, a few photographers, chosen by the two deputy County Attorneys, would be allowed to come around to the front for a few minutes, take a few pictures, and then leave, all as discretely as possible to avoid disrupting the service any more than absolutely necessary.

Apparently, even though the funeral director and this Reverend Anderson had both sat through the planning session and had seemingly understood the importance to the citizens of Cherokee County to see the pain this family was experiencing and see how their elected officials were making sure justice was being served, both men deliberately went to great lengths to ensure that the press was not allowed inside the building. In hindsight, Nathaniel thought he should have put his own people in charge of managing the funeral. The hillbilly preacher and funeral director probably played pinochle with the dimwitted police chief who had his own deputies at the door keeping the press out.

Of course, none of this mattered, anyway. First, the family, in another display of the mindless mentality of the uneducated, chose not to take advantage of the limousines that Nathaniel had so graciously sent, opting instead to attend their son's funeral in their own pickup trucks. By the time the C.A. realized that the people getting out of the dirty old farm truck was the deceased's family, the press had rushed in before Nathaniel could get anywhere near the door to console the mother and escort her into the church. As Nathaniel was fighting his way past the press, some kid got out of the first truck, holding his arm around the mother, and walked into the building with her and the father and their two younger children behind. Once inside the church, this same unknown kid and some teenaged girl took the seats that should have been reserved for Nathaniel. The C.A. still tried to work his way in the pew, but thanks to that kid and the girl there was no room. Nathaniel then tried to get a seat in the back of the church, but by that point the place was so packed with dirt farmers that there was simply no room. As a result, to his utter humiliation, the Attorney for Cherokee County had to spend the funeral standing outside with the reporters, who naturally wanted to know why he wasn't attending the service.

When the funeral was over, the entire church full of people proceeded to their cars and drove over to the Elza Cemetery for the graveside service. This time, Nathaniel was better prepared. He had made sure that his county car would be at the head of the prerecession, right behind the family. He also made sure that the press had maps and plenty of lead-time to allow them to be waiting, cameras in hand, when he got out of his car and met the family before any of the rest of the mourners got in the way. Again, this would have made for great pictures had it not been for the idiotic behavior of the police chief.

When the hearse carrying the deceased and the two vehicles with immediate family (and that unknown kid and his girlfriend) arrived, the police chief sent them along a service road up the back of the cemetery, well away from the awaiting journalists. When Nathaniel's car got to the turnoff, he rolled down his window and insisted on being allowed to join the immediate family, but that stupid police chief steadfastly refused the County official entrance, claiming that the family wanted it that way. So Nathaniel, like everyone else, parked out in front of the cemetery. Then when he got to the gate, two police deputies refused to allow the press and county officials in, again claiming to do so at the family's request. Nathaniel tried to explain that such exclusion couldn't possibly apply to the County Attorney, only to have one of the two irrational hillbilly halfwit cops, one of whom curiously had no neck and looked somewhat like a toad, insist that it applied to him specifically.

So understandably, Nathaniel Cockwright was in an ill mood when he approached the Tidwell family home after the graveside service. Not only had every opportunity of a quality cover photograph already been lost, all of the press had already left town to submit their stories without a single photograph of County Attorney Nathaniel Cockwright. However, knowing that they had purposely kept him out of the funeral, he still felt obligated to pay his respects because there was no way he could prosecute the killer without several more encounters with these daft farmers.

There were at least twenty-five or thirty cars parked around the house. Many of the men, all wearing their Sunday best, were standing out front smoking cigarettes and eating anything from fried chicken to pork chops. Among those standing out front holding a plate of chicken was Police Chief Jefferson Hightower and the two impudent deputies who had refused to allow Cockwright into the cemetery.

Nathaniel nodded his head as he passed the chief and the other farm folk hanging around the front of the house. He preferred not to have to speak to the illiterates of Cherokee County. That was partly due to the fact that he hated the way these dumb East Texans abused the English language, but the real truth was that he always felt like these cow herders and chicken farmers were laughing at him behind his back. He didn't fit in with these people, and he knew it as well as they did.

When County Attorney Nathaniel Cockwright got to the porch steps, the two police deputies stepped off the porch and blocked his way. Nathaniel stopped before them and then looked back at the chief, expecting the empty-headed law officer to at least have the aptitude if not the courtesy to tell his deputies to get out of the way.

"We've been asked not to allow you into the house, Mr. Cockwright. If you'd like something to eat, one of my boys will be happy to go make you a plate," the chief explained.

"I'd like to at least show my respects to the mother," Cockwright protested, partly angry and partly bewildered.

"Please, out of respect for the family, do us this one favor."

Suddenly the screen door opened. The father stepped out, followed by his wife and the young man who had sat next to them at the funeral, along with the teenage girl. The man, unashamedly in tears, shook the boy's hand and then gave him a big bear hug. Next the wife hugged the boy and kissed him on the cheek. She then hugged and kissed the girl. After that the boy turned to face Nathaniel with the girl holding onto his arm. The two brainless deputies stepped out of the way, and the boy and girl came down the steps.

Reaching out to shake Cockwright's hand Jesse said, "Hello, Mr. Cockwright. I'm Jesse Rose. I'd like to surrender."

#

FIRST BAPTIST CHURCH
ELZA TEXAS
2:00 p.m. November 19, 1941

Cherokee-One-Leg climbed gingerly out of his Model-AA pickup truck. He was wearing his only suit, and rather than his old dusty cavalry hat he wore a black fedora. He'd ordered the hat and the suit years before from the Montgomery Ward Company at the insistence of his wife. The suit was black with narrow pinstripes, with pleated and cuffed pants and a kerchief in the front pocket. He had to admit that it was dapper.

This was the second time he'd worn it. The other time was for his wife's funeral. She had spent hours studying the Ward's catalogue picking it out. It was a shame that she had never seen him in it. He had just never found the right time. The old soldier felt a tear come to his eye as he thought about her.

He parked near the back of the large red brick church, knowing his place. A person of color wouldn't walk through the front door. Normally he'd never walk into that church at all. There were churches for the colored folks. But even in Elza, funerals were different. Everyone knew the Tidwells. Paying respects was expected. Cherokee would not be the only colored person there that day, though they all would enter though the back, climb the narrow staircase, and sit in the balcony.

The old church building was a result of the oil boom when there had been a lot of money in the little town. There was probably a time when it was almost full on Sunday mornings, but nowadays the balcony was only opened on Easter, and the occasional funeral.

The church was long and narrow with a stage, for lack of better word, holding the pulpit and choir loft, and an indoor baptism pool behind the choir. There were about a dozen rows of pews with an aisle down the middle, making actually twenty-four pews, all capable of seating about ten people comfortably. The balcony was "U" shaped. In the back it sat over the last five rows of the lower sanctuary. On the sides the balcony continued with two rows.

Cherokee, with the help of his crutch, made his way up the narrow staircase and found a seat along with the other people of color on the right-side balcony. The back balcony would be reserved for the overflow white folks.

The seat on the side balcony was exactly what Cherokee wanted. He was toward the front of the church and could easily look back and see the entire congregation. So far the plan was working as expected. Jesse was sitting with Cliff's family at the front, almost right below Cherokee. From where he sat, the old black man could easily spot anything out of the normal, or in this case, anyone who was not mourning Clifford Tidwell besides that silly C.A. Cockwright.

He spotted the man almost immediately. The Indian fighter's eyes might not be what they once were, but picking out this man didn't require an eagle's sight. Everyone else in the church was with family, but this man was alone. His suit was different. These people were farmers and small town folk. They all wore old, unstylish suits that were bought straight out of a catalog like Cherokee's. This man's suit was freshly pressed and fitted by a tailor.

The man also kept looking at Jesse. Everyone else had their eyes on Reverend Anderson or the choir as they sang, but this guy never took his eyes off Jesse. It was him. He looked just like his brother. It had been five years, but Cherokee had not forgotten the face. There was now no reason to question what had happened to Clifford. The past had, in fact, come back to haunt them.

The plan, so far, was playing out as Cherokee had hoped. Finally, just as expected, the man stopped looking at Jesse and glanced up at the balcony. The two men locked eyes.

#

When the funeral ended, Cherokee worked his way down the stairs and outside as quickly as he could under the circumstances. Even with only one leg, he was still out before most of the mourners. He made his way around to the front and watched as the man walked out of the sanctuary. Again, he was alone. Cherokee kept his distance but didn't let the man out of his sight. It seemed strange, a tall black man with a peg leg and a crutch should have stood out in the sea of white faces, but the old warrior had long since learned that in a crowd like this he was almost invisible. That invisibility didn't bother him. He'd grown accustomed to it, and more importantly, at times like this, it was useful.

The stranger lingered under a sycamore smoking a cigarette while everyone filtered out of the church. He tended to stay somewhat behind the tree, almost as if he was hiding.

Then the man straightened up and watched the steps to the church. Cherokee looked around and saw a young woman coming out. She was the Stoker girl.

She walked out into the parking lot, looking as if she were searching for someone. The man continued to hide behind the tree, watching the girl as she came toward him.

While Cherokee was watching the man, Chief Hightower walked up to the old Indian.

"Thanks for looking after Jesse, Cherokee."

"You knew?" Cherokee answered, while not taking his eyes off the man behind the tree.

"I figured it out. The boys always liked being around you. I drove out by your place yesterday and saw Gemma Crawford's car."

When Jewel got close to the tree, the man jumped out from behind it, surprising her. Startled, she wrapped her arms around him and hugged him. They laughed as he led her to a car.

Cherokee, leaning on his crutch, looked at Jefferson and nodded his head over toward the man and the Stoker girl.

"Do you know that man?" Cherokee asked.

Jefferson watched the man as he held the door of a red 1940 Chevrolet Special Deluxe Coupe convertible open for Jewel.

"No. The girl's Jewel Stoker. I don't know who the man is. Jesse said that she had a boyfriend in Jacksonville. That must be him."

"He's your killer."

Jefferson looked at the old Indian. "How do you know?"

"I just know," Cherokee answered.

As the man got into his car, he briefly glanced back at Cherokee and Jefferson.

Jefferson pulled a notepad out of his pocket and began taking down the man's license tag number. All the other cars began lining up behind the family in the hearse. The man and Jewel pulled out of the parking lot and drove away in the opposite direction.

Jefferson looked up at the line of cars forming up.

"I've got to get over to the cemetery," the chief said.

"When's that Ranger coming back?"

"I don't know. A few days, maybe a week."

"You're gonna need 'im."

#

CHEROKEE COUNTY COURTHOUSE
RUSK, TEXAS
8:38 a.m. November 21, 1941

Cherokee County Attorney Nathaniel Elbridge Cockwright had just delivered the most compelling oratory of his life. In just under forty minutes he had given an address that was eloquent, deliberate, detailed, and quite frankly, an unarguably persuasive discourse. Everyone in the courtroom was brought to tears as he described the inhumane details of the murder. He even garnered a couple of "you tell 'ems" from the audience. Judge Buckner, of course, put a quick stop to the outbursts, but it still served to prove to Nathaniel that he was making his point.

An arraignment in Judge Nehemiah Buckner's court was usually limited to the accused and the arresting officer, but Nathaniel and his staff had made sure that everyone in the county knew what was happening that morning, ensuring that the courtroom was packed with reporters, spectators, and even the C.A. from Anderson county, who just wanted to watch.

Up to this point, everything, again, had gone terribly wrong. The punk kid had waited until late in the day to surrender. By then the reporters had all gone home to file their stories. Had he done it as soon as the funeral was over or even at the graveside ceremony, their picture would have been on the cover of every paper between Houston and Dallas.

As unimaginably perplexing as it sounds, the killer had been sitting right there next to the family through the entire funeral and graveside service, right in front of the entire town, and not a single soul bothered to mention it to the authorities. Even the dumb-cluck police chief knew the murderer was there and didn't say a word.

When he got Jesse back to Rusk, Nathaniel put his deputies to work on the phones, making sure that every paper in the state knew about the arrest. But most of the papers missed getting the story out in the evening editions. He did get it mentioned on WBAP radio out of Fort Worth, though. The result of that was beautiful. The courthouse was packed with spectators for. Even the balcony was full. Nathaniel had hoped for a good turnout, and in fact he had prepared his arrival for it. Normally he would have parked around back in the spot designated for the County Attorney and entered through the small door next to the back staircase. But he anticipated some press, so he'd had Primrose pick him up at home and drop him off on the square in front of the courthouse. He'd climbed the steps, briefcase in hand, as throngs of reporters crowded around him, snapping pictures and asking questions. When he got to the top, he stopped before going in to deliver a few brief comments about justice being served and the safety of the good people of Cherokee County and of course, answer a some questions. He then posed for a few pictures before walking into the courthouse.

#

The courtroom was already crowded when Cockwright arrived, and by the time Judge Buckner walked in, it was standing room only. The defendant was seated to Nathaniel's right, surrounded by a bevy of attorneys, of course. That would play into Nathaniel's hands. He had already planned to play up the fact that this killer had come from one of the wealthiest families in the County. The fact that he had a half-dozen expensive lawyers was not going to play well with these small-town bumpkins.

Nathaniel had just about had it up to his ears with the kid's legal team. No less than four were waiting at the sheriff's office when they arrived back from the funeral with the defendant. They made all sorts of demands, most of which the C.A. felt unobligated to comply to. Most notably, they insisted on seeing their client before the arraignment. That wasn't about to happen. Nathaniel's plan, which he had come up with the moment he'd made the arrest, was to spend the night questioning the punk, hoping to break him down in the wee hours when the kid was exhausted. He had started the questioning as they drove in from Elza, but the dumb brat never said a single word. So when he got him to the jail, he intended to continue the interrogation, and made a good effort, but again, this arrogant little delinquent never so much as opened his mouth. Then one of these overpaid ambulance chasers marched into the sheriff's office with no less than Judge Buckner in tow, ordering Nathaniel to allow the self-important barristers to be present during questioning. On top of that, the judge released the kid without a bail hearing. He set bail and the lawyer posted it standing right there in Sheriff Cadwalder's office.

Nathaniel proudly sat down with all confidence that whatever the defense countered would sound foolish in comparison to the speech he had made before Judge Buckner.

"Thank you for your long-winded discourse, Mr. Cockwright," Judge Buckner said to a round of muffled snickers. "Would the accused like to rebut?"

Nathaniel ignored the admonition. He was used to the judge's sarcasm. The important thing was that the press and spectators had heard what he'd had to say.

The lead attorney stood and answered, "No thank you, your honor."

Nathaniel couldn't help but smile.

"How does the defendant plea?"

The attorney stood again. "He pleads not guilty, your Honor."

"I'd like to hear it from the defendant, if you don't mind Counselor."

The attorney sat down and nodded to Jesse, who stood. "Not guilty, your Honor."

As Jesse sat down, Nathaniel leaned back in his chair, trying hard to contain his elation. Had the dumb kid and his lawyers pleaded guilty, this thing would have been over and done with in a couple of days, but as it was, Nathaniel had the chance to keep this in the headlines for a month or more.

"That will be all for now, Bailiff. Please lead the defendant down to the sheriff's office. I'd like to see the lead attorneys for both sides in my chambers now," Buckner ordered and then slammed down his gavel and left the room.

#

Wilhelm Dinkler III shook hands with County Attorney Cockwright, who for some reason he wanted to call Cockfight, and seated himself in one of the two chairs in front of the judge's enormous mahogany desk. Wilhelm, Wil to his friends, had defended over a hundred criminal cases. This was his twenty-fifth murder case and by far the most publicized. Normally he went to great lengths to protect his client from even being mentioned in the press, but this C.A. had quite a head start. It was rumored around the courthouse that he had contacted the newspapers the very minute he heard about the crime. This, of course, was going to make things considerably more difficult because the jury would, most likely, have their opinions formed before the trial began, which quite frankly was what this idiot C.A. apparently wanted. The fool needed an edge. His speech showed what kind of attorney he was. In Houston, on an even field, Dinkler would have had this thing won on the first day of testimony.

On the bright side, the C.A. had almost no case. A halfwit fresh out of law school could poke holes in his case. Dinkler had yet to lose a murder trial. The C.A. was clearly trying to railroad the kid to further his political ambitions. Dinkler knew all about Cockwright's various failed attempts at running for office.

That's it. He's the one they called 'Cockfight' at some debate.

Judge Buckner, now having changed out of his robe in his private bathroom, walked in and sat down behind his desk. He had his jacket off, and his sleeves were rolled up to the elbow. He was wearing a tie, but the knot was loosened.

Dinkler smiled. Judges were all the same. Heaven help the attorney who walked into those chambers sans coat and with his tie loose, but in all his years in the legal trade Dinkler had never met a judge in his chambers who had on a coat and knotted tie.

"Gentlemen, this case has not even begun, and this kid has already been hung in the press. I had to park two blocks away, and this was just the arraignment. I'm afraid we will have trouble getting a jury. I have half a mind to send it over to Anderson County."

"Your honor," Nathaniel blurted.

"That's what I thought, Cockwright," Judge Buckner said before Nathaniel could finish his sentence. "Now you listen to me. I don't want any more of those half-hour speeches. This nonsense ends here and now."

Nathaniel cringed. "I apologize, sir. It couldn't have been that long, though."

"Thirty-seven minutes forty-eight seconds. I owe the bailiff two bits. I told him you couldn't keep it under forty-five.

"Now, I want this kid to get a fair shake, so quit the foolishness with the newspapers. And, by god, you better not be wasting my time. My phone was ringing 'til almost midnight with people from Elza who claim this kid didn't do it."

"My case is solid, your honor."

"Well you better have more than you put in the brief, because if Mr. Dinkler here spent more than a week in law school he'll chew this up without needing his teeth."

Dinkler simply smiled as he realized that this meeting was to pull the reins in on the C.A.

"Mr. Dinkler, do you have any questions?"

"No, your honor."

"Are you having any more problems with the Sheriff's Office or the C.A.'s office?" Buckner asked, with a glance at Cockwright.

"No, sir. We're not having any problems."

"How much lead-time do you need? I'd like to get this thing over with as quickly as possible."

"I think a week or so will be sufficient."

"Good," Buckner said as he looked down at the calendar on his desk. "Let's start working on getting a jury on Monday, and with some luck we can begin on the following Friday. Any objections?"

Both attorneys shook their heads.

"Good," Buckner said and then looked at Cockwright. "Remember what I said about the press."

#

SHANTYTOWN
ELZA, TEXAS

November 21, 1941

Darnell "Shakes" Blankenship walked along the railroad tracks toward the shantytown holding a rolled up newspaper under his arm. The shantytown wasn't what it once had been. None of them were. Most of the people who had populated these little villages around the country had moved on to California or were slowly finding work.

Shakes, of course, had not.

Oh, he wasn't the hermit he had been a few years before. He spent more time riding the rails and less in his little villa in New Birmingham. In some ways, Shakes was a new man. He was a man with a purpose. He still had trouble with the drink, and he doubted that he'd ever have a job, but he was now a man who knew where he was going and why.

Right that minute Shakes was headed to his little home in the Southern Hotel. In Atlanta, a couple of days before, he had seen a newspaper. He was in the first boxcar headed west by lunchtime.

He walked on past the shantytown and turned up the little overgrown lane that led to New Birmingham. He had no plan. He really wasn't sure what he could do, but the mathematician in him refused to believe that this couldn't possibly be a simple coincidence.

#

CHEROKEE COUNTY COURTHOUSE
RUSK, TEXAS
5:30 p.m., November 21, 1941

Nathaniel Cockwright was having another bad day. He leaned back in his chair and put his feet on his desk. He'd have a drink, but Cherokee was a dry county, and it wouldn't look good for the C.A. to keep liquor in his office when everyone knew that you had to drive thirty miles to get a bottle.

It had all started so perfectly. He had made a grand show for the reporters on the courthouse steps. He then made an excellent presentation for the judge, who apparently knew nothing about presiding over a murder trial.

That was where it all headed downhill. First the judge gave him a pretty good lecture about using the press. Nathaniel expected as much, but he hadn't expected it in front of the defense attorney. Buckner didn't needed to humiliate him and then threaten a change in venue. That was utterly unnecessary. The threat was also not as effective as Buckner may have thought. This case would be a cakewalk almost anywhere. All Nathaniel needed to do was set the scene. No jury would let this one go without a conviction once they got the gory details.

The problem Cockwright had was compelling evidence. The judge seemed convinced that this Houston lawyer could take apart the prosecution, which again, Nathaniel doubted. Still, just a little more evidence would sew it up. He had the kid at the place of death at the time of the murder. He had motive, sort of. And he had the kid openly threatening to kill the victim. With a jury made up of East Texas tomato farmers that should make the case, but Nathaniel would feel a lot better with a little more, especially after the remarks Buckner made.

All day he, Primrose, and Coleman had been down in Elza knocking on doors. Well, it was mostly Primrose because Coleman was almost useless at that sort of thing. Nevertheless every time those two checked in, they had nothing. And by nothing, Cockwright meant just that. It seemed that the whole town had closed ranks. No one wanted to help. Those people who did talk seemed to think that Jesse was a model citizen. Not a single person believed he did it.

Then there was the problem with the two girls. First, the girl at the heart of all this, her testimony could set this thing up. The only problem was that neither of those two bumbling idiots could find her. Elza was not a big place. Coleman and Primrose shouldn't have had any problem, but so far, the two clowns hadn't so much as laid eyes on her. Then there was the murderer's girlfriend. She had to be feeling pretty humiliated since her boyfriend had just killed his buddy because both boys were in love with another girl. In a normal world, she would be ready to sell the kid up the river, but not in Elza. This doll insisted that the punk didn't do it and threatened to call the police chief if Primrose didn't get off her porch.

So when Primrose and Coleman walked into his office after wasting another day in Elza, Nathaniel was, understandably, not in a particularly good mood.

"Good news, boss," Primrose opened with a big smile.

Cockwright closed his eyes and rubbed his temples. He was in no mood for Roosevelt Primrose. "What'd you do, win the Hit Parade?"

Primrose looked at Coleman. "You go first."

"The chief and that Ranger are holding out on us. They got prints off the car."

Cockwright's eyes opened. "When?"

"The day after. The car was down at a local garage and the Ranger took prints."

"Where's the car now?"

"It's being moved to the sheriff's impound yard as we speak."

"Who has the prints?"

"Most likely the Ranger took 'em back to Dallas to have 'em processed."

Cockwright sat up. "If they match the kid's, we've got 'im."

"I'd say so."

"I want photographs of the car, and get me those prints."

"That's the other news, boss," Primrose piped in. "I had a chat with the undertaker. The chief had a kid take crime-scene photographs. He took a lot of shots, and according to the undertaker, he got every detail."

The gears in his head started turning as Nathaniel's day suddenly picked up. "Okay, here's what we'll do. Coleman, get on the phone to Austin right now. Tell them that I want those prints. No. Tell them that you're going to Dallas with the kid's prints and you want them compared right away. Then bring the results back yourself. We're not trusting that dimwit Ranger any more than we have to."

"You want me to drive to Dallas tonight?"

Nathaniel exhaled, trying not to lose his temper. The sooner he got out of this one-horse town the better.

"Take a county car and get a hotel room somewhere halfway. I want those prints in my hand by noon tomorrow."

"Well, I don't know if I can make it back by noon," Coleman debated with a tone that showed he was convinced that he couldn't possibly make Cockwright's deadline.

"Just go and get back as soon as you can," Cockwright ordered in exasperation.

"Yes, sir," Coleman said and immediately turned and got out before a full-blown Cockwright fit.

"Should I get the Sheriff to send someone for the photographs?" Primrose asked, preparing himself for an outburst.

"No," Nathaniel answered, as he thought, "No, I don't want the sheriff involved. You go personally and bring them back here."

Corcwright's mind was churning.

"Here's what we're going to do," Cockwright continued. "We're going to take the whole jury down to Elza to see the site for themselves. Then we're going to pass out copies of the photographs. That will do it. No Texas jury will let this kid off after seeing it up close and personal."

#

MAIN STREET
ELZA, TEXAS
August 7, 1936

As the late-summer heat settled in, so did the change of pace in and around Elza. With temperatures hovering in the upper nineties, farm work tended to shift to the early mornings and late evenings. With their afternoons free, a lot of the farmers who previously had taken advantage of the newly established "Elza Farm Delivery Service" now came into town to replenish their supplies and, more importantly, to catch up on the local gossip that was regularly distributed under the awning at McMillan's. Thus, on this exceptionally hot afternoon, Jesse, Cliff, and Jewel had little more to do with their day than sit on the curb in front of the Palace sipping RC Colas.

"We could sit out here all day and not see her, you know," Cliff piped.

"Who?" Jesse asked.

Jewel and Cliff looked at each other.

"Do we have to go through this every day?" Jewel asked out of exasperation.

Jesse's face showed that he was genuinely confused. "What do you mean?"

"Honestly, Jewel, he's the smartest and dumbest person I've ever met all at the same time."

Jewel began to giggle as Gemma and her younger sister Jettie came out of Anna-Ruth's dress shop and began walking north on the sidewalk. Jesse's eyes focused on Gemma.

"Where do you suppose they're goin'?" Cliff asked, not expecting an answer.

"McMillan's to get the mail," Jewel answered matter-of-factly.

Jesse and Cliff looked at her.

"They go every day."

"How do you know that?" Cliff asked.

"I saw Gemma a couple of weeks ago while you two were off on a delivery. She said they go every afternoon to get the mail and the afternoon paper."

"How come we haven't seem 'em?" Jesse asked.

"Because you two are always on deliveries or off fishin'.

Jesse stood. "Come on," he ordered.

Jewel stood also, with a big grin on her face. "Come on," she ordered Cliff who was still sitting.

Reluctantly Cliff stood. "Great, we get to go watch Don Juan shudder and stammer and generally embarrass the entire male gender."

A few minutes later the three of them came to the porch under the awning of McMillan's General Merchandise store. As usual, a few of the older locals were sitting out front, and with them was Chief Hightower and the Lowery brothers, Toad and Hunker.

When the kids arrived, the two Crawford girls had already gone inside. Jesse, Cliff, and Jewel were in the process of heading in when Chief Hightower stood with a Dr Pepper in his hand and looked down the highway.

"They're here."

Everyone out front stood and watched as a line of trucks with music blasting came rolling east along highway 84.

"It's the carnival," Cliff observed with a sense of excitement.

Every summer for as far back as any of the kids could recall, a carnival had rolled into town and set up camp in a field on the south end of Main Street just past the domino hall. For kids, like Jesse, Jewel, and Cliff, it was one of the most exciting weekends of the year. All the farmers and their families would come in for the event, even folks from as far away as Reklaw, Sacul, and Maydelle would show up.

The kids watched with understandable excitement as the colorful trucks drove past and made the turn up Main Street with music blasting on loud speakers. The carnival always slipped out of town in the night, almost unnoticed, but coming into town, the show did everything possible to draw attention.

After they had passed, Cliff walked over to the chief. "Chief Hightower, did you know they were comin'?"

"Of course. They always send an advance man to lease a lot," he answered with a grin, knowing that it aggravated the boy that something this big was going on without him knowing beforehand.

"Yesterday you and me sat right here and argued about who was the better hitter, Lou Gehrig or Paul Warner. And, you're still wrong, by the way. Gehrig can hit circles around Warner."

"Well, he didn't last night."

"Maybe not, but in twenty years, folks will still be talking about how good Gehrig was, and no one's goin' to remember Paul Warner."

"Well, in twenty years, if Lou Gehrig is still hittin' homers, I'll concede."

"He probably will be, but that's not the point. The point is, we sat here and argued baseball for the better part of an hour, and you didn't feel like it was important to mention that the carnival was comin' to town?" The boy argued with exasperation.

"I guess I figured that you'd see 'em when they got here just like everybody else."

"It wouldn't have hurt for you to mention it."

"Well, Cliff, I didn't realize that aside from keeping the peace my job required me to report all interesting happenings to you."

Frustrated, Cliff turned and walked back to his two friends. "Maybe you should put it on your list of things to do."

Jefferson laughed and took a sip of his Dr Pepper as Cliff joined his two friends who were well entertained by Cliff's frustration with the chief.

The kids started for the steps just as the Crawford sisters came out the door. While Jesse's full attention was fixed on Gemma, Cliff noticed Cherokee One-Leg pull up to the gas pump in his old truck.

"Uh, hi, Gemma," Jesse said with a bit of a shudder in his voice.

As the two girls came down the steps, Gemma looked uncomfortable as she replied, "Hi."

The sisters began walking toward Main Street. Jewel gave Jesse a shove to follow along.

Cliff shook his head in disgust. "I can't take this," he said as he turned and headed over to Cherokee.

Jesse followed after Gemma, with Jewel a step behind. He looked down at the letters Gemma was carrying.

"Did you get the mail?"

Gemma just looked at him as he realized how stupid of a question it was.

"Did you see the carnival come in?" He asked in an attempt to stave off humiliation.

"Yeah."

"They'll probably be open tonight. Are y'all goin'?"

"I suppose so."

"So maybe I'll see you there," he said as he stopped walking, Jewel stopping next to him.

Gemma smiled. "Maybe," she coyly replied and continued walking away.

He watched as she and her sister walked toward their mom's store. Jettie whispered something to Gemma, and they giggled. Obviously it had something to do with Jesse, but he didn't care.

Jewel patted him on the shoulder. "Smooth, Valentino."

While Jesse and Jewel were with Gemma and her sister, Cliff walked over to the old Indian.

"Hi, Cherokee."

The old man just nodded his direction as he began filling his truck.

"Did you see the carnival comin' in?

Cherokee glanced at the boy and shook his head.

"I suspect that everybody in town will be goin'."

The old man smiled at the boy. " I 'spec' that could be interestin'. You keep your eyes open. I'll be on Main Street. Let me know what ya see."

"You won't come to the carnival?"

Cherokee shook his head. "There's some places that folks from 'the Grove' don't go."

Cliff took on a sad look on his face as he realized what Cherokee meant.

"It shouldn't otta' be that way, Cherokee. There's kids in 'the Grove.' They should be able to go to the carnival."

"I know. But that's the way it is."

"You fought in the army. Your son got all those medals. There shouldn't be no place you can't go."

Cherokee smiled down at the boy as he topped off his tank and put the hose handle back on the pump.

"Keep your eyes open," he said to Cliff as Jesse and Jewel walked back over.

Cherokee nodded at the three kids and then walked into McMillan's to pay his bill.

Chapter 11

301 RED OAK AVE.,
ELZA, TEXAS
5:45 p.m. November 28, 1941

J ewel Stoker was uncomfortable as she walked to the front door of the Rose's house. She'd known Jesse all of her life, but she had never been to his house. In fact, she had never so much as even met his parents. That was probably what made her uncomfortable. She had seen them many times, of course. They looked like nice people, but looks could be deceiving. Almost anyone in town would tell you that Garvis Rose was as nice of a woman as you'd ever expect to meet on the surface, but she could easily be as downright mean a person as you could ever expect to meet.

Almost anyone in Elza who owned a store had a story or two about Mrs. Rose. Even George Henry McMillan, who was as affable a person as Jewel had ever known, once remarked that Mrs. Rose considered anyone short of an oil tycoon beneath her. That, naturally, came after she had spent an hour in his store complaining that there just wasn't a decent place to shop in "This entire one-horse town."

So naturally, Jewel was uncomfortable as she stepped onto the porch and knocked on the door. Mr. and Mrs. Rose could be the most gracious and wonderful people in the world, like the Tidwells, and Jewel would still probably not be welcomed. Not after the scene her father had made in the Palace. Had he not gotten drunk and made that scene, Jesse would not be on trial for a crime that everybody in Elza knew for sure he hadn't committed.

It was only a few moments after she knocked that the door opened. To her relief, it was Jesse and not one of his parents. Although she was a little frightened and horribly worried for him, she couldn't help but smile at the sight of him. Jesse, she realized, always put a smile on her face. He was wearing his jeans and a white t-shirt, like usual, the only difference was the stressed look on his face.

"Jewel," he said with a sudden smile.

There was the Jesse she'd grown up with. Jewel had been to the courtroom that morning, but more than once she had thought to herself how much he had changed since she'd last seen him. Suddenly she realized that the difference was that in the court he never smiled.

"Hi, Jess."

Jesse opened the screen, "Come on in."

Jewel smiled politely and shook her head. "It's nice out. Can you come for a walk?"

Jesse could see that she was nervous and understood. Not many people visited the Roses. He glanced over his shoulder and said, "Sure, let me get my jacket."

A moment later Jesse came out, and the two instinctively walked to the street and down the block past the only row of brick homes in Elza.

"I saw you in court today. Thanks for coming."

"Oh, Jesse, of course I came."

"Don't you have to go to work?" He asked.

"I slipped out for a little while. I can probably come for a couple of hours a day. How are you holdin' up?"

Jesse shrugged.

"You must be scared."

"The lawyers say that the C.A. doesn't have case."

"What do you think?"

"I don't know what to think."

"I feel awful. My dad caused all this."

"It's not his fault."

"Yeah, it is. If he hadn't barged into the Palace that night, you two wouldn't have gotten in that fight and you wouldn't be in this mess."

"How is your pa?"

"He's okay. He'll be down at the county farm for another month."

"Hey," Jesse said suddenly remembering. "Cliff said you got a boyfriend."

Jewel smiled broadly. "Yeah," she said tenderly. "He's good to me. I'm really happy. I'm a little afraid to let him meet Daddy, though. He's a little older. You know my daddy. He's not gonna like anybody I see."

"He's gotta meet your dad sometime, you know," Jesse said as he looked down at her belly.

"I really messed up, Jesse. But I love 'im. And he's good to me. I think we might be gettin' married this weekend. We're goin' to keep it a small thing, you know, with all that's goin' on."

The two reached the end of the block and turned the corner onto Main Street without saying anything more.

"I can't believe that Cliff's gone," she said solemnly.

"I know. Every day I think of somethin' I want to tell 'im, but then I realize that I can't."

"I do that too."

"Can't the chief or somebody find out what really happened?"

"Remember when we were kids and that Texas Ranger came to town? He's been lookin' into it. I don't think he's gonna let it go until he gets the guy."

"I remember him," she said with some sadness. "It wasn't long after my mom...left."

Jesse glanced at her, and a knot formed in his stomach.

As they reached Main Street, about a block to the north, Hunker and Toad Lowery were hanging a banner across the street reading, "FREE JESSE." Hunker was standing on an extension ladder, and Toad was on the ground holding it.

Jesse watched the Lowerys in silence and finally looked at Jewel. "Jewel, your mama. She didn't run off on you."

She looked somewhat patronizingly at him. "It's okay, Jesse. Everybody knows that she ran off on me and Daddy."

Jesse looked directly in her eyes. "I saw her that night. Cliff and me, we saw her. She didn't run off on you."

Jewel was stunned. "You saw her? And you never said anything?"

"Me and Cliff, you know, we used to sneak out all the time. We saw her. She was in the alley behind the Palace cryin'. She told us that there were some bad men tryin' to hurt your family. She said that she had to go 'cause they would hurt you."

Jewel started walking slowly up the street. Jesse locked in step beside her.

"One time I took the bus into Rusk and looked up mama in the courthouse records. Then I went to the library and started lookin' though the old newspapers. Did you ever hear of The Tomato Farm near Maydelle?"

"Yeah, I've heard of it."

"My grandmother ran it. She went to prison and killed herself."

Jesse shrugged. "Okay..."

"Don't you get it?" She said. "All those stories people say about my mother were true. She was a prostitute. My mom was a prostitute, and so was my grandmother."

Jesse stopped and stared at her. He had tears in his eyes. "Your mom wasn't," he said firmly.

"What makes you think you know?" She asked, beginning to get angry.

"Because she told me," Jesse answered with a tear running down his cheek. "She asked me and Cliff to take care of you. She knew all the things people said about her, too. Jewel, I don't know anything about your grandma, but your mama, all she did was love you."

Jewel had tears running down her cheek, "How come you never told me this before?" She asked angrily.

"She asked us not to."

Both stood silent. Neither noticed Toad Lowery walking toward them.

"Hey, Jesse. How do you like the banner?"

Jesse looked at Toad and smiled and wiped his eye. "Thanks Toad. It looks good."

"Jesse," Toad began, "me and Hunker, we gotta go testify. You know, on account of us findin' Cliff and all."

"I know, Toad."

"We ain't gonna say nothin' that goes against ya, I promise."

Hunker, having come off the ladder joined his brother and added, "We mean it, Jesse. We already talked about it. We'll lie if we got to, but we ain't gonna say nothin' that helps that County Attorney."

Jewel began to back away.

"It's okay, guys. Just answer their questions," Jesse answered.

"We just wanted you to know. We gotta get this banner up. Good luck buddy," Toad said as he reached to shake Jesse's hand.

Hunker reached out and shook Jesse's hand as well. "We mean, it, Jesse. Me and Toad pray for ya every day."

"Thanks guys," Jesse said with genuine warmth as the two brothers headed back to work.

Jewel had backed a few feet away by the time Jesse turned his attention back to her.

"I gotta get home, Jesse," she said with a crack in her voice.

"Jewel, I'm sorry."

Suddenly she ran back to him and hugged him tightly. Both had tears in their eyes. After a moment she backed away and looked into his face. She then wiped the tear from his cheek and kissed him tenderly.

"I always kind of loved you, you know," she said softly.

"I know," he said. "Cliff told me the night he died."

Jewel smiled, "You were always so in love with Gemma."

"I'm sorry."

She continued to smile as she let go of him. "Don't be. I'm glad it worked out this way."

Jesse just stood there as she hugged him again. "I love you, Jesse. I pray for you too."

She let go and began to walk away. "I've got to go. Rick's gonna pick me up at the house."

"Rick?" Jesse asked.

"My boyfriend," she reminded him.

"What's his last name?" Jesse asked as a cold tension swept through him.

"Hall," she said as she headed across Main Street.

Jesse smiled with relief as she headed away.

#

MAIN STREET – ELZA, TEXAS
Noon, December 3, 1941

Brewster McKinney reached over into the seat beside him and took a leather briefcase and pulled his large frame out of the Ford Coupe. The older he got, the stiffer his body seemed to be after a long drive. It didn't help that over the years he'd broken a half-dozen bones fighting criminals, not to mention harboring a twenty-six-year-old bullet wound. The only serious shoot-out in his Ranger career happened only a year after he'd gotten his star. The fight hadn't lasted more than a minute, and in the end three bank robbers lay dead, but not before the state's newest Ranger got shot.

The Rangers had a tip that the Waco bank was going to be robbed. Young Brewster McKinney and an older ranger by the name of Texas Jack Burnet had staked out the place from across the street. They saw five men walking in together, which was reason enough for concern, but they also had a picture of one of the men and knew that it was on. What McKinney and his partner didn't realize was that the group had left a young crook by the name Eliza Fenwick outside to watch their horses. Had Fenwick watched their horses like he was supposed to, the entire event probably would have ended without a shot, but as soon as his five partners went into the bank, Fenwick walked around behind the building to relieve himself. He returned just in time to see two Texas Rangers standing by the front door of the bank, waiting for the five robbers inside to come out and be apprehended. Fenwick, not being the brightest criminal in the world immediately pulled his gun and started shooting at the two Rangers.

Fenwick's first shot missed McKinney by inches. Immediately Fenwick's five friends came running out. The ensuing shoot-out lasted all of about a minute but resulted in three deaths. McKinney had drawn his weapon and shot Fenwick and then got two more of the bandits as they came running out the bank door. Lying wounded on the ground, Fenwick shot Brewster in the back. It was only a .22, but it still hurt.

Brewster's partner took down the other three. All three of those men were dead. The three men that McKinney shot, including Fenwick, were only wounded.

As Texas Jack said, "Wounded men can still shoot."

It occurred to McKinney that killing came far too easy to Texas Jack, and, maybe more importantly, he did it without remorse, which to McKinney was far worse. Years in the trade can do that to a man. Most of the old Rangers McKinney worked with in those days were like that. Young Brewster McKinney didn't want to become that kind of Ranger.

McKinney had been in a dozen more gun battles over the years, and he still hadn't killed anyone. But he also hadn't made the mistake of turning his back on any more wounded bandits either.

Twenty-six years later, Brewster was reminded of Eliza Fenwick every time he climbed out of his coupe. He also couldn't help but think that it was only blind luck that the wounded bandit didn't killed him.

He'd forgotten to notify Chief Hightower that he was coming back. He really hadn't seen the need. Hightower had made it clear that he wanted the help, and more importantly to McKinney, Captain Little Bigfoot McCullough had ordered him back.

McKinney knocked twice and then pushed the door open. He knew that the chief wasn't at his desk - he could see that through the window - but hopefully Hightower was either upstairs or in the back.

"Chief?" McKinney called as he walked into the police office.

Jefferson Hightower came rushing in behind McKinney. "Corporal."

McKinney turned around to see the chief, somewhat ruffled and out of breath, coming in the door.

"I wasn't expecting you. I was down the street at McMillan's when I saw you turn off the highway."

McKinney nodded and reached out to shake hands. "I apologize, Chief. I should have called."

"Not necessary. I'm just glad that you're back. The trial started yesterday morning," Hightower offered as they shook hands. "I have a little coffee made; you want some?"

"Yes, please."

"They delayed the trial a couple of days. Something about your fingerprints?"

McKinney smiled and sat his briefcase on the floor and relaxed in the chair across from the Chief's desk while Hightower poured two cups.

"I'll explain that. How's our boy?"

"He's holdin' up. He's scared, and he's still not talkin'. He's been out on bail, so at least he's home."

"My Captain has taken a special interest in this case."

"Why's that?"

"A number of things, really," McKinney began. "First of all, that C.A. had one of his boys camped out in my office all last week demanding immediate access to the prints I pulled off the car. He's welcome to 'em, of course, but instead of requesting through normal channels and waiting for us to get the verification on all the prints, he demanded that we give him what we had. That of course was only the deceased and Jesse's. My Captain agreed that I shouldn't hand anything over until every print on the car had been identified. The deputy C.A. called his boss, who immediately called Captain McCullough and ordered him to hand over the prints. Well, between you and me, the Governor himself doesn't have the guts to give an order to Captain Little Bigfoot McCullough. Bigfoot told him he'd get the prints in a day or two. So your C.A. called the Ranger Director down in Austin. This was the second time he's called Director Anthony on this case. That sent up a red flag with both Director Anthony and Captain McCullough, and together they decided that this case needed a little more thorough investigation. So I'm here, and there's nothin' that County Attorney can do about it."

Jefferson chuckled and then got serious. "Did the prints show anything?"

"Before I get to that, what was the name of the woman who supposedly ran off with the carnival?

"Mrs. Stoker. Sarah Stoker."

"What was her maiden name?"

Jefferson leaned back in his chair in thought. "I wish I could remember, Corporal. She married Irwin not long after she moved into town. I'm sure it's on record over at the courthouse. She had a little store. The files are in the back. I'm sure her name's on something back there."

"Was it a produce store?"

"Yeah, now that you mention it. She sold stuff the farmers brought in."

"Her name's Sarah Burney."

Jefferson nodded. "Yeah! That's right."

"You grew up around here, didn't you?"

"Yeah, right here in Elza."

"Do you remember a cathouse over south of Maydelle?"

"'Delilah's Tomato Farm.' Every teenage boy I grew up with wanted to get in that place. Me and a few buddies even drove over there once, but we chickened out before goin' in."

"Deliliah's real name was Juanita Carrillo Burney. "

Jefferson's eyes widened as McKinney continued. "Her father was a rich banker in San Antonio. Their family dated back to way before the Republic. Well, Juanita took up with a soldier. Apparently her old man didn't like him and ran her off. The soldier got himself killed, and she was left with a baby named Sarah."

"Well, I'll be damned," Jefferson uttered in astonishment, partly because of the story itself but partly because McKinney was able to find out all of this information. "Do you think that Sarah was one of her girls?"

"No, just the opposite in fact. I think Juanita tried to keep her shielded from it. That's probably why she was running a store way over here."

Brewster paused and took a long sip of coffee. "I was in on the raid that closed down that house. The Rangers normally don't go after places like that, but there was a crooked lumberyard owner who was caught up in bootlegging, prostitution, and tax evasion. We got him in the sweep. He ended up hanging himself. Juanita got ten years, which was way too much, but the bust got a lot of press, and it had to do with bootlegging and tax evasion so the judge took it out on her. She ended up hanging herself in the Goree Unit. We knew about the daughter and her produce store, but it was a legal business, and their taxes were paid, so we left them alone."

"There used to be a lot of stories about Sarah, even before she left. I remember hearing rumors that she was a floozy and such. I never believed any of those because she was as sweet and innocent a gal as you'd ever meet. So what's Sarah's connection to the Tomato Farm got to do with this?"

"When we raided the farm, one of the customers jumped on my back, and his brother bashed me in the head with a chair. When it was all said and done, the two brothers got themselves a few broken bones and five years in Eastham. Well, when I was researching Juanita, something about those two boys rang a bell, so I went through my old records. Their names were Richard and Peterson Crawford."

Jefferson stared at the Corporal and finally said, "That can't possibly be a coincidence."

"There's more," McKinney, continued. "The prints. Everything on the car belonged to the two boys except for a couple - one on the steering wheel, and one on the gearshift. I wouldn't have caught it if I hadn't looked up those two brothers' names. I crosschecked the prints from the car with the two we pulled when I arrested the Crawfords at the Tomato Farm. Sure enough, the prints belong Richard Crawford."

Jefferson showed excitement. "He's our guy."

"Not so fast," Brewster answered. "Two prints won't get a conviction, and it's sure not going to change the mind of that C.A. But we can definitely question him. His last known address is up in Jacksonville. I talked to the police chief over there. They know all about him. He's been in their jail a half-dozen times for things like drunkenness and fighting, all minor stuff. He's never had a real job. He hangs out at the pool halls. They say he's a runner for a bookie over in Tyler. We've got a Ranger up there lookin' into the operation."

McKinney pulled a mugshot from his briefcase and handed it to Jefferson.

The chief studied the photograph with obvious recognition. "I've seen this guy. He was at the funeral." He paused, trying to gather his thoughts. "That old Indian."

Jefferson paused as he tried to recall.

"Indian?" McKinney asked.

"Cherokee-One-Leg. He lives over in Pleasant Grove, a little black community across the tracks. He's half black and half Cherokee, or at least that's what folks say. The story is that he was a Buffalo Soldier, but I've heard all sorts of stuff about him. I doubt any of it's true, but some say that he was with Teddy Roosevelt's Rough Riders."

"I know who he is. I took Jesse to his house a couple of weeks ago. I checked up on him, too. He served with the Tenth Cavalry. They were Buffalo Soldiers. They started out in New Mexico but later fought alongside the Rough Riders. He was highly decorated - three Silver Stars, two Bronze Stars. There's a note that he was put up for a Medal of Honor but didn't get it because he was half Indian. He had a son who was an officer in the Great War but got killed. His son got a bunch of medals too, but not nearly as many as his old man. What's he got to do with this Crawford?"

"Cherokee was in the parking lot after Cliff's funeral. I saw him and went over to thank him for lookin' after Jesse. He never even looked at me. He was fixed on Jewel Stoker's boyfriend. He said that was our killer. I didn't think much of it. The old goat is eighty or ninety years old. But by God, I'm pretty sure this is the guy."

"He's the Stoker girl's boyfriend?"

"She was hugging 'im and left with 'im." Jefferson paused in thought. "You know what? He was in town that night. The night Sarah ran off. Peterson was at the carnival with the whole family. I remember thinking that it was the first time I'd seen him with his wife and the girls. He had his brother with him. He introduced me. Some people don't like talking to a man with a badge. You know what I mean. Peterson Crawford was that way. I remember thinking that his brother was just like him."

The two men sat silently holding their coffee, looking at one another. Finally, Jefferson broke the silence. "Those two killed Sarah."

"We don't have a body. We don't have a motive. But it sure looks that way."

"We need to get Jewel away from him."

"I agree. But why is this guy back? This ain't the movies. Murderers don't return to the scene of the crime. They usually try to get as far away as possible. And why would he want to kill Cliff Tidwell? And who murdered Peterson?"

"You don't think the boys killed 'im?"

Brewster sat down his coffee and stood. "Where can we find this girl?"

"She works at a Chevy dealership in Jacksonville. I suspect she'd be there this time of day."

#

LONGHORN CHEVROLET
JACKSONVILLE, TEXAS
1:30 p.m., December 3, 1941

Jefferson pulled the Ford prowler to a stop in front of the dealership. The two men had barely gotten out of the car before a chubby salesman in a double-breasted, pinstriped suit met them.

"Welcome to Longhorn Chevrolet," he began with a broad smile. "I hope the two of you are here to buy another prowler."

Jefferson glanced at McKinney, who had a normal, emotionless expression and was clearly not interested in an exchange with a car salesman.

"We're here to see an employee."

"I hope there's no trouble," the salesman said with a concerned look on his face.

"Her name's Jewel Stoker. Would you mind taking us to her?" Jefferson asked.

"Oh, her." The man said with disgust. "She's not here."

"When do you expect her back?"

"I don't know. She's not been in for a couple of days. The boss says that if she doesn't come in or call soon she's not goin' to have a job to come back to."

"Who's her boss?"

"The owner. She's his secretary."

A car pulled up to the front of the dealership, and the salesman began to step back from the two officers who clearly weren't interested in buying anything.

McKinney took the mugshot out of his coat pocket and handed it to the chief.

"Have you seen this man?" Jefferson asked, showing the picture to the salesman.

The man kept looking at the man and woman who stepped out of the car.

"Look, I need to take care of these people."

"Please, can you tell me if he's been in here?"

He glanced at the couple who walked into the dealership and then impatiently looked at the picture.

"Yeah, he comes in here a lot. He takes her out to lunch two or three times a week."

The man was getting more impatient with the two officers.

"Would you mind takin' us to this boss of yours? We'd like to speak to him." Jefferson asked.

"Look, she's not here," the man began somewhat condescendingly. "The boss isn't going to want to be bothered about some floozy blonde who doesn't come in to work. Now, if you don't mind, I've got some customers."

McKinney looked at the chief, who started to speak but paused. Then the Ranger stepped directly in front of the much shorter but heavier man and opened his sports coat revealing his Ranger badge and the Colt automatic handgun.

McKinney looked around to be sure that he couldn't be heard and then said in a soft but even tone, "I'm Corporal Brewster McKinney of the Texas Rangers. This is a murder investigation. Now, you can either take us to your boss, or you can call him from jail to post bond after I arrest you for interfering with my investigation. It's up to you."

Two minutes later the three men were standing in front of the desk of Lazarus Devereaux, owner and general manager of Longhorn Chevrolet. Devereaux had his face buried in a pile of papers and hadn't yet looked up or shown any sign of noticing their presence.

"I'm sorry to interrupt you, Mr. Devereaux," the salesman said with a shudder in his voice, "but these two police officers would like a moment."

Devereaux raised his head. He was a large, overweight man who also wore a double-breasted, pinstriped suit, which McKinney took to be the official uniform of the automobile business. On his desk was a pile of paperwork. To the right was an oversized ashtray with a dozen burned out cigars and an enormous pile of ash. The office was on the second floor with windows behind the desk facing out to the street. The walls to the right and left were covered with hunting trophies, mostly deer, but there were a few elk, and in the corner was a coyote stuffed in a pose as if it were about to attack.

Jefferson couldn't help but smile at the thought that this guy considered a coyote a trophy. Hunker and Toad had killed a hundred coyotes over the years but considered getting only a coyote a wasted day. Of course, that wouldn't keep them from eating one.

"Well, what do you want?" Devereaux asked with pointed impatience.

Jefferson and Brewster glanced at one another and finally, Jefferson spoke. "When was the last time Jewel Stoker came in to work?"

The man was clearly annoyed. "I don't know. You're here to bother me about some blonde-headed secretary? She's not here. She wasn't here yesterday either. Now go leave me alone. Because of her, I've got a pile of work to do."

Jefferson glanced at McKinney, who stepped in front of the little salesman, who then took the opportunity to slip out the door. McKinney then reached into his jacket and took the Colt out of the holster and set it on the man's desk. Devereaux froze as he looked at the gun laying pointed at him.

"Mr. Devereaux, I'm Corporal Brewster McKinney of the Texas Rangers. We're conducting a murder investigation, and we think Miss Stoker may be in danger. Now, you're interfering with our investigation, so you can help us, or I can drag you down to jail where you can sit a day or so for obstruction. It makes no difference to me, but I suspect that making the headlines on an obstruction of justice charge would be bad for business."

Devereaux looked up from the gun on his desk.

McKinney glanced over at the chief.

"When was the last time Jewel was here, Mr. Devereaux?" Jefferson asked.

"The last time I saw her was Friday. She went to that big trial in Rusk. I haven't seen her since."

The chief looked at McKinney.

"Chief, go call one of your deputies and have him go out to her house," McKinney said in a calm and even tone. "If she's not there, have him ask the neighbors if any of them have seen her."

Jefferson rushed to the outer office and picked up the phone.

"That wasn't too difficult, now was it, Mr. Devereaux?"

Devereaux shook his head.

"Has anyone called Miss Stoker to check on her?"

"Check on her? I don't have time to waste calling every dame that decides to skip work. I'm runnin' a business here.

Ditzy broads like her come and go all the time. They never stay long. Soon as they meet some guy they're out of here. If I had my people callin' every skirt that took off without callin' in I wouldn't get any cars sold.""

"Are you telling me that you didn't even bother to find out why she's not been in?""

The man's brow ruffled. "She's a secretary. I only hired her 'cause she's good lookin'."

"So she doesn't show up for four days and you're not even courious?

"Why should I have my people waste time on that broad?" Devereaux belligerently demanded. "What am I supposed to do, send someone out lookin' for some dame just because she ain't come in for a couple of days? She's probably holed up somewhere with that fellow she's been runin' around with. I got a dealership to run. I have to move these cars. I don't have time to waste chasin' down some gal 'cause she decides to quit without tellin' anyone."

Jefferson walked in. "Shorty's on his way over there."

McKinney calmly reached down and picked up the Colt and put it back in his shoulder holster. "Mr. Devereaux, I've dealt with every disgusting kind of low-life vermin there is on this planet, but I can say with absolute certainty that you are the most repulsive human being I've encountered in all my years in law enforcement. I suggest that when we walk out that door you get on your knees and start to pray because if there's so much as a single hair missin' from that girl's head, I'm gonna come back here, put a bullet in your head, and then I'm gonna stuff your fat gut and stand you up next to that damn coyote."

#

ELZA, TEXAS
Saturday August 8, 1936

Jesse and Cliff were walking along Main Street behind Cliff's parents and his little sisters, Rachel and Amy. At the end of Main Street, in the large lot just past the domino hall, the carnival had set up camp. The family could hear the music all the way back to Cliff's house. Carnivals have sounds that are all their own. There was always music, but there was also the faint echo of a barker calling visitors into the sideshows. And above all else rang out the screams of young girls on the roller coaster and Ferris wheel.

The two boys and Jewel spent all afternoon sitting on a curb across Main Street, watching the workers set up the tents and rides. It seemed impossible that so much could come out of a handful of trucks. Such days were purely magical for three kids in a lazy little farm town where the biggest excitement was Herbert Morehead claiming that he lost a cow to a mountain lion. The whole town had gotten in a stir over that one. The thought of a lion of any kind roaming the woods around Elza had mothers locking their little ones inside for days at a time. Cliff, naturally, hadn't bought a word of it. Once the story began to circulate, he asked Toad Lowery if he'd ever seen a mountain lion, and sure enough Toad had never seen so much as a mountain lion track. The cow had probably fallen into a creek and couldn't get out and had gotten eaten up by coyotes or even possibly by a wolf, though that was unlikely because Toad and Hunker hadn't seen a wolf in those parts since they were boys.

So naturally, with the absence of any entertainment, save an alleged mountain lion, the kids could barely contain themselves as they watched the traveling show emerge from the caravan of brightly painted vehicles. The afternoon seemed like the longest of their lives. Late in the day the colored lights began to glow on the Ferris wheel, and the Merry-Go-Round began to turn to the tempo of a pipe organ. The three kids all had to go to their homes where they were forced to endure their typical routines of chores and dinner as if that was a normal Saturday and not the most magical night of the year.

Jesse, of course, had almost no chores, with the notable exception of taking out the trash. That night he had dinner sitting across the table from Garvis. Murdock had driven all the way over to Natchitoches, Louisiana to handle some business with an oil leaseholder and wasn't expected back until late. Garvis, of course, had no interest in going to the little traveling carnival and, quite frankly, couldn't understand why Jesse was so excited about it. Some three or four years before they had taken him to the State Fair in Dallas, which was a far larger and much more entertaining show. The thought of spending a hot summer evening walking around that vacant lot with the foul stench of cow manure emanating from all those dirt farmers disgusted her. But if Jesse insisted on going, she wouldn't stop him. So after dinner Garvis gave her son two dollars, and Jesse went over to the Tidwells, who were more than happy to have the boy join them.

As they walked along Main Street, Cliff repeatedly looked to his right at Jesse and shook his head in disgust. Jesse, whose normal attire, like Cliff's, amounted to a white t-shirt and a pair of well worn blue jeans, opted that particular night to put on his Sunday pants and a pressed, button-down, short-sleeved shirt. Worse still he had his hair slicked back like Humphrey Bogart. Cliff, of course, was all too familiar with the reason for Jesse's sudden concern about personal appearance.

"Why didn't you put on your suit and tie?" Cliff asked with a hint of laughter.

Jesse ignored his friend, having spotted Cherokee-One-Leg sitting on the tailgate of his old Ford across the street from the domino hall. Jesse elbowed Cliff, who was too fixated on the happenings at the carnival ahead to notice the old black man. The two boys glanced at each other, and then Cliff began crossing the street.

"Mom, we're goin' to go talk to Cherokee a minute. We'll catch up to y'all."

"You two shouldn't bother that old man," Susie Tidwell argued, knowing that there was no stopping Cliff once he had made up his mind to talk to someone.

"It's okay, mom. He's our friend," Cliff assured her as he and Jesse headed across the street.

"It's really okay, Mrs. Tidwell. Cherokee's our friend," Jesse added.

Ned, not saying a word, which was his way, glanced across at the one-legged old man sitting next to a bushel of tomatoes with his peg on the tailgate and the other leg swinging. Ned then nodded his head at Cherokee who nodded in return in what was a mutually respectful way of not only acknowledging one another but also showing that the old Indian fighter welcomed a visit from the two boys.

Susie was watching the boys with concern when her husband took her by the arm and said, "It's okay. Cherokee doesn't mind."

"Hi, Cherokee," Cliff said as the boys approached the old man.

"There's a good crowd in town tonight."

"You think that you're gonna sell a lot of tomatoes?" Cliff asked, knowing the real reason the old man was in town.

"Most folks in these parts grow their own tomatoes, but I might get rid of a few," the old man replied.

"You think there's goin' to be some trouble tonight?" Jesse asked.

The old man never glanced down at the boy, but instead he had his focus fixed across the street. "Don't know, but the night's sure got the potential for it."

Jesse looked across in the direction Cherokee was looking. Peterson and Anna-Ruth Crawford were walking toward the carnival from the dress shop with their two daughters and a man Jesse didn't recognize behind them. At the same time, Irwin Stoker pulled his pickup to a stop in front of the domino hall and he, Sarah, and Jewel started climbing out.

Cliff replied jovially, "How could anything go wrong on a night like this, Cherokee?"

Jesse nudged his friend, who looked across at the Crawfords, who were walking toward the Stoker family. As Sarah stepped out of the truck, she looked up at the Crawfords and immediately looked away.

"Is that the Stoker woman?" Cherokee asked.

"Yeah," Jesse replied.

"She knows those two men, and she doesn't want her husband to know it."

"How can you tell that, Cherokee?" Cliff asked.

"She won't look directly at the men, but both are looking at her."

Jesse and Cliff watched as Anna-Ruth Crawford went to Sarah Stoker and hugged her. Sarah was obviously uncomfortable and was trying to keep from making eye contact with the men. The two women exchanged some words and then, smiling, Mrs. Crawford rejoined her family and went into the carnival.

"Wow, you're right," Jesse added.

As the Crawford family walked into the carnival, Peterson looked back over his shoulder at Sarah. When she glanced in his direction, she again quickly looked away.

Irwin Stoker saw the exchange, and he made some comments that upset her, even though she tried to conceal her emotions. Jewel was standing between her parents, obviously embarrassed by their behavior. She looked at the boys and Cherokee but immediately looked down as if not to notice them.

"Those two fight a lot," Cherokee observed. "Your friend is accustomed to it, but it still makes her uncomfortable."

The two boys nodded in agreement but were saddened as well. Jewel was no longer an outsider or a tag-along. The three had become their own little family. When one felt pain, the other two couldn't help but feel it.

"I know the feeling," Jesse confessed.

Cliff looked at him with surprise. "Your parents fight?"

"Not in public," he answered softly and with emotion.

"Did you fight with your wife, Cherokee?" Cliff asked.

The old man looked down at Cliff. "It happened some. Marriage is not easy. But what you just saw was not a normal fight. The husband knows that there is some connection between her and Crawford. What he said to her was for the purpose of hurting her. He's not interested in knowing why she knows Crawford, and he has no interest in protecting her. Whatever he said was intended to hurt her. He's not a good husband." The old warrior paused and then added, "He's not a good man. That woman is tortured, by Crawford and by her husband."

#

As Jesse and Cliff walked into the carnival they forgot all about Jewel's parents. They were two young boys filled with excitement from all the sights and sounds. They started the night with a ride on the Tilt-a-Whirl. They actually rode it twice and still had a roller coaster and Ferris wheel to look forward to.

Almost everyone in Elza could be found on the midway. Even Able McCormack was there, though not particularly happy, having had to shut down the Palace for the night. There were even a lot of people from the neighboring towns, with the notable exceptions of the folks from the shantytown and Pleasant Grove.

Jesse, to Cliff's dismay, had yet to really enjoy himself. He was way too occupied with finding Gemma Crawford, but because of the crowd he'd lost sight of her early on.

As the boys were walking through the midway, Jewel and her parents came off the Ferris wheel. Jewel saw the boys and said to her mother, "I'm gonna go talk to the guys for a minute. I'll catch up with y'all."

"Okay, honey," Sarah replied.

Irwin was still in an obviously unpleasant mood and grumbled as the girl walked away.

"She'll be fine," Sarah assured him.

Looking along the games, Jesse spotted Gemma. He then got his first good look at the man with her father. It was then that he recognized that man. He had been with Crawford at the lynching.

"Look," Jesse said, motioning toward the Crawford family.

Cliff looked down along the games, spotted Gemma, and shrugged. "So what? You're too chicken to talk to her."

"Not her. The guy next to her dad."

"What about him?"

"He was there when they lynched Bucky."

Cliff looked closely at the man and recognized him. "He was standing with Mr. Crawford, wasn't he?"

"Yeah," Jesse said as he watched the two men playing a game, with Gemma, Jettie, and Anna-Ruth behind, watching them.

Just past the games, Cliff spotted Jefferson, looking angry and leaning against a light post while munching from a bag of popcorn. Cliff and Jesse immediately headed his direction.

"What's the matter, Jefferson?" Cliff asked jovially. "You don't look like you're havin' any fun at all."

Jewel walked up between the two boys and nudged Jesse with her shoulder.

"This ain't a lot of fun for me. I gotta stand here all night and keep an eye on the carnies runnin' the games. I already had to shut down the duck shoot," the Chief explained.

Jesse, Jewel, and Cliff looked at the row of games. "What'd they do?" Jesse asked.

"Toad and Hunker were over there, and after missing two shots Hunker pulled that Swiss knife out of his pocket and fixed the sights on the rifle they gave 'im. The next thing you know he was cleanin' them out. The carnie runnin' it came close to punchin' Hunker out and wanted me to arrest him. We settled it by shuttin' down the game. Other-wise Hunker would have gone home with everything they've got."

As the chief was talking, Jesse spotted the Crawfords at one of the games where Peterson and the other man were tossing baseballs at the milk-bottles. Jewel also saw them.

"Have you caught the girlie show yet?" Cliff asked.

"No. And I better not find out the two of you've been in there. I already had to send a couple of Reklaw boys home," Jefferson told them. "Their parents were none too happy about it neither."

"Oh, Jefferson," Cliff replied. "You know we wouldn't try somethin' like that."

The chief glared down at Cliff.

"Well, we wouldn't try it here. Everybody knows us. If we got seen, somebody would tell my pa and we'd end up hoein' fields 'til school starts."

"Don't worry, Chief," Jewel interjected. "If they try to get in that tent, I'll let you know."

Cliff glared at her, but Jewel just smiled.

Jesse no longer heard anything of the conversation. His focus was on Gemma as her family.

"Don't waste your money on the snake man, either," Jefferson added. I saw him while they were settin' up. He's a fellow with no arms or legs."

"No arms or legs?" Cliff asked. "How's he get around?"

"When I saw 'im, he was in a wagon being pulled around by the bearded lady," Jefferson replied, realizing that he had just encouraged the boys rather than deterred them.

"Did she really have a beard?" Cliff asked excitedly.

Jewel, who was standing between the two boys, noticed Jesse's attention was on Gemma.

Jewel gave Jesse a shove with her shoulder. "Go," she whispered.

Jesse just looked at her, and she said, "Go over there and ask her to ride the Ferris-wheel or I'm gonna do it for ya."

He hesitantly walked over to where Gemma was standing with her parents, all the while glancing over his shoulder at Jewel.

Gemma's father and the other man had begun to play another game where they tossed little rubber rings onto Dr Pepper and RC Cola bottles. Jesse and Cliff had tried that one earlier in the evening and come to the conclusion that the rings were too little to fit on a soda-pop bottle.

Jesse walked up to Gemma who had her back to him, watching her father play the game. "Hi Gemma."

She turned to look at him and replied, "Hi," with almost a hint of a smile.

Jettie giggled, causing Gemma to elbow her in the ribs. If Jesse noticed the exchange between the sisters there was no evidence of it on his face.

"Enjoyin' the carnival?"

She looked at him and nodded.

"Have you seen the bearded lady?"

Gemma looked at him and shook her head.

"We were just talkin' about her. Cliff wants to go in there."

For several moments Jesse just stood there looking around trying to think of something to say. Finally he noticed the Ferris wheel over his shoulder.

"Have you ridden the Ferris wheel yet?"

Gemma shook her head.

"Are you goin' to?"

Gemma looked directly at him. "Jesse, are you trying to ask me if I want to ride the Ferris wheel with you?"

Jesse's eyes widened, and he froze at the bluntness of her question. He searched his mind for an answer but could find nothing. Finally he just nodded and uttered, "Uh-huh."

Gemma stepped up to her mother, who was standing next to Peterson, who was now tossing softballs. "Mom, is it okay if I go ride the Ferris wheel with Jesse?"

Jesse was white as a sheet as he nervously watched Anna-Ruth look at him and then back at Gemma. "Okay, but come back here when you're done."

Gemma turned and joined Jesse, who was smiling in relief. As the two walked together toward the Ferris wheel ticket line, Peterson looked back at Jesse.

"It's okay," Anna-Ruth assured him, sensing her husband's disapproval.

As the kids were walking away, Irwin and Sarah Stoker were casually walking down the midway to where Jewel and Cliff and Chief Hightower were standing. The tension from earlier in the evening had subsided and Sarah, though not necessarily enjoying herself, did look less troubled.

Over at the softball toss, Richard Crawford glanced over his shoulder and spotted Sarah. He gave her a big smile, but she turned and tried to ignore him. Richard then motioned with his head for Peterson to look over. When Peterson looked over, Sarah was purposely looking away, but Irwin noticed.

On the Ferris wheel Jesse and Gemma sat without either saying a word. Jesse was nervously searching his mind for something to say. Gemma just sat there enjoying the ride. Finally, Jesse broke the silence. "Are you having fun?"

Gemma giggled and wrapped her arm around his. "You don't have to be afraid, Jesse."

Jesse looked at her, obviously not understanding.

"I like you too," she said softly.

Jesse, still not knowing how to respond, just sat there as the ride turned. Finally after a long pause he thought of something. "Do you like RC Cola?"

She smiled. "Yeah."

"Sometimes we take an RC break on the curb across the street from your mom's store."

"You mean every afternoon between one and two?"

Jesse looked at her in surprise that she had seen them, but Gemma just giggled at him.

He sat there for a few seconds in thought and finally said, "I can bring you an RC sometime, you know, if you want to come out and join us."

Below, Cliff was standing next to Jewel as Richard kept glancing over at Sarah. Jewel didn't seem to notice, but Sarah was becoming visibly uncomfortable as she made every effort to ignore the two brothers. Regardless of her efforts to not look, the man kept smiling and looking over at her, trying to make eye contact. Irwin occasionally glanced back at the Crawford brothers and then at his wife, becoming more and more agitated. Finally Irwin lost control.

From above on the Ferris wheel, Jesse and Gemma watched as Irwin roughly grabbed his wife by the arm and pulled her away. Jewel left Cliff and followed her parents without saying a word.

When Irwin grabbed his wife, Cliff looked at the Chief as if he should do something.

"It's not our business, Cliff."

"It's okay for a man to shove his wife like that?"

"Legally, yeah. Unless she wants to press charges."

Jewel followed as Irwin took Sarah behind the tents. With all the noise of the carnival, Jesse and Gemma couldn't hear a thing, but from their perch they could see Irwin yelling at his wife.

Behind the tents Irwin still had Sarah by the arm. "Who was that, one of the guys you've been whorin' with? We can't go anywhere without runnin' into one of your friends."

"Let's talk about this at home," Sarah pleaded.

"I want an answer now. Did you whore with those two? 'Cause it sure looks like it."

Sarah looked over at Jewel. "Irwin, watch your mouth."

"Answer me."

"Irwin, let's go home."

"Not 'til you tell me the truth. You whored for those two, didn't ya?

"No, I've never done that."

"Then who were those two? 'Cause they know you!"

Sarah yanked her arm free. "I'm not going to do this here. Come on, Jewel," she said as she began to walk away.

Irwin grabbed her as she began to go and hit her hard on the side of the head. Sarah fell to the ground.

On the Ferris wheel, Jesse and Gemma froze as they watched. The ride began to turn just as they saw Jewel run away from her parents, but as they got to the bottom of the wheel they lost sight of her.

The two kids got off the ride without saying a word and walked back into the crowd.

"I've got to go back to my parents now," Gemma explained.

"Yeah, okay. I'll see you Monday?"

Gemma smiled and said, "Okay."

"I'll bring you an RC."

"I like Dr Pepper better," she said with a smile as she walked back to her family.

Jesse watched Gemma walk away, then headed back to where Cliff and the chief were standing. He motioned for Cliff to come with him.

"I'll see ya later, Jefferson," Cliff said as he joined Jesse.

The Chief looked down at the boy and smiled. As long as he could recall he had never heard Cliff Tidwell call him by his title like everyone else in town. "I'll see ya later, Cliff."

Cliff began walking alongside Jesse and asked, "What's up?"

"We got to find Jewel," Jesse answered as he looked everywhere for the girl.

"Something wrong?"

"Her folks had a fight. It was really bad. It was like that day we saw Mr. Crawford and Mrs. Stoker in the alley. Jewel went runnin' off."

"That guy with her dad."

"What about him?"

"We were all standing by Jefferson and that guy kept lookin' over at Mrs. Stoker. Jewel's pa was getting' really mad."

"She's got to be here somewhere. Let's split up," Jesse said as he looked through the crowd.

Gemma's father and uncle were playing another game. She went directly to her mother. "Mom, I'm gonna go to the bathroom."

Anna-Ruth looked at her daughter. "Take your sister with you."

Gemma looked at Jettie and imperceptibly shook her head.

Anna-Ruth didn't catch the nonverbal exchange. The two girls had been perfecting it all of their lives. They were to the point that much of their communication was done more with the eyes than anything else.

"I don't need to go, Mama. I want to stay and watch Daddy and Uncle Rick," Jettie argued.

"Okay. Hurry, and be careful," Anna-Ruth said to Gemma as the girl was already leaving.

She immediately saw Jesse and Cliff looking through the crowd for Jewel.

Boys are so stupid.

Gemma walked between some of the tents and came out behind them where the carnival trucks were parked. She heard the faint sound of crying and looked around and saw Jewel sitting in a shadow against a truck tire with her face buried in her hands. Gemma went to the girl and sat down.

"I saw y'all from the Ferris Wheel," Gemma offered tenderly.

Jewel looked at her as she wiped her eyes.

"My parents fight too," Gemma added.

Jewel sat there for a moment and wiped her eyes and nose, "Not like my parents."

Gemma looked at her, tears swelling. "Yeah. Exactly like your parents."

The two girls stared at each other, both with tears rolling down their cheeks.

Jesse and Cliff met in the middle of the carnival; neither had seen any sign of Jewel.

"Are you sure she's here?" Cliff asked.

"They were behind a tent and she came runnin' out."

"Then she must be in one of the side shows or on a ride."

Jesse looked at Cliff. "She was way too upset to get on a ride."

Irwin Stoker was searching through the crowd as well. When he saw the boys he went directly to them.

"Where's Jewel?" he demanded.

"We don't know, Mr. Stoker," Cliff replied.

Across the way Jesse spotted Jewel and Gemma coming from between some tents. "There she is."

As the two girls approached, Stoker went quickly to Jewel, grabbed her arm and began leading her away.

"We're goin' home," he said harshly as he pulled her away.

"Where's mama?" Jewel asked.

"Who cares?" he muttered as they went.

All three of the kids watched Irwin pull Jewel through the crowd. When they were out of sight, Gemma looked at Jesse and then headed back to her family. Jesse watched and then noticed Mrs. Stoker standing next to the man who was with the Crawfords. She was there only a moment and then began running away through the crowd.

"We should tell Cherokee about this," Cliff said, "but I really don't know what happened."

"Neither do I." Jesse replied.

"What should we do?"

"Where's your folks?"

"They're on the kiddy rides with Rachel and Amy."

"You should probably go join them. Tell 'em that I went home. I'll go out and talk to Cherokee."

"Okay."

When Jesse walked out of the carnival, Cherokee-One-Leg was still sitting on the tailgate of his truck, just as he had been when the boys went in. Jesse went directly to him and hopped on the tailgate.

"Been a busy night around here, ain't it, boy?" Cherokee asked.

"Yeah."

"That Stoker fellow came out with his girl and got in his truck and left. His wife came out a little later and run up the street. She turned the corner down there past the picture-show," the old man explained.

"That man that was with Mr. Crawford. He was standing next to Mr. Crawford the day they hanged Bucky. While I was on the Ferris wheel, Cliff said that he kept lookin' at Mrs. Stoker, and Mr. Stoker got mad. While I was up there

I saw Jewel's dad drag Mrs. Stoker behind a tent and hit her. After that he grabbed Jewel and came out.

The two were silent a moment while Jesse looked down the street at the theater.

"Stay clear of Crawford and that other fellow," Cherokee said.

"I'm gonna go down the street to see where Mrs. Stoker went," Jesse said as he hopped off the tailgate.

Cherokee looked at him. "Be careful. Stay in sight."

When Jesse got to the alley just past the police station, he heard a noise and stopped walking. He could hear all the various noises of the carnival, but faintly down the alley he heard an entirely different sound. He looked into the darkness and then crept softly in the direction of the sound. When he got to the end of the alley he paused next to the rain gutter that he and Cliff had climbed a few weeks before. He then heard the noise again.

He slowly peered around the corner of the police station and saw Sarah Stoker sitting on the little step at the back door of the movie theater crying. He squatted in the shadow and watched her.

At the south end of Main Street, Cliff came walking out of the carnival entrance with his family. His parents were carrying the two girls, who were fast asleep. As they turned to head down Main Street, Cliff looked over at Cherokee sitting alone on the tailgate.

"Mom, I want to go visit with Cherokee. He looks lonely."

"Don't bother that man," Suzie pleaded, but Cliff was already halfway across the street.

"Be home in an hour, son," Ned said in a firm tone that Cliff knew to be an order and not a suggestion.

"I will, Dad," Cliff replied as he walked up to the old Indian.

"Where's Jesse?" Cliff asked Cherokee as he climbed onto the back of the truck.

"He went to check on the Stoker woman," the old man replied with a nod in the direction Jesse had gone.

The Crawford family came walking out of the carnival.

Cliff looked toward them. "Did Jesse tell you about that man with them?"

"Yeah. He said that they were both at the lynchin'."

Gemma looked across at Cliff and smiled as she and her family turned down Main Street to head home. About a block away the family stopped. Anna-Ruth and Peterson seemed to be arguing as the brother was getting into a car. Finally Mrs. Crawford led the two girls away while Peterson got into the car with his brother.

In the alley Jesse crouched low in the shadow of the police station watching Mrs. Stoker weep. Part of him felt like he should leave and let her shed her tears alone. The mother of one of his best friends was having a very emotional moment, and he knew that it was not any of his business. But, he also felt that it was very much his business and she needed someone to look after her.

He watched as she wiped the tears away with both hands. She sat up straight and looked both ways down the alley as if someone might be watching. She then, convinced that she was alone, reached into her purse and pulled out a handgun. She lifted it out, checked the cylinder and then put it back into her purse.

Jesse froze. He'd been around guns all of his life. Everyone in Elza owned at least one. His father kept half a dozen guns in his study at home. Murdock and a group of his work buddies took a regular trip to Colorado each winter to hunt elk. Mr. Tidwell had taught Jesse and Cliff all about how to safely handle and shoot a gun. Jesse, in fact, was a pretty good shot with a revolver, but Cliff was much better with a rifle.

This, though, was entirely different. It was one thing to shoot at bottles on a fence post. But Jesse sensed, accurately as it turned out, that it wasn't bottles that Sarah Stoker was planning to shoot. His heart began to beat faster and his breathing sped up so much that he was afraid Mrs. Stoker would hear him.

Suddenly, the headlights of a car flashed into the alley from the North. It turned into the alley from the highway and slowly crept toward him. He crouched low in the shadow hoping that the car lights wouldn't shine on him as it passed. Sarah stood as the car came toward her. She had the purse hanging on her left forearm with her right hand buried inside.

The car moved slowly and passed the side alley where Jesse was hiding and pulled to a stop, with the back door right in front of him and the car directly pointed at Sarah. Jesse's heart was pounding, as somehow he knew what was about to take place.

The headlights went off and Richard Crawford got out from the driver's side, just a few feet away from Jesse. Peterson got out on the opposite side from where Jesse was crouched.

"Well, Sarah, what was so important that you wanted to meet me in this dark alley?" Richard asked with a broad smile.

"It looks to me like she had a good time. She probably wants another round, Richie boy," Peterson said with a big smile but a nasty look on his face.

Jesse was a little behind Richard and could barely see him in the darkness, but something in his manner made him despise the man. Mrs. Stoker was terrified but also looked determined. To Jesse, Peterson and the other man looked nothing short of evil.

"You ruined my life," Sarah said, staring at Richard as the two men came around in front of the car toward her.

"Now, how did I do that? We just had a little fun, that's all."

"My husband is a good man. He didn't deserve what you've done," Sarah proclaimed with tears streaming down her face.

Laughing, Richard said, "Sarah, I've never met your husband. What did I do to him?"

"I'm going to have a baby. Your baby," she said angrily, no longer trying to hold back the tears.

Richard held up both hands. "Hold on, now. You can't blame that on me. We know what you do for money; besides, how do you know that it's not your husband's?"

"I'm not a prostitute," she said furiously. "I lived behind that house. I never even went inside."

Richard and Peterson both laughed.

"Inside or out back," Richard said, "you're a whore, and ain't no whore gonna blame me 'cause she's pregnant."

"It's yours," she said firmly, indicating that there was no debate on the subject. "You held a gun to my head and you ruined my life. Irwin will divorce me. I'll be out on the street with a baby, and it's all your fault."

Peterson laughed. "Come on, Sarah, this was bound to happen. Girls like you shouldn't get married."

"Why don't you calm down," Richard offered. "Hop in the car, and we'll go for a ride. I hear there's a new roadhouse down by Crockett."

"No. I'm never going anywhere with you."

Richard opened his suit coat and revealed a handgun tucked in his belt.

Jesse froze. The expression on Sarah's face said everything.

"Not this time. You're not going to force me or anyone else to do that again," she said as she pulled the revolver from her purse.

"Rick, she's got a gun," Peterson yelled.

Sarah wasted no time. Richard couldn't even respond.

Cliff was still sitting on the tailgate with Cherokee when he heard a sound from up the street.

"Was that a gunshot?"

Cherokee looked up the direction that Cliff was looking, "Get in the truck," he ordered as he quickly lowered his weight onto his peg and crutch.

Cherokee was too late. Cliff leaped off the tailgate and was running up Main Street before the old Indian had gotten the words out of his mouth.

Richard fell, stunned from the shot as a second bullet ricocheted off the car door.

Peterson leaped at Sarah and grabbed at the gun. She fell to the ground with Peterson on top of her. He punched her violently in the face and her head hit the ground with a thud as a third shot hit the brick wall just above Jesse's head. Peterson stood and began kicking at Sarah's hand. The gun went flying into the brick wall of the Palace. Angrily, Peterson continued to kick Sarah over and over as she lay there crouched on her side crying.

Jesse sat stunned and terrified, not knowing what to do as the man continued to kick her.

Richard sat up with blood streaming from his side.

"Pete," Richard called out.

Peterson looked at his brother, suddenly realizing that Richard had been hit and ran to his side.

"Good god. Get in the car."

Peterson helped his brother get to his feet. Jesse watched motionless as Peterson helped Richard get into the back seat of the car only a few feet in front of him.

Once Richard was in the car Peterson got in the driver seat and slammed the door shut. As his brother started the car Richard looked out the back window directly at Jesse.

Peterson slammed the car into reverse just as Richard yelled, "There's a kid."

As the car backed up Peterson turned his head to look up the side alley next to the police station just as Cliff came running around the corner. Peterson slammed on the brake. The car slid to a stop with the headlights shining on Jesse.

Jesse stood stunned in the headlights as Cliff came to his side. Suddenly, Cherokee pulled his Ford to a stop at the end of the alley where Jesse and Cliff were standing.

Peterson looked at the two boys and then at the headlights shining on him from Cherokee's truck and hit the accelerator and flew backward out of the alley.

As the car was backing out of the alley Richard looked at Cherokee; the old man came hobbling with surprising speed toward the boys.

The kids stood motionless as they watched the car back away. Jesse then looked back at Sarah. She was sitting up with the gun in her hand. She slowly put the gun to her head.

"No!" Jesse screamed as he dove toward her.

She had not seen the two boys prior and was startled and turned her head in their direction. At the same moment that Jesse landed on her, the bullet exploded from the gun and into her neck and then deep into her chest.

Jesse landed next to Sarah as her body fell limp against him, blood pouring from her neck. Cliff, followed by Cherokee, came around the corner and saw Jesse holding the woman as blood flowed from her neck. Cliff came and squatted next to Sarah and Jesse as the old man stood back, leaning on his crutch.

Sarah coughed as she looked at the two boys. "You boys shouldn't be here."

"I'll go for help," Cliff said as he started to stand.

Sarah grabbed his arm, "No."

She coughed again, and blood came out of her mouth. "I'm gonna die. I need to die."

Jesse looked at Cherokee who shook his head. The old warrior had seen bullet wounds before. Some could be saved, but some couldn't. Cherokee had seen enough to know the difference, and this one couldn't be saved.

"Hold on, Mrs. Stoker," Jesse said tenderly. "You'll be okay."

Sarah looked at Jesse and then up at Cherokee and smiled and said weakly, "You can't fix this, boys. I'm not an old Ford."

Sarah coughed some more, and Jesse held her more tightly against him.

"Boys," she began, "take care of Jewel for me. Irwin loves her, but she needs the two of you. Promise me that you'll take care of her."

The boys, with tears in their eyes, nodded as Jesse said, "We will."

Sarah coughed again, and more blood came out of her mouth.

"Did you boys hear all that?"

"Yes, ma'am," Jesse answered hesitantly.

"You know about the baby?"

Jesse nodded.

Sarah coughed some more.

"Don't let Jewel find out. Please, don't let her know what happened tonight. She's innocent. Don't let anybody know. Take my body to the woods. Don't let 'em find me like this. Don't tell anybody about those men. Don't let the Crawford girls know their daddy was here. It will bring so much pain. Nothin' good can come from that. Those are good girls, and they don't deserve to be hurt that way, and neither does their mama. Please, please, don't let that happen. Boys, take care of my Jewel. She didn't deserve a mama like me. She didn't deserve any of this," Sarah pleaded as she looked directly into Jesse's eyes.

As he held her tightly Jesse felt life leave her body.

Both boys silently sobbed as the woman fell lifeless in the dark alley. No one spoke for several minutes, and then finally Jesse let her lay on the ground. The only sound was from the carnival at the end of the street.

Eventually Cherokee broke the silence. "There's gonna be a lot of questions about what happened tonight. You boys shouldn't be involved. I'll go get Chief Hightower. I'll tell 'im that I heard gunshots and came down here and saw a car pull off and her layin' here shot. You two shouldn't be involved."

"No," Jesse said resolutely. "If you do that Jewel'll know her mom killed herself. Besides, they're likely to think you did somethin'."

"That's right, Cherokee," Cliff added. "They hung Bucky for doing less. A colored man and a dead white woman - they'll lynch ya for sure."

Jesse looked at Cliff. "Did anyone else hear the shots?"

"I don't think so. The carnival was makin' too much noise. We only come 'cause we knew you were down here."

"Then here's what we do," Jesse began. "Cherokee, you need to get out of here right away before someone sees your truck. Cliff, you and me will hide Mrs. Stoker behind those trashcans. Then we'll go home. We'll meet back here in an hour. We'll put her in the delivery truck and haul her someplace."

"I can't let you boys do that," Cherokee argued.

"Jewel's our friend and we promised her mama to take care of her. This is where it starts," Jesse proclaimed. "She was right, too. If this gets out, we'll have to tell what we saw. Everybody will find out about Mr. Crawford and that other man, but they won't get in any trouble 'cause she did all the shootin'. But Gemma and Jettie and Jewel will all get hurt. And for what? Mrs. Stoker was right. They don't deserve what will happen. But if we hide her like she asked, well, everybody will eventually forget about it."

"Jesse's right, Cherokee," Cliff added. "We can't let nobody know about this."

"Boys, there's laws. You can't just get rid of a person like she's trash. Somebody's gonna come lookin' for her."

"I know. We'll have to put her where nobody's goin' to find her. And she ain't trash, Cherokee. She's Jewel's mama." Jesse finished.

#

NEW BIRMINGHAM, TEXAS
1:00 a.m., Sunday August 9, 1936

The boys rumbled down the little dirt road past the shantytown in the old Model-T stake-bed. Jesse was driving. The truck was noisy and sure to wake some people, but they had to take that chance.

The two boys met up at Washington's and got the truck. They had to push it out to the road to avoid waking Mr. Washington, which was quite a job. The slope up to the highway was a lot steeper than either boy had ever imagined, and more than once they lost control and let the truck roll back into the lot behind the feed store. Finally when they got it to the highway and started it, they realized that it was way too noisy to drive down the alley without waking someone, most likely Chief Hightower, who would be sleeping right next to where Sarah was laying.

They finally decided to leave the truck parked by the highway and walk down the alley and carry Sarah back. Cliff had brought along an old tarp, so they wrapped her up. Then the two tried to lift her. Neither boy expected that she would be so heavy. The boys were already worn out from pushing the truck up to the highway. They finally decided that it would be easier to push the truck down the alley, put Sarah in and then push it back to the highway.

Once they were finally in the truck, neither boy spoke. They both knew where they were going and what they had to do.

Jesse drove slowly into New Birmingham. Without headlights it was difficult to see, but he could make out the main road and the mine and smelter at the end of the street.

The old Ford coughed as they passed the Southern Hotel.

Inside the hotel Shakes woke with a start. In all the time he had lived there the only sound he had heard at night was the occasional hoot owl. Suddenly it sounded as if an army was passing through. He leaped to his feet from his little bed and crept to the door. Out front he saw an old Ford stake-bed slowly pass by. The truck came to a stop at the old mineshaft.

Shakes crept through the darkness along the main street in order to watch. Two boys got out of the truck. They couldn't have been more than ten or twelve years old. Shakes finally got close enough to recognize them. They were the two boys who visited his little paradise a few weeks before.

He clearly got a look at the one who had tried to come into the hotel.

Shakes watched as the boys lifted something off the back of the truck. It was heavy. Much too heavy for two boys of that size to carry, but they struggled and managed to get it to the edge of the shaft. Though he wasn't sure, Shakes thought that it looked like a body. They then tied a rope around it and looped the rope around the axel of the truck and began lowering it into the shaft. It was all they could do to lower it without losing control. Both boys were on the ground with their feet jammed against the rear tire of the truck as they let the rope slowly slide through their hands. Finally they came to the end of the rope. The boys held tight for a moment as they whispered back and forth. Finally they let go of the rope. A moment later Shakes heard a loud splash.

The boys then got into the truck and drove out of town.

Chapter 12

NECHES RIVER BRIDGE
8:40 a.m., Thursday December 4, 1941

Nathaniel Elbridge Cockwright was on his way to having the day of his life. Up to this point the case hadn't been going as well as he'd planned. The fingerprints had been solid, and there was no question that they belonged to Rose, and there was equally no question that Rose had opportunity, motive, and ability. All things considered, it should be a simple case to prosecute. The kid did it; it was just a matter of convincing the jury to convict.

Wilhelm Dinkler III, however, was not making it all that easy. Dinkler had managed to claim that Rose's prints could be months old, and pointed out that Jesse had been seen in the car any number of times and even managed to produce a witness, well, actually, seven witnesses, who claimed to have seen the defendant behind the wheel of that particular car more than once. It took some smooth talking for Nathaniel to sway the jury. The bottom line, as Nathanial so eloquently pointed out, was that all the witnesses were residents of Elza, and it had become well known that the residents of Elza were almost completely and, quite frankly, inexplicably united in support of the young killer. As a matter of fact, and Nathaniel used this in his argument, at that very moment there hung a banner across Main Street reading "Free Jesse." One couldn't blame them too much.

The kid had grown up in the town, and those people were understandably hesitant to believe that one of their own would do such a thing, another argument that Nathaniel had used. Still, the punk had murdered one of their own. It's hard to believe that the entire town would behave so foolishly. How would these cow-herders feel if the kid somehow got acquitted and went out and did it again?

Fortunately these turnip-growers had someone like Nathaniel to protect them from their own poor judgment. That, of course, is why governments and laws exists. The simple and uneducated elect those who are wiser and better equipped to make decisions that the masses are not capable of making on their own.

Fortunately for the people of Elza, the course of the trial was about to change. Everything had been planned. Nathaniel had orchestrated the entire trial to lead up to this day. He'd managed to get just what he wanted on the jury. With the exception of two, all the jurors were low-income farmers, or in the case of three, wives of farmers. The two exceptions were no less helpful to the prosecution. One of them was a railroad worker who spent most of his days fending off hobos, and the other was a parts manager at the Ford dealership in Jacksonville. None, not a single juror, was anywhere remotely as privileged as the defendant. All it was going to take was for those twelve hard-working citizens to get one good look at the place where this son of a rich oil man left his "best friend," the son of a poor dirt-farmer, to die, and the case would be over. Dinkler could do what he wanted; he wouldn't be able to get that image out of those people's minds.

Nathaniel had arranged for three dozen copies of the crime scene photos to be printed and ready so that each juror, and of course Judge Buckner, could stand on that bridge and look down and see just how brutally this innocent kid had been killed. There was not a jury in Texas that would vote to acquit after that.

Nathaniel stood with a broad smile next to the bridge with Primrose, who had in his hands the photographs. Dinkler, his client, and the three witnesses, as well as the judge, two bailiffs, and the twelve jurors, walked toward them along the tracks. Cockwright couldn't help but smile; he was about to hit a grand slam, and there was nothing this Houston lawyer could do about it.

As they approached, Judge Buckner stepped up on the tracks between the two iron supports of the bridge and addressed the group, "Once again, you are to behave just as if we were still in the courtroom. Jury, until we adjourn to the vehicles, you are not to speak to one another, and any questions to the attorneys or witnesses are to be directed first to me. Witnesses, you are all still under oath. Does anyone have any questions?"

Cockwright rolled his eyes. Of course, those dimwitted hoe-pullers had questions. Only five of them had better than a fifth-grade education.

Judicial integrity was, of course, imperative, but Nathaniel couldn't understand why Buckner was so insistent that there be no outsiders present - not even the press. This case was the biggest story in Texas, and this little excursion was going to introduce the most important testimony in the case. Not allowing the press was going to cheat the people of the state the right to see judicial process played out at its finest.

Nevertheless, despite Nathaniel's protests, the Judge's word was final, and he had decided that the press had to remain all the way down the tracks at the road crossing, which meant that not a single photograph of Nathaniel making his case right above where the bloody killing took place was going to make the morning papers. Once more,

Nathaniel Elbridge Cockwright was going to be cheated out of a guaranteed vote-winning opportunity.

"Since there are no questions," Buckner continued, "Mr. Cockwright, you may call your first witness."

Nathaniel had thought long and hard about how proceed. He could make a long impassioned speech and then call the witness. Or he could start by passing out the photographs and then let the witness speak. Finally he decided to play this with caution. He'd begin by letting the witness tell his story, followed by letting the half-wit police chief tell his story. Then he'd pass out the photographs and ask for the judge to allow the jurors to view the scene for themselves. The way Nathaniel saw it, the more he built up the scene, the greater the impact.

"I'd like to call Mr. Hunker Lowery, your Honor."

That name in itself said everything one needed to know about the collective intelligence of the resident of Cherokee County Texas. Who, other than another back-woods pea-farmer, would name his kid, Hunker? Nathaniel didn't at first believe that Hunker was a real name until he'd had Coleman check the county records. Sure enough, it was right there. Along with his equally dimwitted brother, Toad, who quite coincidentally, looked like a toad.

"Mr. Lowery, will you step up here onto the bridge?"

Lowery walked up to Buckner.

"Mr. Lowery, I will remind you that you are still under oath."

"Yes, sir, your honor, sir," Hunker replied. Chief Hightower had spent more than an hour that morning telling the two brothers how to behave in court. That was all the more difficult since, although court was taking place, they were not physically in a courtroom. The concept of being in court while not being in court completely dumbfounded the Lowery brothers. Hunker especially couldn't understand why he had to get dressed up just to go down to the bridge. He also didn't understand why he couldn't bring his rifle.

"Mr. Lowery," Nathaniel, began, "you were the first to spot the deceased?"

"Yes, sir."

"Please tell the jury what happened."

Hunker swallowed hard. He wasn't accustomed to speaking to large groups of people.

"Well, me and Toad, we'd been huntin'."

"Toad? Would be your brother?" Nathaniel interrupted for clarification.

"Well, yeah. He's right over there," Hunker explained pointing at his brother. "You met him last week, don't you remember?"

"Yes, Mr. Lowery, I remember your brother. I just wanted to clarify for the jury. Please continue."

Hunker paused, not having a clue what the word "clarify" meant. He froze for a moment as he looked at the faces of the jurors, all of whom seemed to know what the C.A. had just said. He finally looked at Chief Jefferson Hightower, who was standing next to Toad. Jefferson smiled slightly and nodded his head.

"Well," Hunker continued hesitantly as he glanced back at the C.A., expecting to be interrupted. "Me and Toad was walkin' across this bridge when I saw the tail of this big gator. I didn't waste no time 'cause gators move real quick, and if ya don't shoot quick ya ain't gonna get no second chance. They'll duck under."

"Where exactly were you and your brother standing when you spotted the alligator?" Nathaniel asked.

Hunker pointed to the other end of the bridge. "We was right over there."

"And where was the alligator?"

"The gator was right down there," Hunker said as he turned and pointed to the riverbed just below where he was standing.

"Please tell us what happened next."

Hunker didn't answer. He just looked down the slope.

"Mr. Lowery, please continue your story," Nathaniel repeated.

Hunker just stared down the slope, now showing some shock on his face.

"Good lord, that's Jewel Stoker," he said as he suddenly leaped off the bridge and down the slope.

"Mr. Lowery, you are under oath," Nathaniel said, almost yelling as Hunker disappeared from sight.

On the opposite side of the tracks Chief Hightower suddenly realized what was happening and ran across. When he got to the side of the bridge he looked down and said, "Dear God," as he looked at Jewel Stoker's mangled body impaled upon a small stump left broken from when they pulled Cliff's body from the same spot.

"Your honor," Nathaniel said in dismay as the judge also ran to look over the side of the bridge.

"Dear Lord," Buckner said when he saw the girl's body lying on her back with a piece of tree stump protruding out of her chest.

"Your honor, please," Nathaniel pleaded,

Buckner furiously whipped his head toward the C.A. "Nathaniel, shut up!" He then looked at one of the bailiffs. "Jimmy, get the jury out of here right now!"

As the bailiff began herding the jury away, Jesse, followed by his attorney, and Toad Lowery rushed across the tracks and looked down from the bridge. Hunker was next to the body.

"It's Jewel Stoker alright," Hunker yelled up. "She's been here a while, Jefferson. The critters have been eatin' all over her. Ain't no gator tracks, though. That one I shot must be the only one around here."

"Get back up here, Hunker," the Chief ordered. "Be careful not to step in any tracks."

Jefferson then turned to the Judge. "Your honor, I need to ask you to get your people out of here."

"Understood Chief," Buckner began just as Nathaniel got to the side of the bridge.

"Your, honor, you can't send the jury off, I need to set the scene, and I have pictures."

"Damn it, Nathaniel, you open your mouth again and I'm pullin' you off this case and sendin' it up to Anderson County."

The judge looked at Dinkler and Jesse, who were standing next to him.

"Mr. Dinkler, I need you to get your client back to the courthouse, right now," Buckner ordered.

Then the judge looked at Jesse who was standing stunned as he looked down at the riverside.

"Are you okay, son?" Buckner asked tenderly.

Jesse just stood there without saying a word. Dinkler grabbed his arm and pulled, but Jesse didn't budge.

"Please, Jesse." We need to go," Dinkler said.

Finally Jesse looked at him and the two walked away.

"Go with them, Cockwright," Buckner ordered to Nathaniel, who was still staring off the bridge.

Nathaniel looked at Jefferson with eyes wide. "You're going to get crime scene photographs of this aren't you?"

"Go!" Buckner ordered, and Nathaniel headed away with a bit of delight.

As they were walking away, the Chief looked over at Toad, who was staring off the bridge. "Toad, you're a deputy again. Go into town and find Corporal McKinney. Also find Shorty and Hobe and tell them that they're deputies, too."

"Does this mean that we get paid again?"

"Yes, Toad," Jefferson answered somewhat impatiently. "You and your brother will get paid. Now go get the Corporal."

Toad headed down the tracks and looked over at his brother who was coming up the slope. "Hunker, we're deputies again."

"Hunker," Jefferson said, looking at the two, "go down the tracks a bit and make sure nobody comes down here."

Hunker nodded and scuffled off with his brother.

The judge watched with disgust as the C.A., now joined by his deputy, walked somewhat joyfully to their car, then he turned to the Chief. "That kid didn't do this, did he, Chief?" He said evenly.

"No, sir, he didn't."

"He didn't kill that kid we're tryin' him for either, did he?"

Jefferson looked at the judge somewhat uncomfortably but also with a bit of new respect. "No, sir, he didn't. We know who did it. We don't know where he is, and we don't have enough evidence, but we know who he is."

"I'm going to put this case on hold, so you can have some more time. The C.A.'s almost dancin' 'cause he's got another murder to prosecute. The papers will be all over this. Most likely they're goin' to be pointin' all their fingers at that boy."

Buckner looked back down the hill, "You've got to get this guy, Chief. This is a mean one. When you and that Ranger get finished here, I want you two to come see me. I don't care if it's after midnight, just come out to my house and wake me up. You got that?"

"Yes, sir, Judge."

Jefferson watched as the judge continued to look down at Jewel.

"Good God, Chief. I'm not going to be able to sleep tonight. I've never seen anything like this."

Jefferson looked down the slope. "That's what I said when we found Cliff."

#

RUSK, TEXAS
9:15 p.m., Thursday December 4, 1941

It had been a long afternoon and evening for Chief Hightower and Corporal McKinney. It was almost noon before Toad had managed to find the Corporal and get him back to the river. They then spent the next three hours searching the riverbed and railroad tracks for evidence. After that the chief and corporal spent the rest of the day driving all over East Texas trying to find Richard Crawford. They were on the way home for the evening when Jefferson suddenly remembered that the judge had all but ordered him to give him a report.

On the way to Judge Buckner's house, Jefferson and McKinney had quite a discussion as to whether it was ethical or even legal to report their findings in an active murder investigation. It seemed all the more questionable considering that Buckner was the judge presiding over one of the murder cases that they were investigating. But, as Corporal McKinney pointed out, for that very reason they had no choice but to obey his demand.

It was after nine o'clock when they finally walked into the judge's home. The house was one of the largest, if not the largest, in Rusk, with an enormous wide, white porch supported by white Roman columns. Inside the house, the judge brought coffee as the three of them settled around a huge mahogany dining room table. Jefferson was somewhat uncomfortable. The only time he had been in a house anywhere near that large was only a few weeks earlier when he first questioned Jesse Rose, and that house wasn't nearly as large as Judge Buckner's.

"I appreciate the two of you coming. I know this is highly irregular, and I'm going to probably have to recuse myself from these proceedings, but it can't be helped. The fact of the matter is that I have a County Attorney whose only interest in this case is getting his face in the papers in order to run for some statewide office. This morning I realized that we have a serious killer running around this county, and the only officials interested in catching him are sitting in this room.

"Tomorrow morning I'm going to call a two week recess. Cockwright will have a conniption, but I'm not going to let him railroad that kid when I know good and well that he didn't do this. Now, what do you two think is going on?"

Jefferson looked at McKinney, but the corporal nodded for him to do the talking. That was the last thing the chief wanted.

He cleared his throat and started to speak. "Well, your Honor," he began.

The judge immediately cut him off. "You're in my house, so we can use names here. My office door says that the name's 'Nehemiah,' but if you call me that I'll have you sent to the county farm. Friends call me Buck," the judge said earning a chuckle from McKinney. The chief was still too nervous to appreciate the judge's sense of humor.

The judge looked at the chief. "Your name's Jefferson, isn't that right?

"Ah, yes sir."

The judge looked at McKinney. "And you're the famous Brewster McKinney."

McKinney just nodded. He was beginning to like this judge.

"Well, Buck," Jefferson paused, trying to gather his thoughts, "I'm not sure where to begin."

"I'll start. Five years ago I came to Elza to investigate a suspicious death," McKinney interrupted, to the chief's relief. "It looked like a man had gotten drunk and his car was broadsided by a train, but the chief here called the Rangers in because he thought there might be more to it. After the investigation, I left town with the only unsolved murder on my record. There was no question in my mind that the man was not killed by the train, but there was no evidence to prove otherwise. The man's name was Peterson Crawford. Interestingly enough, back in '18, I had also taken part in a raid on a brothel south of Maydelle."

"I remember the place," the judge interrupted. "The raid had somethin' to do with that crooked sawmill owner, right?"

"He was the impetus for the raid. But in the process there were two brothers arrested for resisting and assaulting an officer of the law. Their names were Peterson and Richard Crawford."

"I'm following."

"The cathouse was run by a woman named Juanita Carrillo Burney. Juanita had a daughter named Sarah Burney. The girl lived on the premises but apparently was not involved in the operation. As soon as she was old enough, she moved to Jacksonville and later to Elza to run a normal produce business. Sarah later married a man by the name of Irwin Stoker, and they had a daughter by the name of Jewel Stoker."

"The girl we found today."

"Correct," Jefferson said.

"Both killed on those tracks?"

"Barely a hundred feet apart."

The judge thought for a moment. "That's a curious coincidence."

"The one thing I've learned in all my years of trackin' down criminals, Buck, is that there are no coincidences. The bloody car belonging to Clifford Tidwell had prints from three different people. Tidwell's, Jesse Rose's, and two prints from Richard Crawford."

"Good Lord," the judge commented.

"There's more, Judge. I mean, Buck," Jefferson added. "Richard was at Cliff's funeral. He left with Jewel Stoker."

"Is there any connection between this Richard Crawford and the Stoker girl's mother?"

"Nothing that we can prove," McKinney replied. "Sarah Stoker disappeared a few weeks prior to Peterson being hit by the train."

"The story is that she ran off with some fellow in a traveling carnival that passed through town," Jefferson continued. "That story came by Cliff Tidwell and Jesse Rose. Both boys were quite young, but they had a tendency to know everything going on in town at the time. Her husband didn't want her back, so after questioning everybody in town and giving her picture to the county sheriff, we let it go."

"But now you two think that something happened to her."

"I never thought that Peterson was killed by a train," Brewster McKinney began. "My gut tells me that the Crawford brothers had some kind of contact with the Stoker woman; perhaps they were threatening to tell people that her mother ran a whorehouse, or perhaps they were threatening to tell people that she had worked there. I don't know. What we do know is that she suddenly disappeared, and the only people in Elza who seemed to know anything about it were Clifford Tidwell and Jesse Rose. Then a few weeks later, Peterson turned up dead."

"And now Clifford Tidwell is dead, and Jesse Rose is on trial for his murder. You're right, none of this is coincidence. What do you two think happened?"

Jefferson shrugged and looked at McKinney. Up to now, he had tried to avoid piecing together what had happened.

"I think the Crawfords killed Sarah Stoker, and the boys didn't say anything because they wanted to protect their friend, Jewel. I think they were there when Sarah died and promised to take care of Jewel, and that's exactly that they did."

"This Rose kid is willing to go to the electric chair over a promise?"

"There's more than that," McKinney added. "Jesse's girl. She's Peterson Crawford's daughter."

"Is that the pretty little gal who's been sitting behind him in court?"

"That'd be her," Jefferson added.

"He doesn't want her to know what her daddy did?"

"That's what we think."

"What about Richard? Have you located him?"

"I was at his house this morning when you found Jewel's body. His wife claims she hasn't seen him in a couple of weeks," McKinney explained.

"Wife? He has a wife, and he's carryin' on with this young girl?"

McKinney shrugged. Men like Crawford were common in his line, but, of course, judges rarely get the full picture of the people they prosecute.

"There's one more thing, Buck," Jefferson added, finally becoming comfortable. "My two deputies, the ones who were there to testify about finding the body of Cliff Tidwell?

They seem to be the last ones to have seen Jewel Stoker alive. At the time, she was with Jesse Rose."

"Dear god. We all know good and well that the kid didn't kill either of them, but every piece of solid evidence stacks right up against him," Buckner said and then looked directly at Jefferson. "Don't give anything to Cockwright. Not until I tell you to. He'll go wild with it. If not in court, he'll leak it to the press. I'm sayin' that as the judge. Direct all of his inquiries to my office. In fact, all of your communication with him is to go through me. Don't give him anything without my expressed permission."

Jefferson nodded, "I will, Buck."

"What about this Rose kid? Do you think he's in any danger from this guy?"

The two law officers looked at one another. Finally Brewster replied, "He could be. We shouldn't have let him get to the girl."

"I'll call the sheriff and have him put a deputy at Jesse's house tonight, and tomorrow I'll have him put in a cell until you two get this guy."

#

MAIN STREET,
ELZA, TEXAS
August 18, 1936

Jesse and Cliff walked along the street like they did almost every day. Both boys were carrying RC Colas. Jesse also carried a Dr Pepper. Jewel hadn't joined them since the carnival. The boys, of course, knew why.

Jesse and Cliff still hadn't gotten over the shock. He had shaken all night long. His heart had pounded so hard that he felt it in his head. Almost two weeks later, and he still hadn't gotten a good night's sleep. Part of him felt awful for Jewel. She'd just lost her mother and had no idea that she was dead. Part of him was terrified because he knew exactly what had happened and who was the cause. When he did sleep, he would wake up with the fear that he was going to be arrested. Even though at the time he had felt that he was doing something good, he couldn't escape the feeling that he'd done something terrible.

As the two boys came to their regular spot on the curb, Gemma walked out of Anna-Ruth's, crossed the street, and sat down next to Jesse. They left some space between Jesse and Cliff. That was Jewel's spot.

As Jesse handed Gemma her Dr Pepper, she asked, "Y'all still haven't seen Jewel?"

Jesse and Cliff glanced at one another and shook their heads.

"Have either of you gone to her house?"

"Naw, her pa don't like us much," Cliff answered. The two boys had anticipated that someone would ask and had planned the answer. They knew that no one would challenge it because they knew it was true. Actually, it was Cliff who had worked out their plan. Alibis and cover stories were his specialty.

"It's been a long time. She might be sick or somethin'."

"I suspect we'll hear about it, if she is," Jesse replied.

"If I get sick are you gonna just sit on this curb waiting 'til you hear somethin'?" she asked, looking directly at Jesse.

"I'd come check on you."

"'Cause my Daddy likes you so much?"

Jesse paused in thought, "I'd go into Anna-Ruth's and ask your mom."

"I want y'all to go to her house and check on her as soon as y'all leave here," she requested, but it sounded more like an order to the two boys.

Cliff looked at Jesse. "Have fun Jesse."

"What do you mean by that?" Jesse asked.

"I don't have to do what she tells me to do; you're the one that's in love."

Jesse glared at him.

"Clifford Tidwell," Gemma ordered, "if you don't go I'll tell your mother that you didn't have the courage to go check on a sick friend."

"My mom?"

"She comes into the shop every week. We talk."

Chief Hightower pulled his old blue flatbed into the parking spot next to where the kids were sitting.

"About what?" Cliff asked, suddenly concerned.

"She thinks that you and Jettie are gonna get married some day."

Cliff took a long swig from his RC, somewhat relieved. "How come Jettie and not you?"

She just smiled and looked at Jesse.

"Jettie's just a little kid."

"She's just a year younger than us," Gemma replied, rolling her eyes.

The chief got out of the car and walked around to where the kids were.

"What's up, Jefferson?" Cliff asked as the chief leaned against the front wheel-well of his truck.

"Have you kids seen Sarah Stoker?"

Jesse froze as he suddenly had an icy feeling in his stomach.

"Naw, I ain't seen her in a while," Cliff answered, as if lying were the easiest thing in the world.

The chief looked at Jesse and Gemma.

"What about you two, either of you seen her?"

Jesse and Gemma shook their heads. Jesse was terrified. It was easily a hundred degrees outside that day, but his body felt as if it were below freezing.

"Is somethin' wrong, Jefferson?" Cliff asked casually. "You look worried."

"She ain't been home in over a week. Irwin didn't bother tellin' me 'til this mornin'."

"When's the last time he saw her?" Cliff asked.

"At the carnival."

The boys looked at each other. They'd planned this.

"You know Jefferson," Cliff began. "I saw her talking to one of those carnival men that night after I seen Mr. Stoker and Jewel leave."

"What do you mean, Cliff?"

"Well, they were talkin' real close. Like whisperin'. I just remember thinkin' that it was unusual since her husband left."

Jefferson looked at Jesse, "You saw this too?"

Jesse's eyes widened, and he nodded.

Gemma looked at him.

Jefferson snorted and put his hands in his pockets and walked towards his office.

"Thanks, kids."

Gemma looked at Jesse again. She knew something wasn't right with this conversation.

Just then Peterson Crawford pulled his Plymouth sedan into a parking spot in front of Anna-Ruth's across the street.

Gemma stood to her feet. "I've got to go," she said as she handed Jesse her empty Dr Pepper bottle. "See ya tomorrow?"

Jesse smiled and said, "We'll be here," as she trotted across Main Street.

Peterson got out of his car and stared back at Jesse but stopped when Gemma ran up and hugged him.

#

CHEROKEE COUNTY COURTHOUSE, RUSK, TEXAS
December 5, 1941

Nathaniel Cockwright was not a happy man as he took his seat just after Judge Buckner walked into the courtroom. First the judge had spoiled the beginning of his big day by refusing to allow the press to accompany them to the crime scene. And then the rest of his day was destroyed when another body turned up. On the bright side, there'd be another murder trial, possibly with the same killer. All things considered, he could possibly keep his name in the headlines at least until after the New Year. On the other side of the coin, he was going to have a hard time convincing the judge to take the jury back out to that riverside, which was half his case.

Without pulling the heartstrings of the jury, it was altogether possible that he could lose this case. He did still have the pictures. So if Judge Buckner did do something stupid, like refusing to allow the jury back to the river, the brutality of the event was not completely lost. It would have been so much more effective with his impassioned speech right there on the bridge where it all took place, though. Still, Nathaniel wasn't born yesterday. He had one card left to play. Coleman's man at the *Houston Examiner* was aching for a copy of the crime scene photographs. Nathaniel's plan was to let them slip out after the jury got to see the riverside. The photographs would be reported to have come from an anonymous source in the Elza police department. Of course, after the events at the river, Nathaniel didn't know what to tell that reporter.

Judge Buckner slammed his gavel. "As a result of recent events I'm calling a recess in these proceedings until the murder scene we witnessed yesterday," he said with a glare at Cockwright, "has been fully investigated."

Nathaniel jumped to his feet. "Your honor."

Buckner turned to face the jury, ignoring the County Attorney. "Jury, you may all go to your homes and enjoy some time off. You will be notified when to appear again. Do not expect to be called before December 15th."

"Your Honor," Nathaniel pleaded.

"Mr. Dinkler, your client will remain in custody here in the courthouse. Mr. Rose, I'll see to it that you're made comfortable. You will be allowed visitors, but you will not leave the courthouse."

Dinkler stood, "Your honor!" He demanded, but before he could finish his protest Cockwright once again spoke out.

"Court is adjourned." Buckner slammed the gavel, stood, and walked out of the court, again paying no attention to either attorney.

After the judge walked out, a half-dozen reporters scrambled out of the back of the courtroom to find telephones.

Nathaniel Cockwright turned around and stormed out of the room, realizing that even with the photographs hitting the papers the story would be old news by the time court resumed.

At the defendant's table, Jesse sat somewhat stunned. He turned around to face Gemma, who was right behind him with Garvis and Murdock. Throughout the proceedings Gemma had made the drive into Rusk, skipping school. She wasn't worried about missing classes because for one thing she made good grades, and for another, her teacher, like everyone else in Elza, understood. They had not only lost a good friend in Cliff, but the man she and everyone else in town knew she was going to marry was being railroaded into prison. No one from Elza would expect Gemma to be anywhere else; no one except Garvis Rose, of course.

The first day Jesse was been in court, Gemma had accepted Murdock's invitation to ride into Rusk with him and Garvis. During the drive each way, Gemma had listened to Jesse's mother say on no less than four different occasions that it was unnecessary for the poor girl to miss school. There would be plenty of people from Elza to update her on what happened each day.

After that, Gemma drove herself to court.

Garvis was right about one thing. There was no shortage of Elza people in court. The fact was that it was pretty hard to get a seat. If it weren't for Jesse's attorney's saving them a place, there would be no way for Gemma or Jesse's parents to get in. Besides the reporters, who all but assaulted Gemma each day, there were dozens of local citizen from Rusk, Jacksonville, and many other small towns nearby.

Still, as hard as it was to get in, Brother Bill was always there, along with Mrs. Greer and several of the ladies from the Women's Auxiliary. Most of the time Toad and Hunker Lowery were there, though Gemma suspected that they were witnesses for the prosecution. Most notably from Elza though, were the Tidwells. Every morning they were sitting there in the courtroom when Gemma got there. But instead of sitting behind the County Attorney, supporting prosecution's case, the parents of the murder victim sat, quite conspicuously, behind the defendant, a fact not overlooked by the reporters.

So when Jesse turned around, Gemma was sitting directly behind him in a spot that Garvis felt was rightly hers. To Gemma's right, behind the defense attorney, sat Garvis and Murdock. To Gemma's left sat Suzie and Ned Tidwell, something else that got under Garvis' skin, in that she couldn't for the life of her understand just why Clifford's parents felt they had any right to sit so close to her son.

Jesse and Gemma just stared at one another.

"What does this mean?" Murdock asked Dinkler.

"I don't know. I'll request a meeting with the judge to get some clarification. I suspect that the judge is coming to the conclusion that Jesse is being railroaded so the C.A. can get some headlines."

"But Jesse has to stay here?" Gemma asked.

"Yes. I don't know what that's about, but I'll get to the bottom of it."

"I want you to get my son out of here right this minute," Garvis said bitterly.

"Mom, please," Jesse pleaded.

"You have no business staying in that filthy jail. Mr. Dinkler, I want you to march in to that judge's office and demand Jesse be released."

Murdock glared at her, "Garvis!"

"Don't 'Garvis' me. I want Jesse out of that jail."

"Mother, please. One of my best friends was murdered yesterday."

"I don't care. That has nothing to do with this. I'm sorry that poor girl is dead, but you don't deserve what that judge is doing to you."

"I do deserve it," Jesse replied angrily.

"Don't be ridiculous. Now, Mr. Dinkler, go in there and tell that judge that we're taking Jesse home," Garvis ordered.

"She'd be alive if it wasn't for me!"

Everyone froze and looked at Jesse as he hung his head. Years of torment swelled up in him, and tears filled his eyes.

"She'd be alive," he said softly.

The bailiff walked up and said, "Mr. Rose, you'll need to come with me. Miss, Crawford, Judge Buckner said that you're welcome to come along if you'd like."

"I'm coming also," Garvis stated, but it came out more like a demand.

Jesse stood with the bailiff, and Garvis made her way out from the row of seats behind the defendant's table.

"I'm sorry, ma'am," the bailiff replied. "The judge specifically said that Miss Crawford could come and go at will, but everyone else must sign in at the sheriff's office first."

Garvis stood fuming as Jesse and Gemma followed the bailiff out of the room.

#

The bailiff escorted Jesse and Gemma down to the jail in the basement of the courthouse. There he left them with a sheriff's deputy who was sitting at a desk outside of a barred door. The deputy opened the door and led them into a hallway with jail cells on either side. He went to a cell and opened the door.

"The judge sent word that I'm not to lock this door so you can get out and walk around a little. He also said that you're welcome to any visitors you want. He especially said that you can come and visit any time, Miss Crawford," the Deputy explained.

"Do you know what's going on?" Jesse asked.

"We've all been askin' that. Judge Buckner's never ordered anything like this before. The best anyone around here can guess is that he don't think you're guilty." The deputy turned and headed back to his desk. "If y'all need anything, just let me know. That's somethin' else the judge ordered. Anything you want to eat, you just tell us and we're to go fetch it."

When the deputy was back in his office, Jesse and Gemma sat down on the cot next to each other. Neither spoke. Sitting for long periods of time without speaking was not unusual for them. Silence had quit being uncomfortable years ago.

Gemma had been thinking about what Jesse had said about Jewel's death being his fault. There were things about all of this that had her confused. She didn't have any reason to think so, but for some reason the events of her childhood kept running through her mind. She also couldn't stop thinking about the night Jewel's mother disappeared and how Jesse had said that he had been there and that instead of leaving, she really had died.

After a long silence Gemma finally asked, "What was that all about upstairs?"

Jesse sat quietly, trying to avoid eye contact as he searched for something to say. Finally he looked at her and answered, "I can't tell ya, Gem."

"This has something to do with that night - the night Mrs. Stoker died, doesn't it?

Jesse sighed, "Gem, please don't. I can't talk about it."

Gemma stood. "You can't keep your secrets forever, Jesse. Whatever happened that night, it keeps coming back to haunt us. Who else has to die because of this secret? Me? Jettie? When does it end, Jesse? If we're going to get married, you have to tell me everything." She then walked out of the cell.

#

Cockwright stormed into his office, slamming his notes down on his desk. Prestwick, Coleman, and Vivian Yates had followed him upstairs into the suite, but each headed into their own offices.

"Staff meeting, now," Cockwright ordered without looking back to see if anyone was listening. A moment later his three person staff came into the office and took seats across from the large desk where Nathaniel had settled into his chair, still fuming.

For the first five minutes, all four just sat there. Nathaniel was staring, almost at nothing at all. The other three kept glancing at each other and then looking at the floor. No one wanted to look Cockwright directly in the eye. With the mood he was in, he was likely to start firing people.

Finally Primrose couldn't take anymore. "What are we going to do, Boss?"

Without answering, Cockwright turned around in his chair and looked out the window onto the town square that surrounded the Rusk courthouse. People were coming and going from the hardware store and drugstore. The events in the courtroom were the farthest thing from their minds. Judge Buckner was playing games with the prosecution of a killer, possibly a serial killer, and they hardly knew a thing about it. Then it dawned on him.

He whipped around in his chair, "Buckner may think that he can put this off, but if the people demand a trial, he'll have to give them a trial. Until court resumes again, I want all three of you to fan out around the county. Hit every soda fountain, café, diner, and hamburger stand in every town you can find. Start conversations about how this judge wants to set free the most vicious murderer this county has ever seen. Tell people that he's related to the kid. Tell them anything they want to hear. Just make 'em angry."

He then pointed at Coleman. "Get on the phone to that reporter in Houston. Tell him that I've got the biggest story of his life. Tell him that there's been a second murder that was even more brutal than the first and it took place in the exact same spot. Tell him that the victim is the girl that the killer and the first victim had been fighting over. Tell him that if he will come up here over the weekend I'll have him the lead story for Sunday, with photographs."

Cockwright then turned to face Primrose. "Get over to Elza and-"

He paused and looked back at Coleman, who was still sitting in his chair. "What are you waiting for? Get on the phone!"

Coleman got up and walked out of the room.

Cockwright shook his head in disgust and then returned his attention to Primrose. "Go to Elza and get the photographs of yesterday's crime scene from that two-bit police chief. Tell him that it's imperative that we have them right away. Wait - don't ask him for the pictures. He and that Ranger have been givin' me the business from the very beginning. Park on a side-street somewhere and watch for him to leave the office, then break in and take the film."

Primrose' eyes widened. "Are you sure about that, Boss? That's tampering."

"I've had it up to my eyeballs with those two. Get the film. They're rightfully ours, anyway."

#

COLDWELL'S FARM CENTER,
TYLER, TEXAS
August 18, 1936

Stumpy Coldwell was an excessively overweight man approaching his mid-forties. Aside from his weight, there were two outstanding characteristics that could always be said about Stumpy - he never wore a coat of any kind, regardless of the weather, and he was never seen without a half-smoked cigar hanging out of his mouth. Like many men his age, he was losing his hair. At the moment he was also losing his temper.

When Stumpy came home from the Great War in 1918, he returned to the job he'd previously held at his father's Farm and Ranch store selling feed, shovels, plows and even a few tractors. But Stumpy had much higher aspirations than making a meager living selling barbed wire gateposts. His route to France had taken him through New York, where he had seen wealth that far exceeded anything he had ever imagined from his father's little store in East Texas. He also learned that there were ways of acquiring income that did not include hoping that some manure covered farmer in bibbed overalls, which were his biggest selling item, would come in and pay his outstanding bill.

Less than a month after returning from fighting the Hun, Stumpy, who had lost his left arm to an infected shrapnel wound, hence the nickname, approached his father, Buckhorn Coldwell, with an ambitious plan to expand far beyond the little storefront on North Broadway. His idea was to build a giant store out on the new Troup Highway and begin selling much more than just shovels and plowshares. Stumpy argued all night with his father about how the world was changing and how farming would soon be a mechanized industry. The tractor would soon replace the mule, and the merchant who understood that fact would be sitting on a gold mine.

Buckhorn admired his son's aspirations, and even agreed that motorized farm machinery was going to become more and more important in a few years. What Buckhorn Coldwell didn't have was the capital and credit to finance his son's dreams.

That didn't stop Stumpy.

Something else Stumpy had learned in the Army was that there were men almost everywhere with a few extra minutes and a couple of extra dollars who couldn't pass an opportunity to spend those minutes wagering those dollars. It started with a late night craps game in the back of the Farm and Ranch store, but soon Stumpy had expanded his operation to the backs of pool halls and saloons. In time he added a numbers game, which was nothing but a lottery except payoff wasn't likely since the odds were a thousand to one in favor of the house. Pretty soon he was also taking bets on the horses. Some eighteen years later, old Buckhorn was long since dead, and Coldwell's was by far the largest Farm and Ranch store in all of Texas. Stumpy also owned the Ford dealership, and he was thinking of opening another store just to sell things like radios and washing machines.

But the stores were just a way to keep things looking respectable. The real money was in the gambling. There wasn't a pool hall, roadhouse, or honky-tonk within ninety miles that Stumpy didn't have a runner in. Put simply, if someone wanted to place a bet in East Texas, Stumpy Coldwell got a cut.

Stumpy bit down hard on his cigar as he looked out the window at the Plymouth sedan that passed the front of the farm store and circled around back. He'd had enough of the Crawford brothers. He had taken them in when they got out of prison because they'd come well recommended. Of course, they were recommended by another con, and a con wasn't exactly the best reference. Stumpy had made a mental note to not make that mistake again.

Gambling, though not a particularly respectable business, was still a business, and like all businesses it required a certain amount of work. The degenerates who threw their money away on thousand to one odds sometimes needed coaxing. Money didn't simply jump out of their pockets. Stumpy's better runners, the ones who brought in the best money, could easily make a handsome living selling something more legitimate like cars or real estate. They not only had the knack, they also put in the effort to get the job done. Those two Crawford fools couldn't sell water in the Sahara. They spent more time chasing whores than taking bets. The brothers dressed and strutted around like Cary

Grant, but when it came to bringing in a dollar, they were next to useless.

Then the younger one showed up at the back door one night with a bullet in his gut. Stumpy should have left him to bleed out, but then someone would start snooping around, and before long the whole state would know how Stumpy Coldwell really made a living. So for two weeks Richard Crawford had been laid up in the back of Coldwell's. Stumpy had a doctor on call for such a thing. It wasn't unusual for one of his runners to get into a little scuff, but they usually were smart enough to go home and call for help, keeping Coldwell's out of it.

Stumpy had an angry scowl on his face as Peterson Crawford came into the back of the warehouse section of the farm store.

"I want him out of here today," Stumpy ordered.

"Did the doctor say he's okay to leave?" Peterson replied.

"I don't care if he is or isn't. Get him out of here today."

Peterson led as they walked past the stacks of feed to a small storage side room under a glassed-in office. Inside, Richard was lying on a makeshift cot on some burlap sacks of feed. He was wearing a sleeveless undershirt and a pair of slacks. He managed to sit upright when he saw his brother and Stumpy walking in.

"How ya feelin' Rich?"

"Like hell. I still vomit after I eat."

"Well, we got a problem," Peterson began as he leaned against the wall and lit a cigarette. "Sarah's disappeared."

"Who's Sarah?" Stumpy asked.

"She's the whore that shot me," Richard replied.

"Nobody's seen her since that night."

"You two idiots didn't kill her, did ya?"

"She was alive when we left. I hit her and kicked on her some, but she was alive," Peterson answered.

"Was anybody else there?" Stumpy asked.

The two brothers looked at each other.

"Good god you fools," as he reached in his pocket and pulled out a roll of dollar bills. "Here," he said as he handed some money to Peterson. "Get him on the next train out of town. I don't want to see his face for at least a year. No, make it two years. You listen to me and you listen good. Don't you come around here 'til this mess is cleaned up. If this thing comes back to my door, my boys won't just kill ya, they'll run ya through a cotton gin first."

"I'll take care of it, Stumpy," Peterson replied.

"You make sure you do," Stumpy said as he stormed out of the room. He'd put up with enough of this foolishness. The last thing he needed was to have those two fools blow his entire racket because they couldn't keep their hands off an ex-prostitute.

"I can handle the kid. I'll get him to tell me what happened to Sarah. She's probably just run off," Peterson said to his brother once they were alone.

"What if she ain't? What if she's dead somewhere?" Richard asked.

"I tell you, she ain't dead."

"Then where is she?"

"I don't know. I'll find out from that kid."

"There were two kids," Richard said.

"Two? I thought there was just the one."

"No, there were two. And an old colored man."

"Colored man?"

"Yeah, he was a cripple. He was hobbling on a crutch."

Peterson leaned against the wall and thought for a moment.

"You know who he is?" Richard asked.

Peterson thought for a moment and then answered, "Yeah, I've seen him around town."

"You've got to do somethin' about them." Richard insisted. "Because if somethin' did happen to Sarah, they'll pin it on us."

Peterson took a long drag on the cigarette while thinking about the situation. He didn't think he had kicked on Sarah hard enough to kill her. Even if he had, what had happened to the body? The kids knew something, but what was he going to do? He couldn't just threaten those kids; they were likely to talk. Besides, they were always hanging out by the police station. That chief wasn't the brightest cop in the world, but if one of those kids said something to him, this whole thing could send them both back to prison. The old man was the key. Peterson could put some heat on him. If necessary, he'd kill 'im. If he had to, he could kill the old man and the kids. Killin' couldn't be all that hard. It would probably put 'im in good standing with Stumpy, too. The fat man needed people who weren't afraid to get things done.

"I'll take care of it. Let's get you to the train station."

#

TEXAS HIGHWAY 82,
ANDERSON COUNTY TEXAS
10:35 p.m., December 5, 1941

Chief Hightower pulled his prowler into the crowded parking lot of the County Line Roadhouse. Actually, he had no idea what the name of the place really was. It had no sign, but everyone in Cherokee county knew about it. Cherokee was a dry county, meaning that alcohol could not legally be bought or sold, although bootleg hooch was made and sold all over. But if someone wanted to have a good time at a roadhouse or honky-tonk, they had to drive over to Anderson County or down to Lufkin where the alcohol prohibition laws didn't exist.

The County Line Roadhouse was exactly that – the closest place to get legal hooch. Nestled in thick woods, it sat no less than three feet across the Anderson County line and was by far the closest roadhouse to any city in all of Cherokee county. In fact, it was so close to the county line that the entire parking lot was in Cherokee county. Jefferson didn't want to admit it to Ranger McKinney, but in his younger years he and his buddies had spent many a Saturday night dancing and drinking at "The Line" as it was called by almost everyone.

When Hightower found a place to park, the two lawmen sat in silence looking around the lot. McKinney was certain that Richard Crawford was in the place, but the chief wasn't so sure. Crawford had all but disappeared. They learned that he was a regular at the pool halls in both Jacksonville and Rusk. McKinney had talked to his Ranger in Tyler and learned that Crawford ran numbers in that area and that "The Line" was the only roadhouse, so it made sense that he'd be there since he hadn't been seen around the two cities.

A "runner" as the bookies called them, took the bets at saloons and pool halls and then took the cash to the bookie. The next day when the winning number was revealed in the racing forms, the runner would return to pay off any winners and take bets for the next game. Of course, with the odds that the bookies laid, it was rare that there was a winner. Most of the time, when a gambler actually got lucky, the "winner" lost it all on the next bet. For a bookie, a numbers racket was nothing but a way to print money.

Crawford was obviously trying to lay low. But McKinney had busted enough bookies to know that they survived on cash flow from their runners, which meant that Crawford had to keep working or risk the wrath of an angry bookie. If there was one thing McKinney knew, the thing low-life runners feared most was getting on the bad side of a bookie, and the best way to do that was to show up empty handed.

"Red '41 Chevy Coup," McKinney said pointing. "KJ4. I can't see the rest."

The Chief pulled a slip of paper out of his pocket. "3239," he replied. "I think that's our man."

The chief was amazed at how sure of himself McKinney always seemed to be, and how he also always seemed to be right.

"A runner in a car like that," McKinney remarked with a headshake. "Our boy's not a genius. Smart runners try to keep a low profile."

"Well, now we found him, what do we do? We can't arrest 'im."

"We wait a while to see where he goes."

Looking to the right, Chief Hightower noticed an old black pickup pull into the lot and park. He started to mention that Model-AA's were becoming rare when he saw Cherokee-One-Leg climbing out of the cab.

"What is that old Indian doin' here?"

"Is that the old man Jesse was stayin' with?"

"That's him. Cherokee-One-Leg."

The two watched as the old man pulled his crutch from the truck. He was wearing a long blue U.S. Cavalry coat that reached well past his knees. When he got his balance, he adjusted his coat and then reached in under the coat and adjusted a cavalry holster that he had concealed.

"Is that old man carryin' a gun?" the chief asked.

"It looks that way."

"We have to stop him! He's goin' to get himself killed!"

"From what I've read about him, I suspect he's the one who'll do the killin'. But I 'spect we should stop 'im."

The two law officers got out of the prowler and approached the old man from behind as he was slowly making his way to the front door of the roadhouse.

"Cherokee, what are you doin'?" Jefferson asked.

The old man glanced over his shoulder. "The job the two law officers are supposed to be doin'."

"Cherokee, stop," the chief said as he put his hand on the old man's shoulder.

Cherokee stopped and turned with a fiery look in his eye. "They're gonna put that boy on the chair if we don't stop 'em," he said with a glare at the chief.

McKinney had seen the look in Cherokee's eye on other men before. It was the look of a man who was prepared to go to battle and was not afraid to die. The lawman instinctively unbuttoned his coat and slipped his hand under it.

Cherokee looked at McKinney and asked, "Are you expectin' trouble?"

The two men stared at one another as the chief argued, "Cherokee, you goin' in there and getting' yourself shot isn't goin' to help Jesse."

"I ain't goin' to get shot," the old man replied without taking his eyes off McKinney.

"We'll take care of this," McKinney said.

"You're just now figurin' out who we're after. If you had acted when I told you to, that Stoker gal would still be alive."

"You're right. But damn-it, Cherokee," the chief began, still not recognizing the standoff between the lawman and the soldier, "you go in there, you'll be the next one killed."

"We can handle this," McKinney said, sensing trouble.

In the years to come Corporal McKinney would think back on that moment and wonder how it had transpired. Perhaps he had underestimated the man because of his age. Or perhaps he was the one succumbing to the effects of age himself. All he knew was that before he'd had time to get a grip on the .45 under his coat, the Indian fighter had his old army Colt revolver pressed squarely against Brewster's forehead.

The chief froze. Across the parking lot a man and woman had just stepped out of a car and were headed into the roadhouse when they looked over to see the spectacle of an old one-legged black man leaning on a crutch and holding a gun to the head of a much younger white man. The couple immediately darted into the building.

"Cherokee, please put that gun away and let us handle this," Jefferson pleaded.

The old man, still staring at McKinney, slowly pulled the gun away from the Ranger's head and slid it into the holster under his coat.

"I'm going in there," Cherokee said as three men came running out of the building. Two of the three were carrying baseball bats, but the one in the lead had a shotgun pressed against his shoulder.

"I don't know what this is about, but take it off my property," the lead man said as he stopped about ten feet away.

The chief's heart was pounding. A moment before Cherokee had a gun against Corporal McKinney's head, and now some bartender had a gun pointed at him. For a policeman who in ten years of service had never once pulled his gun out of the holster, this turn of events was a bit nerve-wracking.

McKinney calmly pulled his coat back, revealing his badge, "I'm a Texas Ranger, everything's under control. You three go back inside."

"I don't care if you're J. Edgar Hoover, take it off my property."

McKinney then glared at the man. The new breed of Ranger would politely explain that they had business there, and then he'd request that the bartender cooperate. McKinney wasn't the new breed.

"We have business here," McKinney said with a scorching fury, "and we will be here as long as we need to be. Now you will put that shotgun down and leave us be or I'll shut this place down."

"Shut me down? On what grounds?"

"Well, for starters there's a bookie operating in there. And if this house is like every other roadhouse I've ever raided, you have a back room where there's a craps game, and if it's not craps, you've got a couple of prostitutes workin' in there. If it's both you'll be shut down for at least a month. Now, what's it going to be?"

The man was clearly angry but lowered the shotgun and slowly turned around to face his two companions. "Go back in," he ordered.

"You're not gonna to let that Ranger push you around are ya, boss?" One of the men protested.

"Shut up and get inside," the leader ordered as the three walked away.

McKinney turned and looked at Cherokee. "You weren't plannin' to shoot Crawford, were you?"

"No," Cherokee said as he turned and headed toward the door. "You boys better hurry before he hightails it out the back."

The chief looked at McKinney for explanation as they followed the old man.

"The bartender's warning Crawford that we're out here," McKinney explained.

"Then we better hurry," the chief answered, his heart still pounding.

"I don't think we need to," McKinney answered.

The two policemen followed the old man into the building. Just as they got inside they saw Crawford head out the back door. As he went out he looked back at them.

"Should we try to catch him?" Chief Hightower asked.

"No," McKinney replied. "He'll be deep in those woods before we can get to the door."

"What should we do?"

Cherokee smiled and turned and headed back out. "I've got some corn liquor at my place if you boys want talk."

McKinney looked at the chief. "I'm not sure what that old soldier is up to, but I think we just helped him lay his trap."

Chapter 13

Cherokee handed a small glass with homemade whiskey to Brewster McKinney, who sat down on one of the three chairs in the little old house. Cherokee then poured a second glass for Chief Hightower as the policeman looked at all of the plaques, medals, and pictures on the wall above the fireplace that served as a shrine to a long military career. Many of the pictures showed Cherokee in his cavalry uniform standing next to colonels and generals.

"Good lord, Cherokee," the chief commented. "I wouldn't be surprised to see a picture of Custer up here."

The old man settled into a rocker closest to the fireplace and shook his head.

"Custer," he snorted with disgust. "He was a damn fool. My pa scouted for 'im. Pa was smart enough to quit before Little Bighorn. Custer got all his men killed, and the papers acted like he's some kind of hero. If he'd lived he would have gotten court marshalled."

The chief looked at the old Indian and then at McKinney.

The Ranger just grinned and shook his head. The life this old man must have had.

The chief looked back at the pictures. "Is that Teddy Roosevelt?"

343

The old man grinned. "Ole Teddy. The Colonel was a born leader. He didn't know the first thing about fightin' a war, but his men would have followed him straight into hell if he'd led 'em there."

McKinney took a sip of the whiskey while the chief sat down in the third chair. Normally he should have considered arresting a man who was in possession of illegal liquor, but it was late, and the Ranger had much more important things on his mind than some small-time bootlegger. Of course, it didn't hurt that the stuff tasted pretty good.

"What do you know about Crawford?" Brewster asked the old warrior.

Cherokee leaned back in the chair with his glass resting on his good leg.

"Well," Cherokee began, "he had a lot to do with that Stoker woman killin' herself back in '36. And he wants Jesse dead for killing his brother."

The chief's eyes widened as he and the Ranger looked at one another.

"Jesse killed Peterson Crawford?" McKinney asked.

"Yeah, but if he hadn't've I would've. I thought he was gonna kill the kid. Took 'im out to the tracks. I suspect he intended to scare the boy. It was me that he really wanted. He tried to shoot me, but all he got was my peg. I fell down before I could get a shot off. Jesse clubbed him over the head with a piece of Bois de Arc." The old man grinned, "That Bois de Arc is so hard, it's like getting hit with a hammer."

"What happened to Sarah Stoker? You said she killed herself?"

"You remember that lynchin' up in Jacksonville?" Cherokee asked, seemingly changing the subject while looking at the chief.

"Bucky Davis," the Chief commented.

"Mert, his pa, is one of my cousins. They said Bucky raped some gal. The boys, Jesse and Clifford, were there at the hangin'. I don't know how, but they figured out that the oldest Crawford boy was the one who'd raped that poor gal. There was a lot of talk in those days about riots after that, remember?"

"Yeah, I remember."

"I asked the boys to keep an eye on Crawford for me. I guess I hoped that maybe we could prove that Crawford did it, I could turn him over to some of the boys here in the Grove. Well, the kids figured out that Crawford was doin' somethin' with the Stoker woman. They'd seen him talkin' to her a couple of times. One day they climbed up on the picture show and saw 'im hit her."

"That's what they were doin' up there?"

Cherokee nodded. "Well, the night of the carnival she had a fallin' out with her husband because of the two brothers. Stoker left with their daughter, and the woman went walkin' down that alley behind your police station all by herself. Jesse followed to keep an eye on her.

"I was sittin' on my tailgate sellin tomatoes with Clifford when we heard gunshots from that alley. We got there just in time to see the two Crawfords hightailin' it. According to Jesse, Sarah said she was pregnant. He thinks they had raped her. Well, she wasn't one to just take it; she pulled a gun and started shootin' at the two. She hit the younger one, but the older brother got the gun from her and beat her up a bunch. When the brothers took off she shot herself. Jesse and Clifford held her as she died."

"Dear god, they were just boys back then," the chief commented.

"Yeah, it was pretty hard on 'em."

"What about her body?" The chief asked.

"To tell the truth, I don't know what they did with her. Jesse and Cliff wanted me to leave. Remember now, that lynchin' was just a few weeks before. The boys were afraid of what would happen if I got seen with a dead white woman. Lookin' back, I probably should've gone for you, but the fact was that I figured that the boys were right. Nobody would have believed what two kids and a colored man had to say when there was a dead, pregnant, white woman layin' there."

The chief hung his head down. "You were probably right."

"That still doesn't explain what happened to her body," McKinney added.

"Those boys know every armadillo hole within miles. I suspect they used that old Ford stake-bed and took her deep into the woods someplace. That, or they tied some rocks to her and dropped her in the river," Cherokee explained.

"Why are you just now tellin' me this, Cherokee? I don't care about Irwin, but poor Jewel should have known what happened to her mama," Jefferson said.

Cherokee leaned forward and rested his elbows on his knees, holding the glass in both hands. "She begged us," he answered with a break in his voice.

"She didn't want her girl knowin'," he continued. "And she didn't want those two little Crawford girls knowin' what their daddy had done. She was a good woman. She didn't deserve to die like that."

"Are you tellin' me that Jesse's willin' to face the electric chair to keep Gemma from knowin' what a louse her old man was?" Jefferson commented.

"We talked a lot about it, but the boy's got a head harder than that Bois de Arc branch. He won't budge on that. I think he figures he's guilty of murderin' her pa."

"But you said Peterson was going to kill him. He wouldn't have gotten in trouble for that," Jefferson added.

"Either of you ever killed a man?" the old man asked.

Both lawmen shook their heads.

"It stays with you. There's nothin' you can do to wash it off. I suspect Jesse's thought about that night every single day since he was twelve years old. I bet he wakes up at night seeing that guy's face. I know that I do. And that girl of his, can you imagine what it's like to love a girl knowin' that you killed her daddy? All she remembers about her father is that he loved her. She don't know about his bad side. How do you think she'd feel if she found out that her daddy was a rapist? And how do you think she'd feel if she found out that the man she hoped to marry had killed him? That poor boy ponders on those things every single day. That's an awful lot of weight for a young man to carry around. He don't want to die, but he'd rather die than have that girl go through life thinkin' her daddy was a bad man."

#

STAFFORD'S BAR,
LUFKIN, TEXAS
2:15 p.m., Saturday December 6, 1941

Irwin Stoker had been off the Cherokee County work farm for a little over twenty-four hours. He had been drunk for almost twenty of those hours. He was surprised when a sheriff's deputy drove up to the road gang and called his name. The deputy didn't say much about why he'd been called or why he was being escorted to see Judge Buckner in the back seat of a county sheriff's vehicle and not one of the school buses used to haul the inmates. All the deputy said was that Buckner had ordered his release.

When he got to the courthouse, the shackles were removed, and he was given his own clothes. He was then taken through a series of offices that led to the judge's private chambers.

The judge was sitting behind his desk in shirtsleeves. Surprisingly, he stood and came around the big mahogany desk and asked Irwin to sit down with him. He then told the deputy who had escorted Irwin to go. It came as a complete shock when the judge told him that his only daughter, Jewel, had been found dead. He wasn't told anything else except that foul play was most likely involved. The judge then assured him that the Texas Rangers were on the case and those involved would be apprehended within days.

After leaving Judge Buckner's office, Irwin was driven home by another deputy. Forty-five minutes after hearing the news about Jewel, Irwin was drunk. He awoke around eleven that morning with a throbbing headache and not a drop of liquor to help him with it.

The closest place to buy a real bottle of whiskey was way down in Lufkin. Irwin didn't want to make the long drive, but the only other option was to get the corn whiskey they made over in Pleasant Grove. The corn mash would be better than no whiskey at all, but he'd just spent the night drinking that stuff, and the headache he was experiencing was the result. He didn't want another headache. What he needed was some real whiskey.

Six bottles of Old Crow cost him almost all the cash he had in the house.

On the way back to Elza he decided to spend what was left on a hamburger and a couple of drinks at Stafford's Bar on the north end of town. But before going in he managed to drink down about half of one of the bottles of Crow.

He was sitting at the bar finishing up his hamburger when he overheard two men at the end of the bar talking to the bartender about those murders up in Elza. Irwin's ears perked up when heard them first mention Elza, but they had his full attention when they said that the second kid killed was a "pretty young blonde-headed gal."

Irwin sat there with his head down and began to weep.

The bartender was the first to notice the man at the middle of the bar crying over his hamburger. He didn't think much of it at first. It wasn't unusual to see a man crying in Stafford's, especially in the afternoon. Most of the time it was because some poor farmer got his note called in by the bank or some poor oil field worker got fired, leaving him with a house full of kids to feed and no paycheck. This one was obviously a farmer.

Finally the bartender went over to speak to the man. Usually these guys needed someone to talk to. If you give them a couple of drinks and an ear, they would go on their way.

"You want another drink, fellow?"

"No, I ain't got no money for no more."

The bartender looked at the man, who was obviously torn up.

"Here," the bartender said as he refilled Irwin's glass, "this one's on me."

Irwin took a swig, "Thanks."

"You hang out as long as you want. Did you hear about those killins up in Elza? We was just talkin' about it. That 'Alligator Killer' done it again. Got him some gal this time."

Irwin stared at the man without saying a word.

"You okay, fella?" the bartender asked.

"That gal was my daughter."

Suddenly the room fell silent as every head turned his direction.

The bartender was stunned. "Oh, man, I'm sorry. Here have another."

He poured another drink as the two men from the end of the bar moved down next to Irwin.

"My god, man. I'm sorry about your girl. Charlie pour him one on me," one of the men said.

"They can't let that kid get away with this. They ought to go up there and lynch 'im. That's what they ought to do."

#

MAIN STREET,
ELZA, TEXAS
11:00 a.m., Saturday August 15, 1936

It had been another boring morning for Jesse and Cliff. For the third straight day there hadn't been any deliveries. Mr. Washington had said that he thought there would be some in the afternoon. So the two boys were back to sweeping and stocking shelves at the feed store and McMillan's.

They had just finished and were heading up Main Street to see what was happening at the domino hall when Jewel turned the corner right in front of them, just a block past the Palace. It had been three weeks since they had seen her. That had been the night of the carnival - the night her mother had died. Jewel, of course, didn't know her mother was dead.

Jesse and Cliff had both wondered what they would say whenever they saw her again, though they had never discussed it. The fact was that discussing Jewel would just make them think about that night, and both of those boys wanted that memory out of their minds.

Jewel walked up to them with her hands in her pockets. "Hey."

"Hey," the two boys replied simultaneously.

For a moment the three just stood there without saying anything. By now everyone in Elza had heard the story that Sarah Stoker had run off with some carnival worker. Of course, only Jesse and Cliff knew the truth.

Jesse finally broke the silence and said, "I'm sorry about your mom."

Jewel just shrugged. There wasn't much to be said on the subject.

After another moment of silence, Cliff suddenly reached into his pocket and said, "I've got your money."

"What money?"

He handed her some cash. "From the deliveries. You weren't around the last couple of weeks to get your share."

Across the street Gemma came walking out of Anna-Ruth's and headed toward them.

"But I wasn't here," she said to Cliff, somewhat confused.

"We're all partners, remember. The business is part yours."

She smiled and looked at Jesse. "He's just doing this 'cause he's afraid I'll beat him up, isn't he?"

She and Jesse laughed and Cliff frowned as Gemma joined them.

"Hi," Gemma said to Jewel.

Jewel smiled back and said, "Hi." There was a new connection between the two girls that hadn't existed before.

"You guys makin' deliveries today?" Gemma asked.

"Mr. Washington said he may have some this afternoon," Jesse replied.

As they were talking, Peterson pulled up and parked in front of Anna-Ruth's. He looked at the kids gathered together, climbed out of the car, and walked across Main Street toward them.

"If some afternoon you don't have anything to do, you can come over to the shop. I'm there every day," Gemma said to Jewel.

"Okay, thanks. Maybe this afternoon if we don't have a delivery," Jewel replied.

"Why would she want to hang around a dress shop?" Cliff asked.

Gemma looked at him with annoyance. "Because she's a girl and might want to talk with another girl for a change."

"What do girls have to talk about that guys don't?"

Jesse cringed at Cliff's remark.

"I can tell her all about how you're afraid that I'll beat you up," Jewel said with smirk.

Cliff fumed, trying to form a reply as Peterson walked up.

Neither of the boys had seen the man coming, and both immediately tensed at his presence. For Jesse, Peterson Crawford had been the subject of a lot of thought. On one hand, Jesse knew what an evil man he was. On the other hand, Peterson Crawford was Gemma's father. He wanted to tell someone, but other than Cherokee and Cliff, there wasn't anyone he could tell. If he told Chief Hightower what he knew, he'd have to explain about Mrs. Stoker, and they had promised not to do that.

"Hi, kids," Peterson, said with a broad smile as he walked up to them.

"Hi daddy," Gemma said and hugged her father.

"You know, honey," he said to Gemma, still smiling. "I was thinking that we should go to the movies tonight. Would you like to invite your friends? It's on me."

Gemma looked at the others. "You guys want to go?"

Jesse and Cliff were white with fear.

"I don't think I should. I'd better stay home with my dad," Jewel answered.

"Yeah, I don't think that I can, either," Cliff answered. "I'm kind of in trouble."

"You're always in trouble," Jewel commented.

"Yeah, well, Able McCormack won't let me go to the movies this summer, remember?"

"Oh, yeah," Jewel said as she laughed.

Peterson looked at Jesse. "Well how about you, sir?"

Jesse froze. He couldn't think of a reason not to go, and when he looked at Gemma's eyes, he didn't really want one.

"Ah, okay," he said hesitantly.

"Great," Peterson said, still smiling.

#

COLDWELL'S FARM AND RANCH,
TYLER TEXAS
6:00 p.m., Saturday December 6, 1941

McKinney and Chief Hightower were sitting in McKinney's coupe across the Troup Highway from Coldwell's. They had the headlights off, and the car was somewhat hidden in the shadow of a mechanics shop.

The Rangers had known about a gambling setup in Tyler for some time, but they had just recently begun to get a grasp on the scope of the operation. A former runner and current snitch facing a serious parole violation had sung like the proverbial canary. The bookie in charge was a one-armed war hero by the name of Stumpy Coldwell. He had at least fifty runners operating from Dallas to Shreveport and in every town in between. Richard Crawford was one of those runners.

There were four Rangers present for the raid. McKinney and Hightower were out front and three other rangers were out back, along with ten Texas State Highway Patrol Officers. No local police were involved. The Tyler Police Chief was privately notified, but his department was not brought in on the operation out of suspicion that a few of his officers were on Stumpy Coldwell's payroll.

McKinney and Hightower's job was to make sure that no one slipped out the front door. They were only there as support and because their investigation was loosely connected. Under normal circumstances the old Ranger would have taken a much more active part in the operation, partly because of his experience and seniority, but mostly because he didn't like sitting out front away from the real police work. That wasn't possible this time. McKinney had Hightower with him, and although he was gaining respect for the chief as a police officer and investigator, the man lacked the training and experience necessary for a raid like this.

McKinney hoped that Richard Crawford would be picked up. With luck McKinney could get him to slip up during questioning. Criminals weren't the smartest people in the world, and criminals under pressure tended to make stupid mistakes.

The three Rangers would go in from the back. According to the snitch, the store closed at five and the runners gathered at six thirty. They all parked behind the store and met in a large room on the second floor overlooking the warehouse behind the store. Some evenings as many as thirty or forty runners would be there all at the same time. From the cars McKinney had seen pulling around back, this was shaping up to be a good night. He counted forty-five cars. One of the cars was a red '41 coupe.

#

Stumpy stood silently looking down at Richard Crawford, who was sitting in front of him. The room was a large office with windows that looked out over the enormous warehouse behind the Farm and Ranch store. It sat above the storage room where Richard had spent two weeks recuperating after being shot some five years before. Around the room were other book-runners, but alongside Stumpy were three men Richard didn't like seeing.

Stumpy Coldwell considered his gambling business just that - a business. He provided a service in exchange for payment. If a degenerate gambler wanted to win some easy money, he could place a bet with one of the runners, and if he won he would receive his reward. If he lost, well, life was hard. The problem was that sometimes the gamblers made bets on a line of credit and "forgot" to pay. On those occasions Stumpy had to employ people who could retrieve his payment. The three men he used for this particular task were the men beside him. They were old war buddies from the days in Belleau Wood in France.

Richard knew that the boss was angry with him, but he couldn't help smiling when he looked at Stumpy. The large man was standing, as he often did, with his one arm holding the other arm as if he had his arms crossed and resting on his fat belly. Only Stumpy had just the one arm, which Richard found terribly amusing.

Stumpy didn't find anything amusing about Richard Crawford, and he especially didn't like the smirk on his face.

Stumpy bit hard on his cigar and said, "You told me that this mess in Elza had nothing to do with you, but last night a Texas Ranger showed up at 'The Line' lookin' for you."

"I said," Richard argued with way too much confidence for Stumpy, "that they picked up a kid for it, and they did. You've seen the papers. He's going to the chair for sure."

"And what about that girl?"

"The kid did that one, too. He was out on bail," Richard replied with a smile. "I'm tellin' you, Stumpy. I got this all sewed up."

Stumpy grunted. He was beginning to hate this punk. Crawford was just like his brother - a two-bit loser who thought he was George Raft.

"What was that about last night, then? I don't need no Rangers snoopin' around."

Richard slumped in his chair. "Okay, there's a loose end I've got to take care of. But that's it. I'll take care of it tonight and no more trouble."

Stumpy stormed around the room, trying to control his anger.

"What are you going to do, kill someone else? You listen to me, you little punk. You get out of here, and you clean up this mess. I don't want to see you or any Texas Rangers. You get out of East Texas for at least six months or a year 'til this blows over. If I see you again, you get to deal with these three," Stumpy said, motioning to the three large men leaning against the wall.

Stumpy looked at one of the men and nodded his head. The man then grabbed Richard by the coat collar and dragged him down the stairs, through the warehouse, and tossed him out the back door.

Crouched in some brush about twenty yards behind the back door, Texas Ranger Warren Wilson was checking his sawed-off shotgun alongside Texas Highway patrolman Luther Francis when they saw a man tumbling out the back door of Coldwell's Farm and Ranch. Wilson looked at his watch.

"Ten more minutes," Wilson whispered.

The man got to his feet and stumbled his way to a small car and drove away.

"Could you tell the color of that car?" Wilson asked Francis.

"It's dark, but I think it was red."

"Dear god, I hope that wasn't the guy McKinney's after."

"If we'd grabbed him, we would have blown the whole operation."

"Yeah, well you aren't the one who's going to have to explain that to Brewster McKinney."

#

STAFFORD'S BAR,
LUFKIN, TEXAS
9:15 p.m., December 6, 1941

Irwin had been drinking in Stafford's since early afternoon. He'd thrown up twice and passed out once, but the bartender kept giving him coffee, and the other patrons kept buying him food and whiskey. Considering the amount of liquor he'd consumed, he was fortunate to still be alive.

All afternoon and evening people were coming in with new information about what was happening up in Rusk. One story was that the kid on trial was a rich kid whose father had paid the judge to sweep it under the rug. The rich part, Irwin was able to confirm. The kid lived in one of the largest houses in town, and his father was a big dog in the oil fields. That part riled everyone in the bar because they all had been around the oil fields enough to know that the rich oilmen were crooks who made their money off the poor farmers who owned the land they drilled on. Another story had the judge being a relative of the kid, and he wanted to let the kid off. That story, Irwin couldn't confirm but he was drunk enough to say that it wouldn't surprise him none, which was enough to count as a fact to the crowd that was mostly drunk and growing more angry by the minute.

"The judge shouldn't be allowed to get away with this. That boy went and murdered poor Irwin's little girl. Somebody ought to go up there and lynch that rich punk."

#

TYLER POLICE STATION,
TYLER, TEXAS
10:55 p.m., December 6, 1941

Corporal Brewster McKinney had never been so angry in his life. In the past half hour he had chewed the hide off every Texas Ranger on the scene and most of the Highway Patrolmen. If any of the Highway Patrolmen or Tyler Police officers had any aspirations of becoming a Texas Ranger, those dreams promptly changed. No one wanted a job where you worked under a man like that big Ranger, and nobody involved with the raid at Coldwell's was going to escape the wrath of Ranger McKinney.

Chief Hightower didn't know exactly what to do except stay close behind the Corporal and keep his mouth shut. With the mood that McKinney was in, Jefferson feared the slightest remark could set him off.

The two officers, along with two other Rangers, five highway patrolmen, and the chief of the Tyler police department were standing shoulder to shoulder in a tiny observation room looking through a one-way glass mirror into the interrogation room. In the room was a plain wooden table where Ranger Wilson sat across from Stumpy Coldwell.

McKinney was standing squarely in the center of the glass window, blocking the view for most of the other officers present. He knew it; he also knew that no one was going to challenge him. He was working an active murder case, and as far as he was concerned, that far outweighed a punk numbers racket, even if it did pull in a million dollars a year.

McKinney was growing impatient, not that he was a particularly patient man to begin with. Wilson was taking his time. In general, McKinney liked Wilson. He was part of the new breed of Ranger. Wilson was a graduate of the University of Texas with a degree in law enforcement. McKinney grumbled at the thought of it. When he had started there was no such thing as a degree in law enforcement. All you needed was a gun and the guts to go after a bad guy. In the early days most of the Rangers couldn't even read, let alone go to college.

The old days were long gone. There was a time when an interrogation like this would begin with a pistol whipping, but that was a long time ago, which was, the old Ranger had to admit, a good thing. Texas was growing up, and law enforcement had to grow up as well.

But that didn't mean that he had to stand there cooling his heels all night while waiting for that green college kid to get around to asking the important questions. For ten minutes Wilson had danced with this fat bookie without getting to the point. Finally, McKinney'd had enough and barged into the interrogation room and laid a picture of Crawford on the table in front of Stumpy.

"Where is this man?"

Stumpy bit down on his unlit cigar, as was his habit whenever he was angry. Right now he was angry. He had lawyers to handle the legal stuff. He knew that he'd be out on bail in an hour, so this cops and robbers stuff was just academic as far as he was concerned. At worst he'd end up doing six months or a year in Huntsville. He knew that was a possibility when he had started his racket. What angered him was that this thing didn't need to blow up. It was all because of that little Crawford punk, and the proof was lying on the table in front of him.

"I don't know."

"Why'd you have your boys toss him out of your warehouse tonight?"

Stumpy glared at McKinney and then leaned back and said, "Look, I'm a business man. I don't know what you boys think I did to drag me down here, but I'm clean and respectable. But that aside, no matter what you think, I ain't got anything to do with any killin'. We tossed that boy out because I think he killed those people down in Elza. In fact,

I think he killed some woman four or five years ago, too. I don't want nothin' to do with him. If you're after the people who killed those folks, I'm happy to help ya all I can."

"Where do you think he went?"

"I don't know. He said somethin' about cleanin' up a loose end."

McKinney turned around and looked into the glass mirror. All he could see was himself, but he knew Chief Hightower was there.

"Cherokee."

The old Ranger darted for the door.

#

PLEASANT GROVE,
CHEROKEE COUNTY TEXAS
11:45 p.m., December 6, 1941

Cherokee-One-Leg sat still in his rocking chair looking up the long lane from his house. It was a cool night, and he had on his old cavalry long-coat, but that wasn't enough, so he also had a blanket lying across his lap. It annoyed him that the cold tended to bite him so much more as he got older. There had been a time when he and his little brother would have gone hunting on a night like this wearing little more than Arapaho leggings and moccasins.

Cherokee had his army Colt in its holster on his waist and his W.W. Greener double-barreled shotgun was resting across his lap. The Greener was a much finer weapon than Cherokee had ever owned or could ever have afforded, with its crafted inlay and monogrammed stock. It was his finest possession, not because of the price tag, but because it had been a gift from none other than President Theodore Roosevelt himself. After Cuba, Roosevelt wanted to go on a hunting trip into the high Rockies and asked Master Sergeant Julius Caesar Bradford, whom he and most of the army referred to as Sergeant Cherokee, to go along as his guide. Colonel Roosevelt enjoyed hunting like no one Cherokee had ever met. He liked to hunt just about anything from bear to deer and even pheasant and dove. Cherokee understood shooting a bear or deer. Both of those animals produced good meat, and the hides were quite useful as well. But those little birds hardly had any meat worth eating, and they didn't have any hides at all. Still, Cherokee couldn't help but admire the fine shotgun Roosevelt carried to shoot the birds. A month after he retired from the service, a box arrived at his home with the shotgun inside. On the stock was a brass plate with the inscription:

To Master Sergeant Bradford
One of the finest soldiers I've ever known.
Thank you for your years of service.
Theodore Roosevelt,
President of the United States of America

Cherokee's telephone had rung five minutes earlier. It was a signal that there was an unknown car driving through the Grove. The telephone was a new edition to Pleasant Grove. Most of Texas had gained access to telephones ten years earlier, but in places like the Grove, public services tended to arrive later than everywhere else.

He'd really had no need for a telephone, but for lines to be strung all the way out to Pleasant Grove, at least ten residents had to sign up for service. Since Cherokee was one of the few who could afford the monthly bill, he signed up to make it an even ten. Tonight Cherokee was glad to have it.

He watched as a car turned onto the lane about a quarter of a mile ahead. The headlights switched off as the vehicle slowly approached. When the car got about halfway down the lane, three pickup trucks turned onto the lane behind it. They didn't bother switching their lights off. When the car got about twenty yards from the house it stopped. The three trucks continued until all three were lined up, side by side, a few feet behind the car.

Cherokee stood to his feet and stepped to the edge of the porch without his crutch. The Greener was resting in the crook of his arm.

The car sat there, unable to back out and with Cherokee directly in front of it. Cherokee watched as a large black man got out of one of the pickups and approached the driver. The car started to leap forward, but in a flash, the old cavalryman whipped up the Greener and shot a hole in the front windshield. The car stopped suddenly and sat there as the large black man opened the driver's door. The man then took Richard Crawford by the collar and pulled him kicking and screaming to Cherokee's front porch.

"Is this him, Cherokee?" the large man asked.

"Yep, that man's the reason they lynched Bucky."

#

PLEASANT GROVE
CHEROKEE COUNTY TEXAS
12:15 a.m., December 7, 1941

McKinney drove slowly through the small community. There were probably seventy to a hundred homes in Pleasant Grove. Most of the families in these homes were related, though possibly a couple of generations removed. The town had sprung up sometime after the Civil War and had grown with each new generation.

There was something eerie about the town at that moment that McKinney couldn't quite figure out.

Suddenly Chief Hightower said, "Stop the car."

McKinney stopped, not so much because he was told to, but because he felt like he needed to.

"The lights," the chief said. "All the houses have lights on. I've driven through here at night a dozen times, and the lights are always out."

"Everybody's up," McKinney said as he looked around. "Why would they all be up this late at night?"

The chief then whipped his head around looking at every house.

"The trucks are gone."

"Trucks?"

"Everybody here has a pickup. They're all gone," he said as he opened the door. "I'm going to ask somebody what's going on."

"No. We need to get out of here. The last thing they want around here right now is the law. We'll worry about this in the daylight." McKinney said as he put the car into reverse and turned around.

"Do you think Richard got Cherokee?"

"No. I think Cherokee got him. I just hope that tomorrow we don't have another killin' on our hands."

#

THE PALACE THEATER,
ELZA, TEXAS
9:00 p.m., August 12, 1936

Cliff and Cherokee were sitting in the old man's Model-AA pickup two blocks away from the Palace Theater. After they'd made their deliveries and Jewel had gone home, Cliff tried to talk Jesse out of going to the movie with the

Crawfords. The boys knew Peterson had seen Jesse that terrible night.

Jesse didn't know what to do. He wanted to be with Gemma, but he was afraid of her father. He reasoned that Mr. Crawford couldn't do anything to him in the movie theater and certainly wouldn't with Gemma there.

Cliff wasn't so sure, though. When Jesse went home to clean up for the movies, Cliff headed straight for Cherokee's. The two decided that the only thing they could do was sit outside the theater and make sure Jesse got home all right.

"Are you sure your parents don't mind you being out at night?"

"Of course they mind," Cliff said. "I told 'em that I was tired from work. They think I'm asleep."

"What if they check to see if you're in bed?"

"Then I'll get in trouble," he answered matter-of-factly.

"You're not afraid that you'll get a whippin'?"

"Aw, Cherokee. I get a whippin' every few days anyway."

Up the block, people started walking out of the Palace.

"Movie's out," Cliff said.

#

Jesse and Gemma came out of the theater together. Peterson, Anna-Ruth, and Jettie were behind them. When they got across the street, Peterson said, "Anna, why don't you walk the girls to the house. I'll drive Jesse home."

Jesse's stomach tightened. "That's okay. I just live a couple of blocks over."

"Oh, I can't let you walk home alone at night. Besides, I've got to take care of some business." Peterson argued.

Anna-Ruth glared at her husband. She was accustomed to him being away at nights on "business" and clearly didn't like it.

"Honey, you know that a lot of my work takes place at night."

"Okay," she said, somewhat perturbed as she led Gemma and Jettie away.

"Bye, Jesse," Gemma said as she followed her mother.

"Bye," Jesse said as the knot tightened in his stomach.

Peterson turned in the direction of his car. "Come on, Jesse."

Jesse stood still. Peterson then put a hand on Jesse's shoulder.

"Come on," he ordered.

Jesse looked around. Most of the people from the movie were either getting into cars or walking a few blocks up. He could see Chief Hightower in the lobby of the Palace and started to try to move away in that direction, but Peterson tightened his grasp on Jesse's shoulder.

"Get in the car," Crawford said in a tone that was nothing less than a demand.

Jesse tried to run, but Peterson grabbed his shirt collar so tightly that the boy couldn't get free. He then opened his suit coat, revealing a Smith and Wesson .38 Police Special tucked in his trousers.

"I said get in the car," Peterson ordered again with an even icier tone.

With his hand on Jesse's neck, Peterson led the boy to the driver's side of his car.

"Get in," Crawford ordered as he opened the door.

Jesse climbed in and tried to slide to the far side and get out, but Peterson quickly got in and grabbed the boy. With his left hand he pulled the revolver from his pants.

A block up, Cliff tensed as they watched Jesse getting into the car with Peterson Crawford. The boy and man sat silently as Peterson started the car and drove past them and out onto the highway.

Cherokee started his truck and said, "Go home."

Cliff looked at Cherokee. "I'm going with you."

The old man pulled the truck out onto the street and said, "You really should go home."

"If you make me get out, I'm just gonna get on the back of your truck."

Cherokee sat there in the street for a moment, contemplating what to do. He really didn't need another kid along, but he realized there was nothing he could do about it.

"Hurry. We don't want to lose them," Cliff demanded.

Peterson drove with one hand on Jesse and the other holding the steering wheel and the revolver. He didn't want to shoot the kid, but there could be no choice. The brat had stuck his nose where it didn't belong. If he had to kill him, Peterson would drop the kid in the river. They may find him in a few days, but Peterson would say that he had dropped the kid off at home. He'd be questioned, but they wouldn't be able to prove anything.

He turned off the highway onto the dirt county road that headed up and across the railroad tracks. He pulled to a stop on the rise where the dirt road crossed the track.

"You and your friend sure do get around," he said.

Jesse just sat there. His heart was pounding as he searched for a way out.

"So what were you doing in that alley that night?"

Jesse just looked at the man.

"Not going to talk, huh. I guess you're not going to tell me what happened to Sarah?"

Jesse continued to sit there looking at the man as Peterson let go of Jesse's collar and in one swift move whipped his right hand into Jesse's face, hitting him firmly in the nose. Then in a fit of fury, he began hitting the boy over and again with his fist and slamming him against the right side door. As Jesse was pounded on, he tried to open the door, but Crawford grabbed him by the hair and put the gun barrel against Jesse's head.

"You've caused me and my brother a lot of trouble. Now, tell me what happened to Sarah."

Jesse squirmed and tried to pull away, but Peterson yanked hard on his hair and pressed the gun so hard against his head that it left an indentation in his skin. He felt something moist on his face as he realized that his nose was bleeding.

Peterson then looked up into his rear-view mirror.

"Well, it looks like we have company," he said. "I'd bet even money that's your one-legged friend."

Jesse looked back to see the faint outline of Cherokee's Model-AA pickup rolling up the road toward them. The headlights were off, but Jesse knew that it had to be Cherokee.

Peterson opened the door and slid out, pulling Jesse along by the hair.

"You're just a nuisance, but that old one-leg is a real problem. Have you ever watched a man die, Jesse?"

"What are you going to do?" Jesse asked as he fought being dragged by the hair toward the old railroad trestle.

"I'm going to shoot that old man, thanks to you."

"No," Jesse protested, trying to pull himself free.

Peterson dragged Jesse halfway to the trestle and waited.

Cherokee pulled the truck to a stop a few yards behind Peterson's car. He and Cliff could see Peterson up on the tracks, holding Jesse by the hair. The old man stared icily at Peterson and then instinctively reached down to his belt and checked that the flap was pulled back on his old cavalry holster.

"Stay here," he said to Cliff as he opened the door.

Cliff started to speak, but Cherokee swiftly, and far too quickly for a man his age, put his hand on Cliff's shoulder.

"This time, you're stayin'."

Cliff glanced down, and for the first time saw the holstered revolver on Cherokee's belt.

Cliff swallowed hard. "Okay, Cherokee."

The old man climbed out of the truck. He left his crutch behind and hobbled up the slope of the tracks. He had a little trouble because his wooden leg kept pressing into the soft ground. The old man was winded when he finally got up the rise.

Jesse, still squirming, yelled, "Go back, Cherokee! Go back!"

Peterson didn't waste any time. Once the old man was squarely on the track, Peterson fired the weapon. The shot hit Cherokee's wooden leg, causing the old man to stumble to his knee. Cherokee returned fire but aimed high to avoid accidently hitting Jesse. His shot nicked Peterson's right temple.

Cliff leaped out of the truck and ran toward Cherokee.

Peterson was surprised that the old man had fired back and even more surprised that he'd been hit. He raised his gun-hand to his head and simultaneously stepped backward. His foot hit the rail, causing him to fall backwards, taking Jesse with him as the two tumbled down the rise. Peterson quickly got to his feet and rushed up to the track. Jesse fell a little farther down the slope but got to his feet almost as quickly. Next to him was a broken tree limb. He grabbed it off the ground and followed Crawford up the slope. The limb was much heavier than he had expected, but he ran up behind Crawford with the limb in his hand anyway.

When Peterson got up to the track, Cherokee was already on his feet with Cliff beside him. The old man started to fire his weapon but stopped when he saw Jesse come up the slope. Peterson raised his gun to fire just as Jesse's tree limb hit him squarely across the face. Stunned, the man fell limp to the ground, hitting his head on one of the rails.

Both terror and stress erupted from Jesse as the boy hit the man again on the head. He felt the skull crack, but the Bois d'Arc branch stayed intact. Crawford lay there lifeless as Jesse struck the man yet again, releasing weeks of tension that he'd held inside since watching Sarah die.

Cliff ran up the tracks to Jesse's side and stopped his friend, who was rearing back to pound on the man again. The two stood there for several minutes looking at Peterson's bloody, unrecognizable face as Cherokee hobbled up to them. Jesse tossed the tree limb off the tracks and suddenly started to cry. As much as he tried, he couldn't stop himself. Cherokee put his arms around both boys and held them tightly to him. They stood there silently with hearts pounding, sobbing as they looked down at Gemma's father.

Finally, after several minutes, Jesse calmed down.

"Boys," Cherokee said, "we can't just hide this one. We've gotta get the chief."

Jesse wiped the tears from his eyes, "No."

"We can't just hide another one. Folks will believe one person ran off, but they ain't gonna believe it a second time."

Cliff looked up the tracks at Peterson's car.

"Then we let 'em find him."

#

An hour later Cherokee pulled his flatbed Ford to a stop on Main Street and let the boys out. In the distance they heard the whistle of the ten-thirty train headed to Houston. All three instinctively looked in the direction of the tracks, and then the two boys and the old Indian headed off without saying a word.

It had taken them most of the hour to carry Peterson's body back to the car. Once he was in, Cliff started the motor and drove it squarely onto the railroad crossing. Cherokee had a jug of his corn whiskey in this truck, so they splashed most of the jug on Peterson and the seat. They then broke the jug on the track, making sure that it would be found.

#

FOREST
NORTH OF ELZA, TEXAS
1:20 a.m., December 7, 1941

Cherokee-One-Leg was sitting on a wooden chair in an old broken down barn. Around the room hung oil lanterns that put out a dim orange glow. Friends of his grandfather had built the barn nearly a hundred years before. It sat on what was once a thriving piece of farmland but had long since been overgrown by trees and brush. The nearest home was almost a half-mile away.

A dozen men surrounded the old warrior; all the men were black. A shirtless Richard Crawford hung suspended before him. His hands were tied to a crossbeam above. Each leg was tied to a rope that wrapped around a pulley. One pulley was connected to the wall to his right and another pulley to his left. Every five minutes two men pulled on the ropes and his legs were stretched apart another inch or two, and the man would scream in agony.

The door opened and Mert Davis walked into the barn. His face and hair had showed considerable age since the day Bucky was lynched. Mert looked at Cherokee, who nodded. Mert then walked in front of where Crawford hung.

"You were there? You were there when Bucky got hanged?" the old man asked.

Richard was in obvious agony, to the point that he hardly heard the man. It took him a moment to realize what he was being asked.

Richard looked at Mert and shook his head and said, "No."

Cherokee looked over at the two men holding the ropes wrapped around the pulleys and nodded. The men gave the ropes a tug and Richard screamed out.

"Stop," he pleaded. "Yes, yeah, I was there."

"You watched, knowing that Bucky was innocent?"

Richard looked at the man in terror. After a moment he nodded.

"Who raped that girl?"

Richard hung his head in silence. Cherokee looked over at the men with the ropes and they gave it another tug.

"Stop," Richard yelled. "We did it, me and Pete, my brother. But it wasn't any rape. She was one of those girls, you know. They like that."

Mert looked at him in disgust. "She was beaten to a pulp. No girl likes that."

"No, no, we were just playin'."

Cherokee nodded, and the men holding the rope gave it another tug until the man screamed again.

"You dumped her on the side of the road and made her tell folks that Bucky did it," Mert said with a blistering look in his eyes.

"Don't kill me. Please don't kill me."

Mert was repulsed as he turned to look at Cherokee. The years since Bucky's death had paid a toll on the man, but it had also softened the rage. Five years earlier he would have gutted the man and left him to bleed to death, but now all he felt was disgust.

"Give him to the law. We ain't murderers. If the law don't do it, though," Mert said as he looked back into Crawford's eyes, "then we bring him back here, split him in two, and feed 'im to the pigs."

Chapter 14

MCMILLAN'S STORE
ELZA, TEXAS
2:45 a.m., December 7, 1941

A 1940 model Dodge panel van with the words *Houston Examiner* printed on the driver-side door pulled to a stop under the awning in front of McMillan's. The driver hopped out with a bundle of newspapers and sat them on a wooden box next to the front door.

Most Sunday editions of the Houston *Examiner* showed up in places like Elza late Sunday morning or even in the afternoon. The *Examiner's* primary customers were, of course, residents of Houston and the immediate vicinity. A normal run would be loaded on trucks and sent to the delivery points where the papers would be given to paperboys who either delivered them to subscribers or sold the papers by hand on street corners.

The second run would go to outlying areas where the papers often didn't reach their destination until late morning. In most cases, Elza being no exception, the papers would be put in a wooden box on the front porch of a local store. Since the store was normally closed on Sundays, there was a slotted, locked coin box sitting next to the wooden paper box where customers purchased the papers on what was nothing less than an honor system.

From time to time, when there was a major news event or story that warranted it, the *Examiner* would print a Special Edition. An SE, as it was called among journalists, could sometimes double or even triple the sales of a normal run. There were times when the SE way outsold expectations. On those occasions the paper would make a second run, which was a newspaper editor's dream and nightmare at the same time. It was a dream because they made a lot of money; it was a nightmare because some board member would want to know why the editors had missed potential sales because they miscalculated demand. To prevent the latter, the editors made every effort to get the papers to the circulation points as early as possible. Then, hopefully, they could estimate the need for a second or even third run by the sales of the first.

The Sunday of December 7, 1941 edition of the *Houston Examiner* promised to be an edition that might possibly warrant a second or even third run. In fact, the editors of the paper were so excited about their exclusive on the "Alligator Murders" that they printed up fifty thousand extra copies in the first run.

#

PARKING LOT
STAFFORD'S BAR
LUFKIN, TEXAS
9:30 a.m., December 7, 1941

Irwin Stoker awoke in the front seat of his Chevy pick-up. He had the worst taste in his mouth that he'd ever had and a headache to match. Fortunately he had four and a half bottles of Old Crow to help with both.

In his pocket he had two dollars left. Apparently the bartender hadn't charged him for the hamburger or the first two drinks. The various folks in the bar paid for the other ten or fifteen drinks.

As he recalled, somewhere back toward town there was a railcar diner, and the only thing he needed as much as another drink was a few flap-jacks.

In ten minutes he was in Saddler's Diner eating a much-needed breakfast when a man he had most likely met the night before but for the life of him couldn't recall walked up and told him how sorry he was about what had happened to his little girl. He said that no one should die like that, and he couldn't believe that the papers printed those pictures.

"What pictures?" Irwin asked.

A moment later the Houston paper was lying in front of him. In large letters the headline read, THE ALLIGATOR MURDERS. Below were two of Bobby Weatherholt's crime scene photographs side by side. One of Cliff's mangled body and the other of Jewel lying face up, impaled on a tree-stump. The following pages were filled with stories and theories and more pictures. All the stories implicated, if not outright convicted, Jesse Rose of the killings. The stories quoted unnamed sources close to the investigation that claimed that the judge on the case was going to great lengths to protect the wealthy young defendant. One of the stories questioned the judge's integrity, suggesting that the judge was related to the defendant. Another story detailed the wealth of the defendant's family, indicating that the judge might be profiting from the case. All the stories mentioned the name of the County Attorney on the case and how the C.A.'s office was working tirelessly to ensure that justice would be served on behalf of the victim's families.

Irwin took one look at the picture and began to weep. He never even saw the stories. In minutes everyone in the diner was crowded around the old farmer.

Finally, one of the men put his arm around poor Irwin and invited him to come down to church with him. He said that the best thing for a man at a time like this was to be near some people who would pray with him.

By the time the eleven o'clock service started, everybody at the Old Union Road United Methodist Church, Reverend Braswell included, had told Irwin that they loved him and were praying for him and hoped that justice would be served against that rich kid that, "went and killed his little girl." Reverend Braswell completely tossed out his planned sermon on how Joseph resisted temptation with Potiphar's wife so the entire congregation could gather and pray for Irwin in his terrible time of suffering. Of course, Reverend Braswell got a sermon in, it just wasn't one that he had written in advance. This sermon focused on how the true Christian can't sit back and allow injustice, like what was happening up in Rusk with the killer of Irwin's daughter.

In the parking lot after the service, the gatherings were somewhat different than usual. There had been rumors that some good citizens around town were thinking of going up to Rusk to see to it that the pig-headed judge up there didn't let that murderin' kid go free.

Twenty minutes later Irwin was sitting in a Dodge pickup between two men whose names he couldn't recall, in a line of other pickups headed up to Rusk to make sure that justice got served for poor Irwin's little girl.

Irwin, of course, had no idea that all across East Texas, groups of good citizens who had seen the morning paper were also headed up to Rusk for the same reason.

#

CHEROKEE COUNTY COURTHOUSE
RUSK, TEXAS
10:00 a.m., December 5, 1941

Living the life of a hobo taught Shakes a great deal over the years. He learned, for instance, that there are good times and bad times to get arrested. Contrary to what most people might think, getting arrested wasn't always a bad thing. In jail a fellow could find a reasonably warm and dry place to sleep. Jail was also an excellent place to get a couple of good meals. Granted, the food might not be particularly tasty, but when one was living off the generosity of the public, one can't be particularly choosy.

Shakes also learned the best time to get arrested. Smart hobos never get arrested in the morning. If you get picked up in the morning, by mid-afternoon you may be working a chain gang. On the other hand, if you get hauled in during the evening, you will probably get to spend the night before seeing a judge. The best time to get arrested, as any self-respecting hobo knows, is always Friday night. Judges, all judges, take weekends off. That means that if you got arrested for some small offense, you could sit the weekend out in the city jail or a county holding facility until Monday morning when the judge would then decide if it was necessary to send you on to the county farm. With a little luck, the judge would release you for "time served" and you'd never spend a minute in the county lockup.

Shakes usually got arrested for things like drunkenness or loitering. Most of the time he'd be taken to see a judge on Monday and then sentenced to a couple of nights in jail. By Monday he would have already served a couple of nights, so normally he'd be released.

This time was a little different for Shakes Blankenship. He was in for a drunken and disorderly charge, but he had not been drunk, and he was only disorderly because he had made every effort to appear like he was drunk. Shakes was not the man he had been a few years ago.

He'd heard a lot of talk around the country about the murder in Elza. Every newspaper carried something about the "Alligator Killer." On the rare occasion when Shakes was where he could hear a radio, there was always mention of the frighteningly violent killing. Now there was a second killing.

More and more, Shakes was hearing talk that if the court didn't do the job, then someone else would have to do it. He didn't know anything about the killings in Elza. He hadn't even been in town when the first one had taken place. All he knew for sure was that the kid in the cell across from him didn't do it. Shakes didn't know why he was so sure, but he was confident in his position.

"You awake, Jesse?"

"Yeah," Jesse replied from the other cell.

"You want to talk?"

"There's nothin' else to do," Jesse answered.

A minute later Jesse was sitting in a swivel desk chair outside Shakes' cell with his feet propped on the cross section of the cell door.

"What's up, Shakes?"

"You don't remember me, do you, Jesse?"

"Should I?"

"Not really. It was a long time ago. I was just a hobo. Folks don't remember hobos."

Jesse looked at the man, trying to recall.

"You once handed me a watermelon," Shakes said with a break in his voice.

Jesse sat up in the chair. "What are you talkin' about, Shakes?"

"You and your buddy and a girl brought watermelons to that little shantytown outside Elza when you were kids. I was there."

Jesse smiled. "I remember that day. Me and Cliff got in a bunch of trouble for doing it. We had to plant a whole new crop for Mr. McAlister 'cause of that."

"That day changed my life, Jesse."

Jesse, brow wrinkled, asked, "What do you mean, Shakes?"

"Do you remember goin' out to New Birmingham?"

Jesse's heartbeat quickened. He remembered a lot of things about New Birmingham.

"I used to live there," Shakes continued. "I still do, at least part of the time. I made a little apartment in the back of the Southern Hotel. I was there the day you three kids came walkin' through.

Shakes had Jesse's full attention.

"I grew up here in Rusk. I was valedictorian of my High School class. My dad owned the hardware store on the square."

"I've been in there," Jesse said.

"It doesn't surprise me. Just about everybody around came in at some point. I hated that store. My sister and her husband run it now.

"It took a lot of work, but I managed to go to college up in Chicago. I did every kind of odd job you can imagine in those days. I even worked for the county coroner for a time. When I finished school I got a job as an investment counselor. People paid me a lot of money to bet on the markets for 'em. I did good. I made my clients a lot of money. I made a lot for myself, too. I got so busy and full of myself that I didn't even go to my parents' funeral. I felt like I didn't have the time. All I wanted to do was make more money.

"Of course, my sister hated me for that. I can't really blame her. What kind of person doesn't have time to go to their parents' funeral? I gave her my half of the store. I guess that kind of helped make up for the fact that I didn't have time to come back down. The fact is that I didn't want that store. I didn't need it. I was doing too good in Chicago to waste my time on a little hardware store in a back-wood East Texas farm town.

"Not long after my parents died, I met a girl and got married. She was beautiful, but all she cared about was my money. When the market crashed, she sued me for a divorce. She took everything. In just a few weeks time I went from living in a luxury Michigan Avenue apartment to a south side hotel that was infested with rats and cockroaches. I lost everything - my wife, my money, my job. All I had left was a suit and a hat.

"Somewhere along the way I started drinkin'. I don't remember when. Before long my hands started to shake. When I drank, my hands would calm down. At least that was my excuse. I think I just liked the escape that booze gave me.

"That's when I started ridin' the rails.

"When you're hoppin' on trains you sometimes know where it's goin', but other times you don't. It doesn't matter 'cause, well, when you're a hobo you're not really goin' anywhere. I got to the point that I didn't care where the train was headed. I just got on a train to take me to another town where I could do an odd job to buy a meal or two.

"One day I got off a train and realized that I was just a couple of miles from home. So, I walked into Rusk to see my family. I was so used to askin' for handouts by that time that I thought I'd see if I could get one from them. I saw my sister right out there on the square. She pretended that she didn't even know me. I deserved that.

"I was walkin' back to Elza when I remembered exploring New Birmingham as a kid. I wandered up there and found a room in the back of the Southern Hotel. Before long I had me a decent place to live. Only I separated myself from the rest of the world. I felt like I no longer needed anyone else. I felt like no one needed me. The world had kicked me aside, like I was worthless. The truth was, I thought that I was worthless. So I lived most of the time in my private little town where no one would ever come to bother me. It was great. Once in a while I'd go to the shantytown and try and get some food, or I'd catch a train someplace and do some day work. But most of my time was spent in my private little utopia.

"Then one day I was in my little apartment reading a book when I heard some voices. I got off my bed and looked out and saw the three of you. I was hiding in the shadows when you walked onto the porch of the hotel and looked in. I followed when you three went down to look into the old mineshaft. I was across the street while you were looking into that hole.

"I was angry. And I was afraid. You had invaded my home. I had gotten away from the world, and you three brought it back to me. The way I saw it, if someone saw me, the cops would run me out, and I'd be back to living in railcars and shantytowns.

"As I looked across the street at the three of you, I thought about rushing over there and pushing you into the mine. The hole is a deep one. You'd never get out. No one would ever find you, and with some luck no one would come to New Birmingham looking. I'd keep my little home. My life would go on in peace.

"I almost did it, too. I don't know for sure what stopped me.

"Then the next day I went down to that shantytown to barter for a couple of cans of beans. That's what we did in those days, we'd bargain with each other, 'cause nobody had any money. But right after I got there, a cop showed up in a flatbed Ford with some kids who started giving everybody watermelons. You handed me two."

Jesse looked Shakes in the eyes. "I think I remember you."

"Sometime after that the story went around the shantytown that you kids got in a heap of trouble for stealing those watermelons," Shakes smiled. "I hated myself more than ever after that. Y'all were three good kids and I almost killed all y'all.

"About a month after that I woke up in the middle of the night because a really noisy Ford Model-T flatbed went rumbling down the street. I sneaked out and watched you and that other boy lowering something into that mine. I don't know what it was, but it looked like a body.

"I stewed over that for a couple of days, that and the fact that my life had sunk so low that I had almost committed murder for a bed in the back of a crumbling down hotel. Finally one day I went into town. That cop stopped me and asked if I'd seen some woman. He said she'd gone missin'. I told him that I didn't know anything about it.

"I didn't know what y'all put down that shaft, but I knew this. Three kids who will steal watermelons, knowing full well that they'll get in a heap of trouble, so they can feed some folks who don't have enough money to buy dirt aren't going around killing people and hidin' 'em in mineshafts. I thought long and hard about it, and that was the conclusion I came to.

"One day I was in Elza and I notice the steeple on the Baptist church. I hadn't walked into a church since before I left Rusk. I was just a kid back then. I don't know why I went in. I guess that I just wanted to hear what someone else thought about it. That was the day I met that preacher."

"Brother Bill," Jesse added.

Shakes smiled broadly. "Brother Bill. He's one of my best friends now. It sounds funny to say that. Back then I didn't have any friends. Now I have a lot of 'em."

Jesse watched the man who seemed to have nothing but couldn't keep from smiling.

"I went in there to tell him about you kids, but I really never got a chance to talk about y'all. That preacher kept making me tell him about myself. I probably talked for the better part of an hour. I told him about everything - Chicago, the market, my wife, my parents dying. I told him how I was about the lowest person on earth.

"Then he asked me how God felt about me. Well, I thought that was pretty obvious. I was a sinful man and God didn't like me much. Hobos are always meetin' preachers. They're always telling us that God loves us, but we know better. We always say that we know he loves us and we pray with 'em and take whatever handout they've got. Only, this guy didn't leave it at that, he kept pressin' and finally I flat out told him what I thought. I said, 'If God loves me, how come I ended up a drunken hobo living in a ghost town?'

"Then he said to me, 'Shakes, you haven't ended up yet. God started something with you and this life you're livin' is part of it.'

"He didn't bother tryin' to save me or anything like preaches usually do. He just gave me an old Bible and told me to prove him wrong. So I tried. Let's face it. I'm a hobo. I ain't got nothin' and I ain't worth nothin. Why would God want to do anything with someone like me?

"I read that book cover to cover a couple or three times, and all I could find is stuff that backed him up. Finally one night, all alone in my little room at the Southern, I prayed for the first time in my life. Oh, I'd said prayers before, but this was the first time I'd ever really tried to speak to God.

I don't really know what I said. It was something like 'if I'm worth anything to you, take me and use me.

"I think it was that night when I realized that I wasn't a hobo because of all the things I'd done. I was a hobo because of all the things I could do.

"Jesse, back when I first met you, I was a loner without a single friend in the world. Now I have friends in every train depot and back alley from here to Chicago. Somewhere along the way I realized that just because I was a hobo, it didn't mean that I had to be miserable.

"But I still couldn't get the night that you and that other boy came to New Birmingham out of my mind. So about a month after meeting that preacher I bought me a rope, and I climbed down that old mineshaft."

Jesse stared at the man as a cold chill went through him.

"It took me all day, but I managed to get that woman's body out of that hole. I buried her in that little cemetery just past the smelter. I spent over a week workin' on the marker. There was a pink granite corner stone on the old bank building. It took a lot of work but I managed to get it free and rolled it up to the cemetery. I carved her name on it."

Jesse broke down in tears. "We didn't kill her, Shakes, I swear we didn't kill her," he said, trembling.

"I know. Like I said, I worked for a coroner back in Chicago. Capone was around in those days. I saw a lot of shooting victims. I also saw a lot of suicides too. You'd be surprised at how many people either miss or change their minds at the last second only to shoot themselves in the neck and chest. What happened that night, Jesse? Why'd she kill herself, and why'd you boys try to hide her?"

Jesse wiped the tears from his eyes and looked at his new friend. "She was Jewel's mom. You remember the girl who was with us the day we gave you the watermelons? I don't know the whole story. There was this man in town, two men, really. They had hurt this girl; they beat her up real bad, maybe even raped her. Up in Jacksonville they lynched a black guy for it, but it wasn't him who did it. It was these other two. Me and Cliff had seen this one guy meet Mrs. Stoker in the alley across from the Palace, so we climbed up on the roof to watch. We saw him beat her. Then one night I followed her into an alley. Both of the men were there that night. She told 'em that she was pregnant. They just laughed at her. She pulled a gun and tried to shoot one of 'em, but she ended up getting all beat up. I just sat there in the shadow like a coward and watched. When they left she shot herself."

"Are these the same men who killed your friend?"

Jesse nodded. "I think one of them did it. The other's dead. He got hit by a train."

"Why didn't you tell that cop about all this?"

"Before she died, Mrs. Stoker begged us not to tell anyone. She wanted to protect Jewel."

"Why don't you tell anyone now? They're going to throw you into prison, they may even give you the chair."

Jesse wiped the tears from his eyes and looked at Shakes and said, "You remember the girl that came to see me last night?"

"Gemma?"

"Her father was the one that got hit by the train. The other man's her uncle."

Shakes sat back on his bunk and thought for a minute and then looked up at Jesse.

"Have you noticed, Jesse, my hands don't shake anymore? I don't know when it stopped. Just one day I looked down, and my hands weren't shaking. I don't drink anymore either. I'm still a drunk. If you offered me a swig, I'd probably down the whole bottle. But I almost never take that first drink anymore.

"I had everything in Chicago, and at the same time I had absolutely nothing. Now I have nothing, but feel like I have everything.

"Kid, whatever happens in this trial, even if you get sent to jail, you're more valuable than you will ever know. You haven't ended up yet."

#

CHEROKEE COUNTY COURTHOUSE
RUSK TEXAS
11:45 a.m., December 7, 1941

When Gemma stepped out of the car, she was a bit surprised at the crowd in town on a Sunday. There wasn't a single parking spot on the square. She parked a block away on Henderson Street in front of the new laundry and dry-cleaning service. There were mostly men huddled in groups. As she past one group it frightened her to hear some man say, "Somebody' gotta do somethin' about that kid before he murders any more people."

She felt the stare of angry eyes as she climbed the courthouse steps. When she got to the door, she saw a line of pickups pull into town, circle the square and then head off to find places to park.

The judge had been very kind to Jesse and Gemma. He had seen to it that Gemma could come and go all she wanted and that she could bring things like food and books. Gemma's mother had made pot roast, a Sunday tradition at the Crawford house. Normally Gemma would get up and go to Sunday school on a Sunday morning, but the past few weeks had altered her routine to some extent. This morning she waited until the pot roast was fully cooked and packed some into a little Dutch oven to bring up to the courthouse for Jesse.

When she entered the courthouse, a sheriff's deputy greeted her with some nervousness. All the deputies had been very nice, and this man was no exception, but he stood at the door looking out at the crowd with obvious concern.

"What's going on?"

"I'm not sure," the deputy replied. "They started showing up about a half hour ago. If many more show up I'm gonna have to call for help."

"Does this have somethin' to do with Jesse?"

"Have you seen the Houston paper?"

"No," she replied with growing apprehension.

"It's on the desk outside the cells. The keys are there, too. I'm gonna stay up here. You can let yourself in."

Gemma carried the pot down the staircase and into the county sheriff's office. She passed through the office area to a door that led into the jail cells. Just outside the barred door was a desk with the newspaper sitting on it. She put the cast-iron pot on the desk and sat down on a wooden swivel chair to look at the paper. The cover had horrible pictures of Cliff and Jewel. Gemma's eyes moistened as she looked at the two friends she'd grown up with. Their bodies were all mangled and bloody. Next to Cliff was a dead alligator. She almost broke down and cried as she realized that the stories she'd heard were true. The C.A. had rambled on and on about it in court, and it was as horrible an image as she could possibly imagine, but until that moment they were only images in her mind. These were clear and up close. Suddenly the ugly truth of Cliff's slow, brutal death became very real.

Then Gemma looked at the picture of Jewel. Jewel's face was looking up with her eyes wide open, almost as if she were alive, except there was a sharp tree the size of a baseball bat sticking up through her chest. Her body was suspended there looking back at the camera. Gemma broke down and cried. She and Jewel had never been real close. At one time they started to become friends, but that was the summer that her father had suddenly died. At the same time she began going with Jesse. She remembered how, after her father's death, Jesse started coming over to the house a lot to help out with chores. One day when they came home from the shop, Jesse had mowed the lawn and trimmed all the trees and hedges. He began coming over almost every day. As a result, Gemma didn't have much time for other friends. She suddenly regretted not spending more time getting to know Jewel. The poor girl's mother had run away that same summer.

Gemma heard a noise from the crowd outside. She instinctively looked up, realizing that this was going to be a bad day. Gemma quickly took a handkerchief from her purse and wiped away the tears. She couldn't let Jesse know she'd been crying, and sure didn't want him to know what was going on outside. She quickly grabbed the keys and then opened the door to the cellblock and walked down the hall to Jesse's cell.

"I'm sorry I'm late," she said cheerfully as she opened his cell door. "I hope you're hungry."

"What's going on outside? We keep hearing noises."

"I don't know," she lied. "I didn't hear anything."

#

MCMILLAN'S STORE
ELZA, TEXAS
12:50 p.m., Sunday December 7, 1941

The chief and Corporal McKinney were having another unfruitful day. They started the morning by driving out to Cherokee-One-Leg's house, but the old man wasn't home. On the positive side, his truck wasn't there, which suggested that he had left of his own volition and wasn't another one of Richard Crawford's victims. They then spotted Crawford's red coupe parked next to a shed behind the house. The chief immediately feared that Crawford had gotten to the old man, but McKinney knew better. That old Indian fighter was too crafty.

As Chief Hightower pulled the prowler into town, they spotted Toad Lowery in front of McMillan's waving them down. Jefferson feared the worst; the last time he got news from Toad and Hunker on a Sunday morning it was not good.

When they pulled under the awning they saw that Hunker was holding a rifle cradled in the cook of one arm, and over his other shoulder he had a stick with at least five gutted coons hanging from it.

As Toad came to the window Jefferson said, "It looks like you boys had a good morning'."

Toad shoved a copy of the *Houston Examiner* in the prowler window and asked, "Chief, you seen this?"

The chief looked at the cover pictures in dismay and handed the paper to Corporal McKinney.

"Someone broke into my office. That roll of film was in my desk."

While the two officers were sitting in the shade, a long line of pickups drove past on the highway toward Rusk. Both lawmen watched with the interest that only a police officer could understand.

"Is it normal to see this much traffic on a Sunday?" McKinney asked.

"No, there's never any traffic on a Sunday."

A second line of trucks passed. This time one of the trucks was a Chevy pickup with wooden sideboards. There were five men standing in the back. Two of the men were holding shotguns.

"They're goin' to lynch 'im," McKinney said.

The chief slammed the prowler into gear and hit the accelerator. As the car sped off, gravel sprayed all over the Lowery brothers.

#

CHEROKEE COUNTY COURTHOUSE
RUSK, TEXAS
1:15 p.m., Sunday December 7, 1941

When Irwin and his two companions rolled into Rusk, there were already at least a hundred people out in front of the courthouse. His driver didn't bother finding a real parking spot; instead he opted to leave his truck in the middle of the street. By the time they got halfway to the front of the building, a dozen more trucks had done the same.

When they reached the front steps of the courthouse, one of the men with Irwin shouted, "This is the father of the poor little girl that kid butchered!"

In a moment's time the entire crowd, which previously had been composed of little groups, gathered into one large, angry, shouting mass. All the while more and more trucks pulled into town to the point that the streets were no longer passable.

The men with him kept urging Irwin to speak, but he really didn't know what to say. Suddenly, for reasons that he no longer understood, he was now the center of a lot of attention. In all honesty he didn't know if he wanted that Rose kid to pay for Jewel's killing or not. The fact was that he had no idea who killed her or why. Everyone said Rose did it, but he didn't know why they seemed to be so sure.

The truth was that he still had a terrible headache and really wanted to be home with his four bottles of Old Crow.

Before he realized it, he was standing on the top of the courthouse steps, and the angry crowd quieted, waiting for him to speak.

Irwin looked around at the crowed and said, "I don't know what to say. All I know is that my little girl is dead."

"And that judge wants to let the kid who done it go free!" Shouted someone from the crowd.

It took nothing else to light the flame. The mass of angry men rushed up the steps past Irwin and into the courthouse. The deputy tried futilely to hold the door shut and get it locked, but it was way too late, as he was no match for the power of the mob pressing against him. Within seconds they had rushed into the building and down the staircase to the jail.

Jesse and Gemma and Shakes had just finished their lunch. The day before one of the deputies had shown Gemma where they kept metal plates and flatware for the prisoners. At first she was afraid of the man in the cell across from Jesse, but there was something kind and gentle about his eyes. The night before Jesse had told her how he was a nice man who had fallen on bad luck during the depression. Jesse suspected that Shakes had gotten arrested on purpose to get a few good meals. Her mother always made way too much pot roast anyway, so it was no problem to bring enough for three. She even opened his cell, so he could sit with her and Jesse.

They actually had a nice time. Shakes led them in a blessing, and then as they ate he told funny stories about life on the rails. Gemma had almost forgotten all about the newspaper and the angry crowd outside. She finished washing their plates and had just walked back into cellblock when she heard people coming down the stairs and bursting into the sheriff's office. There was really nothing she could do. The entire area was suddenly packed with men. She found herself pushed back into a corner of Jesse's cell. All she could do was watch while the throng poured into the cellblock. A moment later she caught a glimpse of Jesse as the mob carried him out of the building.

When she stepped out of the cell the area was eerily quiet. Shakes rushed to her side, "Are you okay?"

She simply nodded.

The prowler came to a screeching halt a block from the courthouse square. Jefferson had done a masterful job racing into Rusk. For the first time in his career he got to use the siren and lights, which made it easy to get past many of the cars and trucks headed into town. But the highway was narrow and it was difficult to pass more than just a few trucks at a time. Even worse, a number of the trucks seemed to purposely try to keep them from passing.

When they got to the square the streets were blocked with cars and trucks. The two law officers got out of the prowler and began running toward the square. When they got to the lawn surrounding the courthouse, a line of trucks came rambling into town from behind them. These trucks made no effort to stop. Instead, they drove up onto the sidewalks, plowing past anyone in the way. The lead truck was a large pulpwood hauler that simply shoved aside anything in its path.

Irwin was dumbfounded as he watched the mob come out of the courthouse shouting and dragging Jesse Rose. The boy looked terrified, but Irwin didn't really care.

He must have done it. Everyone seemed to know that the Rose kid was the one who killed Jewel.

The crowd carried Jesse to the street corner where someone had already thrown a rope over a streetlight. They had punched and kicked him over and over all the way from the cell to the street. His ears had been boxed so many times that he couldn't hear. When they got to the light pole, Jesse was hunched over on his knees with bruises and cuts all over his face and blood streaming from his nose and mouth.

The two men who had driven Irwin to Rusk, whose names he still didn't know, grabbed him by the arms and led him to where Jesse was kneeling.

"Is this the one who murdered your daughter?" one of the men asked.

The crowd quieted.

Irwin looked at Jesse.

The kid had to have done it; even the newspapers seemed to know it.

Irwin looked at the crowd and then back down at Jesse and then nodded.

Gemma followed Shakes out of the courthouse and stood in horror as the angry mob put a noose around Jesse's neck. Across the street Judge Buckner was fighting his way through the mob.

"Stop this!" he yelled over and again to the mob that seemed to neither listen nor care.

Shakes leaped from the courthouse steps and ran into the mob and grabbed the rope just as the crowd began pulling Jesse up off his feet. One of the men in the crowd hit Shakes with a club, but he held on, keeping Jesse from being pulled up. Then more men began clubbing and hitting Shakes until he lost hold of the rope and fell to his knees.

Suddenly, just as Jesse was lifted off his feet, the new line of trucks came plowing into the square. The streets were blocked with cars, but these new trucks pushed their way though, knocking other vehicles out of the way. At one point they drove onto the sidewalks to get around the blockage. Finally, as they entered the square, they jumped the curb and drove onto the courthouse lawn. In the back of each truck stood two or more men, all holding shotguns. The lead driver started honking his horn as the mob began jumping out of the way of the oncoming truck. One of the men on the truck-bed fired a shotgun into the air.

The crowd stopped everything as the line of trucks pulled to a stop on the lawn between the courthouse and the street. All the men in the back of the trucks were black. Each of them pointed their shotguns at the crowd.

Jesse was swinging with his legs some five feet off the ground.

Gemma watched in horror as the entire square grew silent. To her right, Corporal McKinney came running across the lawn with Chief Hightower close behind. Across the way Judge Buckner fought through the mob to where Jesse was hanging.

"Stop this! Drop that man!" Buckner ordered.

Corporal McKinney rushed into the open space between the black men in the trucks and the crowd holding Jesse.

"Enough!" he ordered as he pulled his big Colt .45 from under his coat. "Let the kid go!"

The men let go of the rope and Jesse fell to his knees, gasping for breath.

"I'm Brewster McKinney of the Texas Rangers. The next man who fires a gun dies," McKinney yelled.

The judge helped Jesse to his feet and pulled the noose from his neck while Cherokee One-Leg climbed out of the passenger side of the lead truck. One of the men in the back of the truck threw a white man from the bed of the truck onto the ground. The black man then leaped from the truck bed, took the white man by the collar, and dragged him to Judge Buckner.

Cherokee stepped up to the judge. "Here's your killer."

Gemma looked in shock as she could clearly see her Uncle Richard on his knees before the judge.

The street grew silent to the point that Gemma could hear her own heartbeat.

Judge Buckner looked down at the man kneeling before him and then at Chief Hightower, who had his gun drawn, and asked, "Chief is this the man?"

"That's him, Judge."

"Did you kill those two kids in Elza?" Buckner asked, looking down at Crawford.

Crawford looked at the judge and then at Cherokee and then looked back at the judge and nodded.

Crawford then looked at Jesse with venom in his eyes, "That kid and his friend murdered my brother."

As the words came out of Crawford's mouth, Jesse looked up at the courthouse steps and saw Gemma staring at him.

Dave Roberson of *The Jacksonville Statesman* had not wanted to make the drive down to Rusk. For the past hour they had been getting wire reports about an attack on the United States Naval Base at Pearl Harbor in Hawaii. Still, the Elza killings were his story, and he had gotten a tip that there might be an attempt to lynch the kid who did it. So duty called, and he made the drive south.

He was shocked when he pulled into town and found all the streets blocked. He found a place to park and got to the square just in time to see the line of pickups barreling over sidewalks and lawns to get to the courthouse.

He stayed back next to Dixon's Drug Store and watched with his notepad in hand. While he stood there, Cherokee County Attorney, the Honorable Nathaniel Cockwright, Esq. walked up beside him and stood watching in amazement while a man confessed to the Elza murders.

In the next few minutes the crowd began to disperse.

Roberson then looked at Cockwright, who had not yet noticed him, and said, "Well, Nate, it looks like your case just blew right out the window, along with your dream of running for Governor."

Cockwright looked at Roberson and asked, "What do you mean?"

"I mean, that a man just confessed. The kid didn't do it, just like everybody's been telling you. It's a shame, too, with the news from Hawaii and all."

Cockwright just stared at him.

"What news from Hawaii?"

"The Japs attacked this morning. We'll be at war by nightfall. Otherwise this world-class blunder of your would have been my lead story tomorrow. It would have been a dandy, too. I'd write all about how a C.A. nearly got a kid lynched because he wanted to run for office."

Cockwright stomach tightened, but before he got to respond, Roberson continued, "But be assured if you ever run for office again, you can bet that what happened here today will be my cover story."

The crowd had spread by the time Cherokee got to Jesse. "You, okay, kid?"

Jesse nodded, but he was clearly in some pain. His eyes were blackened and swollen and he was holding his side.

Chief Hightower took Richard by the arm and led him up the courthouse steps.

Buckner looked at Jesse and said, "Let's get you inside and cleaned up. You may need to see a doctor."

As Buckner led Jesse toward the courthouse, McKinney tucked his pistol back into its holster and looked at Cherokee.

"Cherokee, you sure know how to spoil a lynchin'."

The old man smiled as McKinney helped him up the steps. Ahead, Jefferson had Richard by the arm as he led him past Gemma to the courthouse door.

Richard stopped next to his niece. "He did it, Gemma. He murdered your daddy."

Gemma watched as Hightower shoved Crawford through the door. After they had passed, Jesse stepped up to her. The two looked into each other's eyes.

Buckner stopped and looked at Jesse. "You two take a few minutes." He said as he went inside.

McKinney and Cherokee both nodded in respect to the girl but walked on by without speaking. They knew the kids needed a moment.

"You knew," she said when they were alone. "You knew what happened to my father?"

Jesse just stared at her, searching for words.

"Is it true? Did you kill him?" she asked with tears in her eyes.

Jesse tried to answer, but there was nothing to say. He just nodded.

Tears began running down her cheeks. "All this time. You knew. Way back when mom and me and Jettie would cry for hours wondering why daddy had been out on those tracks, you knew? You were there? You told me that he drove you home that night. All this time you've been lying to me. Why?"

"We were kids and your dad..." Jesse paused. He couldn't tell her the truth.

"That's it?" She said, near sobbing. "That's all you can say? What happened that night?"

Jesse's mind was racing, but he had nothing to say. If he told her what had happened, he'd have to tell her about the lynching in Jacksonville and all about Sarah Stoker and about what kind of man her father was.

"Gem, I can't," is all he could think to say.

"Would you have married me knowing this secret?"

Jesse just looked at her with tears in his eyes.

Gemma looked at him as her broken heart suddenly cooled with bitter hatred. She slapped him as hard as she could on the face and ran down the steps and off to her car.

Thirty minutes later Jesse was sitting in Judge Buckner's office. The judge was in his normal spot behind his big desk. Next to Jesse sat Cherokee-One-Leg. Behind him sat Brewster McKinney and Chief Hightower. To the left sat an annoyed County Attorney Nathaniel Elbridge Cockwright.

"Well, Jesse, it looks like the State of Texas owes you an apology," Judge Buckner began.

"Your honor," Cockwright protested.

"Nathaniel, shut up," Buckner said, cutting the attorney off. "Your antics almost got this poor kid killed. I realize that this is irregular, but Jesse did nothing wrong. This should never have gone to trial."

"Judge you know that man's confession won't hold up; he'll be screaming duress."

"No, he won't," Cherokee interrupted.

Buckner's face showed respect as he looked at the old man. "You seem quite confident, Mr. Bradford."

"He don't want to be free," Cherokee said, simply knowing, as did Crawford, what would happen the moment he was out of jail.

"What about the killing of that Crawford man's brother? That should be investigated."

"And it will," the judge replied. "Jesse what happened that night?"

Jesse looked at Cherokee, who nodded, and then back to the judge and answered, "He took me out to the tracks. I guess he was going to kill me. He dragged me out of his car by my hair. When Cherokee got there Crawford shot at him and hit him in the wood leg. He was about to shoot again and I found a stick and started hitting him on the head."

"So let me get this straight. He had already shot at your friend, and you feared that he might kill you as well, is that correct?"

"Yes sir, your honor."

"Well that settles that."

"Wait a minute, your honor," Cockwright argued loudly.

"No, you wait a minute, Cockwright," the judge said angrily. "How did that Houston paper get that story and those crime scene pictures?"

Cockwright stiffened. He had prepared himself. The judge was bound to ask. "I don't know. The paper said something about a source close to the trial. I suspect it was someone in Elza."

"Jefferson," the judge asked directing his attention to Chief Hightower, "did you give those pictures to that paper?"

"It wasn't me, Buck. I mean, your Honor," Jefferson said, earning a grin from McKinney.

"Mr. McKinney," Buckner asked, "would you mind, in your capacity as a Texas Ranger, going down to Houston to conduct an investigation on behalf of this court to find out exactly how that newspaper got their hands on sensitive evidence in a murder trial?"

Cockwright turned white.

"Your Honor, The Texas Rangers would be more than happy to handle that investigation for the court."

"Your honor," Cockwright began. "I hardly think that's necessary."

"I didn't think you would," Buckner began. "Nathanial, I suggest that you go to your office and type up a resignation letter; that is unless you want to find yourself sitting in a cell downstairs next to Mr. Crawford. And don't even entertain the notion of running for office again. If you run for trash collector in the state of Texas you can count on me being squarely and loudly behind your opponent. Is that understood?"

Cockwright nodded as he looked at the judge, feeling the eyes of every person in the room on him.

"Now get out of my office," Buckner ordered.

Nathanial Cockwright stood and left the room without saying a word or making eye contact with anyone.

Once the former C. A. was gone, Buckner turned his attention to Jesse.

"Gentlemen, we have a problem," Buckner began. "With the radio and newspaper reports of the last couple of weeks combined with that mess in this morning's Houston paper, I'm afraid Jesse isn't going to be safe. He might be okay in Elza, but anywhere else the name 'Jesse Rose' is the same as 'Alligator Killer,' and with what's happening in Hawaii, I doubt that a single paper will report that we got the real killer."

"What happened in Hawaii?" Jefferson asked innocently.

Buckner looked at the faces around the room. Clearly none of them had heard the reports.

"It was on the radio when I left the house. The Japanese attacked our navy base at Pearl Harbor."

"Does this mean we're going to war?" Jefferson asked.

"Probably so."

The room grew silent as everyone considered the ramifications. Finally Jesse spoke up, "I'm not going back to Elza. I'm gonna join the army."

"Jesse," the chief began, "think about this."

"I was going to before all this began. Now it makes more sense than ever."

"You were going to college so you could be an officer. This will be a lot different." Cherokee argued.

"I doubt that I can go to college now. Besides, you weren't an officer. You did okay."

"You probably need to discuss this with your parents, son," Judge Buckner commented.

"Did you see my parents in court, Judge? They aren't parents. They're two people who had a kid together. Cliff's mom and dad were my parents. I'll catch a train and join the army up north somewhere. Maybe my name won't be an issue up there."

"Those stories went nationwide, but you're right, you are probably better off joinin' up outside of Texas," Buckner said and then stood and added as he reached to shake Jesse's hand, "Good luck, son."

#

When Jesse, Cherokee, the Chief, and Corporal McKinney walked out of the courthouse, Rusk was a quiet, empty little town. The only vehicle near the square was the big pulpwood truck that Cherokee had ridden to town in.

When they reached the bottom of the steps, Chief Hightower started to shake Jesse's hand and then wrapped him in a bear hug. When he let Jesse go he said, "I wish I could have done more for you, Jesse. Are you sure you can't fix things with Gemma?"

"She can't marry me now. Actually, she couldn't before, she just didn't know it."

McKinney put out his hand, "You're going to be okay, Jesse. You'll make a good soldier. When the war's over, if you find yourself interested in becoming a Ranger, you come look me up."

"Thank you, Corporal McKinney," Jesse said as he shook the man's hand. "I might do that."

McKinney just nodded, and he and the chief walked back to the prowler.

Epilogue

STONEY'S DINER
JACKSONVILLE, TEXAS
5:30 p.m., June 14, 2014

Jeana had tears in her eyes as she listened to her grandmother tell her story. They had finished lunch over an hour before, and the waitress had just poured a third cup of coffee for the two of them.

"When I finished high school I went to secretary school up in Dallas. After I graduated from there, I worked at that same Chevrolet Dealership here in Jacksonville that Jewel worked at. I was working there when I met your grandfather.

"I was sitting at this booth with a girlfriend from work having lunch one day when I looked down at a paper and saw Jesse's name. He was listed among the Cherokee County boys who were killed at Normandy. We would always look to see if someone we knew had been killed or captured." Gemma paused and swallowed hard, trying not to cry again, "I didn't go back to work that afternoon. I went home and cried and cried. And then I was over it. At least that's what I thought.

"A few years after marrying your grandfather, I was at home ironing his work shirts when there was a knock on the door. We had moved up to Dallas only a few months before.

403

It was the day your mother started first grade. I remember because I was in the house alone for the first time in years.

"I was shocked when I answered the door and saw Shakes Blankenship. He looked completely different, wearing a clean pressed suit but he had the same kind smile he'd had when I first met him at the county jail. He had his wife, Judy, with him.

"I knew the moment I saw him that the visit had something to do with Jesse. After so many years, I had gotten to the point that I didn't think about him much.

"He said that people had started to call him 'Brother Shakes.' He worked part time with Brother Bill at the church in Elza. They showed me pictures of their children, and I showed them pictures of your mother.

"He said that he liked to go by the name 'Shakes' because it reminded him of who he once was.

"I'm not sure why he felt like he needed to come and tell me the story. He may have needed to just get it off his chest, but I think he really felt like it was a way of doing something for Jesse. Most likely he felt that I needed to know the truth. He was right, of course. I needed it. I broke down and cried like a baby all that afternoon. I'd held all of my tears and anger inside for years, not knowing but always wondering what had really happened and why. It felt like the two of them had lifted an enormous load off my shoulders.

"He said that he had slipped out of town with the crowd after the almost-lynching. Given what had happened, no one was going to miss an old hobo. Not long after that started working again as an accountant and eventually he went to seminary to learn to be a preacher. While there he met Judy and they got married. They moved back to Elza, and he worked part-time as an accountant and part-time at the church.

"He told me that he spent a lot of time with old Cherokee before he died and even more time with Chief Hightower.

"It hurt when he told me all the things my father had done. It hurt even more to think that Daddy tried to kill Jesse and Cherokee and that Uncle Ricky was the one who murdered Cliff and Jewel.

"That was the last time I saw Shakes, but for the next fifty years he and Judy were my two best friends, next to your grandfather. I wrote to them almost every week. People did that in those days. Whenever we had problems of some sort, I'd write a letter to Shakes spilling out all of my sorrow, and a day or two later I'd get a reply. He always knew just the right thing to say. In a way he became the father I'd never really had.

"He eventually started a ministry to help the homeless. He traveled all over the country helping to feed people. He helped start organizations everywhere. I used to get postcards from places like India and Mozambique. You saw what it was like today. I doubt that you could count the number of lives he and Judy touched over the years.

"The funeral? That was Shakes? That lady was his daughter?" Jeana asked.

Gemma smiled and nodded. "He went from being a hobo to one of the greatest men I've ever known, all because of three little kids and some stolen watermelons.

"Some years ago I finally got my courage up and went down to the library and did some research. Sure enough, my father and Uncle Ricky had gone to prison for assaulting a Texas Ranger. The more I thought about it, the more it all made sense. My mother and daddy fought all the time in those days, and he was always out until late at night. He didn't have a job, but Daddy always had money.

"My father was a bookie, he a womanizer, and he was a rapist. For all I know he may have been a murderer, too.

And all that time Jesse was protecting me from knowing what kind of man he was. All those years he kept that secret. I hated him, and he was just trying to protect me."

"Do you still love him, Grandmother?"

Gemma smiled and reached across the table and took Jeana's hand. "I loved your grandfather. He was a good man. He gave me a daughter, and I have the best granddaughter I could ever have asked for."

She paused, searching for words as her eyes moistened.

"Jesse would have gone to prison to keep me from knowing what kind of men my father and uncle were. If you had asked me that yesterday, I might have said, no. But right now I think I love him more than I ever did."

ACKNOWLEDGEMENTS

First I must say a special thank you to Deanna Darr for her efforts at editing my poor attempts at writing. Her hard work turned a series of misspelled words followed by misused commas into what you just read. I can't begin to thank her enough.

Secondly, I have to express my appreciation to Dawn at Austin Design Works www.austindesignworks.com for her cover and website design. She did a masterful job and I can't begin to express how proud I am of her work.

I would also like to thank Greg Hill, Kim Cook, John Pevoto, and Carolyn Smith for going through the book for a final edit. It is amazing how many errors a few extra sets of eyes can find.

I hope you enjoyed this yarn. I'm hard at work on the next one. For more information and updates come to my website www.LDWatson.com and go see my pictures at www.LDPix.com.

About L.D. Watson

L.D. is a graduate of the University of Texas at Arlington where he studied film and television. He has a long career in film and video with credits that include television shows, commercials, and motion pictures. Like a lot of people in that industry L.D. has written a number of screenplays including one that was a jury finalist at the Houston International Film Festival.

He's a Christ Follower and a Texan to the core. He likes to say that he owns two types of shoes; flip-flops and cowboy boots. He loves to ride horses but he hates being called a cowboy. As he once said, "I don't dip snuff, I've never owned a pair of Wranglers, and I hate country music, unless you count ZZ Top as country, of course."

Most weekends he can be found driving across Texas with his camera taking pictures for his website www.LDpix.com. His photographic philosophy is simply that, "There's pictures everywhere, you just got to find a way to get them into your camera."

He is writer or contributor on three different blogs and once published a weekly newsletter titled, "Mondays". Currently he is focusing on his two blogs, LD talk and PixTalk. And, of course he's hard at work on his third novel.

54678027R00253

Made in the USA
Lexington, KY
24 August 2016